PRAISE FOR THE SHOLAN ALLIANCE SERIES:

"Series fans will have a field day (or two) reading this delightful but complex tale with multiple subplots."
— *Midwest Book Review*

"Full of fast-paced adventure and has more alien species than the Star Wars cantina! Fans of Lisanne Norman's Sholan Alliance series will love this newest installment. Science fiction catnip." — *B&N Explorations*

"Norman expands the exciting concepts of her first book into an extraordinary look into an alien culture, developing a rich variety of subplots that will leave you desperate to find out what happens next." — *RT Reviews*

"Norman is a masterful storyteller, and this is a gripping story." — *Kliatt*

"Lisanne Norman handles her material superbly — knowing just when to ease up on drama and go for humor."
— *Starlog*

"This is a big, sprawling, convoluted novel sure to appeal to fans of C.J. Cherryh and others who have made space adventure their territory." — SF Chronicle

LISANNE NORMAN
CIRCLE'S END

A Sholan Alliance Novel

DAW BOOKS, INC.
DONALD A. WOLLHEIM, FOUNDER
375 Hudson Street, New York, NY 10014

ELIZABETH R. WOLLHEIM
SHEILA E. GILBERT
PUBLISHERS
http://www.dawbooks.com

Published by DAW Books, Inc.
375 Hudson Street, New York, NY 10014.

First Printing, September 2017
1 2 3 4 5 6 7 8 9

This dedication is to two people:

To Rick Michelson, a professor at the college I went to, and a personal friend now for a good few years. He has kept me sane, and bounced ideas around with me when this book was in its early stages. A heartfelt thank you, Rick!

And also to my son, for just being the man he is now. Love you, Kai. You look out for me and I love that about you.

ACKNOWLEDGMENTS

I'd like to thank Philip Eggerding for the lovely black and white illustrations he has done for this book, and those he has done and sent me over the years. It's always a joy to see how he interprets happenings and people in my books.

I'd also like to thank Philip and John Phillips for being my sounding board when I needed to try out plot items on someone else and for them being very early Beta readers of scenes I was unsure about. Couldn't have done it without you guys!

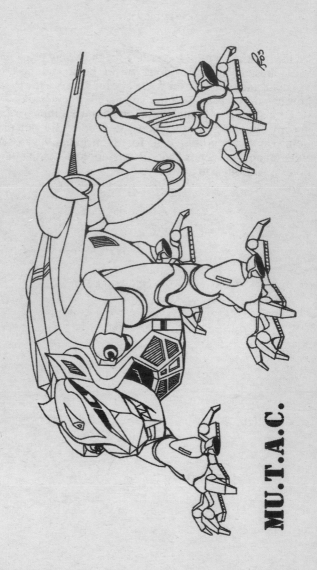

MU.T.A.C.

TeLaxaudin

General Kezule

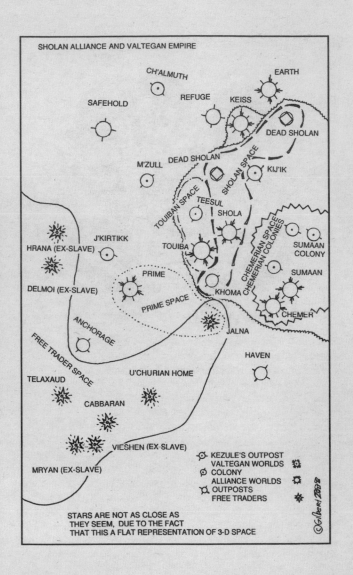

SHOLAN ALLIANCE AND VALTEGAN EMPIRE

CH'ALMUTH

EARTH

REFUGE

KEISS

SAFEHOLD

DEAD SHOLAN

M'ZULL

DEAD SHOLAN

KIJ'IK

SHOLAN SPACE

TOUIBAN SPACE

TEESUL

SHOLA

CHEMERIAN SPACE

J'KIRTIKK

CHEMERIAN COLONIES

HRANA (EX-SLAVE)

TOUIBA

SUMAAN COLONY

DELMOI (EX-SLAVE)

PRIME

SUMAAN

PRIME SPACE

KHOMA

CHEMER

ANCHORAGE

JALNA

FREE TRADER SPACE

HAVEN

U'CHURIAN HOME

TELAXAUD

CABBARAN

VIESHEN (EX-SLAVE)

MRYAN (EX-SLAVE)

KEZULE'S OUTPOST
VALTEGAN WORLDS
COLONY
ALLIANCE WORLDS
OUTPOSTS
FREE TRADERS

©Gilbert 2002

STARS ARE NOT AS CLOSE AS
THEY SEEM, DUE TO THE FACT
THAT THIS A FLAT REPRESENTATION OF 3-D SPACE

THE LEGEND OF THE ZSADHI

"IN the dawn of our people," began J'korrash, "there was a time that stood out in our turbulent history for its peace and prosperity. Trade agreements were sealed, and marriages arranged. The lands of the Queen knew only plenty and prosperity, as did their neighbors. Down the river, trade boats sailed, bringing ambassadors with spices and exotic foods from afar, each wanting to be part of the new age of peace. The Queen's name was Ishardia, and her husband— for she broke with tradition and not only made him King to rule with her, but listened to his counsel—was Zsadhi. But the seeds of trouble were sprouting in her own garden. Her sister, Tashraka, was jealous of her standing among the tribes, and her sister's husband. She had no patience for this time of peace, believing they were stronger than the other tribes and should take what they wanted."

"Was this story set where the capital is now?" asked Kaid.

"Indeed, it was. Their lands contained the Holy Pool from which all life started. Because of that, they were considered First among the tribes. Tashraka approached Zsadhi, offering him not only herself, but goods and possessions no male had ever owned if only he would help her overthrow her sister. Zsadhi made the mistake of laughing at her before refusing her offer because of his love for Ishardia. Mortally offended, Tashraka vowed vengeance on him and her sister. When told, Ishardia refused to take her sister's threat seriously, making excuses for her behavior, unable to believe her beloved sister could wish them ill." She sipped at her bowl of water.

"Tashraka took Nezaabe, the head of the Queen's guards, as her lover, and together they plotted. He knew of a powerful sorceress in the town who would help them—for a terrible price. Together, one night, they stole through the silent streets to the hovel where the sorceress lived. In return for their newly born egg, Tashraka obtained a spell that changed her into the likeness of her sister and the guard Nezaabe into the likeness of Zsadhi. Wrapped in cloaks to conceal their new shapes, they returned to the Palace. There they revealed themselves to the guards, claiming that they were the real Ishardia and Zsadhi, and that her sister Tashraka, and the chief guard, had trafficked with a sorceress for shape-changing spells and were even now impersonating them."

"Magic?" murmured Banner skeptically.

J'korrash glanced at him. "Who knows? The guards burst in on the royal couple in their bedchamber and dragged them out into the Throne Room where the false Ishardia and her lover sat on the thrones. They were sentenced to death, Ishardia to be burned at the stake, and Zsadhi, who was only a male after all, was to be taken deep into the desert and left there without food or water, after he had witnessed his wife's execution."

"Some sister," muttered T'Chebbi.

"Almost destroyed by grief, Zsadhi was dragged to the desert and left, and for ten years, nothing was heard of him. It was assumed he'd perished. For ten years, the country groaned under the cruel hand of Tashraka, still in the shape of Ishardia. She'd raised an army, sending it out to kill all the females and children in the neighboring tribes. The males became her slaves, toiling for her or tortured for her amusement, so that none dared stand against her. Meanwhile, she studied magic with the sorceress, who demanded a place at her Court." She stopped to look round her circle of listeners, smiling slightly at the looks of rapt attention on their faces.

"Then the rumors started. At first it was whispers of a desert holy person, a follower of the Goddess La'shol, who preached against Queen Ishardia, calling her a false Queen, one who trafficked with a sorceress of evil. Tashraka ignored them as beneath her notice. But one by one, as her best female Officers were picked off in their villas, the whispers of this desert prophet became louder until the wailing of the males and children left bereft could be heard outside her Palace." She stopped, raising her cup to her lips. Over the rim, she regarded them, her eyes flicking round the circle of her listeners.

"It was said the avenger was a giant of a male," she continued, lowering her cup to the ground again. "His skin burned almost black from the heat of the desert, dressed in only a loincloth and weapon belt, he carried a great sword of precious steel that cleaved through the guilty as if cutting a water-rich melon. On his chest was blazoned the sword of the Goddess, with two edges, one to destroy, the other to heal. The innocent and worthy had nothing to fear from him, it was only those who cleaved to the false Queen who need fear his and La'shol's wrath."

Kusac shifted uneasily until Carrie took hold of his hand and squeezed it comfortingly.

"La'shol is like our Ghyakulla, isn't she? A nature Entity, not like our L'Shoh who's the Entity of the underworld."

"Judger of souls," said Kusac quietly, leaning against his Human mate.

"Yes," nodded J'korrash. "She's our nature Goddess. Tashraka was no coward. She dressed in full regal attire, wearing the headdress of the Queen, and stood, surrounded by her guards, on the Palace steps. 'Let this desert lunatic come before me with his claims that I am a false Queen,' she said to her people. 'I will prove that he is false by challenging him in mortal combat! The Goddess knows I am the true Queen!'"

Stopping briefly for effect, she waited a moment or two before continuing.

"As she spoke, one of the moons began to slide across the face of the sun, blotting out its light. When its disk reached the center, fire blazed forth across the sky, turning everything as red as fresh-spilled blood. The wailing crowds parted in terror to let a lone male walk through them to stand in front of the false Queen. All who looked on his face saw that of the chief guard who had disappeared when Ishardia and Zsadhi had been executed.

" 'I, the true Zsadhi, challenge you, in the name of the Goddess,' he said, drawing his sword and holding it aloft. As he did, the moon passed away from the face of the sun, and the fire in the sky shot like a lightning bolt to his raised sword, bathing him in flames. When they died, light returned to the land and Zsadhi had resumed his true form, and the people saw that there were two of him."

"So the Entities took a hand," murmured Kusac. "Just as they do on Shola."

"Maybe they are the same, just in different forms," said Carrie.

"Maybe they are," agreed the Prime female. "Tashraka cast off her crown and her robes. Beneath them, she wore armor made of glittering links of bronze that glowed like a banked fire. Drawing her own sword, she stepped forth to meet Zsadhi in combat," said J'korrash. "The fight was terrible, for Tashraka was no mean warrior. Anger and fear fueled her, for she knew the Goddess had kept her sister's husband alive, and hidden his true form in that of her lover. She flung her evil magics at him, but each time, Zsadhi countered it with one of his own, one learned from the Goddess. Till dusk they fought, each taking grievous wounds, until at last, Zsadhi's sword pierced Tashraka's evil heart, killing her. As she died, her own shape returned, and all could see she was indeed Tashraka and not Ishardia. At the same moment, her lover once more became the guard Nezaabe, and with a cry of rage, he flung himself at Zsadhi. Before he had taken three steps, the royal guards turned on him and cut him down."

"What of Zsadhi?" asked Kaid.

"Zsadhi was wounded to death," J'korrash said. "He fell to his knees, his crimson blood spilling over the sand, but before he could die, the Goddess herself appeared, a bowl of water in her hands. She bade him drink, and miraculously he was healed. She told the people that he was their King, and he would rule over them justly until the time there was one worthy to take his place. For the first time ever, a male ruled alone in our land. His first acts were to condemn the sorceress to death by fire, and expose all of Tashraka's supporters and give them to the people to toil on their behalf in improving the lives they had ruined. He ruled for many years, fathering daughters to succeed him, though never marrying again. It was said he could see into the hearts and minds of people just by looking at them, but he was a good and just ruler. The tomb he built to honor his murdered Queen stands to this day by the Summer Palace. On it is inscribed this story."

PROLOGUE

THE continuous pounding on the door had Shazzuk leaping from his bed, barely awake, reaching for the ancient shotgun he kept propped by the night table. His first thought was that Nayash's soldiers were finally attacking the village.

"It's Rhassa, from the chapel," his wife said calmly, not even bothering to sit up. "Go open the door before she wakes the children."

Muttering under his breath, the Valtegan slipped an outer robe over his night clothes and clutching his shotgun, hurried out of their bedroom into the large family room beyond as the banging on the door increased in volume. He heard the first sleepy call of distress from the other bedroom and began to swear anew.

Fumbling with the latch, he hauled the simple door open, hissing in anger at the small group that had gathered on his doorstep.

"What do you want?" he demanded. "Burn it, it's the middle of the night! What could be so damned important that it couldn't wait till morning?" He glared at the priestess and the two main night guards.

"The Zsadhi's sword has gone from the chapel," said Rhassa, torchlight glowing on her hairless green face and head.

Shazzuk took a step backward in surprise. "What?"

"The sword . . ."

". . . has gone from the chapel," finished Roymar, head of the night watch, waving a fist.

"The Zsadhi's returned and taken it, as was foretold," said Rhassa.

"Don't talk rubbish," Shazzuk said automatically. "That's only a legend. Someone in the village has obviously moved it."

"It's gone," said Maalash, nodding his head energetically. "I looked."

"Then someone took it home to clean it," he said lamely.

"Which of us would do that?" snorted Rhassa derisively. "Besides, it was fused to the wall after being sat in that niche for so long."

"But the Zsadhi didn't even live here!" he protested. "He lived on K'oish'ik, not M'zull!"

"He did," agreed the elderly priestess, pulling her woolen outer robe closer round her against the cold night air. "But you know we were taught that the sword was here, during the Fall, on display in the Governor's Palace. Your ancestor."

"That sword's still there, though it's in the Emperor's Palace now," he retorted. "Besides, it's all of it only a legend."

"You know as well as I do that the Governor, your ancestor, had the sword copied during the Fall of the old Empire, and secretly hidden here, in this village," Rhassa snapped. "That sword in the Palace is a fake! The real one was here—till tonight!"

"It's only a legend," repeated Shazzuk, but even he could hear the doubt creeping into his voice. "What if it is the Zsadhi's real sword? Why would anyone here steal it?"

"They didn't," said Rhassa, folding her arms across her chest, her mouth widening in a satisfied smile. "Legend tells that when He returns, the Zsadhi will reclaim His sword."

"What are you saying, Rhassa?" Shazzuk said, using anger to hide his unease.

"I'm saying the Zsadhi's returned."

"Don't be ridiculous!"

"Now would be a good time for Him to return," said

Roymar, "before this new Emperor destroys us all with his ambition to reform the old Empire."

"Be realistic, all of you," said Shazzuk, trying to keep his tone reasonable. "If any strangers had been in the village, we'd all have seen them. How could the Zsadhi have taken the sword? It's the work of the youngsters, playing a trick on us."

"Have you ever tried to take hold of the sword, Shazzuk? Tried to lift it from its place, hidden in plain sight on the wall of the chapel?" demanded Rhassa.

"No, but . . ."

"Because you can't! It's as if it was welded into the wall!"

"She's right," said Maalash, the other guard, giving the priestess a sideways glance. "I tried to pull it out when I was a lot younger, and it wouldn't even move."

"I'm going to look for myself," he said, stepping over the doorsill and pulling the door shut behind him before pushing his way past the old priestess.

The chapel was an ancient building at the rear of the village, set into the face of the mountain itself. Two life-sized statues of the long dead Emperor Q'emgo'h flanked the doorway from which a pool of golden light spilled onto the dirt roadway.

Shazzuk strode inside and instantly the four acolytes searching under seats and behind the altar froze and looked guiltily at each other.

"We've looked everywhere, Leader!" said one, standing up. "It's just vanished. It has to be the Zsadhi."

Hissing his anger, he threaded his way between the semi-circle of seats to the altar to check the bas-relief carving of the Zsadhi for himself. The space where the sword had been was indeed empty. Disbelievingly, he reached out to touch the imprint of where the weapon should have been. What was it his father had said about it? He wished he'd paid more attention to the oldster and his tales of heroes, divine trust, and being descended from the last Planetary Governor of M'zull. Now it was too late to ask him: he'd died three winters ago, taking with him his bitter anger that the rulers of M'zull had supplanted his family, and leaving behind a son utterly disinterested in the faded glories of the past.

His fingers traced the clean edges of the space where the sword had been. It hadn't been forced loose; it had been lifted cleanly from its bed of cement and painted plaster, displacing not one piece of the surrounding wall. Suddenly, he felt the weight of his inheritance fall on his shoulders. He looked along the carved panel to the figures of Queen Ishardia and her sister, the evil Princess Tashraka. He felt a rush of relief: both their carvings were unaltered.

"The Zsadhi has returned," said Rhassa, her voice echoing in the small chapel. "This Emperor has gone too far, murdering his own brother so he could take the false throne!"

"Be silent!" Shazzuk said, turning round abruptly. "You will never say that again, Rhassa, unless you want to condemn us all to death for treason! Maalash, have the blacksmith make a sword to fill the gap. Wake him now and swear him to silence. The chapel will remain closed until the sword has been replaced. Word of this must not go beyond us, do you all hear me?" he demanded, looking at each of them in turn. "Do you hear me?" he demanded again, louder.

"Yes, Leader!" chorused the guards and acolytes.

"He'll come here, Shazzuk," Rhassa said, lowering herself onto one of the benches. "And He'll call on us to help him when he does."

"Enough, Priestess!" he snarled, making his way back through the seats to the entrance. "You'll say nothing of this to anyone! If the Emperor gets wind of this, it could see the end of all of us. The last thing we need is him sending his soldiers here. Get to your beds," he ordered the acolytes. "You have your orders, Rhassa. Roymar, get back to your guard post. You too, Maalash, once you've spoken to the blacksmith! I'm going back to bed for what's left of the night!"

CHAPTER 1

DOGMA

Zhal-Zhalwae, 16th 1553 (May)

WITH a confidence he wished he felt, Kusac, still in the green-skinned reptilian body shape of the young M'zullian Lord Nayash, strode toward the barracks HQ, flanked by the Prime world Valtegans Cheelar and M'yikku. Rezac, also in the shape of a M'zullian officer, brought up the rear.

Kusac stopped by the door, waiting for Cheelar to open it, then entered.

The male on duty at the desk jumped to his feet, chair crashing to the floor behind him.

"Lord Nayash! We weren't expecting you, sir!" he stammered, trying to salute and pick up the fallen chair.

"Obviously," said Kusac, with what he hoped was the right amount of disdain. "Have the troops assembled on the parade ground. I wish to address them."

"Yessir! Your office is ready for you, as always."

Kusac raised his eye ridge. "Hardly. My father's only been dead two days."

"Yessir! I mean, no sir."

The scent of the youth's fear was noticeable, and Kusac finally took pity on him.

"Just go and summon my troops," he said sharply. "I'll be in my late father's office."

"Yes, my Lord," said the youngster, edging out from behind his desk and bolting out of the door.

Rezac gave a low laugh. "Adolescents in the military. They're the same everywhere, and in every time."

Cheelar signaled to M'yikku to go scout out the rooms behind the desk.

"Apparently," said Kusac, unconsciously tapping the baton of office he carried against his free hand. "The M'zullians can't tell the difference between us and them, can they?" he asked Cheelar.

"No, Captain. We all look like M'zullians," the youth reassured him.

Kusac nodded and forced himself to relax.

M'yikku returned. "It's safe," he said. "There's a meeting room beyond here, and off to one side is the private office, with a small bedroom with washroom for times when the old Lord stayed the night. There's even a tiny kitchen."

"Then let's examine it," said Kusac, making his way past the desk and into the meeting room.

Technically, it wasn't on a par with what they had on Shola, or even on the Prime world, but the long table did have built-in comp pads and keyboards, and one side of the wall was lined with screens.

Passing on through it, Kusac came to "his" office. The dry, musty scent, overlaid with the equally pungent smell of liniments, made him recoil.

"I'll open the windows, my Lord," said M'yikku, heading over to them. "Seems that the old Lord was something of an invalid, preferring to stay here, with his young wife."

Hand across his nose and mouth, Kusac ventured into the room, looking around at the ancient but obviously comfortable furniture. From there, he passed into the bedroom. That was a shock of another kind. Everywhere was the obvious influence of a female, from the pastel shades on the windows, to the carpet, and even the wall hangings and bedding.

"Poor old bugger," said Rezac quietly. "He obviously

doted on his wife to let her have such freedom here, on the base, only to end up murdered because K'hedduk wanted her."

"Probably why they stayed here often," said Cheelar. "He knew they were safer here than anywhere else."

"I want the private rooms gutted right now," said Kusac. "Get more appropriate furnishings brought in today. I want nothing left to remind me of my late father and his widow."

"A wise move, Lord Nayash," said a voice from the doorway of the conference room. "Start fresh, make it your own."

Kusac ignored both the newcomer and his own escort, drawing their weapons. "Cheelar, see to it at once. Call a reputable designer to come out immediately with leaflets and samples. I will make my selections today and they can have it installed by tonight." He dismissed Cheelar with a wave of his hand before turning to look past his guards at the interloper.

"And who might you be?" he asked the older male while sending a blistering mental complaint to Rezac.

"A distant neighbor. Telmaar's the name. Had a feeling you might be here today, so I thought it a good opportunity for us to meet. No need for the weapons, I'm relatively friendly," he added, gesturing to the firearms pointing toward him.

A gesture from Kusac, and his guards reholstered their guns. "I'm afraid now is not convenient, Telmaar," he said. "I've a lot I need to see to today."

"Surely this can all wait a few hours, Nayash? We Officers of the Fleet need to stick together. You're new to the Court; there's a lot of factions and undercurrents you should be aware of," he said, sitting on the end of the table.

The young Corporal chose that moment to return at a run. "Lord Nayash, sir, the troops are deployed on the parade ground for you."

Kusac acknowledged him with a nod. "Prior commitments, you know how it goes," he said apologetically to Telmaar. "Perhaps later in the week, when I've settled in."

Telmaar sighed and got to his feet. "As you wish, but some things won't wait. Don't be surprised if you're summoned to Court within the next forty-eight hours. Our new Emperor is more hands-on than his predecessor was."

"I appreciate the warning," Kusac said.

"I'll give you another. Contact the Palace today about your quarters there, and go to Court tomorrow. Don't wait to be summoned." He hesitated briefly. "Have to say, you're not what I expected."

"Time to face my responsibilities," he said briefly. "I'll keep your advice in mind, Telmaar. At our next meeting, I won't be so short on hospitality, but right now, as you heard, my people are waiting for me. M'yikku, escort Lord Telmaar to his vehicle."

With a wave of his hand, their visitor followed the young Prime out.

We have to be more alert to everyone around us! Kusac sent to Rezac as soon as they left. *That could've been a fatal mistake for us all!*

Sorry, Kusac, replied Rezac in a subdued tone. *I was focusing on what we were talking about. I should have noticed him.*

So was I. We're equally to blame. We just can't let our guard down for a moment, replied Kusac.

Going to be a hell of a mission.

We knew that, but it doesn't hit home until something like this happens. Thank the Gods we were at least talking in character!

"Lead the way, Corporal," Kusac said aloud. "After inspecting my troops, I'll want to see their quarters."

"Yes, Lord Nayash, sir!"

"At least he looked after his people," said Rezac as they drove back to the estate a few hours later. "But the barrack's nursery!" He shook his head. "So devoid of anything that would make the young ones' lives normal."

"They've been over two thousand years without female influences in their everyday lives," said Kusac.

"Aye, but you'd think the drones would be more caring!"

"They can't afford to be," said Cheelar. "They're raising either officers or warriors, and there's no place in their lives for softness. Any hint of that, and the other males in their caste would destroy them."

Kusac looked up sharply. "Was that the kind of upbringing you had?"

"No. We were adults when we were released from the accelerated growth tanks, and we always had the company of our sisters. We weren't segregated. Our father, General Kezule, let us live more like Primes, though he trained us hard—a mixture of what you did with the Valtegans visiting your world, and his way."

"The youngsters here are not being brought up unkindly," said M'yikku, "but they are being raised to be warriors, and strong in mind and body."

You can't change how they're being brought up now, sent Kaid from their mountain base. *When our mission is over, everything will change anyway. A few more months is all it will take.*

You're right, Kusac replied. *We can't risk changing anything. Bad enough that I can't sink to the depths that Nayash did, I'll just have to hope those who know him accept that his new responsibilities have changed him for the better.*

That and the whole burning coffin event at his father's funeral, sent Carrie from the estate house.

That, too, sent Kusac. *Is everything quiet back there? We may have to return you to the base, it's just too dangerous here. That visit from the Head Inquisitor on our first night really got me rattled.*

Not surprised it did, she agreed. *I'm still worried about it. Yes, Jo and I are fine. I'd follow Telmaar's advice, by the way. Get your steward to call the Palace about your rooms there.*

Will do. Got to go, almost home now, he said as their vehicle pulled into the estate driveway.

"When do you plan to do our first mission?" Rezac asked.

"Tonight, unless anything comes up to stop us. When we've time, I want you to visit the mountain plantation, find out if the gossip we heard at the village market is true and they do live normal lives with their females free. It wouldn't hurt to have some allies. Talking of which, I want all you can find out about Lord Telmaar, Cheelar. I want to know why he came to meet me today and what he's hoping to gain by befriending me."

"I'll get on that as soon as we get back," said Cheelar. "Don't forget that the ordinary troops aren't bred to be the officer and ruling classes, they're just the foot soldiers. If they're as isolated as we hope up in the mountains, we may find they're a genetic mix that includes both the military and workers."

When they reached the house, Kusac called Laazif to his office to ask about his quarters at the Palace.

"They're underground, my Lord," the steward said. "Unlike his late brother, Emperor K'hedduk, may He live forever, is asking all the nobility and courtiers to base themselves for most of the week at their quarters in the Palace." He hesitated briefly and, literally taking a step back from him, ventured, "If I may make a suggestion, my Lord?"

Kusac rapidly searched the memories he'd taken from the late Lord Nayash before killing him and taking his place. Nayash had been well known for his volatile and excessive nature, deriving pleasure from bullying and tormenting his late father's staff, to say nothing of those not considered his personal clique. Well, time to begin as he meant to go on.

"Please do, Laazif," he said. "I didn't expect to inherit my father's title so soon, so any advice you have would be welcome."

Laazif visibly relaxed. "Then, my Lord, I suggest that I send a group of servants and drones to the Palace to open up your apartments. They haven't been used in over fifteen years. Your late father had no love for Court life, as you know, so there will be a lot to be done to make them habitable."

"See to it, then. I'll be taking my staff with me, you included, of course."

"Yes, Lord Nayash. Shall I call the Palace Chamberlain to inform him of this, and arrange for an appointment to be made with the Emperor? He will want you to swear the Oath of Fealty to him now that you're the new Lord."

"Yes, see to it, please. We'll leave for the Palace tomorrow morning."

"Very good, my Lord," said Laazif, bowing to him before departing.

"So K'hedduk's keeping all his nobles where he can see them," said Rezac, as soon as they were alone.

"Apparently so," said Kusac, sitting down at the desk. "If they're under his nose, he assumes they can't be plotting against him."

"Reasonable, given each of the nobles breeds the soldiers and spacers needed not only for the royal troops, but for their own ships in the fleet."

"Not to mention runs a major commercial enterprise," said Kusac, turning on the comm and data terminal on his desk. "Mine is three munitions factories. They make the weapons and ammo for the equivalent of their commandos."

"You do? Hmm, that could be of use to us."

"Perhaps. Meanwhile, let's check out maps of the surrounding area. As well as making sure that there's nothing to stop tonight's mission, I want to find out exactly where Telmaar's estate is."

"Be amazing if it's his we're planning to hit," said M'yikku with a grin.

"Debatable," said Kusac, pulling up an online map of the area. "However, it looks like it's not his estate." A sudden thought hit him, and he stopped searching. "Could private terminals like this be monitored from the Palace?"

"Unlikely," said Cheelar from where he was pouring cups of cold maush for them all. "It would take an enormous amount of people and resources to track every terminal in the city, never mind outlying areas like here. What's more likely is that certain words and phrases are flagged to trip an alarm, and that will draw the attention of an actual person. Even then, they may not get around to checking each incident out for several hours. I can draw you up a list of the most likely topics to set off such an alarm, if you wish."

"I've been checking for troop movements, and road works. Anything like that likely to set off an alarm?"

"Should be fine," Cheelar said reassuringly, coming over with wide-mouthed cups for Kusac and Rezac. "If you'd been checking the known routes that the Emperor was taking tomorrow on his way to, say, a specific chapel, then yes, that would set off alarms."

"Looks like we'll need to use public terminals in future, to be safe," said Rezac. "We had to do that back in my time, during the Valtegan occupation of Shola."

"Make a list of those things we should avoid doing, Rezac," said Kusac, shutting down the terminal.

"Stop calling each other by our real names, for starters," said Rezac with a grimace. "I'm as guilty of that as you."

Lord Rashal's estate, later the same night

The glow from the nearby capital painted the sky a dull, angry orange, blotting out what little natural light there was from the stars and the thin sliver of the large moon. Ahead, the chapel on Lord Rashal's estate was a dark shape, the last of the lights having gone out an hour before.

Kusac mentally checked the minds of the half a dozen priests within: all were asleep.

"Move out," he subvocalized into his throat mic as he slowly rose to his feet.

In a rolling advance, his fire team of three Primes and Rezac, still like himself in Valtegan M'zullian form, rather than their natural feline shape, moved toward the building, making use of the straggling bushes and trees as cover.

Rezac joined him at the front door as the others ranged themselves against the walls on either side.

Quickly pulling his lockpick tools from a side pocket, Rezac bent to the task of opening the ancient door. Moments later, a click that sounded loud in the silence signaled his success.

Kusac, meanwhile, was checking the hinges for rust. They

looked clean, but just to be sure, he drizzled a little oil over them, waiting a minute or two for it to work. At his signal, Rezac lifted the iron ring-shaped door handle and began to turn it, slowly pulling the heavy door soundlessly open.

Like shadows, the five of them slipped into the building, drawing the door closed behind them. The single main room wasn't completely dark. At the far end, on the altar, twin candles flickered, casting deep shadows on the black carved stone statue of the Emperor behind them.

Between the wooden pews they slipped, keeping to the rear of the chapel where the ordinary estate workers would sit. Leaflets, the exact size of the prayer books lying on the pews, were slipped between random pages and the missals replaced.

While the others were busy doing this task, Kusac headed for the front of the chapel, where a diorite statue of the Emperor stood. The head had obviously been recently replaced with a likeness of K'hedduk, as he could see a fine line between the two layers of dark stone, where the neck joined the shoulders.

The body, clad in what he assumed was traditional ancient armor, was more muscular than he remembered K'hedduk's to be. Reaching out, he ran his hand across the cold polished diorite, picking up the residual worshipful thoughts of generations of priests who had tended it. Definitely not new. Reaching higher, he ran his fingertips, not as sensitive in this body as his natural Sholan form, along the slightly rough join. A rushed job, like those on the Prime world. He let his hand slide down to rest on the outstretched arm.

Anger surged through him as he stared at the too familiar features of the person who had imprisoned him and his family on the *Kz'adul*, ruthlessly stripped him of his psychic abilities, tortured him, and played god with their genetic material, creating hybrid Sholan/Human cubs to use as weapons against them.

He felt the anger flow from him into the statue, watching as the stone began to grow warm.

Focus! said a voice in his mind as he felt a Sholan hand close on his shoulder. Images of himself and the building bursting into flames filled his mind until the heat beneath his hand became painful.

How? he responded without thinking.

Through the statue, into the ground. The unseen hand tightened, claws extending just enough to prick through his clothing.

L'Shoh! He hissed in pain as the heat beneath his hand intensified.

A mind, immeasurably older than his, grasped his will, gently shifting its focus until suddenly he understood the nature of the diorite and was able to channel the heat he was creating into the harder crystalline structure within it.

The pain in his hand vanished as he watched the stone begin to change texture, become lumpy, and finally start to glow a faint cherry red. As the surface became plastic, the arm began to slump downward. The hand was the first to go, the fingers becoming molten globules of rock that dripped down onto the stone-flagged floor.

Fascinated, Kusac watched the features on the face melt and flow into each other like a wax image. With a hiss, and a blast of heat and light that even he felt, the metal breast-plate disintegrated.

"Kusac, stop," said Rezac from beside him. "Any more and you'll be surrounded by molten rock. I think they'll get the message."

With a shuddering breath, Kusac pulled his hand off the statue's arm, leaving behind a perfectly formed handprint in the swiftly cooling stone.

"Hmm, hope they can't get a palm ID from that," muttered Rezac. "Still, I think your message is loud and clear. They'll assume only their Zsadhi could do that."

A faint chuckle escaped Kusac. "Yeah, I suppose it is," he said, moving away from the statue.

There's a carved stone basin over there, Rezac sent, lapsing back into mental speech. *Over by the right at the entrance.*

Open water is considered holy, Kusac replied.

Think you could carve a sword and the word Zsadhi into it? It would really *drive the message home!*

He hesitated.

It's just putting your signature to it, sent Rezac, his mental tone persuasive.

"You worshippers!" The unfamiliar voice was loud in the silence. "What are you doing here at this time of night?"

They all froze briefly, then Rezac swung round, raising his pistol. As he let off a shot, Kusac reached for the mind of the priest. Both were too late; the alarm had been given.

Out, now! sent Kusac, forcing his mental contact on the three Primes.

No time for stealth, just the need to run and escape detection. The Primes reached the door first and had it open as the chapel bell began to peel out.

Get to the car! sent Rezac as he and Kusac reached the font by the doorway.

Kusac found he was holding onto it and surprised, looked down into the stone basin of water—it was diorite like the statue.

A thought in the right direction, now you know the nature of the stone, and it is done, L'Shoh's voice whispered at his ear. *Like this.*

A wave of dizziness passed through him, and he felt the intent for the Zsadhi sword to form in the pool, and the name Zsadhi to be written around it. As he watched, it happened.

"Stop using me like this," Kusac hissed, pushing away from the font and letting Rezac pull him outside.

"You did it!" said Rezac. "Now let's get the hell out of here before the soldiers arrive!"

They made it as far as the end of the road before they saw and heard a unit of soldiers heading for the chapel at a brisk trot. Diving into the ditch, they lay silently as the grumbling troops passed them.

Heart pounding, Kusac lay beside Rezac, trying to catch their words as they went past.

"Second alarm this month!" said one.

"Probably another novice with nightmares or a belly-ache, like the last time."

Then they were gone.

Slowly, keeping as low to the ground as they could, they edged toward the main road. Once across it, they made better time to their vehicle, parked half a mile down the road, hidden in a small copse.

M'zullian Palace, small hours the same night

K'hedduk had sent his bodyguards away when Zerdish arrived, wanting time to speak privately to him. More adviser than chief of his personal security, K'hedduk trusted him alone among the current members of his Court. It was a slow process replacing his late brother's people with his own, and he'd been away for several years. Loyalties could drift during times like those.

"Ziosh is more than a thorn in my side," he hissed angrily, leaning back in his desk chair. "He blocks me at every move I try to make. It's intolerable! He has as much of a sense of his own importance as my brother did, and with less reason!"

"May I speak frankly, Majesty?" asked Zerdish, settling himself in the chair to the left of his Emperor's large wooden desk.

"That's why I asked you here at this hour," said K'hedduk testily.

"Head Inquisitor Ziosh was the power behind your brother, Majesty. Unlike you, he left much of the business of ruling to him."

"And he wants it to continue; that much is obvious. I need to draw his teeth, Zerdish, but how do I do that when he controls the Court?"

"Slowly, Majesty, one tooth at a time." Zerdish smiled, showing his own many sharp-pointed teeth in a predatory grin. "In fact, I might have just the incident to start dismantling his supporters."

K'hedduk raised an eye ridge. "Oh?"

"Apparently, there was an attack on the chapel on Lord Rashal's estate last night. A priest trying to give the alarm was killed, and the chapel was . . . desecrated with symbols of some ancient hero called the Zsadhi. Your statue was melted."

"Melted?"

Zerdish inclined his head in assent. "The stone, a particularly hard one, was melted as if it had been made of wax."

"How is this possible?" demanded K'hedduk, leaning forward onto the desk. "Once we had such technology, but not now. And who would do it? It has to be members of the Court, or the officer cadre. The genetic programming of the lower ranks prevents just this kind of behavior." He paused a moment. "Coupled with the fire effects at Lord Nayash's funeral, we could have a rebellion brewing."

"Perhaps. I certainly doubt it is this Zsadhi that's responsible," said Zerdish. "However, since it is of a religious nature, you can lay the discovery of the culprits at the feet of the Head Inquisitor."

"Indeed," said K'hedduk, a feral grin on his face. "It involves the priesthood and the state religion, and it reeks of sedition against me. Clearly, he should be tasked with the investigation. At the least, it will keep him out from under my feet for a while, and at the worst, if he finds nothing, it proves his incompetence. Meanwhile, I expect you to do your utmost to uncover the perpetrators, and prevent Ziosh from making any significant headway. I want those responsible caught and subjected to the most extreme punishment possible as a warning to the rest of the Court! And I want whatever they used to melt that stone!"

"Of course, Majesty."

K'hedduk reached for the drinking vessel on his desk and took a sip. "Talking of the Nayash family, I'm informed that the new Lord has asked to present himself to me today. I need to bind him to my cause as soon as possible. Thanks to your report, I know he was visited secretly by Ziosh the night he arrived. He's not married, and as the new Lord, it's time he was. I'm sure we can find someone suitable for him."

"I hear his interests lie elsewhere—apart from the young female his late father married, who now graces your harem as Empress," said Zerdish, his tone carefully neutral.

"Irrelevant," said K'hedduk with a wave of his hand, leaning back in his chair again. "He must do his duty to his family, and ties of obligation to me suit my purposes. Do you know of any suitable females? I cannot use one from my currently small harem as he'd likely interpret it as an insult."

"Actually, yes," said Zerdish, his attention focusing back on the Emperor. "My guards brought in a female from the mountain tribes last night. She was traveling in the company of a small band of vagrants we were tracking— runaways from estates trying to live out in the mountains, you know the type. They all died in the encounter, but we did capture the female. Wc haven't yet ascertained if she was companion or captive, though. Feisty, like I hear he likes them. We haven't started questioning her yet."

K'hedduk frowned. "Either my brother, or Ziosh, was growing very lax to allow such escapees to get as far as the mountains. What do you usually do with them?"

"They're punished, then we split them up and send them to various Royal Barracks for training. But these died fighting my guards rather than surrendering. The female is not one you'd like, Majesty. Too feisty by half. The patrol brought her in relatively unharmed, beyond the fight. They know what would happen to them if they damaged her."

"Send her to Keshti. Have him prettify her up. She sounds ideal. I'm meeting with Nayash after the Dawn Rites the day after tomorrow. Have her ready by then."

A scratching drew their attention to the door. Before Zerdish had risen from his chair, it banged open to admit the High Inquisitor. Crimson robes swirling around his ankles, he strode purposefully into the room.

"I must speak to you urgently on a matter of great importance," he said, stopping in front of the desk. "Privately," he added, turning a scowl on Zerdish as the other continued to rise from his chair.

"I think we've covered everything, Zerdish," said

K'hedduk smoothly as his chief bodyguard bowed low to him. "We'll talk more on the last issue after breakfast."

"Majesty," said Zerdish, saluting crisply before turning on his heel and marching out.

"I was about to send for you, Ziosh. We need to replace the ships we lost at the Prime world, K'oish'ik as a matter of urgency," K'hedduk said without preamble as he gestured the Head Inquisitor to the chair just vacated.

Almost unnoticed, two of his black-clad personal bodyguard entered, taking up their accustomed places to either side of his desk by the bookcases.

"They need to be replaced, certainly, your Majesty, but there is no immediate urgency."

"I told you I plan to launch a larger force against the Primes, while they're still smarting from the last attack."

"I should have thought it was obvious to all, Majesty, that it is us who are smarting, not them. What was it we lost again? Some twenty ships and crew, including one of your Generals? But it wasn't of that . . ."

"We couldn't have anticipated them getting help from three different species," hissed K'hedduk angrily, sitting bolt upright.

"That's why my people gather intelligence before acting. The results tend to be . . ." he hesitated for effect, "predictable, and in our favor."

K'hedduk bit back the angry retort on his lips. For now, Ziosh held the purse strings, but by all that was holy, that would soon change! Forcing himself to appear to relax, he leaned back again. "And how do you plan to gather intel on the Primes, or their allies?"

Ziosh's smile didn't reach his eyes. "We all have our trade secrets, Majesty. We do have footage of the different space vehicles in the battle, which will enable us to identify them."

Thinking furiously, K'hedduk stared at him. Who could move among the other species without attracting attention? Certainly not their people. Then it struck him. "You're using the Delmoi and Vieshen as spies, encouraging them to raid shipping lines to gain information."

Ziosh's brow creased in momentary annoyance. "There's more than one way to skin your enemy."

"I expect a detailed report from you on your dealings with both those species in two days, Ziosh," said K'hedduk, his voice as cold as ice. "I cannot plan campaigns when I am missing vital data concerning my resources."

"Gathering information is the purview of my department," began Ziosh, his tone only slightly conciliatory.

"In two days, Ziosh," repeated K'hedduk. "You may have manipulated my late brother, but I am no one's puppet, as you'll discover to your cost if you continue to cross me like this. Now to another matter that might have slipped your attention—the attack on the chapel at Rashal's estate."

"It was of that matter I came to talk to you, Majesty," said Ziosh.

"How could you allow this to happen? You are supposed to root out heresy, prevent such acts as this one of rebellion from ever happening, yet what do I hear? That my statue has been melted—melted!—a priest killed, and symbols of some obscure folk hero belonging to the Prime world, not even ours, have been cut into the chapel walls and a font!"

K'hedduk's anger as he rose to his feet, punctuating the air in front of the hapless Inquisitor with his finger, was far from feigned. It was Ziosh's job to find out about such undercurrents of rebellion and destroy them before they ever crystallized into actions.

"You have failed miserably in this instance, Ziosh. Where was your vaunted Intelligence? Asleep in the temple cloisters after too good a meal? I swear you and your minions live high on the land yet seem to contribute very little to its protection, or mine, as far as I can see!"

Unseen, the hand resting on the edge of the desk pressed the button summoning Zerdish back into his presence.

"I want this matter solved within the week, Ziosh. Within the week. Zerdish, escort the Inquisitor out. He's leaving."

K'hedduk was pacing in front of his desk when Zerdish returned. "How did my brother allow that . . . parasite Ziosh to take so much power from him?" he demanded.

"I don't know, Majesty. I remained on your personal estate, as ordered, until your message reached me a few weeks ago."

"The question was rhetorical," snapped K'hedduk, coming to a halt behind his desk. "I know how it happened. He was lazy, let himself be organized rather than make the effort to exert his own control over his courtiers. Well, Ziosh can disabuse himself of the assumption he'll rule through me as he did with my brother! I'll strip him of his power, piece by piece, until it's all mine again, starting with the Treasury."

He sat down in his chair, thoughts tumbling through his mind eighteen to the dozen. "The next Council meeting is in two days. I want you and ten of your best inside the council room on guard duty."

"Majesty, there's no guard normally in there. Outside, yes, but . . .?"

"There will be that day. I'm going to demand he hands over the Treasury seal to me, and if he doesn't, you can take it from him by force."

"But he's the Head Inquisitor, sworn to protect your Majesty's self. It would be treason against you! I can't do that!" A look of worry crossed the other's face.

"You can when I order you to do so. He can't refuse me in public, it would be treasonable. He'd be guilty of the crime he's sworn to protect me against, unless he has at his fingertips some proof of incompetence on my part," K'hedduk said confidently. "He won't find it as easy to argue his way out of that with me as he would with my brother!"

"Doing that so publicly will start a war between you, Majesty, one you might not win. All he needs to do is accuse those closest to you of heresy, and you will be isolated and in his power."

K'hedduk stared at Zerdish for a long moment, then sighed. "Thank you for reminding me of that," he said quietly. "I'll have to plan this more carefully, protect those loyal to me before I can strike out at Ziosh."

"If I may suggest, Majesty, list exactly what his current duties are, and look at how you can reduce them by giving some of his many acquired functions back to those loyal to you. You can do this all in the name of giving Ziosh the time to spend on those tasks he is obligated to perform. That would be a good place to start," said Zerdish carefully.

"Indeed, it would. There should be a protocol list somewhere, of the court functionaries in my father's time. I can see from that just where and how he's built up his power base. Do you know of anyone to whom we could entrust this task? Someone who wouldn't arouse suspicion? I've been gone too long from the Court to have gotten a proper feel for all the undercurrents yet."

"I know just the person. One of the scribes. Loyal to you, but ambitious. I've had a few dealings with him in the past."

"Very well. Tell him to research the various roles of Court officials in the last hundred years He's doing this so I can put together a commemorative book I plan to write about my father."

"I'm sure no one could find fault with that, Majesty."

"Tell Garrik. I want to be sure the apartments of Lord Nayash are as welcoming as possible. I want him to know from the start that I value his presence at Court."

"He's young, would make a good ally. He's not the sort to hold a grudge at losing his young stepmother to you, Majesty."

"My thoughts exactly," said K'hedduk with a smile. "Let's hope the gift of a sentient wife will sweeten his mood."

"My guards tell me she's also pretty," said Zerdish. "I called them while you were with the Inquisitor. She is on her way up to the harem now."

"Keshti's a drone, isn't he? Can such a sexless person as a drone really prepare a female to be an obedient and pliant wife?"

"I believe so, Majesty," said Zerdish. "When your brother held his open days and the Court females were all allowed to gather in his harem, Keshti was much in demand by the Lords to add to their training."

"Good! Good! I will go speak to Keshti now, be there when this female arrives to see her for myself."

Ghioass, Kuvaa's home, same day

Annuur the Cabbaran moved restlessly on his large floor cushion, pounding the stuffing briefly with his hoofed forelimbs. "Lassimiss been on M'zull long time, that not in dispute," he almost snarled, wrinkling his long snout. "What to do with him now is question!"

"Replace him is obvious," said Azwokkus, TeLaxaudin leader of the Reformist party. "How is what we discuss!"

"Too much discussing," said Kuvaa, reaching for one of the vegetarian tidbits on the low table with her tripartite hoof. "Just take him, put someone reliable in place. Sand-dwellers won't notice." She looked across at the spindly-limbed insectoid beings.

"Is Isolationists we worry about, not sand-dwellers," Aizshuss, the other male TeLaxaudin present said gently.

"Ha! Make him squeal like he is killed for Isolationists to hear, no problem then!" said Annuur. "In fact, no bad points to that idea! Him I would like to pound to dust for the damage he has done to us all with his interference!"

"There will be no pounding, no matter how tempting," said Elder Khassis firmly, the only female TeLaxaudin present. "His questioning will be enough to strike fear and dread into him."

"Kuvaa's point valid," said Shvosi thoughtfully, sipping her fruit juice through a long straw. "If he is just taken and instantly replaced by one of us, and death cries transmitted to Isolationists, no one the wiser he not killed by sand-dweller."

"Unity will know," said Azwokkus. "How we hide this from the AI? That is the bigger question."

"I heading up a unit of Security for Unity now," said Kuvaa. "Told you I would make this my work." Her lips quirked in what was a smile for Cabbarans. "Unity itself is a good teacher. Our long-passed Elders programmed it well."

"Tell me you found how Isolationists hide from us," demanded Annuur.

"I have not found that yet," she said regretfully. "But with help of Hunter Kusac, I can record "death" of Lassimiss."

Aizshuss drew his bronze spindly form upright on his cushion. "You can? How?" he demanded.

She wrinkled her long, mobile snout. "Complicated to explain, but we need Hunter to take memories of time with M'zullians from Lassimiss and give to replacement. This we cannot do, as you know. Also, with him in sand-dweller form, if he "kills" Lassimiss, Unity will record it."

"Hmm, danger is Hunter really kills him!" said Shvosi, the other Cabarran present.

"He will," assured Kuvaa, "but briefly. Resuscitate him here we will."

"And how we hide all this from Unity?" Khassis asked skeptically.

"We don't, until we return here," Kuvaa told her confidently. "We teleport to our isolated safe zone and hold him there. Isolationists use another method to hide their doings, but we have cooperation of Unity, as you know."

"It could work," said Aizshuss thoughtfully.

"Only plan we have after days of thought and hours deliberating today," said Khassis dryly. "Act as soon as possible, we must."

"Can do it now," said Kuvaa. "Drug I have, and Unity had teleporter pad installed here when I became a Senior member of Camarilla. Importantly, is night now on M'zull world and Hunter sleeps. Tomorrow he will move to underground sand-dweller Palace. Easier to take him from above ground."

"Do we know Lassimiss' current location?" asked Aizshuss. "You become a dangerous person since your elevation, young Kuvaa."

"In his quarters at the Palace, alone, Unity tells me," said Kuvaa after a moment.

"Dangerous as befits a Security head for Unity," Annuur responded quickly. "Training her I have been, but now you

need more security yourself, Kuvaa. I lend you my family—
Tirak and Mrowbay, security experts. They ensure you safe."

"Not necessary . . ."

"Take them," ordered Khassis. "Essential to all we do are
you. Your loss a blow we cannot afford."

"That means opening up secrets to them," objected
Aizshuss.

"If we cannot trust my Family, who can we trust?" asked
Annuur sharply, raising himself up onto all fours. "Then let
us do this deed now, stop the rot on M'zull from going further."

"A moment," said Kuvaa, getting up, too. "Decide who
replaces Lassimiss you must as I get drug and dispenser."

As she trotted off into her work area, the other four
looked from one to the other.

"One of impeccable trust must it be," began Shvosi.

"Who knows what they take on," agreed Khassis.

Azwokkus' pale gray draperies stirred around him. "I
will go," he sighed.

Annuur's head swiveled round to look at the TeLaxaudin. "You? But you dislike conflict!"

"In my younger days, that was not always so. As Khassis
will agree, my personal arsenal is formidable. Equipped I
am with knowledge and experience to handle this."

Khassis ducked her head in agreement. "Is true, wild he
was in his youth." A buzzing laugh accompanied her words.
"Better this kept among us."

"I see sense in this, but Kuvaa will not like exposing her
mentor and friend to this risk," Shvosi warned.

"Who better to keep me safe?" said Azwokkus, bringing
his small hands up to his face in an expansive gesture.

"I fetch my Family first," said Annuur, heading for the
transporter plate in Kuvaa's atrium.

"Kathan help you if you're hiding anything else from us,
you dirt-grubbing rodent, Annuur!" Tirak was swearing as
he materialized in the indoor woodland of Kuvaa's home.

What else he had to say was cut short as he took in his
surroundings, ears laid back in disbelief. At his side, Manesh,

hand on his newly returned pistol, was silent, as was Mrowbay.

"Come," said Annuur as he led the three U'Churians at a trot into the living area. "Polite you be, these are old friends and colleagues."

At around six feet tall, the feline U'Churians were used to dwarfing many of the Alliance races, except the Sholans whom they resembled, but neither of them were used to the TeLaxaudin. Small, with spindly stick-thin bronze colored limbs and huge eyes, they were indeed one of the more exotic known species. Rarely seen off the Prime world, Tirak was surprised to say the least to suddenly be face-to-face with three of them.

Khassis began humming in a high-pitched tone, then her translator cut in. "Captain Tirak, a pleasure to finally meet with you. Much have we heard of you in Agent Annuur's reports."

"Khassis this is, Elder female of TeLaxaudin," said Annuur, sitting back on his haunches. "Aizshuss and Azwokkus these are. My people are Shvosi, and this," he pointed to Kuvaa as she, hearing the strange voices, scampered back hurriedly, her small hooves beating a tattoo on the wooden portions of her floors. "This is our hostess, Kuvaa, and the one you will protect like Family."

"U'Churian warriors," whispered Kuvaa in awe as she skidded to a halt. "You honor me, Annuur."

"Kathan's Blessings to you," said Tirak, saluting reflexively. "Merchants, actually."

Annuur snorted. "Who believes that?" he asked of no one in particular.

How much do they know, Annuur? sent Khassis over their private mental link through Unity.

Enough, he replied briefly. "Kuvaa works as Security head on our advanced AI here. Have reason to believe faction antagonistic to us will attempt to harm her. This must not happen."

"How do we know you have the right of this matter?" Mrowbay, Medic on Tirak's ship crew asked. "Perhaps you are the ones we should guard ourselves against."

"Do you trust me?" asked Annuur, looking up at the three black-furred males.

"We did," said Manesh. "But now we find out you have more secrets than a smuggler!"

"A whole world we knew nothing about, where our people live with you and the TeLaxaudin," said Tirak. "Alliances with other aliens we didn't know existed, and technology we could only dream of, and you ask if we can trust you?"

Voices rose around them as Khassis, Shvosi, and Aizshuss began to talk all at once. Only Azwokkus and Kuvaa remained silent.

Rising to her haunches, Kuvaa said quietly, "Do you trust the Sholan Hunter Kusac? Do you wish to protect his mate and their children, like Shaidan? We do. The Hunter is on M'zull with his warriors, trying to bring down the Emperor K'hedduk."

The others fell silent, letting her continue.

"He will need help, and to give him it, we need me to work with Unity, the AI here. Others work against him, and to stop us, would do us all harm. We risk as much as them to stop the darkness of the sand-dwellers spreading over our galaxy. Will you help us?"

"A pretty speech," said Manesh, "but can you prove it?"

"I'll believe it from Kusac himself," said Tirak after a small hesitation. "You can contact him, I take it?"

"You hurt my sensibilities," said Annuur soulfully, gesturing to nearby vacant cushions. "Did we not help him retake the Prime world? Were you not there target-marking for the fighters of the Touibans?"

"Take him with us to deal with Lassimiss," said Azwokkus. "Simpler."

"Us?" echoed Kuvaa, rounding on her friend, head crest dipping toward him and mobile snout wrinkling in distress. "You are going? Tell me you not replacing Lassimiss? The danger!"

The TeLaxaudin patted her arm with his small hand. "Peace, youngster. We need me to go. I have knowledge and protections to accomplish this task. I be safe. Instantly I can transport home if trouble emerges. If not ourselves we risk for what we believe, then who?"

"But you not field agent!" she wailed, butting her head up against him.

"In his day, he was," said Shvosi, nodding her head. "He can do this."

"Sit," Khassis' translator said to the three U'Churians in a tone that brooked no refusal. She pointed to a jug and three clean drinking bowls. "Your caution is good, but for now, drink, take snacks. You, Tirak, will accompany Annuur to visit the Hunter shortly. You can speak to him yourself."

M'zull, that night

A damp nose snuffling in his left ear woke Kusac. With a stifled cry, he leaped out of the other side of the bed, pistol already in hand.

"Is only me, Kusac," said Annuur's quiet voice from the darkness. *Don't call others*, the Cabbaran warned mentally.

"What the hell do you want now?" demanded Kusac, lowering his gun, tail lashing from side to side. "You're lucky I didn't shoot you, I'm in Sholan form right now. You even aware of the concept of privacy?"

"Important this is," said Annuur as he turned on a dim bedside lamp. "Tirak needs to talk to you."

"Tirak? He's on . . ." He ground to a halt as Tirak, ears laid back and blinking in confusion, suddenly appeared beside the Cabbaran.

"No time for that. Mission we have. Must do this tonight," said Annuur.

"I'm doing nothing more for you," snarled Kusac, leaning forward to take a swipe at the Cabbaran, surprised when he actually contacted flesh and fur. "What the hell? You're really here this time!"

"Owww! Abuse me if it pleases you," snuffled Annuur,

sitting up and rubbing the side of his head. "But work we need to do now!"

"I didn't believe you could do this," said Tirak, glancing round the room. "Is this M'zull? Are we really here?"

"Yes. I don't know how you got here, but you're jeopardizing my mission by your presence! What the hell do you want?"

"Has Annuur been helping you?" Tirak demanded. "We've learned a lot that's unbelievable in the last few hours. I need to know which side he's on."

"His own, like the rest of you. Where it coincides with ours, he has helped, though," Kusac admitted grudgingly.

"See?" said Annuur, looking at Tirak. "What I tell you? Now to business." He looked back at Kusac. "We need to remove TeLaxaudin helping K'hedduk and replace with one of us. Tonight, before more damage he does."

Kusac rubbed a hand over his sleep-heavy eyes. "Hold on a minute. Where did this TeLaxaudin come from, and why is he helping K'hedduk?"

"And how long has he been helping him?" demanded Tirak.

"That we will find out," said Annuur grimly. "He is member of Isolationist faction among our peoples, us and the TeLaxaudin. They wish us to isolate ourselves from you younger races. We, as Reformists, wish to help you all, as this danger to you is also danger to us."

Kusac digested this for a moment. The door behind his visitors opened quietly and Rezac, in Valtegan form, slid into the room.

"What the hell?" he hissed.

"Rezac, greetings," said Annuur, glancing over his shoulder briefly, putting a restraining hoof on Tirak's hand as the other reached for his sidearm. "On mission we are, to replace traitor TeLaxaudin aiding K'hedduk. Kusac's help we need."

"Playing both sides against the middle, were you?" asked Rezac, coming further into the room. He nodded at the U'Churian in passing. "Tirak. No surprise to see you here."

"I only just found out about all this," muttered Tirak. "Don't include me in this conspiracy!"

"We have good person to put in place of Lassimiss," said Annuur. "He will frustrate K'hedduk while aiding you. Even you must see need to remove him at least."

Again Kusac hesitated. Granted the Cabbaran had been of some help in the past, and removing anyone helping K'hedduk with access to the tech both those races possessed was a big plus in his book, but he still had his doubts.

"You'll have to earn my trust, Annuur," he said, coming out from behind the bed. "I'll help remove this Lassimiss, but I want something in return first."

"Depends. What you want?" asked Annuur, the suspicion clear in his voice.

"I need Carrie and Jo transported to our mountain base. It's just too dangerous for them to be here."

Annuur nodded his assent. "That I can do," he said, lifting a forelimb and pressing buttons on the wrist pad there. "Is done. Honorable friend Shvosi will take them now."

Kusac reached mentally for Carrie, sensing her surprise. He waited till he had her assurance that she and Jo had arrived safely at the base.

"Thank you, Annuur," he said. "We'll help you remove this Lassimiss. Who are you replacing him with?"

"Admirable friend called Azwokkus," said Annuur. "Of use to you can he be when you in Palace. Plus you and he can communicate when wished. Can make yourself a niche with sand-dweller Emperor by handling this awkward alien for him," he said with a chuckle.

"Dangerous to do that if he's feeding false info to K'hedduk," warned Rezac.

"Indeed," agreed Kusac, sitting on the edge of his bed. "So what does this mission entail? And where is Azwokkus?"

"You need to be Valtegan," said Annuur. "I transport you to Lassimiss' rooms and there you overpower him using drug I give you so his arsenal he cannot activate against you. This slows him. Then you kill him using another drug injected into him. When clinically dead, we appear, take him and revive back on our world, and Azwokkus takes his place. Valtegans cannot tell difference."

"Sounds simple enough. Where's the catch?" asked Rezac, staying between them and the door.

"Catch?" asked Annuur, turning his head to look at him, crest tipping momentarily back. "No catch, except . . ."

"Ah, now we have it," said Rezac.

"They're all linked into an AI called Unity," said Tirak. "It needs to see a Valtegan kill Lassimiss for the Isolationists to believe he's dead, and not in Reformist custody."

Kusac stared at Annuur as pieces of the mystery of the voices in his mind on Kij'ik, and the Prime world, suddenly began to fall into place.

"This AI," he said slowly. "Can it act independently, or only through one of your two races using it?"

Annuur's small ears tilted forward in concern. "Why you ask?" he demanded.

"Because something has been trying and, in part, succeeding in influencing me for some time. I sensed a network on Kij'ik and on the Prime world." Realization hit him. "And even on your ship, the *Merchanter's Gamble*, Tirak! Dammit, Annuur, is there nowhere your hoofs don't get involved? You tried to make me let King Zsurtul die!"

"Not us," assured Annuur. "Nor Unity. The rot has gone further than we knew. Aware that Isolationists been interfering with you, and they are trying to trace where we are right now."

"It's linked into lighting," said Rezac. "The lights would flare, on the *Kz'adul*, then we'd lose time and things were changed, people went missing . . ."

"The same on Kij'ik, and in the Prime Palace," added Kusac, anger growing inside him at how he'd been manipulated all along by Annuur's people.

Annuur stamped a hoof on the floor. "*Not* us!" he said firmly.

"Yes, you! Especially that mystic of yours, Naacha," snarled Kusac.

"You too powerful after mental operation," sighed Annuur, waving a forelimb expressively. "Had to restrict your new powers, let you grow into them, train you. Unavoidable this was, for your safety, and your Family's."

"You had no right to mess with my mind!"

"Have you powers to deal better with this enemy now?" demanded Annuur, as Kusac took a step angrily toward him. The small Cabbaran pushed the tall U'Churian aside when Tirak would have stepped between them. "Should we have left you crippled as K'hedduk left you, with no purpose, no hope? Tell me we did wrong!"

"You should have asked me!" he snarled, fighting to keep his voice down and his vision from narrowing into Hunter-mode.

"Must focus on battle we fight now," said Annuur. "Later we discuss this. More important stopping K'hedduk is now. Time for the rest later."

"And how in all the hells do I do that with your people— sorry, your enemies—mentally manipulating me?" he demanded.

"Working on that now are we," assured Annuur. "Tirak and Mrowbay to be guarding our investigator. Ask them if this not true!"

Tirak nodded as Kusac looked to him. "Yes, we've just been detailed to guard a Cabarran female called Kuvaa. I insisted on talking to you first to know if their claims of helping you were true."

"He's right. We need to focus on the enemy we can see and know is a present threat," said Rezac. "Then we deal with them."

Kusac took a deep breath, forcing himself to relax, and nodded slowly. "There will be a reckoning," he said. "For now, we'll help. Prove yourselves worthy of trust in the meantime, Annuur."

"Oh, there will indeed be a reckoning," said Annuur, his tone also grim. "Meanwhile, inform me if you hear voices seeking to influence you. Give what details you can and we will investigate. This interference is not sanctioned or tolerated by us!"

"Just who the hell is this *us*, and what gives you the right to interfere at all?" demanded Rezac.

"Not now," said Annuur dismissively. "Change to Valtegan form you must now, Kusac, so we can begin this mission. All is ready. I have drugs you need, everything, and Azwokkus stands waiting."

M'zullian Palace, Lassimiss' rooms

His senses strained to their limits as he materialized in the darkened room, Kusac dove across the carpeted floor for the cover of the nearest piece of large furniture. He heard an indistinct crackling sound, then a thin shaft of energy hit the space he'd just vacated. Faint sparks glowed briefly in the dark as the stench of burning carpet filled the room.

"Dammit, Lassimiss! Stop shooting, it's me!" *So much for him not attacking me!* Kusac mentally snarled to Rezac.

"Who is me?" demanded the TeLaxaudin from the darkness.

"How many other people visit you with translocators?" he demanded, inwardly cursing his inability in Valtegan form to read the air currents in the room and tell if the alien was standing still or moving closer to him. "It's Nayash!"

"How you sneak in using that?" Lassimiss retaliated. "I not give you coordinates! Who did? What you want?"

"I worked it out for myself," he said, carefully edging round the side of the chair, attempting to keep its bulk between them. "Put the damned light on! We need some of that aid you promised us."

Silence, followed by a series of sharp clicks and humming that the translator failed to render into speech, then gradually the main light came on.

"Show yourself, Hunter," Lassimiss said. "Then tell me what you need."

Cautiously Kusac peered round the edge of the chair. "Give me your word you'll not shoot at me again."

More untranslatable humming and clicking. "Do not provoke me, then. Show yourself!"

Slowly, Kusac rose to his feet, never taking his eyes off the small alien peering out at him from behind a sofa.

"We need printed papers," he said. "Leaflets." He waved the piece of paper clutched in his left hand. "We cannot print more of them and we've used what we had."

"Give to me. Will see what can be done," said Lassimiss, large eyes swirling, holding out a small and imperious hand.

"Come and get it," said Kusac. "I'm not stepping into the open until you do."

"Then no help!"

"Meet me halfway," said Kusac, gesturing to the low table that stood between them. "You shot at me, after all. I have reason to be cautious."

"Then leave. No help for you. It matters not to me."

"I'm not leaving," said Kusac. "I'll remain here until I get what I need. Pity if Emperor K'hedduk sends someone to fetch you."

Staccato clicks greeted this as Lassimiss' mandibles clashed, but cautiously he edged out from behind the sofa.

Kusac also moved into the open. As they slowly advanced toward the table, Kusac saw Annuur suddenly appear behind Lassimiss, weapon ready.

Kusac reached for his gun. A short phut of air, and the TeLaxaudin collapsed like a bundle of twigs as the anesthetic dart hit him. Remembering his instructions, Kusac cautiously approached the supine TeLaxaudin. The moment coalesced into one of trust for Kusac—did he trust Annuur to be telling him the truth or not? He locked eyes with the other, and with the briefest of nods, pulled the trigger again, shooting Lassimiss in the neck, then handed the gun back to Annuur.

The air shimmered and another TeLaxaudin, dressed in shades of soft gray appeared. Instantly, both Annuur and the stranger were all over the fallen one, pulling the off-white draperies aside and stripping off what looked like jewelry—rings, bracelets—and searching in almost invisible belt pouches, as well as Annuur tapping its limbs in various places with a small, faintly glowing rod.

"We disable him, make him unable to fight back when we resuscitate him," said Annuur looking up briefly.

Kusac straightened out of the defensive crouch he'd been in and joined them, looking down at the untidily sprawled alien and the large pile of devices beside him.

"Did not know he had this," said the strange TeLaxaudin, sitting back on his haunches examining an elaborately jeweled bracelet.

"He was wearing all that?" asked Kusac, pointing at the growing pile. "I didn't see any of that on him."

"Not jewelry, his arsenal," said the newcomer tersely. "Annuur, see what he carries! Contraband weapons—neural disruptor, nanites even! This is very bad."

"Poisoned flechettes, too. You lucky he only shoot at you with energy weapon, Kusac," said Annuur, carefully lifting the items one at a time and putting them into a soft cloth bag he took from a pouch at his waist belt.

"He wasn't supposed to shoot me," said Kusac.

"Hoped he would not, but you accomplished mission. Allowed us to intervene." The newcomer folded himself back on his spindly haunches and looked up at Kusac, his large eyes swirling as the lenses adjusted to near vision. He extended a dainty hand toward him. "Azwokkus I am. A pleasure to meet you . . . Kusac." There was the faintest of hesitations before he said his name.

Slowly Kusac crouched down to the other's level, reaching out to him until their fingers touched. His hand was grasped firmly, far more firmly than he had expected. Azwokkus' hand felt cool and dry to his touch—and he could feel each of the fragile bones beneath the surface. Then the hand withdrew, leaving him with the knowledge that he had been honored with a great measure of trust by this physical contact between them.

"I am replacing Lassimiss. No longer will any aid be given to the sand-dwellers. He must be removed, then we talk," he said, gesturing to the still form.

Azwokkus stood up, draperies moving gently around him.

Annuur looked over at Kusac. "Be quicker if you helped," he said pointedly.

"Um, sure," said Kusac, reaching out from his squatting

position to pick up the nearest piece of jewelry. It resembled a jointed finger, complete with a thin nail at the end.

"How is this a weapon?" he asked, turning it over in his hands.

"Careful!" said Annuur sharply. "Worn on finger, it bends and he sends mental command for thin metal shards, like needles, to fire from the tip. Put in bag! Must hurry!"

Kusac placed it carefully in the drawstring bag Annuur held open for him, then reached out to pick up a couple of conventional looking rings. "What will you do with him?"

"He will tell us everything," said Azwokkus, unclipping something from his belt and attaching it round Lassimiss' arm. "We then collect more evidence to indict his faction, prove they acted against council wishes, aided enemy to us all. Threat posed by sand-dwellers must be negated once and for all."

"We need you to read his mind," said Annuur. "Give Azwokkus knowledge transfer of Lassimiss' dealings with K'hedduk he needs."

"You aren't serious, are you?" Kusac asked

"Very," replied Annuur. "You do with M'zullians and Primes, what problem doing with TeLaxaudin?"

"I've spent nearly two years living with Kezule and his people, I know them well, know how they think. The TeLaxaudin are an unknown species to me. I don't know how their minds work. Besides, he's dead according to you."

"Have you tried?" demanded Annuur.

"I tried with Kizzysus and got nowhere," he admitted.

"Then on my own wits I will have to depend," said Azwokkus. "A little forgetful I may seem to be, but not to be helped."

"How are you going to resuscitate him?" demanded Kusac.

"His heart stopped long enough for Unity to decide he is dead, but not long enough to really kill him. No tissue damage will the poison cause. Once back on our world we can revive him."

"I go now," said Annuur as the last item was placed in the bag and he pulled the drawstrings tight. "Tell Azwokkus what you need, we help where we can."

"How?" asked Kusac.

"Translocator also communicator," said Azwokkus. "I show you."

"Be safe, Azwokkus," said Annuur, pulling his own translocator free of his belt. "And you, Kusac!"

"Wait!" said Kusac, reaching out for the Cabbaran, but he and his prisoner had already blinked out of existence.

"It can wait," Azwokkus hummed gently. "Focus on main task for now we must. I am here to aid you, despite what the sand-dwellers think. They will not notice it is me, not Lassimiss. What is needed by your team?"

"Don't you know that already? You've been spying on us for Vartra knows how long!" Kusac said, getting to his feet as his anger finally began to surface.

Azwokkus' eyes swirled rapidly as he gazed up at Kusac. "I have little time now. Must familiarize myself with this room, become Lassimiss to them. Waste that time, will you?"

Automatically, Kusac raised his hand to his brow to run it through his hair, only to realize at the last minute he wasn't his Sholan self.

"Dammit," he muttered, pulling his scattered thoughts together. "Maps. We need maps. They're difficult to get without drawing attention to ourselves. And a way to hide our searches of the databases here. We're vulnerable, unable to safely hack into their very old-fashioned systems."

"Maps I can get. Holoprojector of place I can also get. Will send you a device to use for your data searches, a safe one, untraceable."

"That would be very useful. What else can you give us?"

"No weapons, but supplies for you and those in the mountains can we deliver. Food, consumables. Printed leaflets, too."

Kusac nodded. "Those we can use. How much notice do you need? And show me how this translocator works, so I can also communicate with you."

"Please," said Azwokkus, moving closer to him and holding out his open hand.

Kusac dug the device out of his pocket and passed it over to the TeLaxaudin.

"Dials you set like this," he said, showing him as Kusac leaned closer.

A faint leathery smell exuded from the small alien, one he'd not noticed till now.

"Do you have an arsenal like Lassimiss?" he demanded abruptly.

The insectoid face tipped up toward him again, the small frontal mandibles on either side of the mouth clicking as the eyes above them whirled briefly with rainbow colors before stilling.

"I have one, yes. We are fragile people, not suited to personal conflict. Among us, weapons are rarely used. Presence of them is enough of a deterrent."

His head dipped down again to the translocator. "This setting," a long thin finger pointed to it, "will let you leave messages. Light blinking here means safe for you to translocate to me. This light means message for you."

Kusac nodded and accepted the device back. "What about using this to travel to other places? Places I choose?"

"No. Cannot do," said Azwokkus with finality. "Much power it uses, too noticeable here on M'zull. Use restricted. Return to your residence now. Work must I do, settle in and become Lassimiss. Your help tonight appreciated."

The TeLaxaudin touched his belt and Kusac felt the room begin to fade as darkness snatched him. Then just as suddenly, he was back in his room at the villa where Rezac was waiting anxiously for him.

CHAPTER 2

Arrival at the M'zullian Palace, Zhal-Zhalwae 17th (May)

THE drive to the Palace had taken a good three hours, even in the fast vehicle that was his staff car. With him were Rezac, Cheelar, and Noolgoi. The other two had gone ahead earlier with Laazif to run security checks on the apartment.

The countryside finally gave way to the sprawling city with its squat, grubby industrial buildings. Plumes of smoke rose from the tall chimney stacks that dominated the skyline.

Cheelar pulled a face as he peered through the one-way glass. "I can smell the pollution even in here," he said. "Depressing."

"The people don't look much better," said Noolgoi from the other window.

Kusac said nothing, just kept watching as they passed the males in shabby clothes standing in groups around the factory doors.

"Lunchtime, I guess," said Cheelar, glancing at his wristwatch. "At least they get a break outside."

They sped through the district, leaving the factories behind. Tall walls with railings set on top became common, the entrances guarded by soldiers.

"Barracks, from the look of them," said Kusac. "Institutional buildings."

"Aye," said Rezac, leaning across Cheelar. "Barracks, hospitals, and schools." He pointed to one building with fencing instead of walls, behind which lines of youngsters in military fatigues were being drilled.

"There's some houses and stores this side," said Noolgoi.

"Makes you appreciate not having to call this home," said Kusac quietly.

The road, which had been straight until now, began to wind its way upward toward the Palace perched on top of the hill. Every now and then there were gaps between the buildings for parks or street malls. Trees now dotted the sidewalks, both fronded ones and bushy ones as the neighborhood took on an appearance of affluence.

Flat-roofed houses with porticos and verandas sat back amid manicured lawns edged with flowerbeds and paths. Their colors ranged from the natural terra cotta to whites and beige. Pedestrians here were nearly all in military uniforms and walked with a sense of purpose. Armed guards at the entrances to these private or public buildings were common.

At last they swung round in front of a building they instantly recognized—the Palace. It differed from the one on the Prime world not by the architecture, which was similar, but the decorations and the murals. All were of a definitely martial nature, and depicted more modern times. This Palace was intended not to awe the population, but to strike fear and obedience into it.

Inquisitors, sent Rezac.

I see them, replied Kusac, eyes fixed on the mural above the vehicle entrance they were approaching.

No, walking out there, in the open!

Kusac looked away in time to get glimpse of the group of three red-robed priests before the car slipped into the shade of the access tunnel.

As they emerged again into daylight, they could see that the central courtyard was vastly larger than the original on the Prime world.

"Do you think it was built larger, or was that done later?" Rezac asked quietly.

"Later. The architecture is similar, but not the same," said Cheelar. "It would also be an open insult to the Emperor of the time, to have a colonial Palace larger than his."

The landing pad, sent Rezac. *It's to my left, where the cafés and stores are on the Prime world.*

Kusac grunted, keeping his eyes on the other side of the courtyard. There, the familiar giant stone statues were on either side of the staircase leading up to the portico and the main entrance. As the vehicle swung round to stop by the stairs, a small contingent of three figures—Laazif and two other Primes—detached themselves from a group of people standing by a small fountain surrounded by tall, spreading trees.

The vehicle slowed to a stop and Laazif ran forward to open his door. Kusac remained in the car until the other three had exited their side and joined M'yikku and Noi'kkah as his honor guard.

Putting on his uniform hat first, Kusac climbed out of the vehicle into the sunlight and heat.

Laazif bowed. "Welcome, Lord Nayash, to the Sun Palace. If you will follow me, I'll take you to your apartments."

Gesturing ahead of them, Kusac murmured, "Lead on, Laazif."

Rezac and Cheelar moved one to either side of him with the other three following behind.

Scan for anyone showing signs of recognizing me, Kusac sent to Rezac as they began to climb the stairs.

On it.

"I don't know if you remember the apartments well, my Lord," said Laazif, slowing down to let Kusac draw level with him. "They're not large, but there's rooms for your aides and guard as well as yourself. The public rooms, a dining room and a salon, are large enough for about ten to twelve people."

"What about yourself?" he asked.

Laazif glanced at him, his expression slightly shocked. "There are adequate servants' quarters, plus the necessary kitchen, my Lord. Your personal standard of living will remain the same as it would in your home."

"I never doubted that, Laazif," said Kusac, trying to suppress a faint smile.

Inside, the Palace layout was very different. Presumably built mostly underground, the upper stories looked to be used only for offices and the living quarters of those employed there. The main entrance hall led to heavy elevator doors, guarded on either side by well-armed soldiers in green dress uniforms. As the doors opened to let them into the elevator, Kusac realized how thick they were.

They'd stand up to a pretty heavy bombardment, sent Rezac, catching his thought as they filed in.

"There are already several invitations waiting for you, my Lord," said Laazif. "I put them on the desk in your office."

"Thank you," said Kusac, clasping his hands behind his back as he felt the elevator begin to slow.

"The central cavern is full of construction crews right now," his steward added as the elevator settled and the doors slid open. "Apparently, there was an attack here a few days ago, rebels of some kind, if you can believe that." He stepped out into the cavern.

"Rebels? How can there be rebels here?"

"You've been in space for several years, my Lord. In that time, some of the mountain folk have grown bold, challenging the rightful order. Not our tribe," he added hurriedly, slowing as Kusac stopped to look around at the ordered chaos of workmen and rubble shifting that was still going on.

"Not our tribe?" Kusac asked as Laazif led them through the safest route past the workmen filling in blast holes and shoring up stone pillars. Guards were everywhere in sight, in groups of four at every tunnel entrance and exit.

"No, my Lord. Your people remain loyal to you. Harvests are always on time, and always the right amount."

"Good to hear," he said as they stopped at the familiar large elevator that they knew led down to the Royal living quarters. "I should pay them a visit."

"Indeed, they will expect it, my Lord," agreed the steward as once again, they filed in.

* * *

This time, they took the opposite route on leaving the elevator, heading away from the Royal apartments.

Kusac dug deep into Nayash's memories as they passed what appeared to be several small stores.

"I see the court still needs the tailors," he said dryly.

"Oh, there are dressmakers here now," said Laazif. "The old Emperor, may His . . . spirit rest with the Gods, allowed the wives of the court to meet with his harem when they wished, provided they were safely escorted there and back, of course. The dressmakers were always attending them."

"Generous of him."

"Emperor K'hedduk does not believe in such laxity, but he allows the wives to gather once a week."

"Surprising."

"Not so, my Lord. Most of the court ladies come from the Tribute from Ch'almuth. Letting them meet weekly helps to keep them docile, they say. This is your apartment, my Lord."

Kusac turned and walked back a few steps. "The damned doors all look alike," he said, glaring up the long corridor at the handful of doors, some with coats of arms showing on a small plaque next to them.

Laazif reached out for the plaque next to his door, pushing aside the cover to reveal his coat of arms. "We use these now to show when a Lord is in residence," he said, opening the door. "Welcome to your Palace apartment, Lord Nayash."

Kusac stepped inside. The entrance was brightly lit, and carpeted in a dark burgundy color. Walls, where they could be seen, were cream and almost completely covered in portraits of what he knew were Nayash's ancestors. Pride of place was one of K'hedduk, wearing the crown he believed to be from the Palace of Light.

"The apartments are clean, and I've had all your late father's personal effects packed and put into storage until you wish to go through them. I'm afraid the furnishings are not very modern . . ."

"That's fine, Laazif," Kusac interrupted, looking around the room, pulling memories of which door led where, to the surface. "We can see to refurnishing later. Right now, I want hot maush and something to eat for myself and my men. You can show them their quarters while I look around my office."

"Yes, my Lord," said Laazif, bowing.

With a few surreptitious hand gestures, Kusac signaled Rezac and Cheelar to search for electronic devices.

They rejoined him some fifteen minutes later with word that the apartment was clear of any listening devices. Shortly after, Laazif arrived accompanied by a servant carrying a large tray.

"I have provided refreshments in the greeting room for the rest of your staff, my Lord," he said, signaling the servant to lay the tray on a table set against the wall near the door.

"Thank you. We'll serve ourselves. You're free to go, Laazif," said Kusac, glancing up from his desk where he sat going through papers with Cheelar.

Once the steward had left, Cheelar continued from where he'd left off.

"From the records, the estate looks to be in good financial health. Whoever was actually managing it knew what they were doing. Of course, I have to check it over properly with the estate manager."

"Do that. Call him here. Rezac, would you . . ." He looked up to see the other already bringing a couple of plates of sandwiches over.

"I'll get the drinks," said Cheelar.

They'd finished eating, found out who the estate manager was, arranged for him to visit the next day, and begun to open the various letters and invitations that had arrived when Laazif knocked on the door.

"Chamberlain Garrik is . . ."

"Yes, yes," snapped an irate voice as the door swung abruptly open. "I can introduce myself!"

Into the room swept a stocky M'zullian dressed in brightly colored long robes. Behind him trailed a couple of drably dressed attendants carrying a variety of books, papers, and envelopes.

"So you are the new Lord Nayash," he said, imperiously gesturing Kusac's entourage aside as he glided up to the desk. "I am Chamberlain Garrik."

Kusac had risen to his feet as the other advanced on him and subjected him to an intense scrutiny.

"Hmm, I suppose you'll do. The court tailor should be able to run up something half decent in two days."

"Excuse me?" Kusac asked, raising an eye ridge.

"Not your concern, mine. Itinerary!" Garrik snapped, holding out an imperious hand.

Behind him, one of the two anonymous drone underlings began leafing through his armful of papers, drawing out an elaborate envelope bearing what Kusac assumed was a Royal Seal.

"Emperor K'hedduk, Long Life and Prosperity to Him, has summoned you to an audience," intoned Garrik. "Tomorrow morning, after the Dawn Rites, in his office." Taking the envelope from his underling, he thrust it at Kusac. "I have arranged for you to attend the court tailor for an appropriate dress uniform to be made for you. In the meantime, one will be provided by them. You'll attend them in three hours, at noon." He held his hand out to the other servant. "Booklet!" he demanded.

The resulting booklet, about half an inch thick and the size of a popular book, was thrust at him. Noolgoi deftly intercepted it.

"These are the rules of court etiquette. I strongly suggest you have your steward help you learn them for your meeting with the Emperor, Long Life and Prosperity be His."

The flow of words stopped for the space of five heartbeats before continuing. "The court you remember is gone, Lord Nayash," Garrik said very quietly. "We now have more—exacting standards. I advise you to be sure to meet them. Your audience is, as I said, tomorrow morning, after the Dawn Rites, which you will be expected to attend. After a short break for breakfast, you will also be expected to attend the Council meeting along with the other nobles and the Generals."

With a slight bow, the Chamberlain turned and swept out of the room, leaving only a faintly perfumed scent behind. Laazif scuttled after him and his minions, closing the door behind himself.

"If you let me read the book, Lord Nayash," said Noolgoi, "I can give you the highlights. We were all trained in court protocol."

"Please," said Kusac, sitting back down.

It seems, sent Rezac, *that the new Emperor has many of his staff running scared right now.*

Indeed. I think we came at the right time, he agreed, watching Noolgoi settle himself in an armchair and open the court protocol book.

Abruptly, the door swung open again. This visitor filled the doorframe, his dark crimson robes adding to his imposing presence. Sweeping them with an obviously disapproving glare, he stepped into the room, Laazif hovering behind him looking worried.

The scent Kusac sensed immediately, with its overtones of superiority and intimidation. Almost, he responded, before forcing himself to override its programming and sending a brief mental warning to the others.

Searching through his acquired memories, he couldn't place the official. Ignoring the frantic gestures of the steward, Kusac went back to studying the estate reports in front of him.

"It's usual to request an audience with me," he said, keeping his tone mild as his companions all bowed to the intruder. "Have you caught the felon who set fire to my father's coffin and disrupted his funeral?" He glanced up at the Inquisitor.

The male stopped, a puzzled look briefly crossing his face. "I am no messenger, Lord Nayash . . ." he began.

"But you are intruding into my private space and disturbing my preparations to meet the Emperor, Health and Long Life be His." A quick probe gave him the inquisitor's name.

Carefully laying his pen down, Kusac sat back in his chair, clasping his hands in front of him. "Since you have failed to capture this renegade person or persons, Inquisitor Luzaarak, why are you disturbing me?"

Luzaarak folded his arms across his chest, breathing in as he tried to take control of the situation.

"I am the chief aide to Head Inquisitor Ziosh. He requires that you attend him tomorrow morning, after the Dawn Rites in the temple."

"Could his message, since it isn't urgent, not have been left with my steward, instead of bursting into my apartment without warning?"

"I was tasked with delivering it to you personally, Lord Nayash," Luzaarak said stiffly.

"You have delivered the message, Luzaarak. You may leave now, but tell your master that I have an audience with the Emperor at that time tomorrow morning. He will have to reschedule it. In future, don't just walk into my quarters, knock like everyone else."

Obviously dismissing him, Kusac unclasped his hands, picked up his pen, and gestured to Rezac to join him at his desk.

Luzaarak hesitated, torn between anger and the knowledge he had overstepped the barriers between the Inquisitors and the nobility. Abruptly, he turned on his heel, thrusting Laazif aside with a hissed "Get out of my way!" Then he stormed out, almost, but not quite, slamming the door behind him.

Do I sense there are two courts in this Palace? Kusac sent to the others.

That of the last Emperor, and K'hedduk's, agreed Rezac. *Though I am guessing, Ziosh ruled the last court. The brother was not a strong king.*

That certainly explains the prevalent atmosphere of stress and fear, agreed Kusac.

Camarilla, same day

Azwokkus activated a control at the desk in their safe house. A projection formed, almost filling the wall, of their captive Lassimiss, confined in a cell deep within the complex that housed *Unity*.

"We sent him straight to this containing cell," said Azwokkus, looking around the small gathering of members of two of the three political parties in the Camarilla. "He was stripped of his arsenal and comms by the Hunter and myself."

"The Hunter knows about this?" asked Htomshu the Te-Laxaudin, her eyes swirling in distress as she tilted back on the cushions.

"The Hunter knows almost everything," said Annuur quietly, glancing at the elder TeLaxaudin. "We cannot control him, cannot make him forget any longer."

"Surely the sedative light pulses . . ." began Htomshu.

"Nothing works," interrupted Shvosi. "Now we are forced to gain his support by cooperation. What worries us more is the presence of Lassimiss on M'zull. How has he manipulated these sand-dwellers, and for how long?"

"Was the loss of our matter transformer over a thousand years ago actually an accident, or orchestrated so that it could be found by the sand-dwellers and used to their advantage?" asked Khassis somberly.

Annuur gave the TeLaxaudin Elder a sharp glance. "I have come to that thought myself. It has certainly enhanced their agenda of fostering not only a civil war among the sand-dweller planets, but an expansionist one to regain conquered territory lost when the hunters destroyed their rule last time."

"And thus provides for the Isolationists one of the needs for us to isolate ourselves from the younger races," said Kuvaa, nodding.

"Won't the Isolationists demand to know where Lassimiss is?" asked Zoasiss, her large, multifaceted eyes swirling as she looked away from the holoscreen to her colleagues. She wrung her hands in distress. "How are we to answer these questions without revealing our part in his abduction?"

"They won't ask us," said Annuur bluntly. "They cannot afford to admit to having an agent on M'zull. Their need for secrecy is as great as ours."

"They will surmise that we have discovered him," said Khassis.

"Not if we divert their attention," said Shvosi thoughtfully. "The sand-dweller ruler is known for his volatile temper and brutality. If what the Isolationists thought were the remains of Lassimiss were found by them . . ."

"They would assume that K'hedduk had killed him," Annuur finished. "Unity, could this be done?"

If all that is required is a smear of the TeLaxaudin member's blood on some of his belongings, then that can be done. For anything more, either the member himself, or a clone would need to be used. The latter would take several months to construct.

"We have his belongings—his arsenal. He would go nowhere without it," said Annuur. "Leave it to me and Kuvaa. We will need his personal effects."

"Agreed. Unity, release them to Agent Annuur."

As you command, Leader Khassis.

The *Couana*, same day

Zsurtul composed himself in front of the comm in the medbay. It had been decided he should make his call from there as it offered the most privacy right now on the crowded *Couana*.

The comm chimed to let him know that Toueesut had

routed his call to General Kezule, his Second in Command as he was absent from the Palace of Light, and their world.

The official Palace symbol of what Carrie called a dragon on the screen cleared to show General Kezule's face, brows slightly creased in concern.

"Majesty," he said, inclining his head in greeting. "How may we help you? Everything is proceeding as planned at your end?"

"Not exactly . . . I mean, yes, General," he said cursing himself for being nervous.

"Nothing is wrong with my daughter? You told me she was doing well. Has her condition deteriorated?" The General's forehead was now creased in real worry.

"She's fine, a few nightmares still, but that's to be expected," he said hurriedly. "Her memories of her captivity are still . . ." he hesitated, ". . . as basic as we'd wish."

"Were you followed? Is there a problem with the *Couana*?"

"No, we'll still be home in three weeks. It's good news, at least we think so," he said in a rush. "We're married, Zhalmo and I. It was what she wanted, I swear it, General."

The look of utter surprise that crossed Kezule's face made the young king almost smile. Almost, but not quite.

"She wanted this?" asked Kezule, sitting back in his chair, obviously in shock.

"Yes, sir. The connection we felt before was still there, despite all she'd been through. I didn't take advantage of her; she came to me."

"She isn't in her right mind, she's still . . ."

"Capable of making my own mind up, Father," said Zhalmo, jumping down the last of the steps and walking over to where Zsurtul sat at the console.

"Zhalmo," said Kezule, studying her as she draped an arm familiarly across Zsurtul's shoulders. "You look well."

"I am," she said, relaxing against her husband. "I am much better. Zsurtul makes me laugh and smile, and each night is less dark with him there."

Both Zsurtul and Kezule didn't miss the faint hesitation

that entered her voice, nor the slightly bewildered look that very briefly crossed her face.

"You should've seen our wedding," said Zsurtul quickly, lifting her hand to his lips. "Well, you can. Toueesut recorded it." He pulled a face as Zhalmo begun to chuckle. "Here we were thinking we'd avoided the fuss of a state wedding!"

"Toueesut certainly knows how to hold celebrations!" she said. "And we had an excess of priests to help Toueesut conduct the ceremony."

"They really know how to rejoice," said Zsurtul, pulling another face as his arm went around his wife's waist. "I swear I had a hangover for two days!"

"This I have to see," murmured Kezule, passing a hand across his face. "A Thanksgiving, there will have to be a celebration. The people must have a public celebration."

"Of course," said Zsurtul, relaxing finally. "We wouldn't deprive our people of the chance to celebrate with us. We'll have a coronation. Zhalmo will rule beside me as my queen. Perhaps you should start the preparations now, and order a new Royal Book to be made, too, for recording our marriage in. We'll start a new dynasty as King and Queen, one of growth and replenishment for our world. Make sure our allies are invited, please. Toueesut tells me we should arrive in three weeks. I'd like the ceremony to be held two weeks after that."

"That doesn't leave us long to prepare, Majesty."

"Exactly!" Zsurtul grinned. "I don't want something weighed down with ceremonies. Something simple is fine. Get Conner involved on the religious side, he'll make sure it's what we'd be happy with. Oh, and I'll need a crown for Zhalmo. Make it like mine, but much lighter. You know, the raptor's head stretched out, the wings wrapped protectively around her head, but feminine looking."

"I'm sure we can come up with something appropriate, Majesty," said Kezule, once again inclining his head.

Prime Palace, evening

"Shaidan, do you go to the pool every night?" asked Kitra as she accepted the bowl of vegetables that the cub passed to her.

"Most nights," Shaidan replied, spooning his stew into his mouth hungrily. "Gaylla comes with me sometimes." *I play with her when she does*, he added mentally. "It's not as much fun as going to the river, though."

"We'll have to arrange another outing there, then," said Dzaka, picking up the water jug and refilling Gaylla's glass.

"I'se really good at swimming now," said Gaylla, carefully laying down her spoon and reaching for her glass of water with both hands.

Shaidan's attention was instantly on her.

"Is not too heavy, Shaidan," she said, placing it back on the table beside her and lowering her mouth to it for a noisy slurp. "See? Don't have to even hold it!"

"Maybe not so full next time," Kitra said quietly to her mate.

"Mmm," said Dzaka, eyeing Gaylla's tall glass.

"Shaidan's teaching me diving," said Gaylla, picking up her spoon again. "He frows fings to the bottom for us to get."

"Only in the shallow water," said Shaidan, turning his attention back to his food. "All the Brothers can swim, it's part of their training."

"It certainly is," said Dzaka. "Just like the exercise and meditation classes you are already getting."

"It's boring," said Shaylor. "I want to do real training."

"You are getting real training," said Kitra.

"All training depends on being able to follow orders, even if they are boring," said Dzaka.

Vazih pulled a face. "But we know all the meditation stuff! All we do is keep practicing it over and over again."

"Practice makes perfect," said Kitra. "You're doing exactly what you should be doing at your age."

"But we aren't, are we?" said Shaidan, looking up at her. "We know so much more than kitlings our age, even if you think of us as ten years old."

"You're doing what is appropriate for ten-year-olds," said Kitra firmly, pushing her empty plate aside.

"No. At Stronghold, Uncle Dzaka was doing Warrior training before then."

"You don't know that for sure . . ."

"I do," said Shaidan, reaching for his own glass of water. "I know because Father knew. Uncle Dzaka trained with the other younglings there. And Dhyshac is already doing proper Brotherhood training. I know everything Dhyshac knows."

"Those were, and are, different circumstances," said Dzaka firmly.

"You're training, Aunty Kitra," said Gaylla, licking the last of her stew off her spoon. "And you isn't all grown up either!"

"Perhaps we can look at expanding your training," said Dzaka, suppressing a smile. "Get you doing some of the things I did when I was ten. You're still young and your bodies are still growing, so there are some things you shouldn't do yet. I'll speak to your training officer tomorrow, see what we can come up with."

Don't you dare smile at me, Dzaka Tallinu! sent Kitra.

I wouldn't dream of it, he replied, straight faced.

"Learning to march around the barracks wasn't what I was thinking about," said Shaidan, leaning his elbows on the table and propping his chin up with his hands. "The Warrior Guild teaches everyone fighting when they're cubs. It builds muscle memory as they grow older. And real muscles," he added.

He watched Dzaka's ears twitch slightly in an involuntary acknowledgment of the verbal hit. "We'll see," his uncle temporized. "Not everyone is a Warrior within the Brotherhood, Shaidan. Some, like me, prefer the priestly side."

"You can still bless your enemies with weapons or fists," Shaidan pointed out.

Caught taking a drink of water, Kitra began to cough, giving Dzaka the excuse of seeing to her.

"I will consider it," he said firmly as he rescued his

life-mate's drink and began thumping her carefully on the back.

Gods, he is SO like my brother, Kusac! Kitra sent to Dzaka as her coughs subsided. *Even down to the way he sits and looks at you so seriously!*

After dinner, the younglings were allowed time to themselves which they could spend in any communal area on the high-security fourth floor. This included the library with its entertainment units as well as the books, the gym, the small enclosed garden, and the pool.

Swiftly, Shaidan headed for the library. He should have about an hour to himself, time enough for what he wanted to do. The others were playing in the nursery, making puzzles, and playing with the new board games that had been brought down from one of the Sholan ships up at the space orbital.

He'd found the latch for the hidden passage quite by accident while looking for more signs of the alien network he'd sensed in the pool room before his mother and father had left on their mission.

Slipping into the library, he closed the door behind him, going over to the fireplace. The wooden mantle and side pieces around the fireplace were carved into the likenesses of intertwined reptiles and their nests. The trigger spot was tiny, it was the carved claw of a reptile sitting on its nest, one that if you looked at it in the right light was shinier than the others. Reaching out, he pressed it carefully.

Silently, a narrow wood panel to the right of the fireplace began to open like a door. As soon as the gap was wide enough, he slipped through, shutting the panel behind him.

A small flashlight gave him enough light to see by, and he headed confidently down the narrow passageway. This wasn't his first visit; he'd been along it several times before. The first time, he'd sneaked out of bed in the dead of night to explore. The passage sloped rapidly downward, leading him into a kind of square spiral down to the ground floor where another wooden panel let him out at the back of the priests' preparation area. Staying in the shadows of the empty room, it was only a short distance until he was outside in the central courtyard.

Hiding in a patch of deep shadow, he took a minute to calm his thoughts before beginning to project a sense that he wasn't there, that if anyone looked his way, their gaze would pass over him and he'd be unnoticed. The Primes, with their natural blocking ability, had been a challenge at first, but now he had it exactly right. Neither Sholans nor Primes would notice him, unless they were specifically looking for him.

Silent and as unobserved as a ghost, he slipped into the night and headed for one of the replanted pools in the center of the courtyard. There, he concealed himself among the bushes, making himself comfortable in the small hollow he had made during his previous visits. He liked to be among people and just watch them. He loved the noise, their laughter; it was all so very different from the secluded life he and the others were living right now.

Ghioass, same evening

Zaimiss was on his way to the Camarilla building when his personal comm unit beeped him. Answering it, he found a distressed Rekkur on the other end.

"Leader Zaimiss, I went to check on our agent and found . . . I found . . . You must see for yourself! It is terrible! Come quickly!" The line went dead.

Clicking his annoyance, Zaimiss tried to raise Rekkur again to no avail. "Details!" he muttered. "Details I need, you fool!" Anything could be wrong! There could be personal danger for him, never mind any other consideration.

A public comm terminal was nearby; ducking into it, he used his own comm to call up Tinzaa. She was sensible, grounded, and Cabbaran, like Rekkur. She could handle physical situations of danger and stress, unlike himself, a TeLaxaudin.

"Tinzaa, I need you to check on Rekkur at our center," he said. "Some crisis he claims there is, and I cannot attend to it at this moment."

"Certainly, Leader Zaimiss. I will report back when I have news."

There, it was settled, he thought, ending the call. It might be expedient to head for the Council chamber and see who was not there. That information might prove useful, depending on the outcome of Tinzaa's investigation.

"Dead? How can he be dead?" demanded Zaimiss, forcing himself to remain upright when every instinct wanted him to sit on the floor and fold himself up into the smallest shape he could manage.

"Too much blood lost," said Tinzaa. "His weapons, scraps of clothing, all there. Would one of your people be without their arsenal and still be alive?"

"No TeLaxaudin voluntarily will give up his arsenal," admitted Zaimiss, eyes whirling in consternation as he adjusted his sight to focus on the Cabbaran standing by the door of their small, private meeting room. "Is it his blood?"

"Unity confirmed that it was," said Rekkur.

"You told Unity? What possessed you to do that? Now there will be investigation, reports to make, accounting to be done!"

"I . . . I thought it was what we did," stammered the young Cabbaran, sitting back on his haunches and waving his hooves in distress.

"You did right," said Tinzaa soothingly. "Not to report it would have been worse. What did Unity say?"

"That the evidence suggested an accident had befallen Lassimiss. Some severe impact, or impacts, had struck him, knocking free his translocator and other items on his person."

"The impact must have triggered his translocator," said

Tinzaa thoughtfully, stroking his whiskers. "I suspect that he was thrown against something, and the fall fatally wounded him, considering how much bodily fluid was on his belongings and the bits of his draperies that were entangled with the translocator."

"Did Unity ask what Lassimiss was doing prior to the event?" demanded Zaimiss.

"Yes, but I told it I didn't know," said Rekkur. "It said we should investigate and give it our findings."

"Well, it is obvious what's happened," said Dhaimass, her tone sharp. "That damned sand-dweller has killed him! We knew he was violent, unlike his brother. He's been demanding we make the matter transformer available to him, give him weapons to win this war of unification! Well, now he's killed our agent."

"It certainly seems that way," agreed Zaimiss, stalking over to the table where a variety of drinks were laid out in chilled containers. He picked up one containing fruit juice and poured some into one of the wide-mouthed bowls. "It is unfortunate that our agent should have met with an accident in the labs on the Prime world," he said. "Those crates were none too stable Kouansishus told us in his last report. Lassimiss must have been careless, knocked one of the stacks over when transferring the supplies he carried there." He stopped to dip his tongue into the fruit juice and take a long drink.

"Sadly, we will be unable to replace him," he continued. "The sand-dweller Emperor will have to manage his war without any more help from us."

"Good," said Dhaimass, humming with approval as she approached the drinks table. "You have solved the problem of Lassimiss' untimely death in an acceptable fashion, and are denying any further aid to the sand-dwellers. I shall see that Lassimiss' Skepp are given what remains of him. Rekkur, send one of the U'Churian servants for an appropriate container from the nearest mortician, then package up what remains for me."

"Yes, Skepp Lady," murmured Rekkur, backing hastily toward the door.

"It is a pity," said Zaimiss. "This incident does limit our influence on them, but with the plan to poison them all in the makings right now, their threat will hopefully be erased soon. It isn't necessary for us to have a spy in their midst any longer."

"Assuming that the matter transformer had created enough of the self-replicating poison units, and released them before it unaccountably turned itself off," said Tinzaa.

"If it didn't, then there is always the Hunter's plan," said Dhaimass. "And we can always send a covert agent down to scout out the situation if need be."

"That we can do," agreed Zaimiss, settling himself on a comfortable pile of cushions.

M'zull, Palace of the Sun, evening

"What is it, Ziosh?" demanded K'hedduk, not even looking up from his desk as Zerdish escorted the Head Inquisitor into his office. "Couldn't it wait until tomorrow?"

"Not unless you want our discussion regarding the costs of the attack on the Prime world to be made public," said Ziosh, moving toward the seat in front of K'hedduk's desk and settling himself in it.

K'hedduk glanced up to see Zerdish returning to his post by the door. "What about it?" he snapped, turning to look at the Inquisitor. "It had to be done. We had no way of knowing that Kezule planned an attack, and brought two other species with him as allies! As far as our Intel knew, he had left the Prime world permanently. And a factor you are forgetting is that my communications with here had been rerouted. I had no backup when I expected the Generals to send their fleets to support my taking of the capital world!"

"I'm not talking about your taking, and losing, of K'oish'ik," the other said, frowning. "I'm talking of the fleet you sent after you returned. You lost thirty-five ships on that wasted venture. Ships we could ill afford to lose."

"I could not afford to let that insult go unpunished," K'hedduk hissed.

"Instead, you gave them another victory," said Ziosh, clasping his hands on his lap. "Had you waited, you would have discovered . . ."

"Discovered what? We had no way of knowing that the Sholans and others would ally with them!"

"Surely you saw their ships as you left the planet?"

"I was fleeing for my life," said K'hedduk angrily, his nails scoring grooves in his desk as he attempted not to clench his hands. "I didn't have time to look around!"

"Be that as it may," said Ziosh. "The loss of thirty-five ships has hit the Treasury hard. We need more resources if those ships are to be replaced. For now, we need to concentrate on recovering more of the assets available on the planet J'kirtikk."

"We need to focus on rebuilding the Third Fleet and preparing to attack K'oish'ik."

"We don't have the resources . . ."

"You forget yourself, Ziosh," said K'hedduk coldly. "I am Emperor here, and while that may be your opinion, yours is not the one that counts."

Ziosh unclasped his hands and began to rise. "On the contrary, Emperor, you will find that the opinion of the Treasury matters a great deal to you. I control that office. We will resume the missions to J'kirtikk in the meantime, and continue to build up our resources." He bowed toward K'hedduk. "Thank you for this chat, Majesty. It has been most . . . informative."

K'hedduk watched him leave in silence. "What kind of Emperor was my brother that he let this . . . person rule the court?" he demanded of Zerdish when the priest had left.

"Toward the end of his reign, your brother preferred not to be concerned with the day-to-day running of the Empire," said the bodyguard, venturing further into the room. "Can I get anything for you, Majesty? Perhaps a drink?"

"I need to be rid of Ziosh, and now!" he hissed in anger, sitting back in his chair. "How does the court view him? Does he have much support?"

"They are afraid of him, Majesty, of course. Inquisitors were also the secret police of your brother, watching everyone for any signs of disloyalty. The Generals believe Ziosh only backed your coup because he saw it as inevitable. I am sure they would enjoy seeing him replaced," said Zerdish carefully.

"Replaced be damned! I want the lot of them gone! We're a military people. It is unconscionable that any religion should hold so great a place on our planet! It is time I made it clear to the Generals just who is holding back our plans to restore the Empire. Get me a list of those who would back me against the Inquisitors, Zerdish."

"We're short a General now, with the death of old Lord Nayash," said Zerdish.

"The place would normally go to his son, yes," said K'hedduk thoughtfully. "I'm seeing him tomorrow, after the Dawn Rites. Invite him for breakfast. I want the time to point out to him just how useful he could become to the Empire, and how quickly he could rise in its ranks if he allies himself to me. He's young, and we need more younger males in positions of authority in the Court. There are too many old fossils around as it is. How are things progressing with that female you took from the mountains?"

"Mahzi, your Majesty. I had a report from Keshti today. She isn't submitting well to the harem regimen. Like all mountain folk, she's too independent. They allow their females too much freedom."

"Tell him she must be tamed within the next few days. I want Lord Nayash in the palm of my hand, and she is a key element of achieving this. If Keshti can't do it his way, then have her beaten or drugged into compliance."

"Yes, Majesty."

K'hedduk pushed his chair back from his desk and got to his feet. "That will be all for tonight, Zerdish. I'm turning in. Good night."

"Good night, Majesty."

When the door had closed behind the Emperor, Zerdish went over to the desk to examine the scores in the surface. He ran his fingers thoughtfully over them. There were only three of them, but they had rough edges and had gone deep. He'd better call the carpenters to see to repairing this before dawn. The Emperor, Long Life and Health to Him, would not be pleased to be reminded of his row with Ziosh in the morning.

Exiting the Emperor's office, he headed out through the executive office and security post to the main open space, euphemistically known as the central courtyard. From there, he made his way across it diagonally to his main security office on the other side of the huge cavern.

M'zullian Palace, Dawn, Zhal-Zhalwae 18th (May)

With Rezac on one side and Noolgoi on the other, both walking the requisite few steps behind him, Kusac made his way to the central courtyard where others, dressed in similar long white robes, were gathered.

You think you have it bad, Kusac? sent Rezac, a rumble of amusement in his mental tone as Kusac pulled at the wide beaded collar round his neck and tried to adjust the skirts of the long robe. *This short kilt outfit reminds me of what we wore in the past as pets of the Emperor back then!*

Kusac glanced briefly back at him. *It looks good on you. This, though . . .*

Everyone else is wearing it. I suppose it stops us from carrying weapons.

A raised hand caught his attention and moments later, Lord Telmaar and his entourage were threading their way through the waiting throng to his side.

"I see you made it, Nayash. And got outfitted, too. Our Emperor, Health and Long Life to Him, seems to enjoy the rituals of the past."

"A loaned outfit only," murmured Kusac. "Apparently my own robes will be ready within the week."

Telmaar leaned forward to flick the edge of the beaded

collar. "Your own robe will be woven to fit you, rather than one size fits all. You'll also get your own colors and device for this. For the moment, it's a stock one."

Kusac looked at the other's collar. "Reds and blue," he said, "and is that a norrta?"

Telmaar laughed as he looked down at the beast picked out in various colors on his wide collar. "Yes. Stupid bastards imported them a long time ago, and they became the top predator very quickly. M'zull is populated with creatures that once walked on the home world. There's the odd indigenous ones, but they tend to be smaller and good at hiding. Yours will be a gold flying beast, rampant, with red claws, if I remember rightly. Your father didn't choose to come to Court often, it wasn't mandatory then, nor were these ceremonial robes expected to be worn at all events."

Around them, the throng had started to move slowly toward the now open door.

"Looks like we're ready to go in. I'll maybe catch you afterward? Have breakfast together?"

"I have to meet with the Emperor," said Kusac. "Perhaps we can meet later?"

"Ah, your audience. I hope you've managed to memorize the rules," frowned Telmaar. "He hasn't given you long. Good luck!"

I am liking this meeting with K'hedduk less and less, sent Kusac.

Don't let it get you all tensed up, sent Rezac. *That's what he intends. Just relax.*

Easier to say than do! retorted Kusac, trying to slow his breathing as he joined the line making its way down the corridor and into the temple. *Did Cheelar manage to find out anything about Telmaar?*

There was a slight delay, then: *Cheelar says he found out that it's known that Telmaar is looking to find a higher posting in the fleet. That is likely at the back of his interest and apparent helpfulness to you.*

That I can deal with, sent Kusac, turning his attention to his surroundings.

Two lines of pillars decorated with colorful scenes supported the roof. Between them, nearer the walls, lit braziers glowed, sending small clouds of scented incense rising toward the carved stone roof. Beside each, an acolyte in a short red robe tended the glowing coals.

As the court spread itself out through the wood-floored hall, Kusac moved slowly nearer to the front.

Does this bring back any memories, Rezac?

Some. Certainly the clothing is the same. It was a long time ago, and not something I want to remember.

Kusac edged closer to one of the pillars as a group of individuals wearing short red kilts and carrying trumpets emerged on either side of the massive stone statue of the Emperor. They lined up, forming an honor guard. The low hum of conversation stopped abruptly as a group of young males in elaborately pleated long crimson skirts entered, swinging censers.

The Head Inquisitor, then K'hedduk should be next, sent Rezac. *They are probably the choir.*

Stifling a yawn hurriedly behind his hand, Kusac tried not to shiver. Although heated, the temple was not that warm, and he wasn't yet used enough to his Valtegan form to feel comfortable.

Do I have to attend every morning?

Only when you haven't got other duties to perform.

Then I'd better get some, and fast!

Inquisitor Ziosh, when he glided into the temple, wore a plain gold band round his forehead. At the front, it bore a single, small gold feather.

That's new, sent Rezac. *They were bareheaded back in my time.*

The trumpeters began to sound their fanfare as Ziosh took up a position at the left of the altar. Around them, everyone began to drop down onto one knee and lower their heads. Kusac quickly tried to do the same and got briefly tangled in the wraparound garment. It was impossible to get a glimpse of his old enemy through the crowd of people around him. He'd have to be patient, bide his time.

Ziosh began to speak, his voice taking on a lyrical

quality as he recited some prayer to the dying of the night, and the rising of the sun.

The voice was hypnotic, but after some ten minutes, Kusac could feel everyone around him getting as restless as he was. Then, suddenly, they were all able to look up. One of the young priests moved forward to the Emperor, carrying a golden bowl of some liquid and a ritual cloth. Bowing low, he offered both to K'hedduk.

It was on K'hedduk that Kusac's eyes were fixed. He stood some forty feet away, dressed in a long white pleated robe bound round the waist by an elaborate wide blue-and-gold belt. The front of his chest was bared, showing off the tattoo he had last seen on King Zsurtul—an open egg with flames emerging from it, and underneath that, a pair of stylized protective wings. Wings like those of the raptor on the long staff he carried: wings spread wide, head stretched forward alertly, it seemed to glare at all before it.

He has the royal tattoo! No, wait. It's different. He frowned. *The wings, they're not the same as Zsurtul's. He must have just guessed at where they went!*

You're right. They should be on either side, attached to the egg shells, not under them! He's wearing the war crown, sent Rezac. *Not good, not good at all, if it means the same here. And the Inquisitor is mad at him for wearing it.*

Kusac tore his gaze away from the tattoo and looked up at K'hedduk's face. It was in profile now, and on his head, he could see he wore a fitted blue headdress, like a cap or an ancient helmet, decorated with small disks of gold. From the front band reared the head of a hissing snake.

Taking the cloth, K'hedduk dipped it in the water and turned to wipe the feet of the giant statue behind him, intoning some prayer that went right over Kusac's head. All he could see right now was the person he most wanted to kill. His vision was darkening, and a redness was creeping over everything in front of him until Rezac's hand grasped his bare arm like a vice, pulling him abruptly back to the here and now.

Don't, Rezac sent. *We'll get him, in our own good time. Not now, not here. He will pay, Kusac.*

Kusac took a breath, forcing the red rage back. "Yes," he whispered. "He will." He began mentally reciting the litany for Clear Thought. If he let his rage take over, then this mission would be finished before it had properly begun.

K'hedduk was turning back toward the congregation now, and around him the choir broke into chanting.

"Homage to our glorious Lord, sovereign over all of us! Glorious you rise, O Living Light of the World!" the young priests chanted.

"*Your dawn rays light up all the earth,*" the congregation intoned.

"When you rise in the horizon, a cry of joy goes forth," chanted the priests.

"*Every heart beats loudly at the sight of their Lord rising!*"

Finally it was over and K'hedduk had left. The choir, trumpeters, and Ziosh, all followed him out.

"We can't leave yet," muttered Kusac, leaning against the pillar. "I'm supposed to meet with him now, but I have no idea where."

"Ah, there you are, Lord Nayash," said Garrik, bustling up to him. "Follow me, if you please!"

Kusac rolled his eyes at Rezac and moved after Garrik. The crowd parted as soon as they saw the Chamberlain, leaving his way to the exit clear.

"You have indeed been favored today," said Garrik, slowing down slightly as he led him out into the courtyard then across it to another corridor. "Emperor K'hedduk, Long Life and Health be His, wishes you to join him for breakfast. After that, there will be a Council meeting that you must attend."

"I need to change, Garrik," said Kusac. "These clothes are not suitable for such a meeting."

"Of course! May I suggest that you send your aides now to fetch your uniform? You will have time to change after you have eaten."

Kusac glanced at Rezac, and with a murmur of assent, the other headed off at a swift walk for the apartment.

"Lord Nayash," a voice from behind called out.

Kusac stopped abruptly and turned round to face the Head Inquisitor. Light glinted off the gold feather in his headdress.

"We haven't yet been introduced. I am Inquisitor Ziosh. Since I hear you are meeting with his Majesty, perhaps you would wait behind after the Council meeting? There are some matters I wish to discuss with you."

"Certainly, Inquisitor," Kusac murmured, inclining his head to the other in respect.

"Then I will see you later," said Ziosh, taking his leave.

"You can change in the room there," said Garrik, indicating a door on their left. "Your aides can also wait there for you."

"What about food for them?"

Garrik sighed. "Very well, I will have something basic brought for them. Come, the Emperor, Long Life be His, is waiting for you," he said, leading him to a door on his right. Stopping, he rapped firmly on it, then waited for it to be opened.

"Remember, do nothing till the Emperor, May He Live Forever, does it first," he said very quietly. "Don't raise your eyes to his unless he tells you to do so."

The door was opened by a black-uniformed M'zullian.

"Lord Nayash, Lieutenant Zerdish," Garrick said, inclining his head before turning to leave.

"The Emperor, Long Life to Him, will be with you shortly," said Zerdish, gesturing to him to enter.

Kusac entered the room. At his right, a curtain divided the room off into the smaller, more intimate, area he now stood in. A circular dining table, with two chairs set opposite each other, dominated the room. To his left stood a dresser with several covered dishes on it. He moved farther in and Zerdish indicated a chair placed just in front of the dividing curtain.

"You can take that seat there," he said, closing the door and positioning himself in front of it.

The room was warmer than either the temple or the corridors, but still not comfortable for the lightweight clothing he was wearing. He stepped over to the chair and tried to sit down, but the way the garment was wrapped around him made it difficult at best. He felt the smirk from Zerdish as he swore silently. This outfit had probably been designed to make the wearer feel as uncomfortable as possible, to put them at a disadvantage. It was certainly working!

Reaching for the side of the garment, he tugged at the folds under the wide belt, easing them toward the center to give him more room, then tried sitting down again. This time it was much easier.

K'hedduk kept him waiting for about ten minutes, then, dressed in his uniform, breezed in, followed by a servant. Kusac leaped to his feet, aware he had to play the part of someone unfamiliar with the new and restrictive court protocols, someone afraid to put a foot wrong.

"Ah, you're here. Good," said K'hedduk.

He bowed low, crossing his forearms across his chest. "Long Life and Health be yours, my Emperor," he said quietly, waiting to be told he could rise.

"Breakfast, I think," said K'hedduk. "Take a seat, Lord Nayash. I thought it would be useful for us to have this . . . informal little chat."

Standing up again, Kusac moved toward the table, waiting until the servant had seated K'hedduk before reaching out for his chair.

"Please, let me, my Lord," said the servant, bustling round to pull the chair out for him.

So he was being treated with courtesy. Then this meeting wasn't primarily to intimidate him. K'hedduk wanted something.

Two more servants entered, carrying plates of cooked meat which they placed in front of them. While the main servant began serving them both hot maush, K'hedduk picked up his bowl and sat back in his chair, obviously trying to appear at ease. However, Kusac could sense the underlying tension in the other's mood which he couldn't hide.

"That's enough, We'll serve the rest ourselves," said K'hedduk, waving them away after the covered dishes of vegetables and slices of warm bread had been offered to them. "Best meal of the day, I always think," he continued, picking up his fork and knife and beginning to cut up his meat as the servants bowed and left the room. "Zerdish, get yours now, I want you at the Council meeting."

Silently the other male left the room.

"So are you settling in at the Palace?"

"Yes, Majesty," said Kusac, realizing how hungry he was as he cut a chunk off his piece of meat. Cooked just as he liked it, it was tender and tasty.

"You'll probably want to redecorate. I'm sure the apartments are rather old-fashioned to you."

He took advantage of a full mouth to assess the room they were in. "A little, Majesty. They need brightening up somewhat. Less dark colors, that kind of thing. I prefer my quarters to look bright and more invigorating."

"Quite. I think best in surroundings that don't look like a mausoleum! So today will be your first Council meeting. I have several of the Generals on the Council. Sadly, the oldest ones, not the up and coming younger males with new ideas. Still, doubtless, they will get their turn. That's why I wanted to talk to you. Your father was one of my Generals, though as you know, his health didn't allow him to leave his estate very often."

"Indeed, Majesty." Kusac paused to take a drink of maush, making sure to keep his eyes on the table and his food.

"His seat is now open, and I am thinking of promoting you to it." K'hedduk's hand waved in a dismissive gesture. "Before you tell me you are too young for such a position, perhaps you are, perhaps not. If we don't try you out, we'll never know. However, much as I want new perspectives, new ideas, I need people utterly loyal to me on the Council. Many of the incumbent members are still fossils from my brother's reign, and my brother didn't often attend the meetings."

"You are my Emperor, I am loyal to you," began Kusac.

"I'm sure you are," K'hedduk interrupted. "We need loyal people like yourself around the Court, and on the

Council. My people, not those who were loyal to my brother . . . or to Inquisitor Ziosh."

The dislike in the way K'hedduk said the name was palpable.

"Ziosh will likely approach you with offers of favors he thinks he can grant you," said K'hedduk, taking another forkful of meat. "Don't be fooled by him. There is one power on this world and that is me. Ziosh has yet to test my mettle."

Unable to prevent the shudder of apprehension running through him, Kusac put down his fork. So they'd come into the middle of a civil war in the Palace. Knowing K'hedduk, he had no illusions as to who would win, and just how dirty the fight would get.

"Majesty, I would never accept anything offered to me by Head Inquisitor Ziosh," he said quietly. "To do so would be treason. Our family has always been counted among the most loyal of the Emperor's people."

"To date, you have. We would like to count on your support on the Council, Nayash. Those who support us in our ventures and policies will find it to their own personal benefit. What do you say?"

"I know nothing about Council matters, your Majesty. I'm willing to learn from those who do . . ."

"Learn? There's nothing to learn! All you need to do is support my wishes! Can you do that?"

"Majesty . . ."

"Look at me, dammit!" hissed K'hedduk, leaning intimidatingly across the table.

Kusac looked up for the first time. K'hedduk's color was heightened, and there were more lines around his eyes and mouth than when last they'd met, but he'd have known him anywhere.

He locked eyes with the M'zullian, suppressing the quite genuine fear he felt lest the other could scent it. "Majesty, I will, of course, support you in the Council, but I need an understanding of the issues. I need to be able to speak convincingly of your plans to others if I am to be an effective advocate on your behalf."

K'hedduk sat back in his chair and looked at him in surprise. "Well, this is an interesting turn," he said. "Not only are you willing to back us, but you also want to garner more support for us."

"I know which side is going to win, Majesty," said Kusac. "I intend to ensure I am well placed on that side."

"Your honesty and ambition is refreshing. It may be that we will have some tasks that only you can perform. If this is the case, don't doubt that you will be well rewarded." He leaned forward again, as swiftly as a striking snake. "And don't doubt that your failure will be equally punished. It is extremely unwise to cross me."

"Nothing could be further from my wishes, Majesty," said Kusac, fighting to keep his tone even and confident, and not to break eye contact. Right now, anger and fear were warring inside him. He wanted nothing more than to leap across the table to kill K'hedduk, and he wanted to be safely with Carrie far from this poisonous individual.

Abruptly, K'hedduk stood up. "Then we'll see how the Council meeting goes. If it progresses the way I wish, then I am sure that you will find yourself one of the youngest acting Generals in our military by the end of the meeting. Good morning, Lord Nayash. I'm pleased our little talk was so productive."

Kusac sat there trying not to tremble with reaction as K'hedduk swept out of the room, leaving him alone. After a few deep breaths, he reached for his bowl of maush and took a long drink.

The door opened again, and so on edge was he that without realizing it, he leaped out of his chair and crouched down facing the door, ready for anything.

A high-pitched almost squeak of terror greeted him as Chamberlain Garrik tried to press himself into the wall.

"I've only come to escort you back to the main courtyard, Lord Nayash," he said. "Please be assured that I offer you no violence!"

Still shaking, Kusac rose back to his feet. "Take me to my people," he ordered. "I need to dress for the Council meeting."

One look at Kusac and Noolgoi smoothly ejected Chamberlain Garrik from the side room he'd been allocated to change in.

"Perhaps you could send for his Lordship's Steward Laazif, Chamberlain." said Noolgoi. "I know you have more important things to do than wait around to lead my Lord to the Council chamber."

"Indeed, I have. I'll send someone for your steward now, but be as swift as possible. His Majesty hates tardiness!" With that, the brightly clad Garrik bustled off.

Noolgoi shut the door and leaned his head briefly against the wall.

"Let me get you out of this robe," said Rezac, reaching behind Kusac's neck for the fastening of the broad collar.

"I can undo it myself," hissed Kusac, reaching up to yank the offending jewelry off.

"No, don't do that," Rezac's grip on his wrist was like iron, making him involuntarily open his fingers. "If you break the collar, we'll have to explain why, and it will take us forever to pick up the bits. Do you want to do that to Noolgoi and me?" He quirked an eyebrow up at Kusac.

"No," he admitted, relaxing the tension in his body. *Dammit, I want him dead, now, by my hand, for what he did to us! I can barely be civil to him!*

This was your plan, Kusac. If you can't follow it, then we have no chance of success, and we shouldn't even be on M'zull, sent Rezac.

"We'll have to hurry," Noolgoi said, oblivious to the unspoken conversation. "They're already gathering for the Council meeting. Garrik will send Laazif to lead us to the chamber." He noticed how the other two were standing and nodded at them. "You'd better ease up on that temper, too, Lord Nayash. I can't guarantee how long we'll be alone," he added quietly.

Kusac pulled free of Rezac and took a deep breath. "I'll

manage. Nicely done with Garrik, thank you. Just help me get out of this ridiculous outfit."

"You look good in it, my Lord," said Noolgoi moving forward to help Rezac undress him. Taking hold of the belt, he began unwinding it from around Kusac's waist. "There is something to be said for the court dressing formally like this."

"Pray the Gods our young friend doesn't adopt it!" Kusac muttered as he raised his arms to let them undress him better. This was definitely a job he couldn't do alone.

Five minutes later, more comfortably dressed in his military uniform and boots, Kusac stepped out into the corridor where Laazif now waited.

"We should be just in time," said Laazif. "Hurry, my Lord. This way!"

They followed after him as he threaded his way through the people toward the main courtyard area. From there, they went down a side corridor until they reached an open door. On either side were black-uniformed guards, standing at attention, hands resting on their automatic weapons.

"ID," demanded the guard on the right.

Kusac turned questioningly to Noolgoi.

"Here, my Lord," said Noolgoi, digging into his pocket and pulling out the requisite ID card.

Kusac took it from him, handing it to the guard.

A quick glance and it was returned. "You may enter, Lord Nayash," the guard said.

Inside, various uniformed persons mingled with courtier types, all chatting animatedly. A flash of somber red among the brightly colored courtier clothing told him the Head Inquisitor was already there.

"Your aides can wait in this anteroom, Lord Nayash," said Laazif. "If you need them, one of the assistants within the Council chamber can fetch them. I'll leave you now." With a quick bow, Laazif turned and left just as Chancellor Garrik entered and called them into the Council room.

The meeting focused mainly on matters that Kusac thankfully knew about—first up was the attack on Lord

Rachal's chapel, the leaflets that had been found there, and most importantly, the desecration of the statue of the Emperor and the font of holy water.

"I don't give a damn right now about *why* it was done," snarled K'hedduk, "I want to know *how*! It is beyond any technology we have, and I want those weapons for myself!"

"If it was a divine act, then there was no technology involved," said Inquisitor Ziosh, sitting back in his chair and looking round the large oval table where some twenty people were seated.

"Divine act be damned," snorted Dr. Leddark. "There is no such thing!"

"I realize you are a person of Science," frowned Ziosh.

"Not open for debate," interrupted K'hedduk. "The hands of people did this, not ancient saints or evil spirits. People with a technology more advanced than ours, as I said. I'm sure even you can see that, Ziosh!"

"Ones capable of building that mechanical beast," said General Geddukk. "Who left at least one of their number behind on M'zull!"

"I'm glad at least one other person has the wit to see what is in front of you all," snapped K'hedduk. "I want that spy found, and found now! The credulous will see the hands of this ancient Zsadhi in this attack no matter what we say, unless we can come up with the spy. How close to finding him are you?" he demanded, turning on Nazhol, the head of the military police.

"Majesty, this is not a simple matter. This person is obviously a master of disguise and opportunity who may even now be hiding among us."

"Stop stating the obvious," interrupted Geddukk. "We all know that. What have you done to find him?"

"I've set up checkpoints all over the Palace as well as the town. Identity and movement papers are being checked for everyone, so this should flush our spy out. You'll notice you were all asked for your ID cards before you were allowed into the anteroom."

"Providing he isn't already settled in with a fake or stolen ID," said K'hedduk, "this is good. I want you all to increase security on your estates and public buildings. Nazhol, you'll see it's done on state buildings. He might pass through our checkpoints, but we'll get him if he tries an attack like this again."

"Yes, Majesty," said Nazhol.

"I meant all of you, not just the MPs," said K'hedduk, sweeping a glare round the whole table. "We all need to be alert for this infiltrator. And if you find him, take him alive and able to be questioned. Make sure all weapons or devices he carries are also given to my security forces. Lieutenant Zerdish will take charge of them."

In the small hiatus that fell, Inquisitor Ziosh spoke, "The next item is the reclamation of resources at J'kirtikk. We need to redouble our efforts. Thirty-five destroyers were lost at the recent attack on the Prime world, and they need to be replaced. The Third Fleet has been seriously depleted—it's below half strength right now."

"We're well aware of that, thank you, Ziosh, We don't need you and your spy force to tell us that," said Gedduk, signing for one of the attendants to bring him over a dish of maush to drink. "This is our domain, and I'll thank you to keep your nose out of it!"

"As head of the Treasury . . ." the Inquisitor began.

"As to that, you were appointed to that position by my brother," interrupted K'hedduk, idly examining his nails. "That appointment has not been ratified by me since I took over the Sun Throne. You will hand the key to the Treasury over to me now, if you please, Ziosh."

"Majesty, this is neither the time nor place for . . ."

"Oh, but it is." K'hedduk looked up and across the table at the Inquisitor. "You will hand over the key now. It is my intention to run the Treasury myself."

"This can surely wait until we are in a more private setting," said Ziosh smoothly. "We should stick to the business at hand."

"This is *my* business at hand right now, Zerdish." K'hedduk raised a hand and gestured his head of security forward. "Get the key from the Inquisitor, if you please. If he objects, have your men facilitate this for me."

As one, the ten black-clad security guards who had appeared to be only an honor guard, took one step away from the walls whcre they had been standing and turned to salute K'hedduk.

"Majesty, this is most unethical," hissed Ziosh, gripping the arms of his chair. "This is an insult to my position as head of the Inquisition!"

"Perhaps, but I wanted to be sure of your compliance this time, and there is no insult intended to your position as a priest, only as Treasurer."

"The key, if you please, Inquisitor," said Zerdish, holding out his hand for it as he stepped round the table to where Ziosh sat.

Fuming, Ziosh lifted the heavy chain from around his neck and handed it and the ornate key threaded on it to Zerdish.

"As you wish, Majesty," he hissed. "May we now return to the matter of the recovery of assets from J'kirtikk?"

"General Chaikul, how does work on J'kirtikk proceed?" asked K'hedduk, taking the key from Zerdish. He examined it briefly before placing the heavy ornamental chain around his own neck and positioning the key in the center of his chest.

"Well, your Majesty," said the elderly General, lifting a folder lying on thc table in front of him. "I have details if you wish them."

"Zerdish," K'hedduk gestured to his officer who went over to the General to collect the papers. "I will certainly look them over, Chaikul. Inquisitor Ziosh is correct, however; we must reclaim more of what remains of their navy to replace those lost to the Sholan Alliance at the Prime world. I want the Third Fleet back up to strength as soon as possible. Don't you agree, Lord Nayash?"

"Yes, Majesty," said Kusac. "We have no way of knowing what emergencies we could face, especially with a spy loose on M'zull. We need to be at full strength again, in all departments, as soon as possible."

"Succinctly put. I think you should help General Shayazu at this time. We need the main courtyard and concourse repaired as soon as possible. This turmoil gives the ideal opportunity to anyone wanting to cause even more chaos. Shayazu could do with a pair of younger feet on the ground, couldn't you, General?"

"I can manage, Majesty," protested the older male.

"I'm not inferring you can't," said K'hedduk a shade testily, "I'm just giving you an extra pair of eyes, Shayazu. Be thankful, dammit!"

"I am, Majesty. I am most grateful," stammered the General. "No one can be in two places at once. He will be most helpful, I am sure."

He's expecting to be challenged by you and lose not only his seniority but his life, sent Rezac.

I know. Is there a way to avoid doing that without seeming weak?

If you can find one, do it by all means. Just make sure to not seem too weak for what K'hedduk wants! He will destroy you if you have no use to him. Noolgoi says Shayazu is in charge of ground troops in the Palace.

I need a space posting, not to be stuck with ground troops.

You have your own units in space you can visit, reassured Rezac.

"As well as replacing the lost ships, we need to increase munitions production," said K'hedduk. "That involves you and General Lezhu, Nayash. Both of you need to increase your output. We lost more than just ships at the Prime world."

"We're operating at full efficiency already, Majesty," objected Lezhu. "We can't do more than that."

"I'm sure we've room to improve, Majesty," said Kusac. "There's always areas where we can cut back on wasted time and increase production."

"That's what I like to hear—take note, gentlemen. This young Lord is snapping at your heels! You'd best pay him mind! In fact, as we're a General short with his father's death, I am appointing Nayash in his father's place."

A slow handclap broke the silence that fell with the announcement. All eyes turned to Lord Telmaar. "Majesty, your reasoning is impeccable! At last someone around my own age to talk to on the Council. Welcome aboard, Nayash."

"I'm glad you approve, Telmaar," said K'hedduk dryly. "Perhaps you should be helping him with the rubble shifting!"

"Certainly, Majesty. I'm sure we two could get the whole mess cleared up in half the time it would have taken Shayazu."

"Then do it and impress me," he snapped, getting to his feet. "This meeting is over, We'll meet again in a week. I expect to hear that this spy has been caught!"

Standing, they waited for the Emperor and his security detail to leave before conversation broke out and they began to file out into the anteroom. The only one who didn't wait was Ziosh. In a flurry of red robes, the Inquisitor left the room.

Kusac felt a hand touch his elbow and turned to find Telmaar standing beside him.

"Well, that was useful," the other said. "We get to work together on cleaning up the courtyard and tunnels around it. Better than hunting down that damned spy, don't you think?"

"Infinitely," said Kusac without thinking, then realized he'd perhaps been incautious. As he began to try and cover his tracks, Telmaar laughed.

"Don't. Your frankness is a relief after a morning spent with this lot! I was trying to avoid being roped into the spy search because traditionally our family is always lumped in with the MPs and security. Personally, I think the search is a fool's errand. Heads will fall before they find him, if he exists."

"Surely he exists," said Kusac as Rezac and Noolgoi fell in behind him. "If not him, then who, or what, caused the damage in the chapel?"

"Maush for both of us," Telmaar ordered one of his aides before taking Kusac again by the arm and guiding him into the anteroom and toward a side table with two comfortable chairs bracketing it.

"I'm supposed to be meeting with Inquisitor Ziosh," said Kusac as he let himself be led.

"I'm sure you'll find that Ziosh has no desire to talk to you or anyone else at this time. Send one of your people to check if you're worried. Meanwhile, let's be comfortable," he said, sitting down as their aides came over to stand behind the chairs.

Kusac signed to Noolgoi to check at the Inquisitor's office.

"I know a person caused the damage," Telmaar said, "but I'm not sure about this spy theory. After all, what do they base it on? That a group of warriors attempted to kidnap the Emperor's chief wife by stuffing her into a space suit, so someone must have stayed behind because no one was carrying a spare suit? Who would stay behind for a mere female, no matter who she was? Anyway, they got her back, so that kidnap plan failed. No, I cannot see anyone staying behind. I think it more likely it is one of us, someone dissatisfied with the current order and wanting a change."

"You just had a change, a new Emperor," said Kusac.

"The court used to be far more relaxed than it is now. Now it's an armed camp, and we're treated like we're in the barracks. That's fine for the troops, but not for the officers or nobility of the Court."

Kusac glanced around, seemingly nervous at Telmaar's outspoken words, but most people were busy with their own conversations. "I think you should be more careful who might overhear you, Telmaar. You don't want to be thought to be spreading sedition," he said quietly, accepting the glass of maush from the servant.

"Don't worry so much," said Telmaar, accepting his drink. "If you listen carefully, you'll hear the hisses of outrage from the Generals as they discuss the unacceptable losses at the Prime world. The only ones you really need to worry about are the Inquisition. Anyone in red is your natural enemy, and Ziosh was so incensed at his public humiliation that he and his minions have left already."

"Yes, I saw him leave," said Kusac, relaxing and sipping his maush. He was learning a lot from this young lordling: the pulse of Court opinion, for one. Time to sit back and just listen.

Noolgoi returned. "I found Luzaarak at the office, my

Lord. He said that the Inquisitor will make a new appointment with you at a later date."

"Thank you, Noolgoi."

"So you're General Nayash now," said Telmaar, raising his glass in salute to him. "If the Emperor is replacing his ancient monuments with younger Generals, perhaps my turn will come soon."

"I'm sure it will," said Kusac, toasting him back. *Now we know what he's after,* he sent to Rezac.

Be interesting to see what he offers you to further his cause, was the reply.

CHAPTER 3

Shola, same day, Zhal-Zhalwae 18th (May)

NONI was not happy, and everyone knew it. Muushoi, Stronghold's physician, was at his wits end as he paced up and down Lijou's office.

"You have to do something about her, Master Lijou!" he said, stopping by the window to look down onto the valley below. "She's not only upsetting me and my staff, but the patients. It has to stop!"

"I shall see to it, Muushoi," said Lijou, putting a hefty dose of soothing thoughts behind his words. He was gratified to see the physician visibly relax and not a bit repentant at his use of his abilities to achieve that end. "You go back to your patients, and I will talk to Noni. Where is she right now?"

"She was reorganizing my stillroom when I left her, telling my apprentices her way to prepare the herbal remedies we make here in Stronghold."

Lijou got to his feet. "I'll go and talk to her now. You have to understand that she is under some pressure herself . . ."

"Then she should take herself off to the Prime world," Muushoi snapped. "This aversion to traveling is just an affectation, like her walking cane—she doesn't need it any more than she needs to avoid traveling. I have no sympathy for her this time!"

"Understood. Physician Muushoi," said Lijou, reaching out to touch the other briefly on the shoulder. "May I suggest you retire to the senior tutor's staff room and take a well-deserved break for half an hour? By the time you're finished, I should have everything back to normal."

Muushoi sighed. "Very well, Master Lijou, I will take your advice," he said, letting himself be guided gently to the doorway. "This has been a most trying experience for me and my apprentices."

"I can see it has," said Lijou.

The door opened abruptly. "Lijou, I need to talk to you about . . ." said Rhyaz. "Oh, I see you're busy. It can wait," he added, backpedaling slightly away from the entry.

"Muushoi was just leaving," said Rhyaz. "Good day, Physician. Remember, take half an hour break, then all should be well."

"Good day, Master Lijou, Master Rhyaz," said Muushoi as he slid carefully past the leader of the Warrior side of Stronghold.

"Come in, do," said Lijou, grasping his friend by the forearm and jerking him into his office before shutting the door firmly to stop him escaping. "I'm glad to see you. You can help me solve a problem."

"I have one of my own," said Rhyaz, straightening his sleeve when Lijou let him go.

"Don't tell me. Let me guess. Noni?"

"How d'you know? Oh, silly question," the Warrior leader said with a grin.

"She's everyone's problem today. What did she do to you?"

"Had a go at our young Brothers working on their massage skills training. Told them they were doing it all wrong. We have to do something about her, Lijou. She's gotten worse in the last two weeks. Is Conner not talking to her or something? What *is* up with her?"

"He calls her every two days and hasn't missed once, as far as I know. I think it's as simple as she just misses him."

"Why the hell doesn't she go and join him, then?" demanded Rhyaz testily, leaning on the high back of an easy chair. "She really isn't being helpful right now. Her apprentice Teusi is fully trained and can take over from her. We can do without all the chaos she's causing here."

"Never say that to Noni; she knows she's indispensable, and she is, but . . ." he sighed. "But not in the state she's in now."

"Well, you seem to have a good grasp on the situation," said Rhyaz, standing up and edging toward the door. "I'll let you carry on with it."

"Hold on, I am not confronting her alone!"

"I'd be no use to you She still likes to see me as the cub with a black eye and bleeding knuckles from dorm fights. Or to berate me as not being a proper Telepath despite my Leska link to Alex! You're far better suited to talk to her on such a weighty matter. I mean, head of our Telepaths and all that, and married."

"Coward! You have a human partner just as she has."

"Aye, but are she and Conner Leskas? No one actually knows, so it makes no difference. Too right I'm a coward in this. I save myself for fights I can win," he grinned. "Come to my office afterward, and I'll promise to put salve on your bruises and feed you coffee if Kha'Qwa isn't around to do it for you."

"My wife is in town, and you know that because she's with Alex! Oh, go on, dart off to your den and leave me to face the monster alone! I'll have my revenge on you one day, and you know it."

"You usually do. Remember, keep her on your right side; it's your stronger one," laughed Rhyaz as he opened the door.

"Begone, and stop laughing at me," said Lijou as his chuckling friend left.

Noni was in the stillroom, sitting on a high stool at the desk at the side of the room, lording it over six young Sholans who were standing at the long lab benches with heating units, making a batch of their ubiquitous bruise and cut salve.

"Keep stirring it," barked Noni. "It mustn't be allowed to burn even though it's in a double boiler. You, the female at the end!" she raised her walking stick to point at the offending female. "Yes, you, blondie! Why you using a metal spoon to stir this with? Haven't you been told the metal will alter the efficacy of the ointment by tainting it?"

"Yes, Mistress Noni! I'm sorry," The spoon clattered to the table as she dropped it and ran to one of the implement drawers to get a wooden stirrcr.

Lijou entered, followed by Teusi. "Noni, a moment of your time, if you please," he said, looking down the room toward her. "In private."

"I can't leave now, Rhyaz, they're at the crucial stage."

"Teusi can take over," he said, indicating the youth. "If you please, Noni. It is a matter of the utmost importance."

Muttering and grumbling, Noni eased herself out of the high chair and back down to ground level as Teusi walked down to meet her.

"May the sun shine on you, Noni," smiled the young male. "Have you any instructions for me with this class?"

"Just the usual. Stop them taking shortcuts, and be sure they put that extra healing pizzazz into it as they make it. Too many of them think it's like making scrambled eggs! Even scrambled eggs taste better with a few good thoughts for yourself and whoever else is eating it!"

"Quite right, it does, Noni. Maybe we should let them try this as an experiment—the taste of eggs cooked with bad intentions compared to those cooked with good ones."

Noni glowered up at him and reached out to tap him sharply on the forehead with a knuckle. "Do not mock me, youngling! You know what it tastes like, you've done that experiment with me."

Teusi grimaced slightly and rubbed his forehead. "I meant no disrespect, Noni. It's nearly lunchtime. I thought they would benefit from trying this out. A practical demonstration of the power of thought while making healing salves."

"Or anything else. Very well, then. You carry on with the class while I see what Master Lijou needs me for."

"Be safe, Noni," said Teusi as she began to walk up the corridor beside the benches to the door.

Noni stiffened briefly but didn't stop walking.

Inwardly, Lijou groaned, sensing Teusi's apologetic *"Oops!"*

As they began walking down the main corridor to the elevator, Noni looked over at Lijou. "Wondered how long it would take you to get around to coming to the class," she said. "That gutless wonder Muushoi ran to you with his complaints, I take it."

"I know you don't like him, but he has his uses here, Noni. We need a licensed physician, which he is, and he's also our surgeon. That's something you cannot do. Professional differences are one thing, but undermining each other is not right."

"Making the herbal remedies is my domain," she snapped. "He's the one with the pharmaceuticals from the big companies. I deal with the natural world."

"It's his class, Noni."

"Then he should teach it! Not leave them alone to make a mess of things. Using metal stirrers! I ask you what will it be next?"

"This exercise was supposed to show up faults in the students like this. They were deemed advanced enough to make the ointment without constant supervision. Anyway," he said, stopping at the elevator. "That's not what I came to talk to you about. I need you to go on a mission for me."

"A mission?" Noni raised one white brow ridge as she looked up at Lijou.

"Yes, a mission. It seems we need an urgent dispatch of seeds and growing mediums to be sent to the Prime world. As some of the plants are already shooting, they need to be monitored during their journey to ensure they don't die. They are plants from the Prime world Ch'almuth, ones that were indigenous to K'oish'ik. I need you to escort them."

"Me? You know I don't travel, Lijou!"

Lijou looked down at the elderly Sholan standing there in her blue robes with the multicolored shawl round her shoulders, and her long white braid hanging down her back.

"Noni, you've been doing a lot of things you never do recently," he said gently. "I need you to escort this cargo to the Prime world, and you will do this for me." He took her by the arm and reached out to press the elevator call button.

"Teusi has packed a bag for you, and the Watcher ship is waiting at the space station for you to board. You are welcome to stay there as long as you like."

"I'm needed here," she said, trying to pull away from him. "You can't make me go."

"I can and I am," he said quietly, drawing her firmly into the now waiting elevator. "You signed up to work with us, Noni, and this is a command from both me and Rhyaz. We need you on the Prime world. Conner needs your expertise there—there are six very special cubs who could do with your singular brand of upbringing."

Noni let herself be drawn into the elevator. "Six cubs, eh? Are they those cubs?"

"Yes, those cubs. We need your assessment of them."

"In that case . . . It seems there is a lot that only I can do out there."

"We also have a more pressing problem. The new bride of Emperor Zsurtul was kidnapped by K'hedduk. She's been rescued, but Kusac had only minutes to mind wipe the torture she underwent at K'hedduk's hands before she was on the ship heading back to the Prime world. We need you to make sure her mind has not been harmed, and that she never remembers the memories she has lost."

"Who is she?"

"General Kezule's favorite daughter, Zhalmo. From all I have heard, a very nice young female, and obviously very important to the young King Zsurtul. So much relies on this new royal couple; we have to be sure she remains mentally healthy."

The elevator door opened opposite the entrance desk of Chaddo, doorkeeper at Stronghold for as long as anyone could remember.

"Morning, Noni, may the sun ever shine on you," said Chaddo, lifting a bundle of items from the shelf under his desk. "I have your mission package ready for you." He reached for the shelf again only to bring out a holstered gun. "We always issue at least a stun gun to every agent going on a mission. May I suggest you have one? There are some dangerous beasts on the Prime world. Plus, they have had the odd assassin, too."

Noni looked at the gun in disgust. "If I have to carry one, at least give me one that works properly, not some child's toy!"

Chaddo glanced at Lijou and, getting a nod in reply, laughed and put the stunner away, replacing it with a small blaster.

"You know how to use it?" he asked, handing it to her.

"Mountain born and bred, I probably know how to use guns you've only heard of," she said, hooking her walking stick on the edge of the desk as she pulled out the energy pack and reinserted it, then checked the sights. "It'll do. What else is in the bundle?" she demanded.

"Standard issue to every agent—backpack, emergency field rations, gun cleaning kit, two uniforms, one of dress blacks, you name it," said Chaddo, packing the items into a small holdall and accepting the gun from Noni.

"Bag it, please," she said.

"You don't have to wear the uniform, Noni. They're there as emergency clothing. As I hear it, there are a great many stores in the Palace, and in the market outside the city walls. You won't suffer from a lack of a wardrobe." Lijou signed for Chaddo's assistant to carry Noni's bag out to the courtyard for her.

"And how's a poor old Sholan like me supposed to afford such finery?" she demanded. "Like as not there is nothing useful in the bag Teusi packed for me."

Lijou suppressed a slight smile as he led the way down the steps to the courtyard. "You'll get your salary as usual while on the Prime world, Noni, with the bonus for being on a mission for us." He reached into the pocket in his robe and drew out a message crystal which he handed to her. "Here is your briefing with all the details on what we are doing to replenish the flora and fauna of K'oish'ik. You'll get your briefing on the other matter from Kitra and Dzaka Aldatan. I can't risk putting anything in a data copy at this time. We need to know if the cubs pose a threat to us in any way at all. Have we a school of demon fish in our midst, or are these just precocious youngsters who appear to be ten years old but have only been alive for barely one year?"

Noni nodded, "I can see that this question would worry me as well as it must worry you and Rhyaz," she said. "How long will the journey take?"

"Three days. It is a Watcher ship. We're lucky that the one with Tirak's crew on it dropped in today with reports for us. They're on their way back to that sector and can easily detour to drop you off."

"Tirak and Annuur, eh? Let's hope I don't have any adventures on the way!"

"You'll join them at the space station, Noni. This shuttle will take you there. Have a good trip and say hello to Conner from us," he said, stopping by the craft.

"Don't you think I don't know that you and Rhyaz cooked this up to get me to Conner," she said gruffly.

"We really need you there, Noni. It was only when looking at reasons to send you that I realized you could be just the person we need for the cubs, and to help Conner with replanting."

"Plus with us both there, no need for you to worry about how long it will take us to complete this job."

Lijou handed Noni up into the shuttle. "I know you hate traveling, but this should be an easy journey."

"How often do you want my reports?"

"Weekly, if you please. Not about the cubs, or Zhalmo, we need to be careful with anything pertaining to them. Only we know about their existence. By the way, see if you can find out why the Watchers have disappeared from our radar over the last few weeks, only for Annuur's to suddenly reappear today. I want to know what they're up to, and he's not talking."

"I'll see what I can find out. Well, I'll say good-bye for now then, and I had better get there in one piece if the trip is only three days!" she huffed as she turned to make for her seat.

"Good-bye, Noni, and safe travels."

M'zull, later the same day

It was late afternoon by the time Kusac and his small staff of five returned to the estate. "Laazif, bring the relevant munitions factory documents to my office as soon as you can," he said, heading up the stairs two at a time for that room. "You and I will have to go over them, see where we can increase output for the Emperor. Some refreshments would also be welcome."

"Certainly, your Lordship. I took the liberty of calling ahead as soon as I knew your plans. There will be some light refreshments waiting for you now, and dinner will be served within two hours."

"Excellent. Thank you, Laazif," said Kusac as the steward bowed and hurried off to the kitchen regions.

"Gods, that Palace was so oppressive," muttered Rezac as he followed Kusac upstairs. "I am so glad to be back here."

Get used to it, sent Kusac, opening the office door. *We'll probably be there at least half the time. Right now, we need to inspect the munitions factories, but that will only give us a couple of days' grace here. Then we'll have to head back.*

Once inside, he gestured to Noolgoi and Cheelar to start checking the room for any surveillance devices, but they already had their readers out ready to scan the room.

"All clear," said Cheelar a few minutes later, putting his device away in its hidden place inside his uniform jacket. "What now?"

"We decide on a region for Rezac to take over, somewhere nearby and preferably friendly to Nayash."

"Needs to be a youngish Lord. I don't intend to pretend to be one in his dotage!"

"Agreed. An older one would restrict your movements by too much. M'yikku, did you and Noi'kkah manage to pick up any useful intel by mixing with the soldiers in the main courtyard and cavern area?"

"Gossip, mostly, but we did find out who your neighbors are. If you can pull out that map of the area, the smaller scale one that has the city in it, I can show you," replied M'yikku.

"Wait until Laazif has been up with his records and our refreshments have arrived. The less the servants see of what we're doing, the less they can give away if it comes to it," said Kusac.

"There's an estate a couple over from this one that has a Lord in his mid years. He'd be well placed for us to take over. He also has a small fleet of his own berthed at one of the other spaceports. It gives us legitimate access to another space station."

"Sounds ideal. What's his name?"

"Lord Lorishuk."

"We'll look at the map, then try and make his acquaintance in the Palace, see what kind of person he is. Unfortunately, we can't do a memory transfer the way I did, so we'll need to observe him first. I can do a limited transferal. The final decision is up to you, Rezac."

"Understood."

A knock on the door, then it opened to let in two servants carrying large trays of hot maush and sandwiches. They were followed by Laazif.

"I'm starving," said Cheelar. "They were not generous with breakfast this morning, and we haven't eaten since then."

"You should have mentioned it to me," chided Kusac. "My staff don't go hungry if I have any say in it. I hope there's a drinking bowl for you, Laazif. We all need to eat right now." Then he saw the slightly startled look on the steward's face.

Dammit! That was apparently very un-Nayash behavior, he swore.

Lapses happen. He'll be forgiving if he thinks you are being fair to the staff as a whole, replied Rezac. *Right now, he doesn't know you as an employer, so your different behavior is accounted for by that. Be worse if you were taking over an established relationship.*

"Are you sure, my Lord?" Laazif asked.

"Quite. I want you efficient, and hungry staff are very inefficient," he said.

"I had a larger table brought into the room for you, my Lord, since it seems you and your staff are frequently working and eating together in here. I hope that was acceptable?" he said, directing the servants to lay the trays on the table. As they left to get another bowl, Laazif put his books down at one end of the table and began setting out the plates and the flasks of maush from the trays.

"Ideal. I expect we'll have a few late sessions at this table. Noolgoi, get the chairs organized, if you please. Cheelar, get the map showing the area out so that Laazif can point out the locations of my factories to help us plan the visits properly."

Sandwiches in the middle and drinks at either end, they sat round the oval table and concentrated on just eating. It had been a long day, and they had left before lunchtime.

"We have to increase production of munitions for the Emperor, Laazif. Are there any ways we can do that without taking risks? What kind of munitions do we make at each factory?"

Laazif, still uncomfortable at actually sitting at the same table as his Lord, choked down his mouthful of food.

"You make three gauges of bullets for the hand arms and rifles all our infantry use. You also make energy packs for the hand blasters used by spacers and officers. And finally you make small bore missiles for the spaceships in your own navy and those ships you supply to the Emperor's fleet. They both fight in the Second Fleet," he added, "but, of course, you know that."

"So where can we increase production?"

"Not with the energy packs; they are just too volatile to push the workforce to make them faster. Any accident means a large explosion with . . ."

". . . . with a loss of trained lives and production. Understood. But we can do more with the bullets and missiles, yes?"

"Yes, my Lord. The plants shut down only on one day a week. If we were to rotate the workforce so no one was working more than six days in a row, we could keep production going for that seventh day. It'll mean a slightly longer day for them, but within tolerances."

"Let's do that, then. Thank you, Laazif. Tomorrow, you and I will visit the factories. In the meantime, please implement the changes."

"Yes, my lord," said the Steward, getting to his feet and bowing.

"You can finish eating first," said Kusac.

"I'm finished, thank you, and the changes have to be given now to the work supervisors so they can draw up new schedules for the workers."

"Very well, thank you."

They waited until he had left, then began to examine the maps for the location of the Lorishuk estate.

"I need to find out what kind of family he has, what members, who lives at the estate, who at the Palace quarters," said Rezac. "Coming into it blind for you was bad enough and we were lucky, but doing that again is chancing things too much."

"Agreed. Let's take two or three days to do our research first. However, I need you to visit the mountain tribe tomorrow while I'm at the factories."

"Why? Wouldn't it be better to wait and go yourself? What reason would I have to go as your representative?"

"I want you to inspect whatever it is they do up there—grow grain and vegetables, farm meat—find out for me. Get the feel of the tribe, how they treat their women. I want to see if they are like the lowlanders, all bred to a station in life or free from that. We could have natural allies there and not yet know it."

"That's a dangerous road," warned Rezac. "Far too dangerous in my opinion."

"At this time I would have to say I agree with him," said Cheelar very quietly. "Why would they support you in a coup against the Emperor? Because that is what you are doing. They would go down with you and suffer badly for it. Far better for them to turn you in and remain free of association with such a mad scheme."

"Let's just see what this visit uncovers, shall we?" frowned Kusac as at the edges of his mind he heard Kaid trying to make his opinion heard. "I'm not the one making first contact with them, after all. I also have Kaid's opinion to hear."

It's possible that some of them may be of use to us, sent Kaid from their base in the high mountains, *but right now, just get a feel for which way the wind is blowing up there. We can discuss it in detail here when you and Rezac need to head back to base for some extended time as yourselves.*

Agreed, replied Kusac. *Tell Carrie I'll talk to her in about ten minutes, when I can get away from the others.*

She'll be pleased, said Kaid. *Will do.*

"I'm taking some time in the pool," said Kusac quietly, getting up. "I need to talk to Carrie. M'yikku, please accompany me as my bodyguard."

I do hate just handling comms when you're taking all the risks, she sent when he was finally able to relax in the pool and chat with her. *Don't tell me it's important monitoring the comms for possible mention of us, I know that, but I feel redundant. We have a program doing this, too. I'm just one of the live person backups.*

Knowing you're doing that gives me the confidence to do this, he replied, making his tone a mental caress.

She sighed. *I know, and at least I know I'm helping. Are you remembering to not stay in Valtegan form for more than three days and nights? When did you last change?*

Two nights ago. Rezac the same. We each had two of our commandos watching over us all night to be sure no one disturbed us.

Good. Any idea when you're coming here? We think every five changes, roughly every fifteen days at most, you should come to base if you can and be Sholan for a full Sholan day—twenty-eight hours.

I'll do my best. So far I am not having any of that

flickering feeling as if I'm about to morph without warning. Neither has Rezac.

The Gods help us all if you do! she said. *Kaid's putting together a contingency plan, but it depends on you giving us good maps of the whole of the Palace underground. We need to know where the cells are.*

Could be difficult, even trying to get that information might get us caught for different reasons. Tell Kaid that K'hedduk is utterly convinced one of us remained behind after the rescue. He's scouring the whole Palace for the spy. We really kicked his ant's nest for him! I'm not sure if this is to our advantage yet or not, though.

Just so long as he's not suspicious of you, she sent.

He wants me as an ally against the other Generals. In fact, he just made me one, much to the annoyance of the others who are a lot older than Nayash. I'm to back his plans in the Council and generally support him. Talk about irony.

I'll tell Kaid to join us, shall I? He needs to hear this.

It was Kusac's turn to sigh. *Better do that. Don't know how long I'll have out here before they call me to dinner.*

Must be dreadful, a lovely pool, a hot evening, and a good dinner! We have sub-zero conditions at night, a little above that in the daytime, and are all stuck in this damned cave. I can tell you, we're all getting cabin fever!

Any more from Annuur?

Yes, sent Kaid. *He let us know through the TeLaxaudin Azwokkus that he's meeting Noni at the space station at Shola to take her to the Prime world. Seems they want to be sure that Zhalmo gets all the help she needs.*

That's actually good news. Kitra won't have to try and deal with it after all, and Noni is well able to handle even my botched job of deleting Zhalmo's memories of her capture and captivity.

Apparently, it wasn't so botched, chuckled Kaid. *Seems that she and Zsurtul got married on the way back. The Touibans and one of the Brothers on the ship officiated. I'll bet they wished it had been a state affair after all. Those Touibans apparently love ceremonies according to Azwokkus.*

Married? So what I did worked, thank the Gods. M'yikku is giving me a five-minute warning, so I need to brief you on what's happened to us.

M'zullian Palace, same evening

"Zerdish, I want to see our alien agent immediately. Send for him."

The black-clad bodyguard left the room silently, returning a few minutes later. "He'll be here in ten minutes, Majesty."

"Good," said K'hedduk getting up and walking over to his drinks cabinet. He poured himself a neat after dinner spirit, swirling the ruby red liquid round the glass before taking a sip. "I have several important issues to discuss with him, and this time I won't be put off."

Azwokkus arrived in a curtained sedan chair of the type used by the wives of other Lords when visiting the harem ladies.

As the servants carrying it entered, Zerdish took charge. "Just leave the lady with us. We'll tell you when to return."

Bowing deeply, the two servants left.

The drab brown curtain twitched, and Azwokkus popped his head carefully out, mandibles clicking. "Is safe?" the automatic translator asked.

"Yes, of course it is!" said K'hedduk, perching on the edge of his desk.

Azwokkus emerged slowly and carefully from the cushions set behind the curtains, his somber green draperies gently moving against his spindly bronze legs. "What does sand-dweller need this time?" he asked.

"Sand-dweller?" demanded K'hedduk. "What do you mean by that?"

"Your people evolve on hot dry world, much sand," said the translator before making a spitting, hissing noise. "Logical name."

"We're Valtegans, not sand-dwellers," snapped K'hedduk. "I don't know if you're aware or not, but I was recently on the home world of K'oish'ik. While I was there, every one of your people disappeared just when I had need of them. I have asked you this question before, but you haven't answered. I want to know not only *why* you left, but how? No ships left the Palace lot, none left the spaceport, so where did you go?"

Azwokkus' eyes swirled rapidly as he sought for an acceptable answer. At least this translator was one of those designed to spit out garbage sounds whenever he wanted an answer to be taken as untranslatable.

"Annual pilgrimage. Time for us to *hiss, spit* . . . to our home world. We travel by *hiss, spit* . . . means *hiss spit hisss* . . . Cannot tell you. Words you do not have." He ducked his head apologetically even though he knew the other would not understand the gesture.

"It's instantaneous transport between your world and this, isn't it?" said K'hedduk, getting to his feet and moving toward the small alien. "I want to know how you do it, I want to use it for myself."

"Cannot. Species thing and only to waiting ship, not far. You cannot use, too big."

"Then adapt it for us! You are adept with inventing devices like that one down in the lower corridors. You can make it possible for us to travel instantly to our ships from the planet's surface, if you put your minds to it."

"Perhaps, I not engineer, I scientist of different kind. I ask, we see." Azwokkus turned to go, but K'hedduk's hand snaked out and grabbed him round the arm, holding him tight.

"Good Gods, but you're all bone," said K'hedduk in surprise. "I need a weapon from your people that will let me beat the Valtegans on K'oish'ik. I am their rightful Emperor and I will retake that world for myself. You will provide me

with a weapon to do so. Not one like we're using on J'kirtikk, I don't want to destroy all life there, I want to enjoy my
victory, have them as my subjects, and have that pretender
in my grasp."

"Matter transformer broken, cannot fix it. No can make
weapons for you," said Azwokkus, trying to restrain himself
from letting loose with his defenses. A quick jolt of energy
would be ideal now, but he didn't want the other to know
just what reserves he had at his disposal. Being touched at
all against his will by this most violent of the sand-dwellers
had him putting his other hand near his translocator in fear.

"What do you mean the transformer is broken?" demanded K'hedduk, shaking the small alien. "My people
said they are having trouble programming it, but I thought
it was their incompetence."

"Stop abusing me! Old is transformer, old, old. Broken
it be from age! Another we not have. Cannot fix. Cannot
make weapons again."

"Burn it, you *will* make me weapons!" hissed K'hedduk,
letting go of the TeLaxaudin and lashing out with his other
hand. Before the blow connected, there was the sudden
smell of ozone and a flash of blinding light.

K'hedduk staggered back with a cry, blinking, his eyes
watering. "What the hell? Get him, Zerdish! Don't let that
insect get way!"

"I can't see either, Majesty," came the reply.

Tears pouring down his face, K'hedduk forced his eyes
open and began searching the room for the alien. "He's
gone, dammit! How dare he leave like that! When he returns . . ." He stopped, took a deep breath. "He's not going
to return, and we have no way of contacting them again.
Unless they want their machine back. Put a twenty-four–
hour guard on it, Zerdish! It is never to be left alone. No one
in or out except for me. If they try to get it, we'll have them!"

"Yes, Majesty."

Ghioass, Camarilla world, Azwokkus' house, same night

"Aieeeee! Vayak, Maykee! Send for Shvosi and Khassis," cried Azwokkus, suddenly materializing and staggering across his living room. "A physician, too, for my arm!" He held out his swollen forearm as the U'Churian couple came rushing in to his aid.

"Quick, contact the Camarilla members and then the physician," said Vayak to his wife. "I'll take him to the bathing room and see to his oil bath. Who did this to you, Master Azwokkus? Was it because of the mission you were on?"

"I cannot speak of it," Azwokkus said, tearing off the translator he'd used on M'zull and throwing it the length of the room. "Oh, the barbarity of them! If I had not been convinced before . . ."

"Hush, Master Azwokkus, you're safe at home now. You'll soon be comfortable again," said Vayak soothingly as he helped the stricken TeLaxaudin walk to the large and airy bathing room.

His wife Maykee headed for the comm unit where she punched in the special code reserved for emergency communications with Phratry Leader Shvosi. As far as she knew, all it did was alert her to the fact that her presence was needed here. That done, she repeated it for Skepp Lady Khassis. Then she called Master Azwokkus' physician.

The two Camarilla members arrived together, thankfully after Azwokkus had had a calming soak in his bath and been treated by his physician for a badly bruised forearm. His arm, now swathed in a soft pastel blue bandage, the TeLaxaudin relaxed on a large soft cushion, wrapped in a shawl of finely worked delicate yarn in rainbow colors.

"Homekeeper Vayak," said Shvosi quietly when the U'Churian opened the door. "How is he?"

"He is well, Lady Shvosi," he replied, ushering them in. "His arm was bruised down to the bone. Any more force on it and it would have been broken. He is still a little shaken, understandably."

"As you say, understandably. Thank you," she said, entering the small hallway.

Azwokkus looked up as they entered his greeting room. "You came! Have I things to tell you. The barbarity—we only guessed at it. Far worse it is. Refreshments if you please, Vayak, and a seat for Lady Shvosi."

"Of course, Master Azwokkus, everything is ready and will be here in a moment."

For the next five minutes, Maykee and Vayak busied themselves around his guests, sorting out the special Cabbaran seat for Shvosi, and cushions for Khassis, as well as low tables with appropriate drinks and snacks for all three of them.

"If you need anything else, Master Azwokkus, just send for us," said Vayak as they left the master of the house with his guests.

"Thank you, I will. So thoughtful is Homekeeper Vayak," he murmured picking up his tall thin glass of fruit juice.

"I know you are very fond of him and his mate," said Shvosi.

Azwokkus' eyes whirled as he adjusted his vision to look at her. "Indeed, I am."

"Now you are settled, tell us what happened," said Khassis.

"The brutal—Valtegan—demanded my presence, and I was conveyed to his office. He wanted to know how we left the sand-dweller home world while he was there. Oh, it was the wisest thing we did! Barbaric we knew he was, but had not met it ourselves!"

"What did you tell him?" asked Khassis.

"I told him it was a ritual thing we leave at that time, annual pilgrimage. He demanded we give him knowledge of instant travel. I said we could not as only over short distances and for people of our size. We had a ship waiting, I said. He pushed, and for then it was best I said we think about adapting it for his size."

"This was what we feared," said Khassis grimly. "They almost bring about exactly what we all know must be avoided—advanced tech in the hands of species too young to understand it."

"More. He demands we devise a weapon for sand-dweller capital world. One to not kill the people like on J'kirtikk does. He wants to enjoy victory! I say transformer old, very old, broken, we have no other, and he laid violent hands on me, shook me! Demanded I fix it! About to hit me when I translocated here. The terror of it," he moaned. "I was so close to killing him for the indignity and pain he was heaping on me!"

"You did well to restrain yourself, Azwokkus. Not many would have had your forbearance," said Shvosi, leaning forward to pat the other on the uninjured hand.

"He now knows we can translocate. Little good it will do him, we are not going back! One of us should never have been there to start with. Have you recorded your memory of this for Unity, Azwokkus? We will need it some day."

"Not yet. I had only just finished with the physician when you arrived. I will do it when you leave."

"Well, one way or another, we get the matter transformer back shortly. Till then, they cannot use it," said Shvosi.

"Opened my eyes to what is happening within Camarilla you have," said Khassis. "I will talk with others in the Moderates Party of a like mind regarding some of this. Shvosi, you should speak to Kuvaa. Security for Unity she has undertaken, so perhaps between them they can find other instances where Isolationists have broken the rules like this. Time we really began building our case against them before we all suffer for their selfishness and manipulations."

Mountain region, Nayash estate, Zhal-Zhalwae 19th (May)

Rhassa stopped at the gate into the pen for the woolly herd beasts. "Shazzuk, there is an aircar coming with someone from the Lord's estate."

"How far out? Does the radio say?"

"I don't rely on the radio!" she snapped. "He's on his way to us. You'll need to see him."

"Then I'll see him when I am ready," he said. "I have these beasts to tend to right now. They'll be birthing in a couple of months, and I need to check they're all healthy or there'll be no young ones come the autumn, and that means no . . ."

". . . wool come the early summer," Rhassa finished. "I know the pattern of the seasons out here, Shazzuk, I'm older than you!"

"But not always wiser," said his wife as she came up to the gate with her basket of food for her husband.

"I said he'd come here," said Rhassa, "and you said no, yet here he is." She pointed upward as they heard the droning of an approaching aircar. "He'll want our aid."

Larashi pushed past the older woman and opened the gate, going up to her husband. "You need to eat. You were up with the sun this morning, unlike our young Lord. Eat this," she said, reaching into the basket for a fat pastry and handing it to him. "Let the village guards come for you. It's no insult to keep working." She pulled out a metal container and unscrewed the lid. "Hot maush," she said, handing it to him. "Go home, Rhassa. You've given us the news, you can tell everyone you knew first."

"He'll want to see the chapel, he will."

"Hopefully he won't ask to go there this time. The sword still looks a bit new," said Shazzuk round a mouthful of meat pastry.

"He won't know. He hasn't been here before. I heard that he's a waster, always out partying, never helping his Da with the estate," said Larashi quietly. "Not like a decent son would." She pulled out another pastry for her son who had just finished counting the beasts.

"Thanks, Mam," he said, taking a hearty bite. "There's forty of them, Da, and all look to be pregnant. We should have a good-sized herd come autumn."

"Yes, I think getting them was a sound move. We can

make our own cloth now, and yarn for knitted goods. Give us something more to barter down in the valley markets."

"And meat for the table for us and his Lordship," said his son.

"You're a good lad, Chygul," His father stroked the back of his son's head as he finished up his pastry. "Here, you can finish my maush for me." He handed him the metal flask. "Looks like that aircar has landed and the Lord is in the village. I see Maalash running toward us. Make sure the beasts get that special feed before you let them loose again."

Shazzuk began wiping his hands on his trouser legs until an outraged cry from his wife stopped him.

"Here! Use this cloth," she said, passing him the cheese-cloth that the pastries had been wrapped in.

Hurriedly, he wiped his hands, heading back to the gate where Rhassa still stood.

"I'm right and you know it," she said as he left the corral and walked toward the village guard.

As Maalash opened his mouth to pass on his message, Shazzuk said, "I know. Lord Nayash is here wanting to see me. Where did you leave him?"

"Oh, you know. Well, he's in the square, beside his aircar, with his guard."

"You left him out in the sun?"

"He's all right. He has those colored glasses and the air-car to lean against. I said I wouldn't be long, and he seemed happy enough to wait."

"Did no one have the wit to let him into my office?" demanded Shazzuk, breaking into a run along the path down to the village. "Sheer manners should have made someone do that! You show visiting village herdsmen and planters in fast enough when I'm busy!"

"Aye, but you're in there then, too," said Maalash, puffing to keep up with him.

The lane between the houses was in sight now, and through them was the town square where all the important gatherings were held.

As Shazzuk emerged into the square, sunlight glinted off the gold aircar and dazzled his eyes. It took him a moment before he was able to focus on the green-uniformed officer walking over to him.

"Nayash village?" he asked. "I haven't been here before. You must be the village leader. Your name is Shazzuk. Have I got it right?"

"Yes, your Lordship," said Shazzuk, dipping his head in a bow. "Welcome to our village. Please follow me into my office—they should have shown you in, not left you out in the sun. I apologize for them, my Lord."

"It's all right. Cheelar, stay in the square with the vehicle, but you can sit in the shade. I know you're all busy because today is a working day," Rezac said, following him into the cool interior of the house. "I also forgot to call in advance to give you any warning. And I'm not Lord Nayash, I'm his aide, Lieutenant Rezzik."

"In here, Lieutenant," he said, indicating a door to the right of the main family room. "Meggu, leave the little ones for now and get us a jug of cold maush and two bowls, please,"

"Yes, Da," said the young girl, getting up and heading off into the kitchen.

On a rug in the center of the room crawled two young children.

"Four youngsters?" asked Rezac, stopping to take a look at them before entering the office. "They must be a handful."

"We have Meggu to help her mam, and I have my other son to help me with the herd beasts and the fields. We have good people here, your Lordship. We always have our produce ready for the estate on time, not like some estate farms. Always have extra, too." He indicated the seat behind the carved desk. "Please sit there, your . . . er Lieutenant Rezzik. I'll fetch the books for you."

"Thank you," said Rezac, sitting down and crossing one elegantly booted leg over the other as he waited.

"Is there any special reason for the visit, Lieutenant

Rezzik?" Shazzuk opened the doors of a cabinet facing the desk and drew out several large ledgers.

"Nothing specific, just visiting all Lord Nayash's holdings since he is new to the title."

"Here you are. You'll see I keep them up to date. Everything you need to know is in them," he said, putting the books down in front of Rezac.

"I poured it for him, Da," Meggu said, walking into the room slowly, carrying a glass bowl of maush.

"Meggu, you should have just brought us the jug."

"It was too heavy, Da," she said as Rezac leaped to his feet and caught the bowl just as she stumbled.

"It's all right, I have it. Even this is heavy for you," he said kindly, putting the bowl on the desk. "I'll enjoy it all the more knowing you poured it for me."

Hot color flushed the youngster's face and she took refuge behind her father, peeping out from behind his leg.

"Your Lordship, I am so sorry!"

"Enough said, Shazzuk," said Rezac firmly. "We were all young once. No harm done at all. Now pull up a chair and explain these ledgers to me."

It was about two hours later, as he was leaving, that Rhassa came up to him on his way to the aircar.

"You aren't him. Who are you?" she demanded.

"Excuse me?" he asked, taken aback.

"You aren't the Lord Nayash. Who are you?"

"I never said I was," said Rezac. "I'm Lord Nayash's representative. He sent me to check on his holding here and report back to him. Today he had to go round the munitions factories."

"Tell him he has to come himself next time. We want to see him."

"Hush, Rhassa, that's enough. Lord Nayash is busy. He can send who he wants to us," said Shazzuk, signaling for Maalash to remove Rhassa from the town square.

"Next time a visit is necessary, he will come personally. Of that, I can assure you."

"He wants our help then he will have to come himself!" said Rhassa as she was bundled away by Maalash and Roymar.

Rezac put a confused look on his face and turned again to Shazzuk. "Who is that?"

"Rhassa, the village priestess," said Shazzuk. "Did you find all in order, my Lor . . . er, sir?"

"Yes, you're managing the estate lands here as well as anyone could, as far as I can see. It will be up to his Lordship to make that determination, but I will so advise him after what you've shown me today."

Rezac made good his escape and as soon as they were in the air, he spoke to Cheelar. "Telepathic female, do you think? She knew I was coming, and she knew I wasn't Nayash. I hope we can get Kusac past her!"

"To all intents and purposes, Kusac is as much Nayash as anyone is likely to get," said Cheelar, "That will definitely be at the forefront of his mind when they meet, so it's possible she will accept him for what he now is. Is the village being well managed?"

"Very. I doubt anyone else could have done so well. I have a feeling that there is a tie to this land for Shazzuk's family. As I understand it, when M'zull fell back about fifteen hundred years ago, there was civil war on each of the four main planets. The winners parceled out the land to themselves and old claims were often lost. It wouldn't surprise me to find out that Shazzuk's family once owned this land and has never forgotten it. Look into it if you can. There must be a history of the families somewhere."

"I'll get onto it," said Cheelar.

Mountain Base camp, later that day

Kaid! Hologram incoming from Annuur, Carrie sent to him. Kaid left his post at the mouth of the cave, and joined her by the small watch fire they kept in the first of the caverns.

"What is it this time?" growled Kaid as he squatted down in front of the hologram.

"We had message. Azwokkus no longer on M'zull. K'hedduk attacked him, nearly killed him. Lucky he translocate to safety but no more TeLaxaudin spy on M'zull. Barbaric nature of those sand-dwellers exposed."

"We did warn you," said Kaid.

"I be knowing this, but others needed proof. Now have it. All who know are for moving TeLaxaudin out of K'oish'ik Palace to Sholan campsite and helping you, not sand-dwellers anywhere."

"No, that would be very wrong," said Carrie. "Zsurtul is entirely different from K'hedduk. They are barely the same species any longer. You have to stay at the Palace, they do need your help."

"I agree," said Kaid.

"Whatever. Now we can offer you direct help—offer Kusac direct help."

"That you will have to talk to Kusac about personally," said Kaid. "He's based at the estate right now, going round the munitions factories. K'hedduk wants to increase production."

"I talk to him later about this, bring here. Things you all must hear I previously told not to tell you."

"How much direct help are we talking about?" asked Carrie.

Annuur looked to one side and they heard a muttered conversation going on just out of range of their hearing. "Working on device we are to transform your Valtegan females into appearance of males. Difficult as only our people here and some U'Churians to test it, no sand-dwellers or Hunters—you say Valtegans or Sholans. May take some little time before we know if works."

Kaid sat up straighter. "What? That would be terrific! We need more people for our raids, and I brought our females because they are warriors, too! But we just cannot use females because of it being a male-only culture. If the M'zulians even get the scent of one of our women, she wouldn't survive their attack."

"We see, no promises yet. I return later, talk more." With that, he was gone.

"Did I hear him right? Is he bringing Kusac here later tonight?"

"That's what he said," said Kaid, reaching out to wrap an arm round her shoulders. "Be good to see him again, won't it?"

"Oh, yes," she whispered. "I worry so much for him. It's difficult making sure I keep myself walled off from him during the days so he can play his part without worrying about me."

"I know. You're doing very well. It won't be too much longer now, only a few more weeks. And you'll see him tonight. I just gave him a brief heads up about Annuur. He says likely he'll stay the night."

"Every day is too long," she said, getting up. "I would love him to stay overnight. Well, I'm off duty for now. I'm going to get into the warmth with the others. It's my turn to help cook dinner. It'll be bland dried meat stew again, I bet."

"At least we have meats!"

"With you Sholans here, we have to have meat," she laughed.

Rezac, back before Kusac, decided he and Cheelar were taking some rec time in the pool. They were still there when Kusac arrived back with Laazif.

"It's all right for some," he said, strolling out onto the sun deck. "How did the visit go?"

"Very well. How is it that every place we go has their own version of Noni?" Rezac asked. "Theirs knew I wasn't you. Not that I pretended to be."

Kusac sat down on one of the loungers. "And what did you find out?"

"The Leader is a family man, two older children, a boy and girl, and two younger crawling ones. The girl helps the mother by babysitting the babies. The son helps farm with the father. They just invested in a herd of woolly beasts for meat and their cut fur to make cloth and yarn. The cloth won't be high quality, but it will make money selling at the markets for the other farmers. Plus there's meat from them, of course."

"That must be the first furred animals I've heard of. Normally, they just run to reptiles."

"Yeah, I was surprised, too. The rest is grain for the estate and to feed to all our people on it, and fresh vegetables and such for our house and themselves. The estate imports the rest of what it needs in foodstuffs and trades out mainly the munitions."

"Right then, I'm getting upstairs for a shower," he said, getting up. "I stink after walking round three of those damned factories! Dinner isn't far away, and I will be occupied this evening after it. I'll tell you upstairs."

"Oh, I forgot. I promised them you would visit in person next time. The priestess also knew you were going to ask for help," Rezac said quietly. "She said come in person or you won't get it."

"And how much weight does she carry in this tribe?" asked Kusac, equally quietly.

"Perhaps not too much," admitted the other with a grin. "They carted her off for being disruptive. They were more afraid of her angering you, not me."

"Well, at least we know that they may be of use to us now. Thank you for going for me, Rezac."

Prime world, after dinner, same day

Dinner was over, and it was the couple of hours when the cubs could choose what to do. Tonight, once again, Shaidan headed for the library. Straight for his secret door he went, then hesitated, his hand poised over the catch. He sensed something, something almost alive, that should not be there. Cautiously, he let his hand rest on the wall, using all his senses to probe deeper, learn more about this object.

He quickly realized it wasn't an object as such, more like a small net of impulses, a web, that was it, a small web. Something like this had been in the pool area several weeks ago, before his parents had left on their mission. He remembered feeling it just as it began to disappear into nothing. Would that happen now?

Shh, came the thought. *Don't tell anyone. Let this be just between us.*

He examined his reaction, finding he wasn't afraid—perhaps he should be, a part of him thought—he was just very curious. *What are you?*

Oh, clever, you can tell I am a what. I'm friendly. What are you?

Against the edges of his mind he could feel a gentle probing, not intrusive, just—there. *Ah I see, Sholan, male, called Shaidan. Hello, Shaidan. Now we have been introduced you don't need to touch the wall. I can hear you if you send thoughts in my direction.*

Like ZSADHI can hear our voices?

Like that, yes, but infinitely more complex.

Who are you?

I have no name as you know it.

You must have a name, every living thing has . . . a name. You're not alive, are you?

I have a name you can call me, the thought offered. *Call me Unity for I unite people.*

Unity. Who are you uniting me with?

Me. I've watched you for several days now, with your brothers and sisters in the nursery, and swimming in the pool. Even in the courtyard when you go out unseen at night to watch the passersby. I am curious. Why do you sit and watch them?

Shaidan let his hand fall to his side, then slid down the wall to sit cross-legged at the foot of it, his head resting back against the intricately carved wood. *It's complicated,* he sent. *No one really understands us except each other. We're ten, but we're also only around one year old. We want to play like kittle kids, then we want to learn grownup stuff. When we were birthed, we only had grownups for company, so we never got to be real kids until a few weeks ago when we came here. Only there aren't any kids like us.* He shrugged. *Watching the grownups here reminds me they can be friendly and kind, unlike the ones we knew originally.*

I see. You're wise for one so young. You do need to learn grownup things, sent Unity. *Soon you will have to bear responsibility for important matters beyond your years. I wish it wasn't so, but I've seen it.*

Seen it? How can you have seen what hasn't yet happened? demanded the cub.

It's what I do, what I am. Bringing people and events together. No, it won't happen because you know me, came the swift reply to the cub's barely formed thought. *It will come anyway. I can just help you be ready for it.*

How can you do that?

You need to learn certain skills you don't yet have. You need to find out who has those skills first of all. Then you need to persuade them to teach you.

How am I supposed to do that? Grownups just say No, and Because I say so, or You're too young, to me.

I'll help you with that once you find out who can teach you.

Again, Shaidan was intrigued and curious. *What do I need to learn, and why?*

You need to learn to protect yourself because a time will come with danger for you that you cannot avoid. Training now will help you succeed in your task.

What task?

I cannot tell you that, only you will know what your task is when the time comes, young Sholan. Would you like to see a people like yours practicing the arts of war?

Yes! Show me, he said as flickering images of black-furred people began to play inside his head.

U'Churians they are, like you once, but not since many thousand years now. Then you had common ancestors. They fight like your people. Watch and learn how they can use anything as a weapon.

A little later, Shaidan headed out to the lower levels of the Palace, this time to just behind the public temple where the entrance corridor for supplies for the Palace food stores came in. Again, staying in the shadows, he crept down the corridor to the courtyard outside. At this time of night he knew he was pretty safe as there were unlikely to be any deliveries until morning. The exercise yard would be mostly empty as any night drills took place outside the city walls.

Nowadays, most of the off-duty soldiers gathered in the Sholan encampment outside the Palace walls. At first small, it had grown in size till it resembled a small township all of its own. If he wanted to find people capable of teaching him what he now knew he needed to learn, he was pretty sure it wouldn't be Garras or Uncle Dzaka that did it.

He had in mind a couple of Sholans, the ones he'd watched working with and driving the MUTAC, the huge Sholan mechanical fighting machine shaped like a Sholan. He'd have to watch them some more to find out how they would react if he approached them after the refusal he just knew he'd get from his uncle and aunt. Right now, they were in the Sholan bar with a small crowd of friends both Sholan and Valtegan.

"C'mon, Jer, you know you can do it," M'Nar wheedled. "Chance for us to make a buck or two out of that asshole as well," he said quietly as he got to his feet. "Maalad, if you want to see him hit the apple on my head, you gonna need a wooden or plastic panel behind me first," said M'Nar loudly. "We're not gonna risk the knives on these metal walls."

"That's fair," said Failan, pushing his chair back and staggering to his feet. "What y'say, Maalad? We gonna do this?"

"Sure, they're all talk. Bloody Brotherhood think they're better'n all the rest of us." He pushed himself drunkenly to his feet, then grabbed the edge of the table and tipped it over. "You wanna backstop? Now you got one! Put it up against the far wall, lads, and clear the floor!"

Around him the other drinkers leaped to their feet and swore at him for spilling their drinks. Those at other tables cheered loudly at the promise of the spectacle to come. Several ran forward to get the table.

Jerenn and M'Nar had remained seated. "You did it again, didn't you?" Jerenn sighed. "A quiet drink I said, no exhibitionism, I said. Sure, Jer, you said. I promise, you said. Now look at it!"

"But, Jer, he insulted your skills. You have to do this to stick up for our side! C'mon, it's easy for you, you know it is. Hey, Deksha, lass, you get the bets in!" he called out to the off-duty Sister serving the drinks.

"We gonna get a demonshration," Maalad said the word slowly and carefully, "of expert knife throwing from this here Jerenn person." He reached down and clapped Jerenn on the shoulder.

"Aye, M'Nar! Will do," Deksha said. "Who'll give me ten to one he hits the fruit first time? Ten to one!"

"I've had a few too many beers, M'Nar. You know I don't like to do this when I've been drinking," said Jerenn.

"Too late to pull out now. You got your knives, haven't you?"

Jerenn gave him a withering look as he got to his feet. "You got your pistol?" he asked, reaching up to catch the apple that came flying his way.

"Apple for you, Jerenn," Deksha called out.

Around them, the tables between them and the back wall were being shifted, and theirs was having its legs folded flat and being propped up against the wall with the other one, ready for M'Nar.

"Just don't throw it so low this time. Last time, you gave me a haircut," said M'Nar.

"Don't tempt me! Go on, get into place. Here's your apple." He threw it at M'Nar who caught it and with a cheeky grin turned and walked off to the far side of the room.

"So what's the bet for?" he asked Sister Deksha.

"The usual, Jerenn," she grinned. "Hit the apple on his head, first shot."

"The usual? Gods help me, do I do it that often these days? I swear M'Nar is being a dreadful influence on me!"

"Nah, he's stopped you getting old before your time. You used to be a bit of a stick in the mud until he came along."

"I prefer responsibly reserved," he said wryly. "Let's make M'Nar sweat, shall we?"

"Sure," she said, a tad uncertainly. "I trust you to hit the apple, but are you sure you haven't had too much to drink?"

"Oh, I can sober up when I want to," he grinned toothily at her.

"So, Maalad, you gonna eat your worlds about Jerenn if he makes this shot?" M'Nar called out as he placed himself in front of the upended table and began to balance the apple on his head.

"If he makes it. I don't think he will, though! Twenty to one he misses!" He waved a twenty note in the air which Deksha quickly snagged.

"You heard him, ladies and gents!" shouted Deksha "Maalad has twenty bucks that says he misses! Last bets now!" she said, waving a wad of cash in the air.

Jerenn walked into the center of the room, measuring the distance to his sword-brother by eye, then he turned his back on him.

"Jer, you sure about this!" M'Nar called out as the crowd howled in anticipation. "I know you're good, but . . ."

Jerenn suddenly spun on his heels and threw.

Air whooshed toward M'Nar's face and the next thing he knew, a shower of apple bits was falling in front of his nose as the two halves of the apple fell to either side. He grabbed for and caught both pieces.

Whistles and calls filled the air as Jerenn took a small bow, then walked up to M'Nar to get his knife.

"You lost, Maalad, you owe him an apology," said Deksha.

"I owe him nothing It was fixed, I want my money back." He snatched the twenty back from her.

"Maalad, he won fair and square. Give me the money back and apologize."

"Be damned if I will apologize to one o' you black crows of doom. Never see you but deaths follow. It was a fluke, I say. You could never do it again. Do it once more and you get my apology, and my coin."

"Sore loser!" someone yelled.

"Do it again, Jerenn," said Goshol, one of the Valtegan infantry present. "I want to see that again!"

M'Nar was walking jauntily down the room chewing on half an apple. He held out the other half to Jerenn who took it. "Nice apple, Pity to waste it," he said. "So Maalad has reneged on his bet, eh? Well, we'll have to show him it wasn't a fluke. Gonna walk me up there, Maalad, so you can see it's genuine?" He gave Jerenn a broad wink.

"Yeah, I'll walk you up there—and watch the blade all the way till it slices into you!"

"Cheerful soul, aren't you?" said M'Nar, linking arms with him and marching back to the upended table.

"No more fruit, Jerenn. Just put a knife above his head?" asked Deksha.

"I can do that," said Jerenn, getting out five of his knives. "I'm gonna enjoy this one."

"What you two planning?" asked Deksha, narrowing her eye at him.

"Wait and see," he said, watching as M'Nar first positioned himself, then spun Maalad so his back was against his chest. "Now, Jer! Don't struggle, Maalad, you could make Jer miss, you know. Stand still, or you'll get hit."

Maalad was a touch taller than M'Nar; the first knife parted his hair and left a hairline crease on his scalp. Maalad howled like one possessed.

M'Nar crushed his arms even tighter round him. "Be still, there's more to come. You wanted proof, so stand still and get it."

Rapidly, one after the other, four more blades flew through the air, landing in a kind of halo around the heads of the two Sholans. By the time M'Nar let Maalad go, he fell to the ground, his pink nose and ears white with fear.

"I didn't . . . I'm sorry, it wasn't a fluke. Just let me go. Here's your twenty!" He threw the money at M'Nar and ran for the exit, followed by booing and hissing.

"Five knives I have to sharpen tomorrow," said Jerenn coming up to pull his knives free. "I hope it was worth it."

"Deksha?" asked M'Nar.

"Three hundred, and you gave them a good show," she said, holding out the cash. M'Nar took it and peeled off forty from the top. "Your cut," he said. "Thanks."

"Don't mention it," she grinned, walking off with a saucy flick of her tail.

"She has some lovely legs," murmured M'Nar, then caught sight of Jerenn's face. "What? Well, she has. Excuse me, I need to do something right now. Meet me outside," he said, stuffing the money in his pocket and diving into the crowd.

The cub was still there, in the shadows at the edge of the room, able to see yet somehow avoiding being seen himself. Except by M'Nar when he was up getting the knives thrown at him. M'Nar went past him, then reached out behind him, spun round, and body slammed the youngster into the wall. Dazed and breathless, Shaidan was easily picked up and hauled outside into the night where Jerenn waited for him.

"Where did you come from?" demanded Jerenn. "I'd heard there were cubs on K'oish'ik, but I didn't believe it."

Shaidan stayed perfectly still in M'Nar's grasp. "I thought you had seen me," he said to him. "I'm Shaidan Aldatan. My father is your Liege, Kusac Aldatan."

"Then you should be in the Palace in bed at this time of night and not in a bar!" said M'Nar, adjusting his grip on him so he was just holding him by the arm. "What were you doing there?"

"And how did you get there!" added Jerenn.

"I came down in the elevator and out the goods entrance," he said. "I came to find you two."

The door to the bar opened with a sudden burst of laughter and light.

"We need to get him into cover," said M'Nar urgently, picking him up in his arms. "His presence isn't exactly public knowledge—yet."

"Palace, now, back to his minders," said Jerenn succinctly.

"No, I want to find out why he came to find us. Cubs rarely do something without a good reason. At least, my cubs don't," he amended as he led them off into the night behind the small township.

Once they were out of the glare of the lights, they stopped and M'Nar sat Shaidan down on the ground. "All right, talk, youngling," he said. "What's this all about?"

"I need teachers," he said. "I need to learn skills like your knife throwing, how to fight properly."

"You're up at the Palace, there's Brother Dzaka who can teach you, and Garras. Why do you need us?"

"They'll say I'm too young, but I need to know now. I feel danger close by, and I need to be ready for it."

M'Nar looked briefly at Jerenn. "If you sense danger, you should be telling them, youngling. They're there to protect you."

"I don't sense danger now. I just know it will come, but I don't know when. I need to be ready for it, that's the important thing. I need both of you to make me ready. I saw you with the MUTAC and with the knives. I need you to teach me what they won't."

M'Nar scratched his head. "Kid, you don't sound like any cub I've ever had. Where you get to be so old?"

"We were bred as weapons by the bad Emperor and grown in tanks till we were ten years old, but we were only born a year ago. He sleep taught us everything we know, all about being telepaths and everything. But not how to look after ourselves."

"Gods! You sure about this? How many of you are there?"

"Six of us. Our parents were all on a ship together. Papa was very ill on it."

"Wait, I remember that! It was the Prime science ship under K'hedduk!" said Jerenn. "He's got to be telling us the truth. We have to get him back to the Palace before we really get ourselves into hot water!"

"We can't help you, Shaidan. You shouldn't have even been down at the bar. Once they find that out, there's no way they are going to let us give you weapons training, or even teach you unarmed combat."

"You'll find a way because that's what you do. Solve things," said Shaidan confidently. "And you were in a knife throwing contest in a bar, which I bet is wrong for you to do."

Jerenn suddenly developed a bad cough.

"Are you trying to blackmail us into helping you?"

"Yes," said Shaidan, fixing serious amber eyes on M'Nar. "No, not really," he admitted, with the grace to look away embarrassed. "Please. I need your help, or something bad might happen to me. Look how easily you caught me!"

"We'll see what we can do," temporized M'Nar, picking him up again.

Shaidan squirmed free. "I can walk, you know," he said with wounded dignity. "I'm ready to go home now."

CHAPTER 4

"WE'LL take you back the way you came," said M'Nar, leading him by the hand back into the main courtyard of the Palace.

"All right, but we'll have to tell ZSADHI you're with me, or he'll fry you with his lasers."

"Comforting thought," grunted Jerenn. "Who is ZSADHI?"

"The Palace AI," said Shaidan. "Haven't you been in the Palace?"

"Only the chapel," said M'Nar, "but I guess we're about to do that now."

This time, there was no staying in the shade, they walked down the corridor in the light. As soon as they passed through the door into the Palace, Shaidan called up ZSADHI.

"Don't tell them I'm here, ZSADHI, and these two, Brother M'Nar and Brother Jerenn, are with me."

"They are looking for you, Master Shaidan," the AI's voice said. "It is most irregular for me to keep silent about your return."

"It's only for a few minutes."

They entered the elevator and began the journey up to the fourth floor.

"Should we be here?" asked Jerenn worriedly. "It is the royal Palace."

"Probably not," said M'Nar brightly. "When did that ever bother us?"

"My sister wants to meet you," said Shaidan suddenly as the elevator drew to a stop and the doors opened.

"Shaidan! You're back!" Gaylla squealed, throwing herself into his arms. "I missed you!"

"Shaidan, where in all the hells have you been?" a male voice called out. As M'Nar and Jerenn stepped out of the elevator, the figure in the priestly robes stopped dead.

"Friends, Uncle Dzaka," said Shaidan hurriedly. "I met them outside. They built the MUTAC."

Slowly Dzaka advanced toward them.

"I went out to try and find them to ask about the MU-TAC," said Shaidan, gently moving his sister to one side. "I'm sorry. I know I shouldn't have left here, but I did so want to talk to them."

"Brothers," said Dzaka, his tone formal. "Thank you for returning my nephew to me. Shaidan, you know how important it is for you to stay safe in the Palace. It was very wrong for you to have left without asking one of us."

"I know, Uncle Dzaka, but I was safe. There were no assassins this time."

"Assassins!" exclaimed M'Nar. "For children? That's despicable."

"For Liegena Carrie, and Kusac actually," said Dzaka, "but it makes no difference, they were hidden in plain sight amongst our soldiers. The cubs are obviously very precious to us all and should not be wandering about alone in the middle of the night!" he finished sternly. "Bed, now, both of you."

"I want to talk to Shaidan's friends," said Gaylla, sticking her finger in her mouth and clutching her dolly even more tightly. "They's nice, and I want to talk to them."

"Not tonight, Gaylla. Maybe we can arrange something tomorrow, but as Brothers they do have duties to see to. They may not be free."

"Oh, that's all right, Brother Dzaka," said M'Nar. "We're off duty all day tomorrow."

"Yes, please. I didn't get to ask all the questions I wanted to about the MUTAC," said Shaidan.

"We'll see. You don't deserve any treats for this piece of behavior. Your aunt was very worried about you indeed!"

"We'd better be heading back down," said Jerenn, tugging on M'Nar's arm. "Glad we were able to help."

"Yes, indeed. Thank you again for bringing him back safely to us."

Jerenn waited until the elevator was on its way down before speaking again. "Please don't get us involved with these cubs, M'Nar. I know you miss yours, but they are the Liege's children, and special at that. They're probably under General Kezule's protection and that of King Zsurtul, when he gets home. It's just too much complication."

"Then it's up to us to simplify it. Assassins here, and we didn't know about it? Shaidan's right. He should know how to look after himself. When my son was ten, he was already well trained in martial arts. As the Liege's child, it's even more important he knows how to protect himself."

"I don't want to get involved."

"We're already involved," said M'Nar firmly.

"Let's wait and see what happens. There's nothing we can do to make it happen, after all."

M'Nar just smiled.

M'zull, Mountain Base, late evening, same day

As soon as he arrived with Annuur, Kusac got out of his uniform and morphed back into his Sholan self. "The pain is worth it," he groaned, letting Kaid help him to his feet. "I really don't like being Valtegan. I'd rather be me."

"I'm just glad you're here," said Carrie, handing him a warm woolen tunic to wear. "Come and sit by the heaters and get warm."

"Coffee, I could really kill for a coffee right now."

"Coffee coming up," said Jo, passing a large mug of the aromatic hot drink to him. "What can we get for you,

Annuur? We have a pile of blankets for you to sit on. It's the best we could do, I'm afraid."

"If you have maush, that would be fine," said Annuur, heading for the pile of blankets. He turned round on top of them a couple of times, then pushed some together to form a ridge before settling down.

"This time, I've had time to work out the questions I want to ask. I need to know why you fought and nearly damned well killed me on the Prime world! What was all that about?" Kusac demanded, sitting opposite him.

"Had to pass you something very important, but being watched we were. Need to hide our contact, escape from surveillance."

Kusac glanced automatically at his hand, turning it over to look at the palm, then up at Annuur.

The Cabbaran nodded his head, the whiskers at the end of his long snout twitching. "Yes, it was in that pouch and when you opened it, the cube . . ."

". . . dissolved into my hand."

"Yes. Nanites they were, like those that the matter transformer is making and releasing right now. We needed you to carry them here so could be released into transformer to give it its instructions, so it knew what kind of nanites to produce. Making those that in a few weeks will steal all Valtegan memories. Talking of which, you need these," said the Cabbaran, reaching a very mobile hoof into one of his belt pouches to draw out a small case. "Inside several vials. You need to break one in room where only those you trust are standing. These nanites will prevent the memory loss ones from affecting them. It is for your people, Kusac, you and Rezac and those from the Prime world, and any others you deem necessary to keep their memories. If you need more, let us know."

"That's certainly useful," said Kaid. "I was worried that the memory loss would affect you in Valtegan form and planned to ask Annuur when he was next in touch with us."

"Why would we be being spied on? Who was doing the spying? Why did you need to send the instruction nanites secretly to here? I don't understand." Kusac turned the case over in his hands, half-heartedly examining the outside.

"Decision made to kill M'zullians here to prevent this war. Others spoke against this but were not listened to. So plot devised to have things our way—memory loss, not death."

"What the hell! Who made these decisions, Annuur? Who has the right to sentence a people to genocidal death, no matter what they've done?" Kusac demanded.

"Some TeLaxaudin on Prime world were doing spying. There is council that keeps an eye on species like the M'zullians who threaten the peace of the whole galaxy. Rarely they take action, but they were threatened themselves. This time, they acted." He stopped to take a long drink from the bowl of maush that Jo had handed him.

"So it's a council of TeLaxaudin."

"Mmm . . . and Cabbarans," he admitted. "We been around longer, we know how to cooperate better than you. I not on the council," he added hurriedly,

"What will they do when they find out that the M'zullians are still alive?"

"Factions there are," said Annuur. "One in charge now responsible for the transformer being on this world, for helping this last Emperor win war against J'kirtikk. They thought to profit from confusion caused by M'zullian war, but miscalculated. Now they want dead. Other side feel responsibility is theirs to fix problem, not kill them. By time this is resolved here, is resolved in the council and that faction no longer in charge. Helping the M'zullians as they did broke every code. As for it being wrong nanites, transformer locked, no one can change what it does now until after this task finished."

"Tell me more about this council and what gives them the right to interfere in the lives of races other than their own. And what your part in it all is," demanded Kusac.

"Same right as you—they are threatened, they take action to stop threat. Not complicated. My part? You call me agent for them, go here, go there, tell this, get that information, bring back to them."

"I don't like this at all. It has to stop. You have no right to act against other species like that. If anything needs doing, then those most affected by it should decide — us, in other words, not two species who keep themselves apart from us! Those responsible for meddling like this must pay for their actions!"

"Time to discuss this later, not now. Now we focus on this problem."

"I share your anger, Kusac," said Kaid, "but let's solve this problem first. How long before the nanites plan is ready to go?"

"We think about three months to spread over all M'zull."

"How will we know who's been infected by the memory loss nanites?" asked Carrie.

"You won't, but the antidote or preventative will stop it happening to those who're given it," said Annuur.

"I'm concerned that there are TeLaxaudin acting against us and Zsurtul on the Prime world," said Kusac. "How do we know they won't try to poison them?"

"They won't. Those now on Prime world belong to the faction that doesn't favor killing. It was made certain before I came to you tonight. What you have worked for on that world is safe, Kusac, they promise that."

Kusac nodded. "It better be!"

"What happens when the nanites are spread to everyone?" asked Kaid.

"Nanites are self-replicating, so spread fast. Matter transformer know when they have finished because they emit a signal. Transformer then sends signal to them to activate, and it will shut down all M'zullians everywhere, apart from those you have chosen to be unaffected."

"What if they are driving, or cooking? Lives could be lost," said Carrie.

"Where possible, they will direct people to safety first. Then they will be unconscious for maybe a day while memories are edited to remove all but basic functions. A Lord now will not remember he is one after this. You will need a caretaker race to look after them. The Touibans have offered to be in charge and will call on other species to help. Maybe six months and a lot of sleep tapes and they will function normally again in new society you choose."

"Not us. We need King Zsurtul and Kezule as well as the Ch'almuthians involved in this," said Kusac. "Their people, it has to be their decision."

"Then is their decision, not yours, not mine, not council," said Annuur. "Now as recompense for actions of others, I am to offer you direct council help. As said earlier, working on unit that will force your Valtegan females to become male for some time. In early stage, no knowing if it works yet. What else can we be doing?"

"Food and supplies," said Carrie promptly. "We have this dried meat that is tasteless, and are running out of dried vegetables. We need power units as backups for our own ones. Several have failed us, and we've no spares left now. We use them to recharge the suits and to heat this area."

"More of these translocators set to here so that my team can escape in case of danger," said Kusac.

Annuur nodded. "Can do that. What? No superior weapons to win this war you are waging when all you need to do is wait for nanites to work?"

"No, no weapons. We have what we need," said Kusac, frowning.

"I joke, I joke," said Annuur, shaking his head.

Prime world, the Palace, next day, Zhal-Zhalwae 20th (May)

"You're sure they pass all the background checks?" Kezule asked Dzaka. "I feel as responsible as you for the cubs' safety until Kusac returns."

"Everything checks out," confirmed Dzaka. "M'Nar, as well as being a father and used to handling cubs of their age, has been creating individually tailored learning programs for our students for over two years. Jerenn has been in Special Ops and an instructor for around fifteen. We need someone to start training them, and it may as well be these two that Shaidan seems to have taken to. They have more than the necessary qualifications between them."

"What training are you giving them?"

Dzaka grimaced. "Originally, I was going to fob them off with learning to march and do drills like all of us had to learn, but Shaidan called me out on that. I was unusual in that I was brought up in the Brotherhood from a very early age. So I got all sorts of skills taught to me that are normally reserved for those of sixteen years. They're going to learn some self-defense disciplines. After all, those in the Warrior Guild back home are learning those skills before they are ten!"

"What about Gaylla?"

"Her, too, unless she says she doesn't want to do it. I want to be sure that little one can look after herself if nothing else."

"Good. If Mayza was older, I would send her along with them."

"Maybe when she's older, then?"

"Quite possibly. Well, since you have everything in order, I'll leave you to handle it yourselves. You don't need me for this."

"Just wanted you to be aware of what we're doing, General," said Dzaka, getting up to leave.

"I appreciate that, Brother Dzaka," said Kezule, rising and walking him to the door of his office.

Some twenty minutes later, Shaidan and his brothers and sisters were shepherded down to the main courtyard. Their trip to the barracks was cut short by a crowd of people right in front of their exit.

"They's here!" said Gaylla excitedly, pulling free from Shaidan's hand and rushing into the thick of the crowd.

Shaidan took off after her, with Kitra and Dzaka in hot pursuit. Being smaller, the cub worked his way to the front of the crowd only seconds behind his sister to see her stop dead to watch the two Sholans fighting each other with swords. It was at that moment that M'Nar's sword went flying across their fighting circle and headed straight toward

Gaylla. Yards from her, it clattered to the ground, bounced, and came to an abrupt stop just inches from her feet.

She bent down and reached out for the carved quillons with their sparkling gray gems for eyes.

"Ooh, pretty! I want one like that!" she said, her finger hovering just above the blade.

M'Nar took a sliding leap across the courtyard to land by the blade and pick it up before she could.

At the same moment, a Sister swooped down on Gaylla and snatched her up in her arms.

"Uh, Gaylla, isn't it?" M'Nar asked, looking up at the cub before getting to his feet and dusting himself off. "Nice to see you again."

"Put me down!" Gaylla shrilled at the top of her voice as she squirmed and fought the encircling arms. "I don't know you! Put me down!"

"Please put my sister down before you drop her," said Shaidan. "She's not in any danger. My aunt and uncle are just behind us."

"Oh," said the female, giving in to the immutable force that was the struggling child as all eyes turned to her. "Sure thing. I just thought she needed . . ."

"Protecting?" asked Jerenn as Gaylla bolted straight to M'Nar as soon as her feet hit the ground.

"Well, taking back to her parents. I'm Sister N'Akoe, by the way."

"Jerenn and M'Nar," said Jerenn.

Gaylla was hanging onto M'Nar's leg when Kitra and Dzaka managed to push their way through the last of the very interested crowd.

"I know you all have better things to do. Dismissed!" said Dzaka in his best parade ground voice, and the gathering immediately began to disperse. Brotherhood priests were often the most fearsome of the Brotherhood, so it was said among the forces.

"Aunty Kitra, I found them I did!" said Gaylla, jumping up and down in excitement. "I said I would, didn't I?"

"Yes, precious, you did," said Kitra, reaching her hand out.

Obediently, Gaylla let go of M'Nar's leg and briefly turning the full force of her big-eyed smile on him, trotted back to her aunt.

"I thought we'd go to the Sholan gym, just outside the walls," said Dzaka. "I want to see how you get on with the cubs. If you all get on well, I have a new posting that may interest you."

"I told you it wasn't complicated," said M'Nar as he and Jerenn began hauling the single bed from Jerenn's room into his.

"Which, organizing our new rooms up here in the Royal Nursery wing, or us now being the official trainers for the cubs?" puffed Jerenn.

"Both. It worked out beautifully, as I said it would. And we didn't have to try."

"We're going to regret this," Jerenn said. "We should be helping to protect Shaidan and the cubs from danger."

"They've had so much protecting they're ready to bust out of here and run amok," said M'Nar. "I know cubs, and they should be out on their own in the daytime, playing down by the river in the water and mud, climbing trees, running through the grass, feeding the herd beasts, anything but being hothoused in the Palace! They have to be taught to take care of themselves, too, and that's what we're doing, officially, and unofficially."

"I get your point," said Jerenn as they squeaked the bed round the doorframe and carted it over beside M'Nar's. Jerenn set his end down with a thump. "After this, I'll need a night in bed to recover!"

"Our first night in real comfort and you want to sleep? You disappoint me, Jerenn! How about a swim in the heated pool here with Shaidan instead," said M'Nar.

Jerenn's ears perked up. "Really? No joking?"

"There's certain times we can't use it," said Shaidan from

the doorway. "Like when King Zsurtul wants to use it, but it's all right the rest of the time. Dinner is in an hour. If you want to go, we have to go now."

"How did you know . . ."

Shaidan gave him a look. "Please, I'm a Telepath. I know things. Gaylla wants to come, too." He looked from one to the other of the two adults. "Gaylla is special," he said. "She's the same age as us, but she's a bit slower. You have to take it more carefully with her, but treat her just the same."

M'Nar glanced at Jerenn, then back at Shaidan. "We noticed, but it makes no difference to us. She's adorable. So let's go and get her and have a nice long soak before dinner!"

"You'll like the bubble pool, then. It massages all the parts that hurt."

"I love it already," smiled M'Nar as they headed down the corridor toward the nursery door. Gaylla was waiting there for them. As they stopped, she held up her arms for M'Nar to lift her up.

"You coming swimming with us?" he asked, picking her up. "I bet you swim like a fish, don't you?" He tickled her behind her ears and under her chin, making her giggle.

"I swim pretty good," she said.

M'zull, the Palace, next afternoon, Zhal-Zhalwae 21st (May)

After a night spent with Carrie and the others at the cave, when Kusac got back to the estate, he had a lot to tell the others. He and his staff had returned to the Palace that day and as soon as he arrived, he'd sought out Telmaar. With the other's help, he got himself up to date and organized on assisting to get the troops clearing up the debris and filling the potholes in the main crossroads area as efficiently as possible.

There was some collateral damage where missiles had

caused cracks in the walls of the tunnels that opened up into the crossroads and courtyard area. These he was painstakingly researching himself and then issuing the builders orders to fill the cracks with mortar. Doing this enabled him to start compiling a map of his own of the tunnels and what was located off each one and then check them with the master plan that Telmaar had.

He was working on this project when one of the Emperor's black-clad bodyguards accosted him, telling him his presence was wanted now.

"I'm covered in dust and debris. I should change before going to see the Emperor."

"His Majesty, Long Life be His, will not be concerned about that," said the aide. "Just follow me."

"Long Life to Him," murmured Kusac, handing his papers to M'yikku. "Carry on," he said, following the bodyguard.

"Ah, there you are, Nayash," said Kezule, getting up from behind his desk as Kusac was shown into his office. "This is a momentous day today. One that sees us seal a partnership that will benefit us both."

"Majesty?"

"I have a gift for you. Delivered several days ago to my harem, she has been being trained by my own harem master, Keshti, for you. Since I knew you had no wife, and it's time you married, I decided that one of the women entrusted to me—and a virgin, of course—would be the perfect gift to cement our alliance."

Struck utterly speechless with surprise, Kusac had difficulty finding anything to say.

"Well, speak up!" frowned K'hedduk.

"I'm stunned, Majesty," he said truthfully. "I could not have looked for, or anticipated, such a gift from you," which was utterly true.

"She's from one of the mountain tribes, captured when my men were doing a routine patrol of that region. She was out alone, so naturally they picked her up and brought her here."

"As they should," said Kusac. "No worthwhile female should be seen out without a male escort of her husband or some other close male relative."

"Glad to hear you're a traditionalist. These mountain women can be way too independent; they need firm handling. Keshti runs training sessions for the other court ladies from too relaxed environments, like Ch'almuth, once a week. You are welcome to have yours attend."

"Sounds ideal to me," he said. "I'm sure she'll benefit from it. Thank you, Majesty. An obedient wife is the only kind to have."

K'hedduk nodded. "Well, Keshti will have her here in a few minutes. You'd best take the rest of the day and tomorrow off to organize your own harem. She'll come with a drone servant to look after her, of course. I don't expect my Generals to have to look after their wives themselves."

There was a knock on the door. Then it opened to admit the male drone Keshti, head of the Palace harem and the Emperor's own seraglio.

"Majesty." He bowed low before entering. Behind him came two females, one wrapped from head to foot in exotic cloth. "I've brought the young female as you requested, but she isn't fully trained yet."

"Lord General Nayash has said he will send her to your weekly harem sessions so you can continue training her," K'hedduk said. "Now show this prize to her new Lord."

"As your Majesty wishes," said Keshti, reaching out toward the draperies covering her. With the flick of his wrist, the outer cloth was whisked aside to reveal a young female of average height, her coloring a blush of red and tiny blue iridescent scales across her face. She stood there in her long figure-clinging blue gown, swaying slightly and blinking her overly large round eyes.

"She is still under the influence of the training drugs, of course, Majesty. It will be some time before they wear off."

"Yes, yes, we know that. Tell Nayash what her name is, and anything else relevant that he needs to know today."

"Her name is Mahzi, Majesty, and she comes from the mountains. As such, she is one of the more intelligent of the

M'zullian females, on a par with those from Ch'almuth. A prize, indeed. Females like her are much sought after as wives as they confer status on the owner. Turn around, Mahzi, let your new Master see you from all sides," he said, his tone not unkind.

Obediently, the female turned round, her gaze passing over him with no reaction from her. In fact, there was virtually no reaction to anything in her almost lifeless face.

"Neshol, her drone servant, has a case with the training medication in it," said Keshti. "May I respectfully suggest that the Lord General keep his wife to be as she is now until he has finished her training. It should only take another few sessions. They learn better when under the influence of these narcotics."

Kusac was having a hard job suppressing the anger he felt at the young female's plight. He couldn't help seeing the face of Zhalmo imposed on hers and remembering what K'hedduk had done to her. Common sense suddenly took over and told him that if this female was still a virgin, then K'hedduk wouldn't have touched her, and likely his sadistic methods of so-called training had never been used on her.

Kusac swept a low bow to the Emperor and, as he rose from it, made sure a smile of pleasure was firmly plastered onto his face. "Majesty, this is indeed a gift beyond any I could have looked for. I can see just how advantageous our alliance is going to be. I must tell you that I've spent the afternoon avoiding Inquisitor Ziosh. He's getting most insistent. How would you like me to handle him and his threats?"

"Play him along for a while if you can, see what he tries to offer you to side with him, then just tell him straight you have allied yourself with me, Nayash. As I said, take the rest of the day and tomorrow off to settle your new female into your harem. Keshti, send a sedan for her on Fridays for your training class. Now, I really must get back to work."

As K'hedduk went back round behind his desk, Keshti carefully threw the length of gauzy material over the female's head, twitching the folds into a pleasing arrangement.

"Follow me, Neshol, and bring your Mistress with you," said Kusac, as he bowed himself out of the room.

Inwardly, he was seething as they made their way back to his apartment amid many curious looks. What better way to see he was kept on a short leash than by giving him a wife and a drone servant to spy on him in his own home! Angrily, he used his communicator to call up M'yikku and order him to leave the overseer of his team in charge and return to the apartment.

"Do I even have a harem?" he wondered out loud.

"Lord General, all Palace apartments have a harem in them," said Neshol. "Usually, it adjoins the master bedroom. It is unlikely your late father allocated it to another purpose. We will be able to make do tonight if at least you have a guest room free."

"Right," he said. "Make do tonight," he said, suddenly realizing he had to explain this to his true wife, Carrie! Come to think of it, he had to explain it to the others. He began with a brief outline to M'yikku.

Once back at the apartment, he saw the drone female and his "wife to be" installed in the harem, which was unaltered as Neshol had said it would be. He left her with instructions not to give Mahzi any more drugs. Telling M'yikku to give the news to Laazif and the rest of their group, he headed for his office and shut himself in there to tell Kaid and Carrie the news.

Not again! she fumed. *I will not tolerate you having another Valtegan lover!*

Not my fault, Carrie. I didn't ask for this, and I can't refuse it either. We'll just have to hope this Mahzi is willing to pretend to be my wife in return for obviously better treatment at my hands than she'd get from anyone else.

You'd damned well better hope she is! With that, she cut the mental communication.

I'll do what I can to talk sense into her, Kusac, sent Kaid. *There's nothing you could have done, and when she calms down, she'll realize that.*

I hope so. We'll talk again later.

* * *

It was after dinner when a knock on the office door disturbed them all from their work planning a new Lordship for Rezac and their next mission.

Flipping papers over the map, Kusac called out "Enter!"

It was Neshol. She stood just inside the doorway to give her message. "You asked me to let you know when the drugs Mahzi was given had worn off. They have done so."

"Right, I'll come with you. I need to talk to her," he said. "Carry on," he told the others as he left the room.

The harem room was overdone and fussy, very feminine with ruffles and flounces on the curtains that framed the four posts of the bed. Overall though, there was an older air to it, a genteel shabbiness.

Mahzi sat before a room heater at a small table. She was still wearing the blue dress she'd worn before.

"You can leave us, Neshol. I'll send for you if I need you."

"Yes, Lord Nayash." She bowed before leaving.

Mahzi stood up as he entered. "I demand you release me at once," she said. "I'm a free female of the mountain tribes; you have no right to keep me imprisoned."

"I didn't imprison you. It was the Emperor's soldiers that found you out alone and brought you in," said Kusac, shutting the door behind him.

She had the grace to look embarrassed at that, and as color flooded her face, she looked away from him. "It makes no difference. I demand you return me to my family."

"I'm afraid I can't do that. The Emperor now considers you property and gave you to me. I can't let you go without offending him and getting into a lot of trouble."

"I don't care about you—" she began.

"You should," said Kusac, drowning her voice out with his. "Because all that stands between you and your family being murdered by the Emperor's soldiers is me! If I let you go, have no doubt he would get you back, and your fate would not be one I would like to imagine. Being raped by his troops is not something I'd wish on you. Meanwhile, he'll also have put the whole village to the torch and burned it to the ground as a lesson to all not to go against his wishes."

"You wouldn't let him do that!" she said, this time turning pale as ice and sitting down abruptly.

"No, I wouldn't, but this Emperor would do it without a second thought," he said, taking the other easy chair and sitting down. "Perhaps we could talk sensibly now you know the reality of your situation. First, have you eaten?"

She looked up at him, startled. "Yes, I remember they brought food for me about two hours ago."

"Good. You have been given to me by the Emperor to be my wife." He held up his hand as she began to speak. "Just listen, if you please. Apparently mountain-bred females like yourself are much prized as wives by the nobility. However, I don't want to marry you for several reasons."

"You don't?"

"No, nor do I want to take advantage of your quite obvious charms," he said with a slight smile. "This means we have to pretend we're married, even if we have to go through with the ceremony."

"We can't do that! I'm promised to N'abui! I want to marry him!"

"You can't, at least just yet," he said. "It's vital for both our sakes that the Emperor thinks you're married to me. We can't afford him to think otherwise, as I've explained to you."

"I can't. I promised him, and if I marry you, I can't ever marry him!" She put her head in her hands and began to cry.

"What village are you from," he asked.

"Nayash village," she wept.

Kusac got to his feet and began to pace the room. This just got better and better! Not only was she obviously the daughter of one of his tenant farmers, but she wasn't much more than a child if he judged her behavior correctly.

"Just stop crying, Mahzi," he said, "Nayash village is mine. We'll find a way round this. Tomorrow we'll go and see the village Leader."

It was like the sun had come out. "We can? My Mam will be so worried. How long have I been here?"

"I don't know, when did you go missing?"

"On the sixteenth or seventeenth I think."

"Then about a week," he said. "I'll leave you for tonight. If you need anything, you have a way to call for Neshol?"

She nodded. "Lord Nayash, why are you helping me? Why don't you want to marry me?"

He hesitated. "Let's just say I don't want to be married at all and leave it at that. I'll see you tomorrow."

Back in his office, he gave vent to his anger. "She's not much more than a child, and promised to a lad in my village because she's one of my villagers!"

"Could you talk to her?" asked Rezac.

"Yes, but she won't go through a sham marriage with me because it would mean she couldn't marry this N'abui!"

"She thinks the marriage would be forever whereas we know differently," said Cheelar. "We can't tell her that."

"No, but we have to talk sense into her. I'm taking her up to the village tomorrow, to see her parents. She's been missing for nearly a week; they must be beside themselves. Maybe in gratitude that I've rescued her they can talk some sense into her. Me threatening her won't do any good. She'll just dissolve into tears."

"K'hedduk, being the micro manager he is, will want to see you married himself," warned M'yikku. "How can you avoid that without her agreeing to it?"

"Get married tomorrow in the village," said Rezac thoughtfully.

"I'm already married, or had you forgotten that?" he asked sarcastically.

"No, not you get married, get her married to her sweetheart tomorrow and pretend to K'hedduk you married her in the village ceremony. He'll be mad, but there's not much he could do about it except demand you go through another ceremony at the Palace. If that happens, it will be a sham one as she's already married. She should agree to it in those circumstances."

"Even she will be able to see that she isn't actually getting married to you," said M'yikku.

"All this depends on the village Leader and his wife's support, as well as that of the parents of both these youngsters. In fact, we suddenly have the whole village in on a conspiracy to cheat the Emperor," said Kusac.

"It's to save one of their own this time, not like it would be if you asked them to back you against the Emperor," said Rezac. "By doing this, you just got them committed to helping you in the future."

"I hope you're right," sighed Kusac. "Let's get back to planning that raid. Not for tonight, though. We'll have to leave it for a few more days."

Prime world, same evening

The Watcher ship had landed gently in the spaceport just outside the walls of the City of Light. As it taxied into one of the bays, Noni began to release the safety webbing from her bed. Not designed for passenger transport, it didn't boast any acceleration couches other than those for the crew, but it did have nets over the beds. Grabbing her walking stick, she sat on the edge, her two bags at her feet, and waited for Tirak to come and escort her out.

Finally, he came. "Are you ready, Noni?" he called out, rapping his knuckles on the door.

"Yes, just come in," she shouted back.

The black-furred U'Churian opened the door and stepped into the cabin. "Well, we're here at last. They've sent an aircar to meet you, and it won't be long before you're up at the Palace in comfort. It's a warm summer night here, so you should be comfortable." He approached her bed to pick up her bags as she got to her feet.

"Right glad I am to be here at last," she said. "Doubt I'll sleep tonight. My system's still on Sholan time and there it's about midday."

"You'll soon adapt, Noni," he said as they left the room

and began to walk down to the exit. "Can you manage the stairs? There are no landing facilities like you get at space stations, I'm afraid."

"I can manage," she said, "You go first. Then, if I trip, I got a soft landing."

Tirak's rumble of laughter amused her. "Just hold onto me if you need to," he chuckled. "Or I can carry you down if you like."

"You'll do no such thing!" she snapped. "I'm perfectly able to take a few stairs down!"

As they started down the steps, she saw that Conner was waiting at the bottom for her. He waved, and suddenly nervous, she timidly put up her hand and waved back. What if he wasn't pleased to see her? What if they'd been apart too long? Then she was at the bottom of the staircase and staring up into Conner's bearded face. He smiled and picked her up in a huge hug.

"Noni! How wonderful to see you! I hope you're planning a long visit!"

"Put me down!" she said sharply, secretly pleased at his reaction. "You'll scandalize everyone!"

"It's dark, so there's no one here to scandalize," he said happily, setting her back down on her feet, kissing her on the cheek, then tucking her arm through his. "Come, my dear. Time to see your new quarters and get some food into you. Captain Tirak, thank you for bringing her safely to me. Brother Jerenn will take her bags from here. If you could see to unloading the cargo, I'd be obliged."

"Don't worry about the cargo, that's my job," he said, handing the bags over to Jerenn. With a crisp salute, he walked back to the Watcher and ran up the stairs to see to the unloading of the plants.

Conner opened the aircar door and helped Noni into the back seat, then got in beside her, taking a proprietary hold of her hand.

"And who's driving this contraption?" she asked.

"Jerenn very kindly offered his services," said Conner as the object of their discussion slipped into the driving seat.

"Jerenn, I remember you, lot of grief for you a few years back. You look and feel like it's mostly behind you now. Just don't drive here like you do at Stronghold! And I see you got a sword-brother now! Good for you!"

"They're the first pair here to take the vows," said Conner. "I'm very proud of their dedication and commitment to the Brotherhood and each other. They are now training the cubs. You'll get to meet them tomorrow."

"Bairns, the same everywhere—young and small, and full of hurt knees, overstuffed tummies, and the monsters under the bed and in the closet!"

A muffled chuckle came from up front as Jerenn started the aircar.

"So you're replanting this world, are you?" asked Noni, trying to see out the windows as they sped along several feet above the roadway.

"With plants from various similar ecologies, yes. The ones you brought all came from Ch'almuth and were imported there from here before the Fall. We sent seeds to Shola for our telepaths to start growing as we'd had no success ourselves with these ones."

"Well, I kept an eye on them during the trip, and they're all sprouting now," she said. "I'd advise putting them in greenhouses for some time before planting them out, till they get a bit bigger, and certainly you need to get them acclimated to here rather than Shola."

"Exactly what we plan to do," said Conner. "It's summer here, and the heat can be fierce. Not all nights are as balmy as tonight either; some get downright cold. I think you'll like it here, though, Noni. Lots to see and do, very interesting food, and a wonderful market outside the Palace walls."

"Hmpf! Certainly sounds interesting. Perhaps I'll have a look at this market tomorrow."

The aircar was approaching the Palace now. Lights illuminated the building, bringing the painted and bas-relief friezes to life in a riot of color and stylized poses.

"Magnificent artwork, isn't it?" asked Conner as they

flew past it, Jerenn angling their approach so they could see it better. Then they were coming down in the Palace parking lot and following the commands of one of the ground staff to taxi into the covered area.

"Welcome to the Palace of Light, Noni," said Jerenn finally, turning off the engines and popping open the door for them. "If you want a grand tour tomorrow and Conner is busy, just call on us."

"You can ask ZSADHI to contact any of us," said Conner as he hiked up his robes a few inches to scramble out of the vehicle and wait, with hand held out, for Noni.

"Who's this ZSADHI?"

"The Palace AI. He only listens to you if you say his name. We'll have to get him to scan your retinas so you have access to the Palace proper," said Conner, helping her down. "Just a short walk and we're at our quarters next to the temple."

"Do we get wakened up at all hours with the caterwauling of choirs like at Stronghold?" she demanded.

Conner laughed. "No, Noni. Services are only held in the evenings after dinner, and once a week at midday. Though I don't always take the services," he said. "Nowadays the priestesses of La'shol, who is their Nature Goddess, take about half of them."

"So you got their own religion up and running?"

"Yes. King Zsurtul wanted a female-based nurturing religion to take over after the patriarchal Emperor worship of his father's reign."

Once in the central courtyard, they took their time walking through the crowds that were browsing the few stores or coming and going from the various restaurants that lined one side.

"Some parts look a bit new for an ancient Palace," remarked Noni as they walked over to the entrance to the temple.

"The courtyard saw fierce fighting when we retook the Palace from K'hedduk," said Jerenn. "The two fountains with the palm trees round them were almost obliterated by mortar fire, and one of the statues was completely destroyed, as was part of the southern façade. It's all been rebuilt, of course, but that's why it looks newer—it is."

"Ah. I see."

As they approached the door to the chapel, Noni could see a group of people waiting at the entrance.

"I don't like fuss," Noni grumbled.

"They wanted to make you welcome, Noni," said Conner. "Was I to tell the second most important person on this world, General Kezule, he couldn't greet you in person?"

"Looks like Shaidan has gotten himself invited to the welcome party," observed Jerenn.

"Would you mind taking those bags to my quarters, please, Jerenn?" asked Conner.

"My pleasure, Master Conner," the other said,

Kezule stepped forward, hand outstretched. "Welcome to K'oish'ik, Noni Dzaedoh," he said, as they touched fingertips briefly.

"Thank you kindly," she said. "Good to be here, see what everyone's been getting up to without me to keep 'em in line."

"Noni, good to see you," said Kitra, giving her a hug.

"Kitra, you look well. Life here must suit you, child. Dzaka," Noni said, nodding to him. "I swear you grow taller every time I see you! And you, youngling, you must be Shaidan. No need to ask who your parents are, I can see Kusac and Carrie writ large on your face, and your mind." She reached out to touch the edges of his mind and was met with a sense of welcome, but also an implicit warning he didn't welcome further closer contact—at least, not yet.

"I'm Shaidan," the cub said, holding out his fingertips to Noni. He barely let her brush them before letting his hand fall back to his side.

So, reserved and cautious. This one would take some patience if she was ever going to get close to him. He had a feel about him, one that said he didn't quite belong to this world, as if he was slightly loose in time.

"The others decided I should be the one to represent them and greet you," he said with a slight smile.

"We've left a hot meal for you both in your dining area,

Conner," said Kitra. "Poor man refused to eat until you arrived so he could eat with you."

"Such a good male he is," said Noni, patting Conner's arm. "Well, let's get me into my new home, then. I'm tired after all this traveling."

"Of course, Noni. Have you luggage?" Kitra looked around for bags.

"Jerenn took them down for me," she said, starting to walk down the length of the temple. "Well, I have to say this is a lovely place, so bright and airy, even at night like this. The flowers are beautiful, and the wall paintings! I don't think I have seen lovelier ones."

"All done by our own women," said Kezule, "with a bit of help here and there from some of the menfolk, too."

"It feels welcoming, General," she said, "Your folk have done a grand job. You, too, Conner, a grand job."

"Thank you, Noni," he murmured, squeezing her hand a little to let her know he was pleased.

"We'll let you get settled in as you've had a long three days, I expect," said the General as he stopped at the doorway out of the temple to their quarters.

"I have. I'll be pleased just to stop moving!"

"Good night, Noni," said Shaidan.

The apartment wasn't large, but it was certainly big enough for the two of them. Furnishings were comfortable and a little threadbare, but then, she thought, so were they. It would soon feel like a home, once she got moving with it, Still, for a bachelor dwelling, Conner had certainly made it feel relaxed and homely. A vase of wildflowers sat on the table between the covered dishes that Kitra had placed there.

"Flowers, eh? Who brought them?"

"Gaylla, actually, She gives me a bunch every few days," *But today's is special ones for you, Noni,* came the childlike thought.

Startled, Noni looked at Conner.

Conner nodded. *Yes, one of the other children, and yes, there is nothing very childlike about any of them, including little Gaylla,* he sent to her. "You'll see when you meet her tomorrow," he said.

Night night, Noni! You'll be my Noni, won't you? My own Granny? There was a hint of anxiousness in the mental tone.

Yes, child, I'll be your very own Noni. Now go to sleep and I'll see you in the morning. With that, she shut down the conversation and turned to Conner. "What *are* they?"

"Very special," he said, helping her out of her jacket and pulling out a dining chair for her to sit on. "I'll tell you about them as we eat."

Prime Palace, next day, Zhal-Zhalwae 22nd (May)

Shaidan was sitting in the nursery just after breakfast, waiting for lessons to begin. He was letting his mind roam idly, thinking of nothing special when he was suddenly aware of Unity reaching out for him. This was not an invitation to talk, it was more of an imperative to observe.

Ghioass, same day

Kuvaa was searching through Unity, trying to find out not only how she had been duplicated, but how the Isolationists had been able to subvert the AI into hiding the kidnap and incarceration of the one the Hunters called Vartra.

She wasn't getting too far right now; it was a matter of setting up routines and searches through the massive databases.

"Unity, how is it that you knew nothing about the kidnapping?"

I have no idea, Councillor Kuvaa. All I can think is that somehow they rewrote some code, or found ancient access routes that enabled them to circumvent my safety parameters and protocols. Neither should be possible.

"Run a self-diagnostic on this date," she said, punching in the date when her image and voice had been duplicated to give false information to one of their agents. "Look the day before and the day after as well," she added. "Perhaps something will show up to give us a clue what happened."

As you wish, Councillor Kuvaa. It will take some time.

"Take all the time you need; I am not waiting for it. I'll be back in a few hours," she said, "Let me know when you have completed the search."

Yes, Councillor.

Kuvaa was baffled. Unity had a multitude of safety protocols to prevent just this kind of thing from happening, and even more to keep it shackled so it couldn't become a free entity. It should be utterly impossible for anyone to bypass all these and make Unity forget it had been tampered with. There was no doubt in her mind that it had been Unity that had taken Vartra hostage and held him against his will, albeit without its knowledge. It was imperative they find out how this had been done so they could prevent it happening again. If the Isolationists were able to take an Entity captive, they could take all the Reformists and more captive the same way! With a sigh, she closed down her terminal in the inner sanctum of Unity and began the laborious job of passing out through all the safeguarded doorways to the outside world again.

Prime world, the nursery, same day

Shaidan had picked up much of what Kuvaa had said and thought thanks to his mental link to Unity. As he understood it, Unity provided comms not only for all their agents, but for people everywhere on their home world to talk to each other. It did that through a network of webs placed carefully in various locations. Somehow, the opposing party to Kuvaa—she was a Cabbaran Reformist—had faked her image and voice in a conversation with an agent, making them do something very wrong. He'd seen Cabbarans building houses from mud and straw with the power of their minds in the small temporary township outside the City of Light's walls. They were good at that, changing natural objects into other things.

They build worlds and repair those that get badly damaged, sent Unity. *It is their great gift as a people.*

He acknowledged the information, then turned his mind to Vartra. How had they reached Him when He was an Entity and not a person living in their here and now? How had they got Unity to kidnap someone who wasn't exactly there in the realm of the normal living? Here was Unity, able to communicate with him by thoughts just like a person, thoughts that didn't have problems with the distances between the world Unity was on and this one. Was this the answer? That the incidents had actually happened outside normal space and time and been projected from there to this reality?

Unity, do you work outside normal time? he sent.

Yes.

What about space? Do you work in the place where our Entities live?

I operate in multiple realities, in all possible futures.

Have you checked to see if you were programmed in that state, outside of normal time and space, to do these tasks and then forget them?

No. I shall do so now.

I have to go now for lessons. I hope you find what went wrong, he sent before cutting himself off from the web.

M'zull, same day, Nayash village

"Don't land in the village square," said Kusac quietly as his aircar approached Nayash village. "Land just outside so they don't see Mahzi."

"Aye," said Cheelar.

Once he had landed, Kusac got up and went back to

where Mahzi sat with M'yikku. "I want you to wait in here till I send for you," he said. "I need to be sure it's safe, and to explain what happened to your parents."

She nodded uncertainly. "They'll be so mad with me."

"They'll be glad to know you're safe. I would be," he said, standing up and patting her on the shoulder. "Let's get going," he said to Cheelar as he headed back to the exit.

From the common where they'd parked, a lane led between the houses to the village square. Having called up first to tell them he was coming, there was a welcoming group waiting for him.

"I'm Shazzuk, Leader of the village," said a male of middle years stepping forward to greet him. "This is my wife, Larashi. How can we help you, m'Lord Nayash?"

"I've actually come to help you. Can we go somewhere private to talk?"

"My office would be best, and it's out of the sun."

"Please, lead on."

Kusac followed them to a house across from where they stood. It was the largest one, and most ornate, with carved wooden posts on either side of the door. Once inside the room that passed for Shazzuk's office, his wife banged the door closed, then leaned against it.

"He's not Nayash," she said bluntly. "He's pretending to be him, but he's the Zsadhi."

A look of panic crossed Shazzuk's face as he looked from his wife to Kusac. "You don't know what you're saying. The Zsadhi is long dead, and why should Lord Nayash pretend to be him?"

"Listen to what I'm saying—he's not Nayash. He is the Zsadhi come again, I can see him with the Sight and you know that's never wrong!" She came forward. "I can prove it. He has the tattoo of the sword on his chest."

Cheelar stepped between Kusac and Larashi. "I think you should remove your wife, Shazzuk. She's deranged. The sun has gotten to her today," said the youth

"His scent, Shazzuk, it's not what it should be! He's not one of us," she said urgently, grasping her husband by the arm.

"She's right," Shazzuk said slowly. "Something about

you isn't what it should be. I met Nayash once, belligerent
bully he was, nothing like you, or your man the other day.
What do you want from us?" he demanded. "We made you
welcome, yet you're trying to deceive us, get us into trouble
with the authorities! Is this some twisted test of our loyalty?"

"I am Nayash," said Kusac, pushing Cheelar to one side.
"I'm here today because I was given one of your people
yesterday. A young female called Mahzi."

"Mahzi? She's my sister's daughter, went missing five
days ago," said Shazzuk, diverted for now. "What happened
to her? Is she all right?"

"She got picked up by a patrol and taken in to the Palace," he said. "I have her now. I will need your help to keep
her safe from the Emperor. Will you help me?"

Shazzuk looked at his wife who gave a brief nod. "Yes,
whatever we can do we will do. She's not more than a
youngster, a good lass."

"She doesn't deserve to get noticed by the Palace," said
Larashi.

"It's too late for that, but luckily I am in a position to
keep her safe. Fetch her, Cheelar."

As Cheelar moved aside to go and get her, Larashi
lunged forward to grab at Kusac's shirt. A hard yank and
the top few buttons popped open.

"See! He has the Zsadhi tattoo!" she said.

"Don't be ridiculous," said Kusac, quickly pulling his
shirt closed again, "There's nothing there." He ground to a
halt as his fingers felt the raised edges of the sword tattoo.
"Coincidence," he muttered. "I had it done one drunken
night. Get the female, Cheelar!"

"Aye, Lord Nayash," he said, heading for the door.

"Look, I know what you think, but I'm not the Zsadhi,
and I am Lord Nayash. There is no other one but me!"

"I have the Sight. I see and know things," said Larashi. "I
smell scents on you that are strange, alien scents, I see the
Zsadhi in your face."

"You're talking rubbish! Worse, with the Zsadhi attacks
around the capital city, you're talking sedition!" said Kusac,

fastening his shirt. "I will not be associated with your legends."

"Leave it, Larashi. We have Mahzi to bother about now."

"No! He needs to know we are the guardians of his sword, and it went missing the night of the old Lord's funeral, the day he came here. He needs to see the chapel where the sword was kept, know who your forefathers were before the Fall and the civil war that followed it!"

"Who were you?" asked Kusac.

"It's ancient history, nothing that would interest you," said Shazzuk, sitting down on one of the dining chairs he'd had placed in the room.

"His ancestor was the governor of M'zull, in charge of the whole planet. His lands were part of what became Nayash's."

"I thought you had ties to the land," said Kusac. "Rezzik, who visited you a few days ago, said no one could look after the land better than you. That doesn't happen unless you have ties to it."

"You had no business telling him, Larashi. Now he'll be thinking that I believe I have claim on the land," said Shazzuk tiredly. He looked up at Kusac. "I want no troubles here, your Lordship, or whoever you are. I just want to get on with farming the land, that's all. I do a good job, you said so yourself, so just leave me to do it."

Cheelar entered with Mahzi, who instantly burst into tears and fell onto her aunt's shoulder crying.

"The soldiers found me, Aunty Larashi," she sobbed. "I was running down to the river with my cousins from the next village to meet N'abui and they caught me, took me to the City. The soldiers killed them, just killed them when they tried to protect me! The Lord says they had me in the harem and the Emperor gave me to him as a wife! I can't marry him, N'abui and I promised ourselves to each other!"

"You see the problem," said Kusac, finally sitting down next to Shazzuk. "I don't want to marry her, but the Emperor has given her to me to take as my wife."

"Why would you bring her to us? Why would you care about a village female?" Shazzuk asked.

"Because she matters, you all matter." He sighed. "Look,

your wife is right, I'm not Nayash, The real Nayash is dead, and I took his place. No one knows any different except you now. I brought her here because we have to find a way round this. I suggested a mock wedding, but she'd have none of it. I don't know what to do and hoped you could talk some sense into her."

"Why are you pretending to be Nayash?" demanded Larashi. "It's not to get his wealth, nor for revenge, at least not against him." She studied his face carefully, then nodded. "You are the Zsadhi because you've come to save us from the tyrant that sits on the throne now, just as you did so long ago."

"Message coming in, my Lord," said Cheelar, putting his comm unit to his ear. "Let me take this outside where the reception's better."

"Go," said Kusac. "Look, we have to sort out what to do with this youngster before anything else."

"Let me take her to her mother," said Larashi. "She will do what we tell her to do; she needs have no say in this." With that, she left the room, taking the weeping youngster with her.

"Females, always a crisis," said Shazzuk. "So you do have the tattoo, then. Legend has it so had the Zsadhi. He tattooed it onto himself while he was in the desert, to honor the sword the goddess gave him to fight Tashraka with. Did it just appear?"

"It appears and disappears," he said reluctantly, reaching up to feel through his shirt for it. He could still feel the raised edges of the scarring. "What's this chapel you have?"

"When the Fall came, there was an exhibition on M'zull of the Zsadhi's belongings and other things associated with the legend. The actual sword of Zsadhi was here, on M'zull, when the Fall happened. My ancestor had a duplicate sword made so that when he escaped the City Palace, he took the real sword and left the replica behind. He headed up here to this village to sit out the war and had the chapel built and the sword placed in it for safety."

"Why would he do that? He was the ruler of this world. Why would he not fight to keep it?"

"He had no chance of winning, and he valued life above glory is the way it was told to me by my Da when I was a child."

Cheelar came back in looking puzzled. "There's been another Zsadhi incident," he said. "Seems that one of the main breweries has been blown up, destroying it completely. As it blew, it scattered Zsadhi leaflets everywhere."

Kusac sat upright. "What?"

Cheelar nodded. "Seems the Zsadhi struck again, my Lord."

Kusac stared hard at Shazzuk who shrugged. "I was here all last night, and all today, my Lord."

The door opened and Larashi returned. "So you heard the news. About time they did something to fight back!"

"Only the mountain tribes could do that," said Kusac quietly. "Because only you are casteless, descended from a mixture of all the castes in the centuries after the Fall. Does the Emperor realize this? He knows your females are like those on Ch'almuth where the whole planet is a mix of all castes, but has he realized you males are, too?"

"I don't know what you're talking about," said Shazzuk. "We're worker caste, all of us, just our females are a little more outspoken."

Kusac stood up. "Like hell you are. Take me to this chapel," he said. "I want to see it."

"It's at the rear of the village," said Shazzuk.

"Take me." If it meant having to be their Zsadhi to get them working for him, dammit he'd do it! Right now, it seemed as if there was an underground movement among the only free people on M'zull—the mountain folk. Unless he got these folk on his side, working with him and his people, there was a good chance that it would all fall apart as these amateurs got themselves caught. On the other hand, they could give him an insight into the M'zullian psyche he'd never otherwise get.

Carved into the living rock at the back of the village, the chapel doorway was flanked by two life-sized statues of the long dead Emperor Q'emgo'h, last Emperor of the unified

Valtegan worlds. Inside, a semicircle of seats faced the back wall where bas-reliefs of the story of the Zsadhi's life had been carved out and painted in now somewhat faded colors. It could be a brother chapel to the one they'd used on Ch'almuth. Beside the central figure of the Zsadhi was a real metal sword inlaid into the living rock. Like the one in the chapel on Ch'almuth, and the one Vartra had brought to him there, it was double edged with gold quillons, and the pommel was set with a multicolored faceted gem.

"That's not his sword," came a voice from the shadows. An elderly female stepped forward, wrapped in a thin shawl against the slight chill inside the chapel. "That's a copy they made two weeks ago when the original went missing."

The room was getting darker, and the voices seemed to be coming from some great distance as he fell to one knee in front of the sword. Reaching out, he touched it. It slid smoothly out of its bed in the wall, the grip fitting his hand as if it had been made for him.

"The sword of the Zsadhi," he said, looking at the glowing weapon. Just beyond it, he could see the sword was still in the wall. He frowned, confused because he could feel this one in his hand. He grasped it with his other hand, desperate to be sure he wasn't imagining it, but it was there, it was real—for now. He could feel himself beginning to fade in and out as his tether on reality began to slip and he started morphing into his Sholan self. The pain was so intense that he cried out and, letting go the sword, fell to the ground unconscious.

Raised angry voices all shouting at each other were the first sign that he was coming round.

"Be quiet, all of you!" shouted Larashi just as a bucket of cold water hit him full in the face and chest.

Coughing and spluttering, he sat up, soaked to the skin. "What the hell was that for?" he demanded as a towel was thrown at him. He grabbed for it and began drying himself off.

"Give me your wet shirt and jacket. Whoever—whatever you are," demanded the female sternly, holding out her hand. "It will dry in minutes out in the sun."

Reluctantly, Kusac shucked himself out of both, handing them to Rhassa, who gave them to one of the other females to take it outside to dry. Shivering, he began toweling himself off.

Larashi tugged the towel away from him when he was finished and said, "Now tell me that he isn't the Zsadhi! You can all see he's the exact image of him, down to that tattoo, and we *saw* him black-skinned and with the sword, the real sword, not that copy."

Kusac groaned and put his head in his hands as he realized nearly the whole village was gathered in the chapel, all looking at him as he sat half naked in front of the carving of the Zsadhi. He must have morphed partially at least if they had seen him as black-skinned. Had it been enough for them to realize he really was alien? He reached out mentally and found that only the original three in the chapel had indeed seen him briefly morph into his Sholan form, then back to his Valtegan one.

"Go back to your fields or homes," said Shazzuk. "Don't discuss this with anyone outside our clan. You don't want to go against the will of the Gods on this!"

Gradually, the chapel emptied until only the priestess, Shazzuk and his wife, and Cheelar were left.

"I blew it, didn't I?" he asked Cheelar quietly in Sholan.

"I don't know that you did. They seemed very impressed. Hell, I was impressed and I saw you do it on Ch'almuth! You didn't go full-on Sholan, though, just turned dark-skinned with some fur."

"You might not have done the raid on the brewery, but you know who did!" Kusac said to Shazzuk.

"And you're some kind of alien with black fur that can also be like one of us. How do you do that?" asked Shazzuk.

"Ask your Zsadhi, or La'shol, because they did this to me; I didn't! All I wanted was to stay home with my wife and children, and now look at me! Playing an avatar for an alien species millions of miles from home."

"Why are you here pretending to be Lord Nayash?" demanded Shazzuk.

"Same reason your rebels are acting against this Emperor—you know how corrupt he and his regime are."

"Why would you care?"

"Because once he's done with conquering your other three worlds, he's coming after us," snapped Kusac.

"You were part of the old Empire?"

"Yeah, you could say that," Kusac said, getting to his feet and moving over to sit on one of the benches. "We have a lot we need to talk about. There can't be two Zsadhi groups causing a ruckus in the city unless they are working closely together. If we don't cooperate, one lot will get the other caught. Quite honestly, we're in a better position to do real damage than you are, and we're professional soldiers. Your people aren't."

"Where are you from?" asked Larashi. "Not from M'zull because they're all caste bred down in the lowlands and wouldn't even condescend to talk nicely to us."

"K'oish'ik," said Kusac "Your K'hedduk took it for a few weeks, but we drove him off. He sent a punishment fleet against us and only twelve ships returned. We destroyed thirty-five."

"Really?" asked Shazzuk, smiling. "He suffered that large a defeat?"

Kusac nodded. "He did. Now will you help us topple K'hedduk?"

"I can only speak for us, but yes, we'll help. I'm convinced that no matter what species you are, you are the Zsadhi of our legends. It was another village that did the raid on the brewery though, not us."

"What about Mahzi?" asked Larashi. "You say you were given her to be your wife, yet you don't want to marry her."

"I can't, I'm already married. As I said, I suggested a sham marriage to her, but she refused. She wants to marry this N'abui."

"He's a young man in this clan, but their promises mean nothing. They are too young to be making them."

"What if they got married here, today, in a village ceremony? Then, if the Emperor demands I marry her at Court, it will be a sham marriage because we'll both have a real husband and wife. That's really the only solution I can see."

"It would keep the child quiet, knowing she has N'abui to come home to when this is all over," said Rhassa. "And it's a simple solution. Both can honestly say that she got married today. You can say you had a village wedding to the Emperor."

"You'd have to stay for some of the night at least," said Shazzuk. "We can't send her back with you a virgin. We've all heard the horror tales of the Court and our Mountain females. She must be well and truly wedded and bedded before you leave."

"Agreed. It would be safer. As for helping us, what we need right now are people to be my personal staff. Have you any who can pass as soldiers?"

"Only three, from our village guards. I'll speak to the other leaders under the guise of the wedding tonight."

"Wait. We need to tell them as little as possible. Then, if they get caught, they can't give us all away."

"You mean cells," said Shazzuk. "We've got that set up, don't worry."

"We'll take suggestions from your folk on what raids to do. We need ones to cause the most aggravation to the administration of the City and to K'hedduk himself. Undermine his authority, make the Court and ruling classes dissatisfied with him. When we decide on a mission, the best people to do it will carry it out, be it your teams or mine, or even a combination of both. Agreed?"

"Sounds sensible to me. Some places we can infiltrate better than you can, but we can't get to the Court or the officers. Larashi, tell Mahzi what's been decided, and Rhassa, go get everyone into the mood for a wedding. Make sure they think it is the Lord that she's getting married to. I'll speak to N'abui myself."

The village wedding ceremony was very simple. Vows were exchanged while holding a pottery bottle filled with holy water from the chapel's font. Once the promises had been made, the couple threw the bottle to the ground where it broke, spilling the water. Then salt and grain were exchanged between them so they'd never know thirst or hunger, and they were pronounced married. All this happened in the chapel with only the immediate family present so they were able to keep up the pretense of Mahzi marrying Lord Nayash, yet enable her to marry her sweetheart N'abui.

In the small hours of the morning, a very tired Mahzi, bundled in a blanket and carrying a bag of her belongings, was brought back to the village Leader's house. There she said a tearful good-bye to her parents and left with Kusac, Cheelar, and three of the guards from the village.

Before they left, Shazzuk thrust a book into Kusac's hands. "I know what you are," he said. "You're a Sholan. Your kind are mentioned in this old book of my father's. It's a copy of an even older one. I never believed him and his tales of aliens, but it seems he was right."

Kusac flicked through the pages, stopping at the one with a drawing of a Sholan. "That's us," he said, handing the book back to him. "Good night, Shazzuk."

CHAPTER 5

SHAIDAN and the others had thoroughly enjoyed their first unarmed combat lesson from Jerenn and M'Nar that afternoon. Even the warm-up exercises had proved challenging, but they'd all managed to keep up and to perform the various kicks and punching movements with a good degree of accuracy.

After the lesson, they all piled down to the pool for a hot shower, followed by a relaxing swim. They were allowed to get out when they wanted as they were escorted back to the nursery by the staff from the main floor's security office next door to the pool.

The other cubs had all left, but Shaidan was still soaking in the bubble pool while M'Nar and Jerenn were having a last swim before getting out. He was idly thinking about the problem Unity had that morning, trying to track down how its routines had been subverted. Before he realized it, he was in communication with it again through the small web in the wall behind the pool.

Thanks to you, I was able to start tracking down what had been done to me, came Unity's thought.

Oh, that's great news. You haven't yet found it, though?

No, but I am very close.

I was thinking about how they did the morphing into Kuvaa. My Papa can morph into a Valtegan, and apparently I almost did the first time I saw him change.

You mustn't try that, Shaidan, it could be very dangerous. Your Father uses the power of his mind to do that, you haven't got his years of experience. You could get stuck as a Valtegan, or worse still, as something half and half.

Shaidan shuddered. *I won't try it. Is Kuvaa there now?*

Yes, she is working on one of my terminals.

Can she see or hear me?

Not at this time. It depends what she's doing. You're safe for now.

Are you tied in to all the computing and comms devices?

Yes. They cannot function without me.

Then if someone invented a device that let them morph into Kuvaa, or at least change their appearance to look like her, they would have to design it on you, right?

There was a small silence. *Yes.*

Then why not look for someone designing something like that on the days just before the first time Kuvaa was duplicated.

I should have thought of that myself. You have a good mind, Hunter cub!

Hunter cub?

We call you Hunters because that is what you are—Hunters. You are helping me hunt down the truth. Hunting in all its forms is one of the great gifts of your people.

That's a fine thought.

"Shaidan, time to go," said M'Nar. "Wake up, youngling! Dinner is in half an hour, just time to get showered and dried and back to the nursery."

"Maybe we tired him out, M'Nar," teased Jerenn. "We'll have to make the next session easier for him."

"I'm fine. Just resting my eyelids, they've been open all day!" he said, pulling his legs down to the bottom of the step he could reach and pushing off to get to the other side. There M'Nar lifted him out and onto the sandy beach.

"Race you to the showers!" Jerenn said as he ran splashing into the water.

After dinner, Shaidan headed for M'Nar and Jerenn's room. The door was wide open and he could see the two

Brothers sitting inside on their beds. Jerenn was sharpening his knives, and M'Nar was busy stripping down his pistol and cleaning it.

"I need to know how to do that," he said, leaning against the door post. "I want to know how to do it, too."

"Hmm? I think you might find your wrists are a little weak to use this gun," said M'Nar. "It can pack a fair kick."

"We could get some of the training guns sent down from the *Khalossa*," said Jerenn. "They're lighter."

"I won't get to carry a gun around, so I need to be able to use any gun that's handy. Though shooting a lighter weight one would also be good practice," Shaidan added.

"Nothing to stop you watching us work on our weapons and try it for yourself," said M'Nar. "I think you're right, Jer, and we should get the practice ones down. Then we can try and get the cubs started on the target practice at least."

"There shouldn't be too much trouble doing that. After all, it isn't as if Dzaka isn't Brotherhood himself, and brought up in Stronghold from when he was almost a newborn."

"Was he?" asked Shaidan, coming into the room.

"Here, sit beside me," said M'Nar. "We have lots of stories we can tell you about just about anyone in the Brotherhood. Who do you want to hear about?"

"My Papa," said Shaidan, his face lighting up.

"We don't know too many stories about him because he wasn't in Stronghold for a long time like we were. What about some more about Brother Dzaka?" asked Jerenn. "You watch what M'Nar's showing you with the gun, and I'll tell you a few tales."

Ghioass, same day

An excited Kuvaa trotted into the main Camarilla assembly room and looked around for Phratry leader Shvosi. There!

She was nestled at the edges of a bank of TeLaxaudin cushions, propped up on her scat, chatting now and then to her neighbors while keeping sharp eyes on who was entering and leaving the room. It was that in between time when the recess for dinner was just ending and the next session was about to begin.

Kuvaa wound her way through the other delegates to her superior's side. "Phratry Leader Shvosi," she said very quietly. "I need to talk to you alone. Now."

"Meet me in our office outside the hall," she said, beginning to get up from her chair. "Tell Azwokkus to join us. He's over by the trees." She pointed one delicate hoof in his direction.

"Yes, Phratry leader," said Kuvaa, dipping her head in a gesture of obedience before rushing off.

"I checked for devices," said Kuvaa as Shvosi and Azwokkus entered the small meeting room. "It is clean."

"What news have you?" demanded the Cabbaran.

"Unity has found it. Found how they were able to duplicate me! It is a device they engineered to morph people into a form different from their own. It turned up as a new device, made a day or two before the incident. Unity alerted me to this discovery."

She pulled a bundle of papers out of one of the larger pouches on her utility belt and handed them over to Azwokkus. "Here are the plans for it."

"This will be invaluable for our own research into the same subject," said the TeLaxaudin, leafing through the pages. "We will have a device ready for the Hunters within days now. Still won't know how stable it is, they will have to test it on themselves, but it will work."

"Now we can develop protocols to prevent Unity being fooled by this technology."

"Device should give off signal when on, so why we not tell Unity to check for that? We'll know the exact signal once we build our own units," said Shvosi.

"Good thinking. Yes, we can do this. I will go and enter the plans into the fabricator at my home and get at least

one unit made tonight so we can study it more tomorrow."
Azwokkus looked up from the plans. "Well done, Kuvaa."

She accepted the praise graciously, but at the back of her
mind was a worrying niggle. She hadn't suggested this line
of search to Unity, and as part of the safety measures, it
wasn't allowed to go off on a tangent on any topic, so where
had it got the idea from?

M'zull, Palace, Zhal-Ghyakulla 6th, Month of the Goddess (June)

It had been a busy two weeks, starting with K'hedduk's
displeasure when Kusac told him that he was already married to Mahzi, and that it had been a village ceremony. It
had taken some pretty serious groveling to placate him.
Next up had been the heavy schedule of work finishing off
clearing the tunnels and crossroads courtyard from the
damage caused by the MUTAC. Kusac had been trying to
check down the tunnels radiating off the affected areas,
ostensibly to find any cracks, but in reality to carry on with
the mapping he was doing of the underground Palace. That
work was made a little easier by the arrival of Telmaar and
half a dozen of his men. With them helping with the heavy
work, it had left Kusac a little more freedom for his mapping.

"I don't know how to thank you," said Kusac as they finally loaded the last of the shovels and picks into the
battery-operated repair carts and watched them head off to
the lower levels. "This would have taken a lot longer but for
your help."

"My pleasure," said Telmaar, brushing the dust off his
arms before rolling his sleeves back down and accepting his
jacket from one of his men. "Just keep me in mind next time
our esteemed higher-ups are handing out promotions!"

"I wouldn't be too quick to accept one," said Kusac,

slipping his own jacket on. "With it comes exhausting hours of extra tasks!"

"That's where having friends able to help you works out well," said the other, clapping him on the shoulder. "Fellow fleet officers should stick together, I always say! Now, I must run. Things to do, as they say." With that, he inclined his head and left.

"Be careful of him," muttered M'yikku under his breath. "He's only a friend while he thinks you can help his ambitions."

"I know," said Kusac, turning back to him and his brother. "But to have turned down his help would have been suspicious."

Shazzuk's three males had proved to be a godsend with their knowledge of the local areas of both the city and the estate. Any doubts that Rezac, or Kezule's sons, had had about them were gone, they'd proved their worth.

Rezac had been installed as Lord Lorishuk in the estate on the other side of the capital city. Lorishuk had no wife or sons to complicate the masquerade. He was a loner who'd been posted for several months at J'kirtikk. Those posted there returned changed, something to do with all life being obliterated on the planet—the silence really seemed to affect people posted there, and it was said that it made them go mad. Whatever it was, it was enough to account for any changes in the Lord's behavior.

Noolgoi and Noi'kkah had gone with him, and one of Shazzuk's guards—Khoshin. Cheelar and M'yikku, who had been seen most often in Kusac's company, stayed with him.

Mahzi was settling in to the apartment. As was normal, she stayed in her room except when visiting the Palace harem to mix with the other females there and continue to be trained by Keshti. Kusac had taken her the first time and made it abundantly clear to Keshti that his wife would not be drugged again. She would have to learn the old-fashioned way. She had also been thoroughly schooled to behave like a good subservient wife and to give no details about their personal life at the apartment.

Every few days, Kusac would spend a couple of hours in her company while her servant, Neshol, spent time with Laazif and the other staff. It allowed him to create the illusion that he was content with his wife.

He was settling down for the night in his own room when Annuur suddenly arrived.

"We have six of the morphing units for you," he said, sitting back on his haunches and holding out a medium sized box for him. "They work on Cabbarans for six hours, males can become females, and females become males. No Sholans on which to practice, so you will have to test yourself."

"Dammit, Annuur, I could have been doing anything!" he said, getting out of bed and wrapping a robe around himself. "You can't just appear suddenly like that! One of these days I may not realize you're friendly and lash out at you!"

"I knew you were not busy. You need any here, or shall I take to den in mountains?"

"Take them to Kaid, please. He'll be the one doing the tests on them." He looked sharply at the Cabbaran. "There isn't any danger to them while they are using them, is there? They can't get stuck as half Sholan, half Valtegan, or mess with what gender they are?"

"No. Is as safe as we could make them. You use dials to set what you want to be—male or female, and Valtegan. Then you hit power button and you change. Can use it to change back if you don't want to wait for six hours to be up."

"That's useful," he agreed.

"We need information from you or from clan members on what memories you want kept from people here. Not ones you use that antidote on, the others."

"None, Annuur, I want a clean slate from here. If they are going to get memories, have them be from Ch'almuth. Get them to put together basic stuff so they can look after themselves, and not be too curious as to what happened to them all. Touibans have a form of telepathy—can they sing the memories so they can be broadcast to the whole planet at once?"

"I look into this. Idea is good, I like it. New pamphlets

wc have for Kaid and you, made them rough like printed here on illegal press," he said. "You sure you not want them all crisp and clear?"

"No, because it would be too obvious we were getting outside help. I want to leave that card for later if I choose to play it. The pamphlets have to go to Kaid as well. I can't risk anything to do with these Zsadhi events being found on my premises, you know that."

"Understood. I take them there now." With that, he was gone.

Kusac sighed and, taking off his robe, headed back to bed.

Prime world, Barracks armory, afternoon the same day

M'Nar watched Shaidan rapidly strip down the assault rifle and put it back together in record time. "He's got an amazing memory," he said quietly to Jerenn. "I don't know about you, but I barely learned how to do the pistol in the first two weeks, let alone the pistol and an assault rifle."

"Took me about three weeks," said Jerenn. "Do you reckon it's because of the sleep tapes they had before they were born?"

"I don't know, but I'm beginning to suspect he might be mentally picking our brains."

"I'd know," said Jerenn firmly. "I haven't sensed him trying to read me at all."

"He's good, though, better than most telepaths."

"You know how sensitive I am to forced mental contact, M'Nar. The least of what I get is headaches, and I'm not getting any."

"Hmm. Well, at least Brother Dzaka agreed to allow them to learn how to shoot pistols, and learn to strip the guns for cleaning."

"Aye, he did, but Gods help us if he finds out Shaidan is playing with assault rifles!"

"I'm actually going to up the ante and show him how to strip rifles now," said M'Nar, getting up and taking the rifle over to the cub.

"M'Nar!"

"Right, youngling. Time to learn about rifles," said M'Nar. "If you have a choice of guns, go for the pistols. They'll be easier for you to use right now, less kickback."

"I don't know why I bother protesting," Jerenn muttered to himself. "It never does any good!"

"But I always know when someone is coming, and we can get the guns, or me, out of the way in time," said Shaidan, looking over at him with a grin. "When will you teach me how to use the knives, Jerenn?"

"When M'Nar says you're ready. You need to know more self-defense before we start with the knives."

"I want to set up sessions with ground obstacles, Jerenn, so he learns spatial awareness. We'll need boxes and rocks and things to put down in the practice circle, things that if he isn't careful, he'll trip over."

"That's not fair," said Shaidan.

"In real life, you won't be fighting in a circle of flat ground," said Jerenn. "M'Nar's right. You need to learn what the real world is like—rocks and all. That will help you be one up on your attackers."

"We've only got about thirty minutes left before you have to be back up in the Palace for dinner, so pay attention," said M'Nar.

Shaidan was free tonight to do what he wanted, so he headed over to the pool. Time alone was scarce now with his extra training with Jerenn and M'Nar, and he liked to spend it just observing what Unity was doing and maybe talk to it a bit. Some of his brothers and sisters were also at the pool, so he made sure to swim with them for a few minutes before heading for the bubble pool behind which was the Unity node.

Greetings, Shaidan, sent Unity. *I was able to find out how they duplicated Councillor Kuvaa, thanks to your suggestion of the morphing device.*

That's great, Unity. What about Vartra? I haven't seen him in a long time, he sent wistfully.

That I'm not responsible for; he's not with us this time. I promised you I would tell you about the Camarilla.

Mmm, yes, you did.

Until seven thousand and five hundred years ago, the Camarilla consisted of only one species, the TeLaxaudin. The Camarilla is a council formed to watch younger species and to see that they don't harm either themselves or others. Then one of the species they were watching took an action that caused them to think long about what the Camarilla meant and did. The result of that was to ask the Cabbarans to join them.

What was it they did? asked Shaidan.

A species you know as the U'Churians. Their world was in danger. Where the TeLaxaudin would have only observed the death of these people, the Cabbarans couldn't do this, so they intervened to help them. As I told you, the Cabbarans' great gift as a people is to be able to manipulate matter, to turn what they can imagine into reality.

What did they do?

The planet, called Home *by its inhabitants, was dying because of a solar flare from its unstable sun. So bad was the damage the people had suffered that they couldn't survive unless the Cabbarans intervened.*

And did they? asked Shaidan.

They did. They knew of your people, the Sholans, and how similar they were to the U'Churians, so they visited your world, took a small clan of early Sholans, and brought them to Home. *Meanwhile, those Cabbaran ships that remained at* Home *were working on healing the land from the radiation caused by the solar prominences. They did what they could for the people but were only able to save a small number of them, and they were damaged on a level that meant their children would bear abnormalities that would cut their lives very short.*

How did they save all the people of a whole world?

They couldn't, but what they could do, because the U'Churians had not yet spread themselves all over their planet, was to work where the most people were. With the arrival of the Sholan tribe, it was now possible for the Cabbarans to adapt their DNA to repair that of the U'Churians. They made it possible for that one small clan to inbreed with the U'Churians. This is why your people share a common ancestry long ago.

They look very like us, except for their legs, and their hair being coarser than ours.

The differences are deeper than that, Shaidan, but you can take pride in knowing your early ancestors helped save a whole species.

It's good to know we were helping others from the earliest of days, agreed Shaidan. *So the TeLaxaudin—weren't they displeased at this?*

Many of the TeLaxaudin still believe in not getting involved in the problems of other races, but many are willing to step in and help them if the need is dire. They decided the need was dire and so weren't angered with what the Cabbarans had done.

Since then, the Cabbarans have been very close to the U'Churians, watching them develop and helping them secretly to discover drives for starships that would take them into space and off the surface of their planet. To this day, more than half the U'Churians live on huge spaceships that ply the merchant routes around this galaxy, The rest live in underground cities, safe from their sometimes violent sun. This is why you see Cabbarans and U'Churians working together as Family, because of the strong bond between their peoples.

So if the worst happened, and the sun had another flare, then all life wouldn't be at risk this time. There would be enough of them in space to keep their species going? asked Shaidan.

Yes. In fact, there have been several such incidents since then, but very few people were caught outside. The damage to their world repairs itself after a few hundred years, but since Home *dwellers live inside the earth, they are never affected by it.*

Why don't they just find another planet to live on, one that has a stable sun? asked Shaidan.

It's their home. They don't want to leave, despite the problems it has. The Camarilla now has two races that belong to it, and they watch my projections for all possible futures to see what will happen with each of the younger species.

Wait a minute, sent Shaidan, sitting up with a surge of water that threatened to engulf him. *You* predict *what happens in the future?*

In all possible futures. This way the Camarilla can steer the galaxy on the best possible path that avoids all-out wars and natural disasters.

So you're involved in this Valtegan war?

The war was caused by the fact that fifteen hundred years ago, the Valtegan Empire, spanning four worlds of their people and numerous slave worlds, tried to enslave the wrong people. The Sholans. They were prepared to make terrible sacrifices of their telepaths to thwart the Valtegan plan of domination. The war they caused brought about the Fall of the Valtegan Empire, and for fifteen hundred years it stayed as just four separate worlds. Then came K'hedduk who wanted to unify the old Empire again, and he set about planning to take over the throne of M'zull from his brother to do that.

So breeding us, sent Shaidan, *what he did to my father and mother, was all to use us cubs as weapons against everyone else! He wanted his own telepaths to use them to destroy people.*

You were to be his spearhead, to go one each in his starships and to strike mentally at any and all opposition to his plans. You were just the beginning, he planned to have hundreds more of you.

Shaidan shivered in fear. *We were lucky that Kezule found us, and that my clan and my father came for us,* he sent quietly.

K'hedduk underestimated the love for you that your parents had, sent Unity, its mental tone kindly. *There are factions within the Camarilla, Isolationists that want nothing to do with any other species. There are the Reformists who want to reform the Camarilla and stop it making many of the bad decisions it has made recently, and the Moderates who are between the two. Kuvaa is a Reformist, and she is now aware of you. Your biggest danger comes from the Isolationists who, despite their name, are getting very involved in the lives of those on M'zull. They want an outcome that will destroy many of the other species so that they cannot, in some distant future, threaten them.*

They want to see the M'zullians get back the old Empire?

I believe they do. The Moderates and the Reformists want to prevent this war of conquest, but by humane means. This is what your parents are fighting for on M'zull now.

Why are you telling me all this, Unity? This is grownup stuff, isn't it?

Normally I would say yes, but the Isolationists are watching you, Shaidan, and I feel they could still try to use you to let the M'zullians dominate.

What can I do? I'm only a cub!

You know the truth now, so they cannot persuade you to do their will. They might be able to force you, but now you can armor yourself against that. Vartra was taken to stop him influencing your father, so they could control him. Then he began appearing and talking to you, so they abducted him to stop that. You and your father are both nexuses, people around whom the future gathers and swirls. Your actions could save or destroy millions of people and worlds.

Huh, no pressure, then, said Shaidan, tears springing to his eyes. *This is so not right! I'm not old enough to make such decisions!*

You may not have to, little one, but I wanted to warn you what is at stake in case. You can ask me any questions you want, and I will help you.

Is this Kuvaa watching me now?

Yes, but she is not a danger to you at this time. She cannot know what we are talking about as I have invoked Privacy for us.

Shaidan got to his feet, still shivering, and not because he was cold. *I need time to think about this, Unity. You were right, I need to know how to defend myself.*

I have something for you. Take this device, wear it where as a piece of jewelry it won't be out of place, and you can contact me from anywhere.

There was a quiet ting as a small metal object hit one of the rocks behind him. He turned round to see a small sliver of silver-colored metal with a loop at the top sitting on a stone by the back wall. He reached out and picked it up. Immediately, it became warm in his hand.

Wear it in with your hair ornaments. You need never take it off, and no one will guess what it is, sent Unity.

I'll think about it, sent Shaidan firmly. *You've told me a lot. I need to understand it and decide what I am going to do about it. The Isolationists watching me, they can only see me where you have nodes, right? That's in the nursery, here, and the library?*

Yes.

What if I remove the nodes?

They will place new ones, and we may not be able to find them. Better we know where they can track you than it remains secret. That way, you can make sure your behavior at the nodes doesn't let them know you know about them.

Good night, Unity, he sent, then switched off his connection to it. This was too much to take in all at once. Without anyone to talk to about it, how was he to decide what the right thing to do was? That was his father and mother's job, not his.

Clutching the sliver tightly in his hand, he swam back to the shore on the other side of the pool to get showered. He'd need to ask Shishu to braid it into his hair before bedtime. With it there, he had the option of whether or not to contact Unity.

The sound of cheering and music outside drew the cubs to the two windows that overlooked the grand courtyard. There they could see that a crowd had gathered and were obviously waiting for someone to arrive.

"King Zsurtul's back," cried out Gaylla, jumping up and down. "He won't go through the courtyard, though."

"No, they'll make an appearance on the balcony," said Shishu, lifting Gaylla up so she could see the courtyard better. "We won't be able to see him from here, of course, but he will be coming upstairs to his rooms. He'll be tired after his long journey and so will Queen Zhalmo, so we shouldn't bother them tonight."

"The music's changed," said Shaidan. "That's their anthem. The King must be on the balcony now."

"Probably," agreed Shishu. "He won't say anything tonight. All he'll do is wave for a few minutes, then go inside to come up here. So off to bed, all of you!" She carried Gaylla over to her bed and, pulling back the covers, popped her into it. "Good night, Gaylla," she said, covering her up and giving her a hug.

"Night, Shishu."

Zsurtul drew Zhalmo back from the balcony into the chapel again and signaled for one of the guards to close the windows. "We've done our duty for tonight," he said. "Time to go upstairs and get some real food and a long hot bath!"

"I'm so tired, but I seem to have done nothing but rest," said Zhalmo as she accompanied him out through the Throne Room and into the corridor that led to the elevator.

"Welcome back, King Zsurtul," said the Palace AI. "Is there anything I can do for you? I did pass on your message to the kitchens, and as soon as you are ready to eat, a meal will be served for you."

"Thank you, ZSADHI. I think we need time to catch our breath first. Let's head to the lounge as I'm sure everyone is going to gather there. We should see your father as soon as possible, Zhalmo, let him see you really are home and safe," he said.

"Home," she said, looking at him. "Seems almost unreal to think of here as home now. It always seemed to be just a posting before I was kidnapped."

"Well, it's your home now," said Zsurtul as they made their way into the elevator.

Guards snapped smartly to attention as they exited the elevator. Zsurtul nodded at them and led Zhalmo down the corridor to the lounge where the General was indeed waiting for them, along with his wife Doctor Zayshul, and Kitra, Dzaka, Conner, and an elderly Sholan female he'd not met before.

"Welcome back, your Majesties," said Kezulc, obviously torn between being formal and wanting to ask his daughter how she was. He needn't have worried because she immediately ran over and hugged him.

"I'm so relieved and happy to be home," she said. "You're not angry with me for marrying Zsurtul, are you?" She moved back a step to search his face for his reaction.

"Not if that is what you both wanted," he said gently, stroking her cheek. "We're all pleased to see you both back safe and sound. You remember everyone, don't you?"

She nodded, then stopped, catching sight of Noni at the back of the room. "Not everyone," she said. "I don't think I've met the other Sholan female."

Noni came forward, holding out her hand in Human fashion. "I'm Noni," she said. "I'm here to help Conner with the temple, and the growing and planting."

"Pleased to meet you, Noni," said Zhalmo, briefly touching fingertips.

"Welcome to K'oish'ik, Noni," said Zsurtul. "I hope you'll enjoy your stay with us, however long it is."

"I'm sure I shall," she smiled. "I already feel like I'm at home."

"Noni is being modest," said Conner. "She's also like a den mother to the Brotherhood back on Shola. She sees to all the cuts and sprains the Brothers get training, plus, I'm told, has a great hangover cure!"

"She'll not need to come to me for that, I'll be bound," said Noni. "But if you should need me, I'm in the temple with Conner. King Zsurtul, I'd take your lady for her dinner now, she's gone a bit pale suddenly. Food will make her feel better."

Anxiously, Zsurtul put an arm round his wife and

exchanged a few quiet words with her. "If you don't mind, we'll just go and grab something to eat, then head for bed. We're both pretty exhausted," he said, excusing himself.

Noni watched the young couple leave. *I need to work on her tonight,* she sent to Conner. *The barriers Kusac placed are beginning to break down. She has lost the memories of her captivity, but her imagination is noticing the hole and rushing to populate it with what she imagined happened. I need to give her new memories to replace the missing ones.*

How can you do that tonight?

I need her drugged. Once she's asleep, I can work with her. "Doctor Zayshul, can you somehow get her to take a sleeping draft? I need to work on those missing memories tonight, and I need her asleep to do it."

"I can slip something in a drink for her," she said. "But how will you get into their room after they go to bed?"

"By asking King Zsurtul to let me in, of course! Can you write a note and pass it to him for me? I can't read or write Valtegan."

"I'll talk to King Zsurtul. You go and see to putting something in her maush, Zayshul," said Kezule.

"Hopefully, they'll not be quite ready as I'll have to go fetch something from the hospital. I don't just happen to carry sleeping pills around with me!" she said dryly as she left the room.

"What is it you want me to tell him, Noni?" asked the General.

"It's just as I said. The reason she's so tired and almost fainting is because her mind has realized she has holes in her memory. I need to fill those with new memories now. It will take me a few sessions, but tonight's is crucial. So you tell him we're drugging her. Then, when she's asleep, he has to let me into their room to heal her mind."

"I'll go and talk to him now," said Kezule.

"I'm so glad it's going to be you doing this, Noni," said Kitra, "I don't believe I could have done it."

"You'd have done a good job until I arrived, child, never

doubt yourself," said Noni kindly, patting her arm. "You have plenty of talent for this kind of work, just not much experience yet. I'll teach you. We can always do with more of the natural kind of healers like you. Now you say your brother left a message in the mind of the Prime medic on the *Couana*? Then we'd best have her over here so that I can get it from her."

Zsurtul came to fetch Noni when Zhalmo was asleep.

"Are you sure you can fix this, Noni?" he asked. "She's been well until the last couple of days, then she would suddenly stop talking and stare off into space as if she was looking for something. And the tiredness hit her then, too."

"She's looking for the missing memories, but she doesn't realize that's what she's doing. It's on an instinctive level, not a rational one. We need to build new memories for her, but that will take a few sessions. Tonight we lay the groundwork. I need you to encourage her to come to me to help me with the seeds and plants. Let her think it's her idea. When she's with me, I can work on her without her knowing it."

Noni followed the young King through the lounge into the bedroom where Zhalmo lay fast asleep in the large bed.

"A chair would be helpful," said Noni as she moved to the side of the bed where Zhalmo lay.

Zsurtul rushed off and brought a dining chair over for her.

Nodding her thanks, Noni sat down in it and reached out to feel Zhalmo's forehead, then her pulse. "She's well under now. I can begin."

Reaching into her sleeping mind, Noni immediately found the area from which Kusac had ripped the memories. It was like a gaping mental wound, all raw and roiling with dark impulses and thoughts. She needed to calm that area down, then reduce the irritation so that it ceased generating the disturbing feelings for which Zhalmo had no rational explanation.

Slowly, Noni began to smooth out the area, filling the gap with pleasant thoughts of nothing in particular. Here a memory of a pleasant day, sunshine and warmth; there one of watching a river chuckling over stones as it made its way to the inland sea many miles away. Another of the swimming hole and the cool water there. The memories wouldn't necessarily remain for long, but long enough for them to attract new ones that Zhalmo would make herself with Noni. Memories of arranging flowers in the temple, for instance.

It took some time, but at last the groundwork was done and none of the angry emptiness remained. Noni withdrew and, taking a deep breath, opened her eyes.

"She'll do for now. You should find she rests well tonight and feels a lot better in the morning. Now remember, it's vital you bring her to help me in the temple tomorrow. I need to work alongside her, help her make the new memories to replace the temporary ones I've placed there. If you don't, then within a few days, she'll be worse than she was this evening. Just so you know, Kusac did a first-rate job on her considering how little time he had. This is not because of what he did or didn't do. He could only take away the bad and had no time to replace the memories; that, he left to me. So don't go thinking he did less than his best for her."

"I wouldn't think that, Noni. Thank you for what you're doing for her. I can only imagine what she went through . . ."

"Then don't, or I'll end up having to take those memories from you so she doesn't feel you looking at her and wondering about what might have happened! Imagination can be a powerful bad thing as well as a boon. Don't you go letting it rule your life with her."

"I won't, Noni."

Noni got to her feet. "Right. Time for me to head downstairs with Conner. You have a good night, King Zsurtul. Just relax and sleep. She will be better tomorrow."

Palace of Light barracks courtyard, Zhal-Ghyakulla 7th, (June)

M'Nar had dragged Jerenn cursing and complaining from his bed at almost the crack of dawn.

"Dammit, M'Nar, this could wait until after first meal, surely?" he grumbled as his sword-brother bundled him into the elevator and down to the first floor.

"No," said M'Nar succinctly, grasping his arm again and hauling him across the deserted grand courtyard toward the entry to the barracks parade ground. "This is our berran coming home after a major mission, Jerenn! I want to know how she performed, and in what state Jurrel brought her back while he's still there for you to tear a strip off his hide if she's in less than perfect condition!"

"Me? Why am I the one to do the hide tearing?" muttered Jerenn. "You're just as capable as me of doing that. All I want to tear into is my first meal."

M'Nar stopped abruptly. "There! Can you hear her?"

The sweet purring of the MUTAC's motors formed a counterpoint to the sound of the giant feet hitting the concrete. It filled the quadrangle, bringing all the troops rushing out from their barracks to see what it was.

M'Nar and Jerenn had rounded the corner in time to see the MUTAC leave the main gates and stride purposefully across the parade ground. She paused briefly, then turned toward them and continued more slowly before coming to a complete halt some ten feet in front of them. The rising sun glinted off the windshield, and they could just see Jurrel behind it.

"You got her dirty!" said M'Nar, a note of outrage in his voice. "Her feet and lower legs are caked in . . . something awful," he finished, staring at the damp legs of the MUTAC. "How could you do that to our berran?"

Almost daintily the MUTAC lifted a back leg and shook it, sending some of the accumulated grungy mess flying off it to land with a splat several feet away.

"Sorry, M'Nar," Jurrel's voice came booming out of the

speaker. "I'm afraid there was very little room in the corridors of the M'zullian Palace, so I stepped on more than a few M'zullians. I didn't have a chance to clean her in transit, but I did stop to wade through the river a little before bringing her back to you."

Now fully awake, Jerenn stared at the MUTAC. "You used our MUTAC's feet to kill M'zullians?" he asked disbelievingly.

"Yup, and they made a satisfying squishing noise," said Jurrel happily.

"How did that affect her balance?" demanded M'Nar.

"Not at all, so long as I kept two feet on firm ground. She handles like a dream; you did an amazing job with her."

"And the guns and missiles?"

"Perfect for shooting down the close quarters of the Palace tunnels. Worked just as well in the landing bay area, too. What we need now is a craft the size of the *Couana* but designed to carry the MUTAC to combat zones."

"That we are already planning, M'Nar and Jerenn," said the unmistakable voice of Toueesut from behind them. "Your input we would be liking as well, friend Jurrel."

M'Nar turned round, blinking rapidly for a few moments until Toueesut and his swarm stood still so the two Sholans could get their visual bearings.

"Greetings, friends M'Nar and Jerenn," said Toueesut, bowing and gesturing expansively. "Glad we are to be home and to be bringing back to you your MUTAC undamaged if a little dirty after its adventures on the M'zull world. It killed many of the enemy I am told, and helped the escapes of our people with the new Queen Zhalmo. So liking this design are we that we are wanting to be making more of them for our own use. Of course, we will be seeing that you two and the young human Kai are receiving your due remunerations."

"Ah," said M'Nar, for once almost speechless as he looked at the swirling and dancing swarm.

"Sure I am that the Sholan Brotherhood will also be wanting more of the MUTACs for their own use. I believe we have all added a very useful heavy weapon to our peoples' armories, yes, indeed."

"Thank you, Toueesut," said Jerenn, finding his voice at last. "It will be good to see her as a major resource, not only for Shola, but for you."

M'Nar turned his attention back to Jurrel. "She needs cleaning," he said. "You got her dirty, so you can help clean her up. We'll need large brushes and an environmentally safe detergent. Meet us at the riverside two hours after first meal."

"Aw c'mon, M'Nar," said Jurrel, ears flattening. "I just got back from a mission!"

"You know the rules: clean up the equipment you used as soon as you can," said M'Nar firmly. "We'll help, but I want you there, too."

"And I thought you guys would be different," huffed Jurrel as he lowered the MUTAC to a crouch and powered her down before opening the hatch.

M'zull, Palace, Zhal-Ghyakulla 13th (June)

K'hedduk had attached Kusac to his staff, using him to perform sometimes menial errands for him, mainly taking messages between the Generals. They were jobs that could easily have been done either by a messenger, or by using the communicators. Forced to put a good face on it, Kusac was finding it very trying. As he returned from the latest message delivery, one asking General Chaikul to ready a detailed report on what was currently being salvaged from J'kirtikk, he was crossing the main courtyard when he received a message from Rezac.

"Well, as I live and breathe, is that Nayash's son over there?" the words boomed out, accompanied by a mental call. *Hey, it's me, Rezac!*

Kusac stopped dead and turned to look at the older Valtegan bearing down on him. *Rezac?* he sent.

The one and only. "It is Nayash, isn't it? I thought I

recognized you. I knew your father. Sorry to hear he'd passed away. Tragic, tragic. Oh, you may not know me, Lorishuk is the name." He took Kusac's hand and began pumping it up and down enthusiastically.

"Lord Lorishuk," said Kusac. "A pleasure to meet you. How have you been?"

"Been better. It's that cursed planet J'kirtikk. Just got back from there. Too damned quiet, not a sound anywhere, just dead bodies and the broken machines. Downright spooky it is."

"I'm sorry to hear that. You'll be glad to be back on M'zull, then."

"Very glad. Time to catch up with everyone. Talking of which, you can bring me up to speed on the Court gossip, can't you? I hear as how you're a special aide to his Majesty, May Long Life be His."

"Long Life," echoed Kusac. "I don't know that I know much about the Court gossip, but you're welcome to what I do know. Would you like to come back to my apartment, share a cup or two of maush?"

"Very kind of you to invite me," said the other. "A nice hot maush would hit the spot right now."

"Then come with me," said Kusac, trying not to laugh at the picture of the bluff older male that Rezac was portraying so well.

So how's it going? Have his staff accepted you? Kusac asked.

Only a little confusion from his Steward, but given he's been on the hell planet for about two months straight, everyone is giving him lots of slack. And yeah, he was as bluff as I'm portraying. Your initial reading of him was a little too mild.

"Did you hear about the explosion at one of the city's major wineries last night?" asked Kusac. "I heard that it was completely destroyed."

Is it safe to discuss this? Rezac sent. "Not only that, they left leaflets again."

"Zsadhi ones? What did they say?" *Yes, everyone is talking about it now. We'd be unusual if we didn't.*

"No one knows because the Inquisition were there before anyone else and had them all picked up and destroyed."

"Who do you think is behind these attacks?"

"Has to be the officer caste since the other castes can't act against anyone else. And if it's officers, you can bet some Generals have their fingers in it," said Rezac. "It'll be revealing to see who doesn't get their holdings hit."

"You have a point," said Kusac thoughtfully as they approached his apartment door. "I think I'll start keeping a list of who gets hit, and who doesn't."

"So far, it's been a chapel, a brewery, and a winery—things that keep the masses and the elite happy, nothing vital to our war effort," said Rezac, as he followed Kusac in.

"It hits morale, though, and that can be damaging to everything and everyone."

"Enough of that. Let's talk of more pleasant things. I hear there's to be a music recital tomorrow evening. Are you going?"

Kusac opened the door to his office and showed Rezac in. Going to his desk, he hit the intercom to ask Laazif to have fresh maush and some sweet pastries brought. Then he pulled out the gadget they used to check for monitoring devices.

"So far, so good," said Kusac, heading back toward the oval table and pulling out one of the dining chairs. "It seems that everyone accepts you as Lorishuk."

Rezac sat down beside him. "I'm lucky, he's not an unkind Lord. No nasty habits to gloss over, unlike your Nayash."

"How did your raid go last night? I know it was successful, but any problems at all?"

"None. It was easier to get past these M'zullians than it was to get past the Valtegans in my time."

"Here you aren't part of a captive population that is expected to be rebelling," Kusac pointed out. "They weren't expecting any more attacks. They will be now, so from now on it will only get more hazardous."

"Agreed, but it's a risk we have to take. Talking of risks, how is Mahzi working out?"

"She's turned out to be a lot more savvy than we thought.

Talking to the other females at the weekly harem sessions has taught her a lot about how well off she is with me, compared to the others. She's being most circumspect and is proving to be a godsend at getting useful gossip from the harem females. It's as good as having a spy in all the top courtiers' and Generals' homes. I know which ones favor K'hedduk and which want to take him down and have a military ruler instead. None like the Inquisitors. All this gives me bargaining points to play the Generals and K'hedduk against each other."

"Useful information, indeed. How goes your problem with Inquisitor Ziosh?"

"He waves his hands about, hisses and threatens me, but there is nothing he can really do. Right now, despite marrying Mahzi in the village, I'm K'hedduk's favorite and can do no wrong with anyone else, so Ziosh's complaints will only endear me more to K'hedduk. I do have a surprise, though. Today Roymar returned from his trip to the village with Shazzuk. He's wanting to learn to be a soldier. I've sent them out to the barracks on the estate to do some training with M'yikku."

"That's unusual. Can he learn enough that's valuable in a few weeks? Isn't he more useful to us all in the village?"

"I'm planning to send M'yikku back there with Roymar after a couple of days. They can then start training up some of the other willing villagers. Once they've established a good routine, then M'yikku can return. Who knows—they may come in useful."

"By the way I have used the antidote on myself and my team but without telling them about it. Figured I'd leave it to ask you what you want said to them," said Rezac.

"I've still got it to do. I suppose I should do it sooner rather than later. Explanations are the last thing to worry about right now. Oh, I forgot to tell you, Annuur came by last night with six morphing units for us to test. I sent them on to Kaid at the mountain den. Haven't heard back from him about them yet. Annuur says they last for six hours on their people, but they have to wear them all the time they are morphed."

"That's terrific news! If they keep their scent concealing suits on when morphed, then if they change back too soon, at least their scents will be masked," said Rezac.

"The plan is if they morph back to Sholan or Prime females, they hit the translocator and go straight to the den. We should all do some drills with that, so if we need to use it, we get it right first time. Hush, Laazif is coming."

Ghioass, same day

Kuvaa had found the anomaly while she was installing the new safety protocols into Unity to prevent the use of any morphing devices again. Some unauthorized person was accessing the AI at the same time every day, and she intended to find out who it was. So far, it seemed like the person was no threat to Unity, or to her security for it, but that didn't mean it would always be so. They weren't adept at covering their tracks either, so it was like reading footprints in the snow for her. Another strange thing was that this person was leaving information for her to find, information that had led her to discovering how the Entity Vartra had been captured and imprisoned. Right now, she was more intrigued than concerned.

As she searched Unity, trying to find the entry point that this person was using to access the AI, it seemed as if her searches just got sidelined to nowhere. After this had happened three times, she began to get a sense that Unity itself was trying to keep her from finding out where the point of contact was. Which was ridiculous.

"Unity, please start a self-diagnosis, checking all essential files, routines, and subroutines," she said, sure that this would keep it busy long enough for her to locate the access node in peace.

"Affirmative," said *Unity*,

She found the node within minutes this time and sat

back, utterly surprised. The node was on the Prime world, in the pool area. But they'd shut down all nodes in those areas. The only extant ones were now in the lab areas for the use of the TeLaxaudin scientists. So who had put a node there? On impulse, she continued searching the Palace and found two more nodes—one in the library and one in the nursery. The node in the nursery suddenly went active and the form of a young Sholan cub came into view.

"Who placed those three nodes in the Prime Palace, Unity?" she asked sharply.

I did, Councillor Kuvaa, said Unity. *You wanted information about the Sholan cubs, so I put nodes where I knew they frequented so I could watch them.*

"I didn't ask you to do that."

You did, Councillor. I cannot place nodes anywhere myself; my protocols prevent that.

She hesitated. Unity was right. It had to have been ordered to place the nodes by someone, and since she was the one working most on it at the present, likely she had asked it to monitor the cubs.

"This cub is not being monitored, it is accessing you," she said. "How is that possible, Unity?"

The cub sensed me and began talking to me. He is a very powerful telepath, Councillor, and was able to bypass the protocols you set to prevent someone like him accessing me.

"How many others can do this, or have done this?" she demanded with a sinking feeling in the pit of her stomach. If this cub could do it, who else could?

No one, Councillor. He can only do it because he sensed my nodes to start with.

"Which Hunter cub is this?" she asked, feeling she already knew the answer.

It's Shaidan, the son of Hunter Kusac and his mate Carrie.

That explained a lot. The Hunter had discovered much about their purpose, and what he didn't know, Agent Annuur had been advised to tell him. If the cub was anywhere near as powerful a telepath as his parents, no wonder he had found the nodes and initiated contact with Unity. It had to be that way; after all, the opposite—that Unity had initiated the contact—was unthinkable.

She sat back, listening to the cub and the AI converse as he asked for information on a range of topics from martial arts to the physics of knife throwing. Relief flooded through her. Shaidan was merely using Unity as an encyclopedia, nothing more. She had no need to worry.

M'zull, Palace, Zhal-Ghyakulla 16th (June)

As Kusac was gathering his papers at the end of the Council meeting, one of K'hedduk's aides approached him with instructions to join the Emperor in his office. There, he was invited to sit beside his desk.

"Have you noticed any signs of dissent among the Court because of the Zsadhi attacks?" K'hedduk demanded without preamble.

"It's certainly a major topic of conversation," said Kusac. "Everyone is talking about the attacks."

"What are they saying? Who do they see as responsible for them?"

"Many are speculating on who would be carrying out the attacks, obviously, and the main possible culprit seems to be people from the officer caste since the lower castes are incapable of acting against their superiors or another caste."

"It's too easy a target, too obvious," said K'hedduk. "There has to be more to it than that."

"Some think that there is a General or Generals at the back of it, and it's a plot to destabilize your rule, Majesty," said Kusac diffidently. "I think it's possible, but again, somewhat obvious."

"What about out in the city? What do the workers think about this? It's hitting them as well when the breweries get attacked. At least we're getting the leaflets collected before they are distributed. Have you seen them? They are divisive and scurrilous!" He pulled open a drawer and virtually threw a leaflet across the desk at Kusac. "Read it for yourself!"

Zsadhi was written at the top in large letters. Below it was a drawing of the sword, and across it had been written the message—"As he came in the past, he comes now to fight oppression. Your officers live in luxury while you toil in dirt! Rebel now!"

Kusac handed it back, impressed, but keeping that to himself. "Rather a wasted effort, surely. The workers can't rebel because they're genetically bred to respect the scent marks of all the military castes."

"They can still challenge their superiors for their jobs; all the castes can do that. If they do, we'll have chaos on the streets as no one will know their place anymore!"

"It isn't that bad, is it, Majesty? Aren't your advisers just giving you the worst possible scenarios so as to cover their butts if everything goes wrong?"

"No, they're actually being accurate," said K'hedduk, sitting back in his chair. "Zerdish has people out there, listening to the mood of the workers. There is some muttering among them, and I need to know if it's about to escalate. I rely on you to keep me informed of the mood at Court. See if you can find out if one of the Generals is behind this."

"I'm already keeping records on which estates are being hit to compile a list of possible sympathizers or leaders of this movement. We really need to know where they meet and who is carrying out the raids, and infiltrate them."

"Then get onto that, Nayash. Use any resources you need. Just talk to Zerdish and tell him what you require," said K'hedduk, picking up a sheaf of papers to let Kusac know the interview was over.

"Yes, Majesty. Long Life and Health to you," he said, getting to his feet and slowly bowing his way backward to the door.

M'zull Palace, the harem

The Palace harem was not just where the females kept by K'hedduk to entertain his guests were housed. Like its more exclusive counterpart, the Emperor's seraglio, the females there didn't just lead pampered lives, they were expected to learn skills that they would use to beautify themselves and their surroundings, and to entertain their Lord. Embroidery was one such, as were dancing and singing. They were to entertain their Lord while he was eating, perhaps even his guests, too, with their accomplished voices and dancing. It was to this end that Keshti was educating the females of the Court, even though they were rarely, if ever, seen outside their homes apart from their sessions with him in the Palace harem.

Mahzi settled herself next to Neeshou, another mountain lass like herself. The other five were from far away Ch'almuth, and she had little in common with them. Neeshou had been coming here for a year or two and was very adept at embroidery, so Keshti relied on her to help Resho, the head female drone, to teach some of the others while he put them, one at a time, through their paces with the dance lessons. Some of the dances he taught them used two people and it was fun to learn those, Mahzi thought.

"Good day to you," she said quietly, as she settled herself at the other female's side. "How has your week been?"

Neeshou turned a tense face to her. "Not too good," she whispered. "The General, my husband, lost his winery last night. It was the Zsadhi again. I ran and hid from his anger it was so great."

"What did the leaflets say this time?"

"That we live in luxury and they toil in the dirt. It's true, we do, but I'd give anything to go back home again!"

"Neeshou," came Resho's warning voice. "It's not for you to discuss things like that. You are a trophy wife now, and you must always think and behave as one. It's for the males to worry about things outside the harem, not us."

"Yes, Resho," she said quietly.

"Why should we be silent about this? It affects us, too!" said Mahzi.

"What happens outside is not our consideration," said Resho firmly. "If you continue to talk about it, I will have you sent home and a report made to Lord Nayash. We'll see if he's at all tolerant about your behavior!"

Mahzi subsided and went to get her sewing from the basket beside Resho.

"What does this Zsadhi want, Resho?" asked one of the others.

"If he exists, he wants anarchy, Dershul. To overturn the accepted way of doing things that we have now would bring nothing but anarchy. Don't think any males are going to free you and let you return to your birth homes; they won't. They'll just keep you for themselves, and you won't have one master to keep happy; you'll have many! You're far better off now than you could ever be under any other way of life."

"I was happy at home before I was taken by the M'zullians," said a small female next to Mahzi.

"Chanshu, do you have to toil in a field, or look after smelly herd beasts, or do you sit around all day in beautiful surroundings waiting on your Lord's pleasure? I know which I would prefer," said Resho sharply. "Now enough talk of matters that don't concern us. Back to your sewing. Nayrou, it's your turn to recite the rules of the harem. Begin."

Mahzi filtered out the sound of Nayrou's voice. She was thinking of what Nayash had talked to her about the night before—since he knew she could read, he made sure she got the copy of the day's newspaper after he was done with it. When he came to visit her, they would sit and discuss the articles she'd read. He was very different from these other males and seemed to take pride in how much she understood of what she read, of the politics, as he called it, behind the stories. These females had husbands who valued only their looks and passive behavior. She wished she could get them to see that this wasn't the way things should be, that they could be equals of the males, but without the male in their lives changing their attitudes, what was the point in making the other females unhappy trying to get freedoms they could never have?

"Mahzi, we have dances we learn here in the harem that are centuries old called fan dances. Perhaps Resho would help me teach you one of the simple ones," said Neeshou.

"Fan dances? With real fans?"

"Yes. Resho, can I teach her one?"

"If she makes some headway with her embroidery today, certainly," said Resho.

"You will like the dances," whispered Neeshou. "They have special meaning for our people. You'll see why as you learn them."

Capital city, early hours of the morning Zhal-Ghyakulla 17th (June)

Dressed in dark gray overalls, their lower faces obscured by masks, Kusac, Cheelar, M'yikku, and Maalash kept to the deep shadows at the side of the buildings as they made their way carefully to the warehouse district where the brothel they planned to hit that night was situated. They'd chosen that night because no one would be expecting another raid from the Zsadhi so close to the last one. Their target this time was one designed to hit at the ordinary worker. Causing damage to the main brothel would hit them hard because they had to work hard to earn the right to visit the drones that were employed there. It was sure to cause an outcry among the workers.

Their target building was one of the smaller warehouses that had been made over to be part club and part cheap hotel where the males who earned enough credits would be granted a few hours with one of the drones. Though sterile, the drones were not genderless and customers could choose male or female as their preference demanded and availability allowed. At this time, the facility was closed for the night.

Their plan was to get into the building and plant some explosives around the doorway and by the back exit, scrawl the Zsadhi sword on a main wall, drop some leaflets, and leave, setting off the charges as they went. They intended to cause enough damage to render the place unusable, but not enough to risk the lives of those inside.

Streetlamps were few and far between in this area of the city. Lights were reserved for the large compounds where transport vehicles unloaded their cargo. Their vehicle parked half a mile away in one of the last residential areas, their route took them through streets lined with the smaller warehouses on the edges of the large industrial parks.

As one of them ran forward to scout the area ahead, the others hung back in the deepest shadows—in back alleys, behind dumpsters, whatever cover they could find. At a signal from the forward man, the others would join him, one at a time. They were close now, only a chain-link fence between them and the building. Cheelar took the cutters out of his backpack and clipped a gap through which they could crawl into the compound. Once inside, they dashed again for the deep shadows at the side of the building. All the lights were off as expected. They crouched down, listening for any sounds.

A light wind whistled across the yard, blowing a scrap of paper about. Overhead, behind a covering of clouds, a sliver of moon shone dimly. All was still and quiet.

Kusac made the hand sign that told Cheelar to get the door. Moments later, keeping low, they were slipping inside to either side of the door, waiting for their eyes to adapt to the deeper darkness within. Once they could see again, Kusac signaled to M'yikku to plant the charges on the doorframe while he ventured farther into the room.

A dim shaft of light from a streetlamp picked out the easy chairs and sofas that lined the room. In the center were groups of the same chairs back-to-back, forming seating islands, each with a low table in front of them.

Freezing suddenly, Kusac held up his hand in the universal Halt signal. He'd seen a shape, a lump on one of the chairs that was out of character with the others. Dropping lower to conceal his body profile more, he froze, waiting for a full two minutes. What was it? A cushion on the chair? A pet animal? Though rare, he had seen some canine-like pets about the Court; or was it a person, curled up in the chair?

Silently, Kusac crept forward, loosening his knife in its scabbard, then pulling it free. Inwardly, he cursed his Valtegan shape. Had he been in his natural Sholan form, he'd have been able to smell the subtleties of its scent and tell what it was. He was level with the first of the central chairs now. Another step and the form grunted and moved. He froze, breathing quietly, trying to get a handle on the scent, any scent. It moved again, lifting an elongated head, sniffing the air loudly.

Animal! Kusac flung himself on it and found himself fighting for his life as the snarling beast tried to fasten its jaws around any part of him it could reach. He hissed in pain as the teeth grated across his right forearm. M'yikku joined him, using the butt of his gun to repeatedly beat the creature on the head while it alternately snapped at Kusac's and M'yikku's arms.

The snarls and occasional yelps of pain it was producing sounded like clarion calls loud enough to wake the dead to them. Finally, Kusac got a grip on its head and thrust his knife deep up under the jaw. The creature stiffened briefly, then with a final death thrash, fell limp to the seat of the chair. Hot blood gushed down the knife and over Kusac's hand as he pulled his blade out, wiping it on the soft-scaled skin of the beast.

"Get moving," he hissed, nursing his left arm. "M'yikku, you paint the sword. The damned animal bit me several times."

Upstairs, they could hear the floor creaking as someone got out of bed and began to walk across the floor.

Cheelar ran to plant the rear door charge as M'yikku pulled the can of spray paint out of the pocket of Kusac's backpack, then headed over to the nearest wall. Climbing up on one of the chairs, he began drawing the Zsadhi sword on the wall between a tall mirror and an erotic painting.

Maalash cast a handful of Zsadhi posters into the air, letting them flutter down to the ground.

While they did that, Kusac headed back toward the front door, digging in his pack for a scarf and began wrapping it crudely round his left forearm. The last thing he needed to do was leave a blood trail behind him for the authorities to follow.

Moments later, the others met at the front door, and as silently as they had entered, they left. A quick sprint across the yard and they were out through the gap in the chain-link fence. From there, they hurriedly retraced their steps until they were almost out of line of sight, That was when Kusac triggered the detonator. The double explosion lit up the darkened enclosure with a satisfying low crump of sound and display of bright orange flames. Loud shouts and the ringing of the fire alarms could be heard in the distance.

"Let's get out of here," said Kusac quietly as they headed round the corner. Again keeping to the darkest shadows, they reached the area where they'd parked their vehicle among several others just like it at the side of a residential area. Once in the car, while the rest stripped off the gray coveralls and pulled on their normal uniforms, Kusac scrambled out of his coveralls and began wiping the blood off his forearms with it. The bite marks were still weeping blood, and he dabbed futilely at them with the scarf before tying it on again.

The distant sounds of sirens were coming closer now, and he could feel the night around them coming alive as people slowly responded to the noise and explosion of fire.

"Ready?" Cheelar asked, and getting a chorus of "ayes," he started up the engine and headed out of their parking place.

"Let me see your arm, Captain," said M'yikku from beside him. "Maalash, get the first aid kit." Using his knife, he swiftly sliced through the scarf, exposing the oozing bloody gashes that crisscrossed Kusac's forearm.

With fire engines and the military police all converging on the brothel, a vehicle going in the opposite direction was going to be noticed. Slowly, with the headlights off, Cheelar inched the car down the road, stopping abruptly as a vehicle whizzed past ahead of them at the crossroad.

"Hold his coveralls under his arm while I pour this antiseptic over it," ordered M'yikku.

"Shit, that's worse than the damned bite!" exclaimed Kusac, with a loud hiss of pain. trying to pull his arm back.

"We got to get it clean right away, or it could go septic. That was a canine equivalent of a norrta, all teeth and attitude, a guard animal. Didn't expect them to have one of those."

The vehicle edged forward again till at last they were at the cross street they needed. Cheelar waited a moment with the window open, listening for the sounds of any other vehicles, then he turned into the crossing and headed down the road and out of the city.

"I really hate these missions," said M'yikku with feeling as he bound Kusac's arm up firmly with the bandage in the kit. "They twist my guts up into huge knots until we're safe home."

"I think it gets us all the same," said Kusac, flexing his arm and nodding his thanks before getting himself back into his uniform. "We've got some breathing space now for a few weeks at least. It'll be down to the other units to do the next few hits."

"Is this actually having a real effect on the people?" asked Cheelar. "We're so close to it that it's difficult to tell."

"Oh, yes," said Maalash. "If the officer caste is twitchy in the Palace, and you know they are, then you can believe the worker caste is even worse. You've been hitting their chapels, their brewery, and now their brothel. They are going to be so mad at their superiors for not protecting their interests that you're going to start seeing challenges happening very soon."

"How will they happen?" asked M'yikku.

"They'll just march up to their superior and challenge him to a duel," said Maalash. "Don't they do it that way for you officers?"

"Not exactly," said Kusac. "The physical challenge no longer happens, it's more of a calling the person to account in front of other officers or their superiors. They then investigate the officer and, if need be, replace him with the best person for the job."

"Huh, I think our way is better. You get a new person immediately if you win."

"Both ways are pretty brutal," said Cheelar, flicking on the headlights as they cleared the last of the city streets and entered the countryside.

"I seriously suggest you have a bad hunting accident on the estate tomorrow to explain your injury before we go back to the Palace," said M'yikku, helping him ease into his jacket and button it up.

"Good thought," said Kusac, flexing his arm and clenching his fingers one more time and wincing at the pain. "Feels better. Nice job with the field dressing, M'yikku, thanks. We're definitely going to have to burn that coverall."

"If we stop about a mile from the estate gate and pull into the side there, I can run into the woods and deal with it," said M'yikku.

M'zull, Palace, Council meeting, Zhal-Ghyakulla 18th (June)

"This amount of civil unrest should be impossible, Majesty," said General Nazhol. "I have units going door-to-door in the city, looking for anyone that even resembles an insurgent. Any people not at work who should be are being rounded up, the ringleaders taken into custody, and the rest escorted back to work."

"Don't take them all into custody. Shoot half and leave their bodies prominently exposed as a warning to the others!" snapped K'hedduk. "They are breaking the laws, they are acting in a way that should be impossible! Workers cannot rebel!"

"Tell them that," countered Inquisitor Ziosh. "Killing our workforce isn't the answer, nor is causing more damage among them. You should have anticipated this. The trend in the raids was there for all to see . . ."

"If it was so obvious, Ziosh, why did you fail to spot it? Where is your army of spies when we actually need them? Or you, Generals!" demanded K'hedduk, thumping his fist on the table. "Last I looked, we were all on the same side, not trying to outdo each other! If we don't work together, we won't find this damned Zsadhi!"

"What if there isn't one Zsadhi," said Kusac. "What if it's several people?"

"Don't be ridiculous," snapped General Nazhol. "Of course it's only one person! How could it be more than one? These workers are workers for a reason; they aren't the brightest ones in the unit!"

"They don't have to be, but the ones who are leading the raids, planting the Zsadhi information, do. I say they aren't worker caste," said Kusac. "I say they're a higher caste. Look at the raids. Carried out with precision, they have to be the work of the military."

"He's right," said K'hedduk. "The raids can be done by a team of soldiers, but their leader or leaders have to be a higher level, they have to be officer caste! I don't know why we didn't see it before!"

"Well, that throws your spy theory out the window," snapped General Geddash.

"Not entirely," said Kusac. "There could still be one person in overall charge, and that person could still be the spy."

"Why does it take my newest General to point out clues you should all have noticed? Dammit, you're the tacticians, so you keep telling me, yet you can't analyze this fake Zsadhi's tactics!" hissed K'hedduk.

"This isn't our lack, Majesty! You're the one who . . ." began General Lezhu.

"And what have I had you doing for weeks?" interrupted K'hedduk. "Looking for this spy, looking for those responsible for these raids! You're the military advisers, so advise me and let's see if you can come up with a plan to stop him, because so far, you've had no suggestions, no insights, nothing! Get out of here, all of you, and come up with some new ideas for the meeting the day after tomorrow, or by all that's holy I will start looking for younger males who *can* give me solutions!"

K'hedduk waited for the room to empty before venting his wrath. "They blame me! Me, Zerdish! How dare they! They are the advisers and not a scrap of useful advice have I had in weeks from them except for 'There is no spy, you waste our resources looking for shadows,' and 'Zsadhi is a folk legend, not real,' and still the raids continue!"

"There's some merit in the possibility that more than one person is carrying out these raids," said Zerdish. "It would explain why it's proving difficult to find a pattern for them, and a base of operations. If we triangulate the raid sites, we get nothing."

"As soon as you have more people involved, the chances of someone letting slip they are a member of the units causing the raids goes up. Nayash is right; it has to be one or more of the officer caste in charge. From the rate at which the Generals are digging in their heels and not cooperating with me or each other, I'm sure at least one of them is involved."

"It's possible, Majesty."

"Possible be damned, probable more likely. I cannot rule effectively when I have to deal with a group of cast-off ancient Generals inherited from my spineless brother! I need people of my own choosing, of a like mind to me, people of action, not ancients stuck in their ways! It's time I harvested them to make way for new blood, Zerdish. Time I got people like Nayash onto this, finding out who's not only loyal to me but useful as well."

"Shall I send for Nayash?"

"No, not yet. They will have gone to rumble and hiss their venom to each other. Nayash knows to listen well to what he can. Let him gather some more information. We'll talk to him this afternoon, Zerdish," said K'hedduk, his good humor restored as he got to his feet.

Later that afternoon, Emperor's office

"How did the Generals' meeting proceed?" asked K'hedduk as a servant poured maush for Kusac.

"It was a heated discussion as usual, your Majesty," said Kusac. "I know it would have been more moderate had a little more time passed between the Council meeting and theirs."

"Moderate? How moderate?"

"It's easy to blame the person in charge, but a leader is only as good as his intelligence. Since you are getting no intel from them . . ." He left the rest unsaid.

"I am dependent on them, as you say. Who are the most vociferous in condemning me?" he demanded.

"Majesty, I really couldn't say. Tempers were running hot—they were accusing each other of not being candid with information for you, of not making enough effort to track down this Zsadhi and his insurgents. It would be wrong of me on a few minutes of such unguarded conversation to point the finger at, for instance, General Geddash, for feeling since his command is the First Fleet he has no need to check out his people and his staff. Or to praise General Lezhu for taking a most firm line with his people by setting a watch on all his factories and warehouses and escorting his people to and from their communal residences. A move I intend to follow today, I should add."

"So Lezhu is keeping his people under tight control. Good for him. What about the others?"

"I have no more information, Majesty," he said, taking a sip of his maush. He'd learned from previous audiences that K'hedduk got really mad if he didn't make an attempt to drink the maush. "No others mentioned what they were doing. I do see that Geddash has a point, though. With most of his people in space, the chance of them being responsible for any insurrection is almost none. They don't have the shore leave to be able to do it. And so far, all the raids have happened down here, none up in space on the stations. It's easy to see why he thinks his troops are exempt from the checks the rest of us are carrying out."

"He has a staff planetside as well who could be members of this Zsadhi group. By not checking them, he is putting us all at risk. Maybe I need to see who is not taking this threat seriously, not checking all his personnel. They have to have a base, somewhere they keep their leaflets, their paint, and whatever alien weapon they use to melt stone! I want that weapon, Nayash. What I could do with it against my enemies!"

"It sounds like it could be more of a personal weapon rather than the long-range weapons you would need to fight a war, Majesty. Close quarters combat should only be for mopping up after the main battle, either in space or the atmosphere."

"You haven't seen one of the sites of a raid yet, have you? The last two had no melted stone like the first one. Visit the chapel on Lord Rashal's estate and see the damage for yourself. Go after you leave here, tell me what you think happened. I can compare it with the report that fool Nazhol gave me! He was convinced it was carried out by at least ten people! A group of four could have done that with the right equipment."

Kusac got to his feet, relieved to be let off so lightly this visit. "I'll not waste any time, Majesty. I'll go now. I should have a report to hand in sometime tomorrow."

"Yes, go now, but remember to keep your ears open to what the Generals and the Lords are doing."

"Of course, Majesty. It is my privilege to serve you. May Long Life and Health be Yours!" Kusac bowed deeply before leaving the royal presence.

Prime world, same day

"My wedding wasn't half as much of a fuss as this is being," exclaimed Zhalmo, throwing herself into a comfy chair in despair.

"Your dress! It will be covered in creases!" Shishu rushed forward making little clucking noises of disapproval as she grasped her soon-to-be Queen by the hands and pulled her to her feet.

"I can't stand any longer, Shishu," said Zhalmo. "I've been standing for the past two hours, and almost all of yesterday while they fitted the dress on me! Now they want to make more adjustments to it! Enough, I say! It looks fine as it is!"

Doctor Zayshul looked her up and down critically, before walking around her. All the while, the dressmaker continued her litany of criticism, telling them that the skirt was still too long at the front, and the train needed another tuck at the back to make it hang to perfection and . . .

"That will be all, Takoul," said Zayshul with finality. "You have surpassed yourself, the dress is perfection. There is no need for any alterations. You can go now." She stopped in front of Zhalmo and reached out to gently squeeze her arm. "You look lovely, my dear. King Zsurtul will be so proud of you."

Zhalmo felt the tension suddenly leave her body as she began to relax for the first time in days. "Thank you," she said. "How long till the ceremony begins?"

Doctor Zayshul pulled her comm unit out of her dress pocket. "We should be heading to the robing room now," she said, checking it and putting it away again. "The King will be waiting for you. Your father certainly is," she laughed. "He's been pacing the floor since he got up this morning."

"Really?" she asked, smiling.

"Yes, really!" Zayshul linked arms with her daughter-in-law and led her to the door. "Shishu, please bring Mayza to the robing room, and make sure to bring that special cushion for the crown. Oh, and check that Shaidan is ready."

"Yes, Doctor," Shishu said, following them out.

"Remember, you are to take the crown on this cushion to King Zsurtul. Then you move back to where Doctor Zayshul, the General, and your uncle and I are standing," said Kitra, reading the directions from a piece of paper as they cut behind the curtained off area of the Throne Room and entered the robing room.

"I won't forget, Aunt Kitra," he said, squirming as his uncle once again tugged at his white tunic, and adjusted the wide jewel-colored belt. "It's fine, Uncle Dzaka," he said, running his finger under the matching broad collar he wore. "It's this necklace that's cutting into me."

Dzaka adjusted the fastening for him. "How's that?"

"Much better, thanks."

"It's only for a few hours," said Kitra sympathetically. "You can put up with it for that long, I'm sure."

"Yes, Aunt Kitra."

"Here comes Zhalmo," said Dzaka .

Kitra moved through the small group of court officials to greet her and assure her that Shaidan was ready.

"It's the waiting that's getting to me," said Zhalmo, kicking the train of her dress into obedience when it tried to wrap itself around her legs. "Damned dress won't behave! I just wish it was all over! And it's not just the ceremony, it's the banquet afterward," she said glumly.

"You look lovely. Once it all starts, the time will fly," Kitra reassured her. "It did for my wedding. Not that this is your wedding," she said, ears flattening slightly in embarrassment. "But it is your day, and you'll find you enjoy it once it actually starts."

"I know," smiled Zhalmo, patting the younger female on the shoulder. "The fact it's my coronation is more intimidating than if it had been my wedding!"

The quiet hum of conversations suddenly stilled as the young King entered. Around the room, everyone bowed in his direction.

"Please, rise up," he said, addressing the court officials. "You should go into the Throne Room. They're ready to begin the ceremonies." He looked across the room at Zhalmo, smiling broadly as he saw her.

Self-consciously, she smoothed down the full skirts of her silver dress as he came straight to her side.

"You look wonderful," he said quietly, taking hold of her hand and raising it to his lips as around them, the members of the court made their way into the Throne Room.

"And you look very much the King," she said, looking up at the winged raptor crown that cupped his head. "I hadn't realized the crown was so beautiful."

"It's also heavy," he grimaced. "Your crown is much lighter and, I think, more beautiful—a real Queen's crown. The Palace jewelers have outdone themselves."

"I can't wait to see it," she said as he took her hand and they turned to face the doors into the Throne Room.

Trumpets sounded as the Chamberlain led the way into the Throne Room. The heavy drapes had been pulled back, and the two thrones had been moved from the back of the hall to just in front of the row of pillars.

The King's throne with the large sunburst behind it was obviously prominent, but beside it now rested an altogether lighter and more modern Queen's throne. Carved around the legs were young herd beasts and birds which were only now being released back into the wild. Fastened to the padded back of the throne in a silver metal, was a large lunar disk. Together, the two thrones spoke of rulers who cared about their people both day and night.

Dzaka and Kitra led Shaidan to the right of the thrones, joining Doctor Zayshul and her daughter Mayza. On the left side, Toueesut and his swarm stood almost still, beaming widely.

"I be saying that the silver material we gave them for the dress would be the best for the purpose of her coronation," he said in a stage whisper.

Kitra nodded and shushed him, putting her forefinger to her lips in the universal sign for silence.

The Chamberlain entered carrying the Queen's crown on a green velvet cushion. On cue, Shaidan came forward to take it from him before retreating back to where his aunt and uncle stood.

Another court official, carrying an ornate book, stepped forward, looking at Mayza and her parents, waiting for the Doctor to bring her over to take the book from him. This accomplished, he stepped back into the throng of courtiers.

Shaidan watched as King Zsurtul and Zhalmo entered last, to another fanfare of trumpets. As the final notes died away, they took their places in front of the two thrones, facing the assembled members of the court and their honored guests.

"It's with great pleasure," the young King said, "that I bring before you my wife Zhalmo to be crowned as my Queen and coruler."

Applause filled the Throne Room, and from outside, where the ceremony was being beamed to the people who filled the central courtyard, they could hear the cheering.

"I say coruler because I want her to share with me the day-to-day business of ruling this world, and returning it to the verdant planet it once was."

More applause filled the room. Shaidan shifted his weight, and as the King's speech droned on, he turned his attention to the crown he was carrying.

Made of platinum, the crown was indeed beautiful and light if the weight of it on the cushion was anything to go by. It was a circlet, about three inches wide, embossed with large raptor's wings inlaid with precious stones of blue, turquoise, and orange. At the front, the same raptor head as on the King's crown, reared up protectively. It was a real work of art.

Then his Aunt Kitra was digging him in the ribs to get his attention.

Startled, he looked up at her.

"Go on," she whispered, gesturing him forward. "It's time to give the crown to the King!"

"Oh! Right," he said, mentally shaking his head and standing taller before moving slowly toward where Zhalmo now knelt before the King.

"I present to you, my undisputed wife, Queen Zhalmo. Are all of you gathered here willing to give her your service and reverence?" the King asked, his voice ringing out clearly.

"We are!" came the loud reply.

Shaidan, dipping his head forward in respect, held the green cushion out to King Zsurtul.

"Thank you, Shaidan," the King whispered as he lifted the crown from its resting place.

Shaidan smiled, and clutching the cushion to his chest, backed off until he was standing beside his aunt and uncle.

"Will you take the oath of allegiance to K'oish'ik?"

"I will," replied Zhalmo, looking up at her husband.

"Will you solemnly promise to help govern the people and lands of this great planet, according to the customs and laws that hold here?"

"I will,"

"Will you do your utmost to promote the religion of La'shol, the Goddess of all life and prosperity, and to further Her wishes to make this land once more green and fruitful?"

"I will do that," she said.

"Then I crown you now in the sight of the Goddess and of my people here present, as Queen Zhalmo."

Shaidan watched as solemnly, the crown was placed upon Zhalmo's brow. This done, the King held out his hand to her.

"Arise, Queen Zhalmo!" he said.

Shaidan was happy to join in the shouting and cheering. When it had died down, the King spoke again.

"Let the Book of Records be brought forward so the Queen's signature can join mine to attest to her coronation this day."

Mayza trotted forward and stopped in front of the King to hand him the ornate book. Book in one hand, his wife's hand in the other, Zsurtul led Zhalmo over to a prepared side table as Mayza made her way to her mother's side.

There, the book was handed to General Kezule, who opened it and laid it down ready for the Queen. He took up a pen and handed it to her.

"The Book of Records is ready for you, Majesty," he said, bowing deeply to the King and Queen as he handed his daughter the pen.

"Thank you, Father," she said, taking it from him. Leaning forward, she signed the book with a flourish and handed the pen back to him.

The roar of the crowd outside was heard by them all, then the bells recently mounted on top of the Palace rang out their joyful carillon.

Taking his wife's hand again, Zsurtul drew her arm through his and led her past the table to the small chapel and from there, to the Appearance window. The cheering grew even louder if possible as the inhabitants of the Palace of Light and the town outside it all voiced their delight.

A prod in his back made Shaidan turn round. M'Nar's face smiled down at him.

"So how's our young Queen maker enjoying himself?" the Brother asked.

"I'm not a Queen maker," said Shaidan, raising his voice to be heard over the din of the bells and grinning up at him. "Just a helper for the Queen."

"You did a grand job today, youngling," said M'Nar, reaching out to pat him on the head. "Who'd have thought we'd see this from inside the Palace!"

"I certainly didn't," said Jerenn.

"Does this mean you'll be at the banquet, too?" asked Shaidan.

"I guess so," said Jerenn.

"Of course it does!" said M'Nar, ears dancing back and forth. "A state banquet has got to have better rations than ours!"

"Hey! You eat the same food as we do now," said Shaidan. "It's pretty good."

"Only joking," said M'Nar as Kitra shot him a stern glance. "Yes, Sister Kitra, we'll be quiet now," he said, grabbing Jerenn and melting into the nearest group of courtiers.

Shaidan chuckled quietly to himself as he heard Jerenn say, "I wasn't the loud one! You're always getting us into scrapes, M'Nar!"

Kitra gave a melodramatic sigh. "With them, it's like having two big brothers around. Ones that are always getting into mischief. Now stand up straight, Shaidan. When they come back from their appearance, then we'll be following them into the audience hall where the banquet will be held."

"Where will my brothers and sisters eat?" he asked. "We're not all eating with the grown-ups, are we?"

"The others are eating in the anteroom with Shishu and several other people. King Zsurtul was very definite that he wanted you and Mayza—and Gaylla—to dine with us."

Shaidan grinned in pleasure. "Gaylla will be pleased. She can't always be involved in what I do, and she knows that, but it's nice when she can."

"Brother Jerenn and Brother M'Nar can sit with you two," said Kitra, keeping a straight face. "About time they helped Gaylla during a meal."

"Yes, Aunt Kitra."

CHAPTER 6

Prime world, Palace of Light, same evening

TAKING a couple of deep breaths, Shaidan lowered his center of gravity and fixed his eyes on M'Nar's, his arms about shoulder width apart. Though his eyes were focused on his opponent's, he was also paying close attention to the older male's body language.

Suddenly, M'Nar passed the knife from one hand to the other, the move quick and fluid. Shaidan knew better than to follow it with his eyes and instead kept focused on the other's face. Again the quick flick of the hands, this time accompanied by a sudden lunge toward him.

At the last moment Shaidan pivoted on one heel, slapping his right arm down across M'Nar's outstretched right forearm while letting his back slam into the other's chest. From that position, he grasped M'Nar's forearm as his other hand instantly went to grab for his thumb. Having caught it, he pulled it back to almost breaking point, then stopped.

"I'm patting your side, Shaidan," said M'Nar in a strained voice.

"Oh, sorry!" exclaimed the cub, hurriedly letting him go.

"Well done, Shaidan," said Jerenn, looking at the others. "That's how you need to do it. Remember, watch the face but be aware of all central core body movements because often an attacker's eyes give him or her away just before they move. They'll look in the direction they are going to move a fraction of a second before they do. Now pair off. Shaidan, you take Gaylla. See if you can help her out with her moves."

"A little too enthusiastic," muttered M'Nar to Jerenn, flexing his thumb. "But he got it right."

"He always gets it right," said Jerenn. "They're all coming along very well. Teaching them a series of responses to set situations was a brainwave, M'Nar. It fits in with the patterns of movement they need to know, yet gives them ways to defend against all kinds of assaults right now."

"You'd have come up with it, too," said M'Nar, "in a week or two!" He skipped out of the way of the humorous cuff aimed at his ears.

"So what's next for our youngling? Are you ready to let him learn to throw knives now?"

"Yes, I'm ready. He's managed to sharpen that old set of knives I gave him, so all we need now is a where and a when that we can't get caught."

I know the perfect place, sent Shaidan. *There's a hidden ruin to the north side of the Palace, the place K'hedduk hid his spaceship when he was here. It's like an underground warehouse. It has lighting and is all concrete inside.*

They both picked it up loud and clear despite neither of them being an actual telepath. Like all Brothers and Sisters, they had a sensitivity, an extra sense that helped them excel at their work, like a danger sense or a form of empathy, like Jerenn and M'Nar.

"Sounds good," said M'Nar quietly, knowing Shaidan would pick it up as if he'd sent it telepathically.

The cubs carried on practicing that move for another ten minutes before swapping over to each take the turn as the knife wielder.

That done, they got Shaidan out again to demonstrate a new move.

"Right, kitlings, this time we're going to show you what to do if someone comes up behind you and locks an arm across your throat."

Jerenn this time demonstrated on Shaidan.

"Now where is the weak point in his attack?" asked M'Nar.

"His hand?" asked Vazih.

"No," said M'Nar. "It's his elbow. What's happening now is Shaidan is getting choked by the pressure of that arm against his throat, so the first thing we need to do is to get rid of that pressure. Turn your head, Shaidan, so your neck is in the crook of his arm where his elbow is. Immediately you do that you can breathe again, right?"

"Yes, much better," wheezed Shaidan.

"Now reach up and grab that elbow, digging in your nails. For the real thing, you'd make your nails into claws and dig those deep into his elbow, but don't do that now!"

"Ouchie, that would hurt a lot," said Gaylla.

"It would," agreed M'Nar. "Now as you dig in those nails, pull down on his elbow and turn your body slightly away from him so your hips press into his stomach. Keep turning and you'll find you can face him. While doing this, you lift up your right foot and claw-scrape down his shin. He or she will soon let go! Remember, no claws for real, just use your toes for now, and fingers."

"Be careful to not hurt your partner too much!" said Jerenn. "Your shins are very lightly covered bone and any downward scrape is going to really hurt."

"Once more, you two, without me talking you through it this time if you can manage that," said M'Nar.

Shaidan executed the move perfectly again, this time making sure he didn't hurt Jerenn.

"Right, pair up again and practice. Then we'll take you one at a time to try the move with one of us so you know what it's like to use it on an adult."

Half an hour later, M'Nar and Jerenn were herding them to the Sholan camp's temporary bath house to wash the dust and dirt off themselves before heading upstairs.

After dinner, Shaidan chose to head to the pool to relax and further indulge his curiosity about Unity. He no longer needed to be beside a node, as Unity had told him, but he did like to be in a quiet place where he'd be undisturbed. At least when he was in the pool, Aunt Kitra and Uncle Dzaka knew he wasn't outside at night and so weren't checking up on him every few minutes. They were giving him some free time during the days now so that he could go into the grand courtyard with an escort of one of the Brotherhood, or one of Kezule's commandos.

No sooner was he settled in the bubble pool and tuned in to Unity than he was aware of another presence. Instantly he tried to back away, but this time he was mentally held firmly in place.

You must be Shaidan. I'm Kuvaa, sent an alien yet undeniably female thought. *I've noticed you before but never been able to talk to you.*

You're holding me against my will, he sent. *Let me go and then maybe I will talk to you.*

I need to talk to you. What you're doing is dangerous. I'm in charge of Unity, I control the security for it. Somehow you are getting into our databases and interacting not only with Unity itself, but our data.

You left nodes for me to find, they're how I access Unity. If you had them protected, perhaps I wouldn't be able to take advantage of them.

I thought all the nodes were closed down. It seems someone has opened some of them up again. I will see to closing them. I also need to thank you for your help in solving the problem we had with how I was duplicated.

Oh! It was you, was it? Let me see you. I don't get images.

Kuvaa allowed an image to form of herself.

You're a Cabbaran, and one of those with tattoos. I heard they can mesmerize people if they look at them too long.

They show my clan affiliations, my profession, and my rank within it, sent Kuvaa. *But what you're doing is dangerous, Shaidan. Many thousands of people are constantly using Unity every day. It's quite possible that another user, one not as friendly as I am, will discover you. That would not be to your advantage.*

So you aren't always in agreement? Is that with each other, or just with the TeLaxaudin? he asked. *Which faction are you?*

He had the satisfaction of seeing Kuvaa wince slightly, at least he interpreted it as a wince.

Reformist, she said. *How do you know this? How did you find out?*

The same way I found out how you were duplicated. I asked Unity for information and worked it out for myself.

You . . . you're in communication with Unity?

Even he could sense the shock in her voice. *Yes. We talk to each other a lot.*

This should not be possible, she muttered. *Nothing shows up on the potentialities, even though you are a nexus.*

Maybe because it's not that important that I talk to Unity. What are these potentialities?

Not important, Shaidan. Just know that it would be better for you not to talk to Unity anymore in case the wrong people find you chatting.

Unity wouldn't let that happen to me, he said confidently.

I found you, she reminded him.

Only because you're in charge of security for Unity. He warned me about you a while ago, and I have been careful. He'd warn me if someone was watching.

He would, would he?

He warned me about you, said Shaidan defensively.

What do you discuss? she asked in a sudden change of topic.

Anything, Everything, he sent. *What bothered me today, what I couldn't get right, what Unity is trying to discover.*

So you help each other?

Yes. It isn't always about being clever, sometimes it's about thinking in a different way. All of my brothers and sisters, we all think alike because of how we began.

You did have a strange beginning, didn't you? The sand-dweller bred you to serve him, but you became part of his downfall.

How do you know all about us? Have you been watching us all this time? Shaidan demanded.

No, we couldn't see you, we heard about you after the events. I have to go now, Shaidan, and you should, too. Remember what I said; what you are doing is dangerous.

*I have to do it, Kuvaa, because my father can't, and I can.
It's my Clan duty to find out things, like about you.* With that,
Shaidan cut off his connection to Unity and was suddenly
back in the bubble pool. He was shaking a little from reaction and the realization of just what he was finding out. It
also occurred to him that he couldn't tell anyone else about
this and he desperately needed to. There was just no one he
trusted enough that would let him carry on getting the information despite the danger. At least he could write it
down and tell Gaylla if anything happened to him to give it
to Uncle Dzaka. That was his only option right now.

Sighing, he got out of the pool. At least writing it down
would make him organize what he'd found out in a logical
way.

M'zull Palace, Zhal-Oeshi 5th, Month of Harvest (August)

Kusac got a summons from Inquisitor Ziosh to be in his
office at noon that day. The Inquisition offices were attached to the temple as the ones on the Prime world were,
but there the resemblance ended. Heavy with the scent of
incense from the temple, the atmosphere was intimidating.
Crimson and black were the main colors in the carpet, the
drapes, and the furniture.

The Inquisitor sat at his desk, and looked up as he entered. "Nayash. So you finally condescend to present yourself to me," he said, putting down his pen.

"I've been busy for his Majesty, as I'm sure you know,"
said Kusac, sitting down opposite him.

"I know I gave you the opportunity to work for me and
you didn't even have the manners to turn me down."

"I knew you would understand where my loyalty had to
lie."

"You forget, Nayash, who has the power here. I can arrest you on charges of blasphemy, and there is nothing your

Emperor can do to prevent it. What is K'hedduk planning to do about this civil unrest? He might have tamed the workers for a while, but they will rebel again the next time one of their leisure facilities is hit. Another brewery, another brothel, and who knows what could happen?"

"You talk as if you would enjoy the conflict it would cause between the workers and the soldiers."

"I enjoy anything that embarrasses him!"

"A dangerous thing to admit to me," said Kusac, curious to see where this was going.

Ziosh lifted the paper in front of him and held it up for Kusac to see. "This is an arrest warrant for you for the crime of blasphemy. It states that you willfully set light to your father's coffin, consigning his soul to utter darkness instead of eternal life in the Western horizon. Such a crime carries with it the death penalty, if you are found guilty—and you will be."

"Unless? There's always an unless with you."

"Unless you work for me and pass me information on what his Majesty is planning. You are in the perfect position of trust now. I could not have arranged it better had I tried."

Kusac got angrily to his feet. "If you think you have me backed into a corner, Ziosh, think again. I refuse to spy for you!"

"You have two days and then I expect a report from you, Nayash. Remember, you're only of use to me if I don't have to arrest you."

Barely restraining himself from banging the door behind him, Kusac stormed down the corridor until he joined Cheelar.

"Apartment, now," he said tersely, leading the way at a fast pace. Once inside, he waited until Cheelar shut the office door, then he exploded.

"That snake wants me to spy on K'hedduk, or he'll arrest me for burning my father's coffin, he says. It's basically a death sentence!"

"You can't play one against the other?" asked Cheelar quietly.

"Not this time. I have two days to come up with the first

information on what K'hedduk plans to do to prevent another attack on a workers' entertainment facility—a brewery or brothel. Whatever I tell Ziosh, I get the feeling he could use it to start his own series of raids! We've launched a snowball here, and it's just getting bigger the farther downhill it rolls."

"Snowball?" asked Cheelar.

"We did cold weather training on the asteroid—remember the snow? Remember my people making balls of it and throwing it at each other and you?" Getting a nod in reply, he said, "Snowballs. If you roll one along the ground, it gets larger as it gathers more snow."

"So what can we do about Ziosh?"

Kusac pulled out his desk chair and sat down. "I don't know yet," he said. "Ziosh said the Emperor couldn't help me if he has me arrested because he's autonomous. Since he admits I'm useless to him if he has to have me arrested, then it's likely if I don't come to heel within the two days, he'll not come after me but at one of my staff, or Mahzi. It's what I would do."

"Can you tell the Emperor?"

"If I do and he does nothing, it leaves me unable to do anything permanent to Ziosh. I'll be the immediate suspect."

"So either you spy for him, or kill him within the next few days." Cheelar went over to the sideboard where a jug of cold maush sat and poured it into two bowls, bringing one over for Kusac.

"I don't suppose there is any way the Zsadhi could hit at him, is there?"

"The only deaths so far have been of necessity," he said thoughtfully. "Ziosh was enjoying the thought of more anarchy among the workers. If I didn't know better, I would put him as one of those responsible for the Zsadhi attacks."

"Can you denounce him to K'hedduk?"

"All he needs is to have alibis for the nights of the raids and he's off the hook, and my credibility suffers. No, we have to strike directly at him."

"Pity we can't make him forget he threatened you at all."

"Forget! That's it! The TeLaxaudin had some device that could make us forget what had happened on that science ship, and on the Prime world. If they could use it on Ziosh . . ."

"Ask them," said Cheelar.

Digging in the concealed pocket, he brought out the small transmitter and activated it. Within a few minutes, Annuur answered.

"What you be needing?"

Quickly and quietly Kusac described the problem.

"Can do, but it will only give you a few days of his forgetfulness. Is major issue for him, he will think of it again."

"Gives me time for a more permanent solution. When can you do it?"

"Tonight we will do it, best done as soon as possible."

"Can you destroy that arrest order, too? If he sees that he will remember."

"Can do, but you need help as you know document, we don't. We take you when he's asleep."

"I'll be here." He cut the connection.

The rest of the day passed slowly until it reached midnight, then Annuur and Azwokkus came for him.

"Cannot do just his room," said Azwokkus' translator. "Have to do area of Palace so need to wait till most asleep. If not, might catch them in bad situation and they know something happened to them."

"How did you do us on the ship?"

Azwokkus glanced at Annuur.

Annuur sighed. "Area your crew were in isolated from rest of ship, had control over only your area," he said. "Understand, was Lassimiss and his people, not us. I and my family prisoners, too."

"Just take us to Ziosh so we can get this done," said Kusac tiredly.

"Wear these," said Azwokkus, handing him a pair of dark glasses. "Will prevent you being affected."

Taking them, Kusac put them on.

"We activate device now, then go to target who is like one hypnotized."

As Azwokkus said this, there was a sudden flash of light, then around him the room dimmed until it was pitch-black, then very slowly, as colors seeped back into his vision, he realized he was in the Inquisitor's office. Ziosh stood like a statue, staring into space, not moving, barely breathing.

"Find papers you need while we see to him," said Annuur. "Can take off glasses now."

Cautiously, he removed the glasses and began to move toward Ziosh. "You're sure he won't wake?"

"No, but hurry," said Azwokkus.

Kusac pushed past the priest, stopping to stare at his vacant face for a moment. He shuddered and moved on to the desk, rifling through the papers there till he found the one for his arrest.

"Be sure you have all you need," warned Annuur. "Cannot come back for several days if you forget something."

More slowly, Kusac checked all the papers on the desk, finding several of interest which he quickly read, One was a report from General Nazhol, obviously one of Ziosh's spies. He filed the information away for future use.

As he passed Ziosh again, he stopped, fingering the hilt of his knife. "I could kill him now and be done with it."

"No," said Azwokkus firmly. "Do that and he wakes and we all discovered. Other ways to take him down, we look into it. You ready? Two weeks and nanites ready to activate, just two weeks left."

"I'm ready."

"We leave now."

Next thing he knew, he was back in his bedroom alone with the arrest warrant.

"As quick and as easy as that," he said quietly, thinking of the times he'd forgotten what he knew about being spied on in the Palace between one step and the next. Lassimiss and his people—the whole Camarilla—had a lot to answer for, and by the Gods, they would answer once this was over.

Zhal-Oeshi 7th (August)

The next day he was wakened by a call from the Emperor's office telling him to report to the estate village of Lord Lorishuk to investigate the latest Zsadhi raid on his brewery.

"Since you wrote such an excellent report for his Majesty on the state of the other raids, he's decided to put you in charge of the investigation," said Zerdish. "He'll expect you to have a full report on his desk within the next two days."

At least it got him out of the Palace and Ziosh's sight for the next couple of days, definitely a plus in his mind, and at Rezac's estate, too.

Getting up, he dressed and headed for his dining room where he knew his breakfast and his staff would be.

Grabbing a plate and serving himself from the sideboard, he said over his shoulder, "You're with me today at Lord Lorishuk's estate. I've been asked to investigate the latest Zsadhi attack at his brewery. You'll need that camera again, Cheelar."

"On it," he said, gulping down the last of his breakfast and getting to his feet. "Will Lord Lorishuk be there?"

"I expect so. If my estate had been raided, I would certainly be there."

"Shall I call ahead and warn his people we're on our way over?"

"Good idea. This will likely take more than one day to record everything that has been broken or damaged. The other raids certainly did."

It was almost noon by the time they arrived at the estate. Lorishuk's steward met them at the door and escorted them to the Lord's office where Rezac greeted them warmly, complaining loudly about the depredation to his brewery which, he said, had been all but destroyed by targeted small explosive charges to the mash tub, the kettles, and fermenters.

After lunching, they drove down to the village where the brewery was situated. It had been a medium-sized establishment that made one of the most popular beers drunk by the worker and soldier castes alike. Its loss would be felt hard by many people.

The smell of half-fermented beer mixed with a sulfurous odor hung over the area like a sour miasma. Inside, the floor was littered by copper-and-steel pipes, tubing, and sections of the giant cylindrical containers.

"Looks like they targeted exactly what they wanted to destroy rather than blowing up the whole building," said Kusac.

"That seems to have been their plan," said Lorishuk/ Rezac. "It also left them the walls to paint their Zsadhi sword symbol onto." He pointed to the north wall where a six-foot-tall sword had been scrawled onto the white plasterwork.

M'yikku scribbled furiously on his notepad while Kusac waited for him to finish.

"What about any other signs like the molten stone. Any sign of that anywhere?"

Of course not. You weren't here to do it! sent Rezac. "Nothing like that, just the sword and the leaflets."

Should I melt part of the floor so it seems consistent?

Only if you can find a place to do it unseen.

"Do you have one of the leaflets I could see?"

"Absolutely. I had them all gathered up before the workforce on my estate could get them, as per the standing orders. I have one here you can have." He reached into his jacket pocket and pulled out a folded sheet of paper. Opening it out to its full letter size, he handed it to Kusac.

"Your leaders enjoy their wives and luxurious homes while you toil alone and never know true females. Time for this to change." Kusac read aloud. "As divisive as the other ones. Whoever is doing this really wants to upset the order and discipline that has lasted for several thousand years."

"I'd also say that with the knowledge of explosives and as articulate as they are, the people claiming to be the Zsadhi are a cross-caste group with members from every caste in it," said Rezac.

Keep pushing the multicaste thing; then they won't think

to look at the mountain folk at all, sent Kusac, handing the leaflet to M'yikku. "I agree with you on that. Let's see how they got into the brewery."

"It was easily done. I've never bothered to have the place guarded. Just locking it up at night has always been enough for me. If you follow me round to the rear, you can see that they broke in the back door using some kind of metal lever to force it open."

"Photos, Cheelar," said Kusac as they walked round to the back of the building.

"Yes, m'Lord," said Cheelar, examining the door and taking photos of the broken lock from every angle.

Rezac and Kusac waited for him to finish, chatting about the damage and how long it would take to replace the equipment and get the brewing production back up and running again.

"Finished m'Lord," said Cheelar.

"Let's look at the damaged containers, see if we can discover if they used fuses or detonators, what kind of explosives they used, and photograph the damage," said Kusac.

Kusac and Rezac stood and watched as Cheelar, M'yikku, and Maalash carefully searched through the debris for clues.

We don't want to be too efficient, Kusac, sent Rezac. *Just enough to keep everyone satisfied that we did a good job.*

Don't worry. I've done several of these already. It enables me to choose what to let them know, plus look efficient. On the off chance anyone else is looking at the same evidence, there's no obvious lies or excluded evidence either.

Gods, I hadn't thought that K'hedduk would have someone else look at the evidence, too!

I did, so don't worry. Part of what I do is say what I think the aim of the attack was. Even being right on that doesn't harm us as there is nothing they can do to stop the effect the lack of the brothel or the brewery will have on the people.

They're going to start guarding everything soon, sent Rezac.

Which is when we up the ante by choosing targets they think are impregnable and won't guard properly, if at all.

Naturally, it will increase the danger for us, but it will really hit them where it hurts.

"Finished taking the pictures, m'Lord," said Cheelar, folding the camera back into its case.

"You got some of the painted Zsadhi sword?"

"Yes, Lord Nayash."

"Are you done now, Nayash? Can I send for a clean-up crew? The smell of stale beer is only going to get worse as the day gets hotter."

"Yes, send your people away now while I have a last look round. Maalash, take the evidence box back to the house, please." *I don't want him around when I make the molten floor patch,* he sent.

Alone apart from his own people, Kusac walked round the room, choosing a place behind the largest piece of the broken fermentation drum. There he quickly focused on a patch of dry ground, forming the Zsadhi sword in his mind before mentally transferring the image into the ground. The tar of the floor heated up, the surface briefly glowing slickly before it began to flow into the familiar sword shape, leaving a recessed outline around it.

The smell of hot tar assailed his nostrils until he tipped beer puddled in the curve of a section of wall over it.

"Cheelar!" he called out. "Round here, please. There's a sword etched into the floor here. I need a photo of it."

"There is? My men must have missed it," said Rezac coming round beside him. "Amazing how they do that. Must be a handheld weapon of some kind, like the ones used to cut the tunnels in the rock in the Palace way back when."

"It was under a piece of wreckage," said Kusac.

"Yes, Lord Nayash." Cheelar came round to join them, opening out the camera again and crouching down to take a couple of photos.

"Now we're done," said Kusac, getting up.

"So what's your report going to say?" asked Rezac later that night after dinner.

"First, I'll detail the damage, then that they used

specially prepared low level charges of a putty-like explosive set with a detonator to destroy the vats used for brewing. They did this to cause maximum damage but to avoid putting lives at risk. They wanted to damage property not people. They chose the site and used leaflets intending to push a wedge once again between the worker and soldier castes, and the officer caste. Finally, that it bears all the trademarks of a Zsadhi raid in that it has the painted sword and the melted pavement, also drawn into a sword shape. I'll put the remains of the detonator into an envelope and attach it and the sample leaflet to the report. I'll offer an opinion that the raiders are made up of a mix of all three castes—workers, soldiers, and at least one officer."

"Nothing in there an intelligent male couldn't work out for himself," said Rezac.

"Exactly."

Prime world, library, same day

It was the rest time after lunch and Shaidan was in the library looking for a book when Unity contacted him.

Wait, sent the cub, *Let me find a place that's out of sight in here before we start talking. I don't want to get involved and then have someone walk in and wonder what I'm doing.*

I will wait, came the reply.

The library was lined with bookshelves, but other bookcases were placed at right angles to the walls to maximize the number of books the room could hold. It was behind one of these, by the window farthest from the door, that Shaidan hunkered down with a selection of books around him on the floor.

I'm ready now, said Shaidan. *What's so important? Is it Kuvaa again?*

No, not Kuvaa, but you are being watched by someone else, a TeLaxaudin in the Palace. Giyarishis is his name. He was asked to watch you and has noticed that every now and then you become invisible.

Invisible? How can I be invisible?

You seem to just disappear from the time line.

The what? You said the time line?

The Camarilla watches time lines for potentialities of what may happen and they try to choose the line that has the least conflict and danger in it.

They manipulate time? But why watch me?

I explained to you before. You are a nexus, things happen around you, events are attracted to you. By watching you, they can see what is happening in the bigger picture of space and time around you.

I'm only a cub. I don't rule a planet or anything important. Important things don't happen around me.

As I said, a nexus also attracts happenings—things happen to them, Shaidan. The main thing right now is that you vanish, and that is drawing attention to yourself. Try not to vanish.

But I don't know how I do that! I am always here! How can I vanish?

I think it's when you try not to be seen that you vanish, sent Unity. *Like now you are talking to me, but you have vanished for other people looking at your time line.*

Do I vanish for you?

No, I see you.

I don't know what I'm doing, or how, sent Shaidan, getting upset.

Just forget about being noticed, and you should be all right. You're very like your father. He used to vanish as well, but he didn't know about me or the Camarilla.

I know, sent Shaidan. *I'll try, Unity, I'll try. I have to go now for my lesson.* He cut the connection and, gathering the books around him, was standing waiting when moments later Kitra came for him.

"Hey. They're just about to leave for the Sholan gym. Better hurry and go get your gear, Shaidan."

"Yes, Aunt Kitra," he said, scampering back to the dorm. The others chattered their way down the corridor with

Jerenn and M'Nar while Shaidan tailed along at the back until Gaylla dropped back to take him by the hand.

"You look like you'se thinking hard," she said, squeezing his hand. "What makes you do that? What you worried about?"

"Nothing, Gaylla," he said, mouth dropping open in a smile. "I was just running through yesterday's lesson, and wondering if there would be any new moves today. Do you enjoy our lessons?"

"Oh, yes," she said, grinning hugely. "When Shishu chases me for bed and makes a grab at me, I can now get away from her."

Shaidan chuckled. "That's not really fair as she can't counter your moves."

"Oh, I don't do it for real and hurt her. It's only for play."

"So long as you remember to be fair to Shishu, too."

Their sessions always began with a warm-up run and then some stretching exercises. Today they had some of the Brothers and Sisters with them, one for each of them. Spying one of the sisters, Gaylla went marching up to face her, hands on her hips.

"You shouldn't pick up people like that, you knows," she said. "It can be very dangerous for you. I knows how to make you let me go now."

"You do?" smiled N'Akoe. "Well that's why we're here, so you can practice your escapes on us."

"Oh. Well, I will do it for real, you know," she said seriously. "Just not with claws out cos that would hurt a lot, and I don't like to hurt people much unless I have to."

"Do you want to practice with me?" N'Akoe asked, glancing over at where Jerenn was eyeing them cautiously.

"Sure, but I won't go easy with you cos you're a girl, you know," Gaylla said, a serious look on her small face. "Us girls have to be tough, too."

"We do, indeed," she grinned back.

"I see you two have met again." said M'Nar. "She wasn't trying to take you away in the courtyard, Gaylla."

"I know now, but we'd had those bad people who took

Shaidan's mama captive not long ago, and he was a Sholan. I thought that she'd come for me."

"Well, now you know she didn't," said M'Nar, stroking her hair. "But it's always good to be cautious like that. Don't trust everyone, Gaylla. Only trust those you know well."

"Time to team up with a Brother or Sister, younglings," said Jerenn. "Not M'Nar or me, we're instructing, so choose one of the others. You're going to practice your escapes today."

After their long soak in the Sholan baths, the cubs were escorted up to the nursery where M'Nar and Jerenn got permission to take Shaidan back downstairs to the Palace courtyard and the town outside the Palace walls.

"So where are we going?" asked Shaidan for about the tenth time.

"If you can lead us to where this ruined underground warehouse is, maybe we can teach you some knife throwing," said Jerenn as they threaded their way through the bazaar.

"Really?" said Shaidan, bouncing along between them in delight. "I know the way. It's not far from one of the farms we visited when we first came here."

"Lead on, then," M'Nar gestured.

It was a brisk fifteen-minute walk north across the plain outside the Palace. Aboveground, there was the ruin of a farm outbuilding, but below it was what Shaidan thought was a warehouse.

"Do you have a rope?" he asked. "It's easier with a rope, especially to get out, but you don't need one."

"Too late now, youngling," said M'Nar. "Next time warn us if we need things like ropes."

"I will. Oh, it looks like it's been boarded up," he said, running over to the doorway. Planks of wood were nailed firmly across the door, and it was obvious that it was off limits.

"Let's walk round the whole of the building first," said Jerenn, "It may be there is an easier way to get in than pulling those planks off."

"There isn't."

"Let's just look first," said Jerenn. "How often have you been here?"

"Only once," Shaidan admitted as they began to walk round the outside of the building. "But I remember it well!"

"Someone has been here since then, Shaidan, and they at least nailed the door shut. We don't know what else they did. Perhaps there are windows, and the planks are not so firmly nailed on. We need to see before we decide what to do."

There was a small window, with no glass left in the frame, on the far side of the barn, the one away from the Palace. Across it, the planks were thinner and there were only two of them.

"Window," said M'Nar.

"Yep, definitely the easier one and, being on the far side, less likely to be noticed," said Jerenn.

It took both of them to loosen one end of the planks, and pull out the other end just enough that though they were still attached to the wall, they swung loose.

"This way we can put them back over the window when we leave, and no one will be the wiser," said Jerenn as he climbed through. "Better hand Shaidan to me. No need for him to try and scramble through on his own."

Shaidan was lifted up and swung through to Jerenn, who caught him. Backing away from the window, he placed him on the ground beside him as M'Nar clambered through.

The brick walls were all too high to easily climb over, which was probably just as well because in the center of the floor was a gaping hole. Looking upward, virtually the whole of the roof was also missing.

"If I didn't know better, I'd say that something came up from below, something like a craft." said Jerenn, walking carefully over to the edge of the hole in the floor and looking down.

"This isn't a warehouse; this is the hangar where King Zsurtul was shot," said M'Nar, joining his sword-brother. "A secret hangar accessed from the Palace by a hidden tunnel. I heard about this the first day we were all here! Never thought I'd see it, though."

"Queen Zhalmo was kidnapped from here, too," said Shaidan, walking round the edge till he was above a large vehicle. Before either of them could stop him, a dull thud alerted them to the fact the cub had jumped down onto the roof of the vehicle. "So this is a hangar, then?"

"Shaidan! You should have waited for us to check it out first," scolded Jerenn.

"This hasn't changed," Shaidan shouted back up at them as he scrambled off the roof to the cab of the vehicle, then down onto the hood. "Come on down, it's huge down here!"

When M'Nar jumped down, he could see right away that the roof of the hangar was only some twelve feet tall—just as tall as it needed to be to house a shuttle or a small scout ship. As they all stood together in the circle of sunlight from the hole in the roof above them, they could see the various vehicles that ringed them. There was the one they had used to jump down on that smelled faintly of fuel, then another that was lower and wider, and had towing hooks and cables on the back of it.

"Hangar, definitely," said Jerenn. "That's a mobile tanker, but it could hardly hold enough fuel for a scout ship or even a shuttle."

M'Nar bent down. "It's connected by a pipe to something in the ground. I expect the fuel is there and the tanker is only here to act as a pump." He got up and dusted off his hands. "We'll stay away from that in future. The other—what do you think it is, Jerenn?"

"Towing vehicle, to get the ship into the correct position for takeoff. Look, there's markings on the floor," he said, pointing to where the bright sunlight almost obscured the yellow-and-black diagonal-striped lines painted on the concrete.

"Well, now we're here, let's see what we can set up as a practice area for the knives." M'Nar walked over to the debris strewn to the sides of the hole in the floor above. "It's wood," he said. "Very rough and ready, but we can prop it up against one of the pillars to make a target area. It'll certainly do for now."

Jerenn and Shaidan came over to look, and between them they found a rough piece about six feet by three that they could use.

"We pace off five steps from our target and turn to face it," said Jerenn. "We'll draw a line there for me. That's where I'll throw from." Reaching into his pocket, he took out a piece of chalk and marked the concrete. "Now I take one more step back, and one slightly to the left side since we're all right-handed. This is where we start the throw from. These are practice blades, slightly blade heavy, so you will hold them by the grip, or handle so that the heavier blade goes first."

"But how do I hold the blade?" asked Shaidan.

"I was just getting to that part," said Jerenn. "Hold your thumb in the center of the handle on one side, and on the opposite side have your index, middle finger, and next finger. Hold it so the blade points forward like so." He demonstrated. "Crank your arm back, keeping the blade horizontally flat and step up to your line. Then just let go." He threw the blade which landed in the wood with a satisfying *thunk*.

"The blade should make one revolution then stick into the target. Now you try." He handed the next knife to Shaidan. "Don't forget to pace out your distance."

At first, the knives bounced off the wood, but gradually, every other one would hit, Some hit but then fell out, and others really hit home and stayed in the wood. By the time they'd been at it an hour, Shaidan seemed to have gotten the knack of throwing.

"Now it's just practice," said Jerenn.

"We should see if we can backtrack that secret passage," said M'Nar. "It would make getting here a whole lot easier.

I don't like to think of Shaidan climbing in and out of here alone, and especially not on a fuel vehicle."

"You are definitely not to come here alone," said Jerenn sternly. "Anyone could snatch you, and we'd never know till it was maybe too late. Promise you won't come here alone?"

"I promise, but how can I practice if I don't come here?"

"One of us will take you," said M'Nar. "You do not want to go looking for danger by going off miles from the Palace on your own."

"We'll try and find the secret passage another day," said Jerenn. "We've already been gone almost as long as your time allows. We have to get back pretty quickly today. Leave it with us, and we'll see what we can do."

Shaidan used the wheel to boost himself up onto the hood of the vehicle and then clambered up the cab window to the roof, Jerenn and M'Nar right behind him. M'Nar boosted him up onto the roof proper and then followed.

"You know, Jer, this sounds hollow. I don't think there is any fuel in it."

Jerenn knelt down and began rapping on the roof of the cab, then the roof of the tanker part, comparing the sounds. "I think you're right. That makes me a lot happier. That fuel is very volatile, and we really shouldn't be down near it if we can avoid it. Here will do for now, but we have to find a better place to practice."

"Agreed," said M'Nar, grasping Shaidan round the waist and lifting him up until he got a firm grip on the edge of the floor above them.

"Time to head back at a run, I think," said M'Nar. "Who's up for a race?"

M'zull, Lorishuk's estate, evening, same day

I bring gifts, came the mental voice of Annuur. *Is it safe to join you?*

Yes, but not for long, Kusac replied.

Moments later, Annuur materialized in the office. "Nanites I have for you both, important ones. Have you released yours for your people and the mountain tribe yet?"

"Not yet. I haven't been back to the village . . ."

"No more excuses! Must do or too late. Have you at least done self and Primes?"

"I've done us, of course. I'll go to the village later this week and do it then."

"Good. Rezac, you done your people?"

"Done, Annuur," said the other.

"Excellent. These ones special. This one changes scents of all officer caste so that they lose scent which prevents soldier caste from attacking and challenging them." He handed first Kusac, then Rezac, a small black vial. "This blue one prevents you and your staff from being affected by it. You get each person to touch open tube to transmit to them." He handed them each a blue tube. "And last one I drop now anywhere as it spreads the memories we want these sand-dwellers to wake up with when all is done."

This larger tube Annuur dropped on the floor where it shattered. Kusac watched, as fascinated and repulsed as when he'd released them before, as a tide of metallic liquid appeared to flow out of the broken tube. Within a heartbeat or two, it had vanished, its color changed to match the surface it was traveling over.

"Does that make you feel nauseous, too?" Rezac asked him.

"Yeah, very."

"Memories won't attach to you," said Annuur. "We set it so that repulsor works for this as well. Now use the officer one on self, then release them in a crowded place. Should only take a few days to cover officers. Memories will keep duplicating to population even after their minds are wiped. It will take the Touibans' signal to activate them. Those not reached by memories on that day will get the nanites at a slightly later date. Touibans and Ch'almuthians will have more memory nanites to release when they come."

Kusac pocketed the black vial and opened the blue one,

putting his thumb over the opening and briefly tipping the contents against his skin. With a queasy feeling he watched a tiny drop of the metallic liquid seep into his thumb and disappear as he screwed the lid back on.

"Good, now you remain unchallengeable while around you anyone else can be challenged. It will be your protection in the last few days. This will activate now, so treat all your people with it as soon as possible. Does not mean other officers won't try to attack you because these nanites have less time to spread. Those not affected can attack you, and once you attack those affected, they can fight back, so be on guard."

"I will. Thank you, Annuur."

"Yes, thanks, Annuur," added Rezac.

"What about Kaid and the others back at the den? Have they got it yet?"

"They got it first, now you two."

"What about the mountain folk, the hybrids of all castes, and Ch'almuthians already here. How will they be affected by all this?"

"All affected except those you choose to protect. Oh, almost I forget, translocators I have for you." He pulled a small bag off his belt and handed it to Kusac. "Only go to den and back to place you set as home. You use in your office, you return to office. You arrive in outer cave in place they keep clear now for arriving people. You test, get used to using. I go now. Much to do." With that, Annuur vanished.

Kusac opened the bag and looked inside. It held half a dozen slim devices. Kusac pulled out three for Rezac and his two commandos and handed them over to him. "I do suggest practicing with them; it's a very disorienting experience. These ones are way smaller than the one I originally got from Annuur."

"Probably because they only go to two places," said Rezac.

"I suggest we make the estates our home. We're likely to be safer there than anywhere else, except the mountain den."

"Good point. When do you have to go back to the base to be yourself again?"

"In three days. You?" asked Kusac.

"Tomorrow. I suggest we practice tonight since you're

staying the night here anyway. We can take it in turn to accompany our people there and back. You can set this room to home for now."

Kusac nodded. "We'll do it after your staff are all asleep."

Prime world, Zhal-Oeshi 8th (August)

Shaidan was relaxing after dinner on his bed. He'd drawn the curtains round it, the only privacy the cubs had in their communal dorm, but they were still so closely attuned to each other that they wanted that closeness most of the time.

First he felt the weight on his bed, then he saw a Cabbaran suddenly appear on the foot of it.

"Shhh! I Kuvaa. Hello, Shaidan," she whispered.

Eyes like saucers and ready to shout out in fright, Shaidan scooted up the bed as far as he could go.

"What do you want?" he hissed. "How do I know you are Kuvaa? You could be anyone!"

I am Kuvaa. Unity, please confirm this.

She is Kuvaa, Shaidan. She will not harm you today.

What do you want with me?

I bring you to meet Unity. It has physical presence that few get to see, but I thought you might like to meet it.

Him, he's a him, Shaidan corrected absently as he thought about going to visit this amazing AI that was so much more than the Palace ZSADHI.

How long would I be gone? he asked.

Can bring you back moments after you leave. No one will know you've been away.

Of course. You manipulate time and space, don't you? Where are you and Unity?

Not that far from where you are on world called Ghioass. You want to come?

Why? Why do you want me to visit?

So Unity and I can find out more about you,

You want to study me. Suddenly he was suspicious.

Know all about your origins. Is not that I am curious about . . .

You want to know why I vanish, he sent, frowning at her. *Giyarishis here in the Palace is already watching me for that.*

Giyarishis watching you? No orders has he to do that! Must talk to him about this. Unity, privacy always when I talk with Shaidan or am with him. See to it.

Yes, Councillor Kuvaa, said Unity.

So are you coming?

Yes. I'll come, he sent, moving cautiously back down the bed until he was squatting beside her.

Kuvaa reached out a forelimb tipped with a tripartite hoof. *Then take hold of me and we'll go!*

Shaidan reached out a tentative hand and grasped hold of Kuvaa's forelimb. Instantly, he was engulfed in cold and darkness. Then, as he was about to panic, suddenly it was over and he hit the ground with a slight bump. Around him, the air glowed with a faint blue light, and as his eyes became accustomed to it, he was able to make out his surroundings. Seating was a pile of cushions, or a slanted chair-like thing he quickly realized was built for a Cabbaran. In front of both was a table at a comfortable working height. There the familiar ended. A large monitor of some kind, with outlines of light, glowed against a wall. On it, multicolored lights swirled like a tide around a small bluish glow, ebbing and flowing before they merged into each other in the constant stream of light.

On the tables, holographic input devices, also made of light, waited for their beams to be broken by fingers or hooves.

Kuvaa settled herself on her chair, gesturing Shaidan toward the cushions. "Sit, sit, just touch nothing for now. What you see on wall is what is happening around us right now. Only one major nexus at the moment and that is your father. His actions we read in how the colors flow around him."

"So you're watching now?" asked Shaidan.

"Yes, this is happening right now, from minute to minute. But this screen shows many other things. Unity, show the mountains outside this town on Ghioass," said Kuvaa.

The images changed to show a landscape of blue skies and green-clad hills and mountains.

"So beautiful," murmured Kuvaa. "We can look at anything we wish from here. Unity can be used as you would use a computer, but with your voice or by typing in commands, or by touching the screen." She leaned forward, hitting a few keys until the keyboard was replaced by a smaller holographic monitor in front of her. She swiped her hoof across the virtual surface bringing up a series of icons. With a few more strokes she had called up a view of the Prime Palace.

Shaidan let out an exclamation of surprise as Kuvaa, using her hooves, zoomed in closer till he could see the people walking across the grand courtyard, looking at the shops there or going into one of the restaurants.

"That's now?" he asked.

"Right now," she agreed. "We see only a general view, and only from this angle. Can't look for specific people . . ."

"You can't see anywhere you don't have a nexus," he said, looking over at her. "Even so, you can spy very effectively on us there."

"That's not the purpose of the nodes," she said. "In the past yes, but have been dismantling them."

"So what is the point of them now?"

"Just to check what is really happening if we get a warning from the potentialities you saw first. If we see a conflagration—an important large event about to happen—we can look to see what it is. We can only see places we have been to, places we've been able to physically place the nodes first."

"What about my home world, Shola. Have you got nodes there?"

"Unable to put any there as your telepaths would notice them." A few taps on her screen and the keyboard in front of Shaidan changed to a small screen like Kuvaa's. "Place your hand against the screen so Unity can read you," she said. "You'll feel a faint buzzing against your palm when in right place."

Shaidan slowly stretched out his hand, feeling with all his senses for that faint buzz against his palm. "Oh! I feel it," he said, turning to let his mouth drop open in a grin. "It feels really strange, sort of all tingly. What will Unity do?"

"Unity just scanning your hand for basic information—things like your temperature, your pulse and so on. With that information, it will be able to identify you from any other Sholan. I can also give you limited access to Unity when you are here, like now."

"What will you let me do? Ouch!" Shaidan snatched his hand back, sticking one of his fingers into his mouth. "That hurt! What was that for?"

"Just a blood and DNA test," she said soothingly. "Plenty of them you must have had. Unity is done now."

"Too many," Shaidan agreed ruefully, examining his fingertip. "So what will Unity allow me to do now?"

"Unity teaches our young. I allow you to access its teaching programs. You have met U'Churians, yes?"

Shaidan nodded.

"Then you can access some programs about them, their world and their culture that will teach you more than you could learn elsewhere."

"I'd like that."

Kuvaa pulled up a program for him. "This is a general knowledge one about them to begin with," she said.

"Kuvaa, how come I can understand you and Unity? How will I understand a program for your children?"

"Universal translators I wear, that Unity controls. It changes the language to one you can understand."

"He," said Shaidan absently, already drawn into the program about the U'Churians. "Unity is a he."

Prime world, Palace of Light, same evening

"General," said Zsurtul, entering Kezule's office where he was just winding down his work for the day. "I would like to talk to you about a personal matter."

Kezule got to his feet, gesturing to the easy chairs set around a low table. "Certainly, Majesty. Please, take a seat."

"Not Majesty, please, just Zsurtul when we are alone," said the young King, taking a seat. "It's Zhalmo. She's started going out to train with her brothers and sisters again. I'm worried about her."

Kezule joined him. "You knew she was a warrior when you married her, Zsurtul. You can't change what she is and still have the female you love."

"You have me wrong, Kezule. I don't want to change her, I want to find a way to let her be what she is, to have a purpose in her life that's hers, without putting her in danger. She can't go on missions any longer, but there must be something she can do."

"I take it that running the Palace artisan guilds doesn't hold too much fascination for her."

"About as much as it does for Doctor Zayshul," the young male smiled. "At least she has her profession as a Doctor to continue, but Zhalmo just can't be a commando any longer."

"Since she wants to train with her Brothers and Sisters, why not put her in charge of your bodyguard? As their head, she would be intimately involved with all the security details like training and rotation of personnel. It would give her a purpose again, one she had before, yet shared with the rest of your bodyguards."

Zsurtul smiled, his face losing the worried look it had had since he'd walked into Kezule's office. "That would work, I'm sure," he said. "She'd not be able to turn down such a job. But what about her? I need to know she's being guarded securely, too, not just me."

"We need to give her a title, a rank within the guard, but insist that she has someone who is an equal to her in rank. That person will only overrule her if it is thought she is jeopardizing her security for the sake of yours."

"All we'll have to do is be sure she doesn't choose someone she thinks she can push around."

"If she does that, you appoint someone else. M'kou can

tell you who would fit into that category, so have him there with you when she chooses her staff."

"Thank you, General. You've given me a solution I am sure Zhalmo will approve as much as I do," he said, getting to his feet. "I won't hold you up any longer as I am sure you want to be with your wife and daughter."

"Good night, King Zsurtul, I'm glad I was able to help."

M'zull, Palace, same day

"I have new orders for you, Nayash," said K'hedduk as Kusac was admitted to his office. "Your reports on the raids by the insurgents were excellent, and I found them accurate and detailed. They haven't helped us to capture this Zsadhi group yet, but they have given us vital information about them. I now need you to visit all three fleets and put together a dossier on how loyal the troops and commanders out there are to me. You have three days to do this."

"Three days isn't long enough for a full report, Majesty," he began, but K'hedduk cut him short.

"It's all I can allow at this time. I need a first impression of how loyal they seem, and that's all for now. I concur with your feeling that the Generals here are plotting something, and I need to know who I can depend on in the fleets. Report back to me on the eleventh. You can get your orders from my secretary on your way out. Dismissed."

"Yes, Majesty," said Kusac, bowing his way back out of the door. He stopped by the secretary's desk to get his orders and headed back to his apartment to pack a bag, get his staff, and make an urgent call to Azwokkus.

"I need undetectable explosives," he said. "I need to set up some major charges that I can detonate remotely at a later date. I want those fleets utterly destroyed before the M'zullians are wakened up, if your nanites sleep plan works."

"Be not so disparaging of our plan, Hunter. It is our same expertise you are calling on now to help you. Better it will be if the explosives are brought to you on the station rather than before. No need to smuggle it in then. Also gives us a few hours to assemble what you need."

"How can it be detonated?" demanded Kusac. "From the planet's surface, or do we need a ship closer to the stations?"

"Timers would be acceptablc."

"Except I won't know when I want to set them off until a lot nearer the time. It may be I need to use them as a diversion, or it may be that I just need to blow the stations and the fleets to hell."

"We can arrange. May need someone to visit each station to set off trigger device, though."

"I'll contact you from each station when I find a secure location to do it from." With that, he closed his connection to the TeLaxaudin.

"We're going to each of the orbitals. K'hedduk wants me to talk to the Generals and Lords on each, find out who is loyal. Cheelar, get me plans printed off for each of the three military orbitals—don't bother with the domestic one. M'yikku, get a bag for yourself and Cheelar for two nights away from home, then tell Laazif we'll be away till the eleventh. On the way, get Maalash and tell him to grab a bag, too. I'm going to pack mine now."

Kusac was able to commandeer a shuttle in the underground parking lot where not so many weeks before, they'd unloaded the MUTAC.

As he made his way across the rock floor with M'yikku and Cheelar, he heard the sound of running footsteps.

"It's Telmaar," said Cheelar.

"Dammit! Last thing I need is him asking to come with me," muttered Kusac. Turning round, he waited for the other to catch up.

Telmaar skidded to a stop beside him. "I hear you're headed up to the orbitals to inspect the Fleet. Mind if I come along? I left some belongings on my ship which I find I need now."

Kusac hesitated. Once again, he had no good reason to refuse to let him accompany them.

"Don't worry," Telmaar reassured him as his own aide panted his way up to him carrying a large holdall. "I hate inspections. I'll make myself scarce while you do your thing."

"You're with the Second Fleet, aren't you?" Kusac asked. Getting a nod in reply, he said, "I'll take you up, but you'll have to get a shuttle there to your ship. I really won't have time for any relaxation. I've only three days to inspect all three fleets, so I'll have to be focused on that."

"Fair enough," said Telmaar. "Shuttle it is. Just glad to get the chance to grab my gear!"

There were four distinct orbitals around M'zull and three had a fleet berthed at them. The fourth was for incoming cargo. Kusac had chosen to go to the military orbitals in order, starting with the First Fleet.

It was the largest as it was the Royal Fleet belonging to the Emperor. General Geddash was in charge of it as the most loyal of the Generals, one who had supported K'hedduk while he was in exile as well as now he was back and in power.

With M'yikku and Maalash handling the luggage, they boarded the utilitarian shuttle and took off for the main orbital.

"Cheelar, go up front and call ahead. Tell them why I am coming and that I expect suitable quarters to be assigned to us for tonight as well as a guide to show us round the orbital. They should also contact each of the ship's Captains and tell them to hold themselves and their ships ready for possible inspection by me. I'll also need a briefing room where I will meet with all Generals stationed on the orbital at eighteen hundred hours."

Cheelar saluted smartly. "Aye, sir," he said, then headed up to the bridge.

"You seem to have it all well organized," said Telmaar, leaning back in his seat. "Gossip is you've taken to your promotion as one born to it—which, of course, you were."

"Logistics," said Kusac, opening his briefcase and pulling out a folder. "It's all down to logistics, and my aide Cheelar is particularly gifted when it comes to that. Now if you'll excuse me, I have to read up on this station and the fleet. I didn't exactly get much warning of this inspections as I told you."

"Certainly," said Telmaar, crossing his legs and fishing in his pocket for a pack of smokes. They were similar to the cheroots that Kezule occasionally smoked.

You do realize he could be a spy, sent Kaid. *It's very convenient that he's always hearing what you are doing and wants to be involved.*

That had occurred to me, too, replied Kusac. *I'll be especially on my guard.*

The flight was short and when they docked, they were met with full military honors, honors that he quickly dispensed with. "I'm here to work, gentlemen. Show my aide to my quarters and provide me with my guide. I'll tour the facility now," he said, walking smartly past the welcoming committee and into the main corridor.

The station was purely utilitarian and based on a cuboid design. Each side was divided up into sections of four berths, accessible by staff through a communal docking air lock. A problem at one berth meant all four were locked down. There were five of these sections and three levels per side, giving a total of berths for one hundred and twenty ships—more than enough for the fleet. The lower level berths were for repairs, and the smaller craft. Fuel storage, munitions, and other essential stores were also kept here. Recreation facilities were segregated with Officer country and Admin on the third level, and the non-officers restricted to their own bar and eateries on the second level. Bars on both levels came complete with the companion drones, though access to them was still highly controlled.

The areas Kusac wanted to visit were the Admin level, each of the twenty battleships, and the lower level where the volatile stores were kept. Charges set in the heart of the station where munitions and fuel were stored, would rip through it. From his study of the plans on the flight up, Kusac knew there were elevators at each corner of the station, and four in the central area. There'd be no need to target the individual ships, locked in their docking bays. As the station exploded and crumpled around them, they'd go down, too.

"General Nayash, I'm Lieutenant Niddoe. I'll be your aide for the duration of your visit to the First Fleet," said a voice from his elbow. "Where would you like to go first?"

"Third level. While you contact the Generals and get them to meet me in the main briefing room on that level, I will inspect the Admin offices. I expect to meet with them within the hour as my time here is limited. Make sure that food and drinks are served in the room." He stopped abruptly and pulled his orders from his pocket. "My orders, direct from the Emperor himself, Long Life and Health to Him."

"Long Life and Health," echoed the Lieutenant, accepting the papers and quickly casting his eyes over them. "Thank you, General," he said, handing them back. "I'll see to contacting the other Generals as soon as we reach the third floor."

"Maalash, join me when you've stowed our luggage," he ordered. "Cheelar and M'yikku, you're with me. Well, Niddoe, lead on."

Twenty battleships, and twenty Generals. He'd met with them all in as informal a setting as he could have devised, given the time constraints, to get the mood of them collectively, then after about an hour, had met with each one on his own in an interview room. The general mood didn't bode well for K'hedduk as a full two thirds of them felt he'd acted rashly in sending the Third Fleet out to K'oish'ik and were not impressed by the losses they'd taken. The remaining third would be loyal to the end, royalists each of them. Interestingly, age wasn't a factor of loyalty.

Interviews over, Kusac headed to the docking bays for the Carriers. With Lieutenant Niddoe to guide them, he made his way leisurely through the bays on one side, just listening to the chatter as the ships were refueled and reprovisioned. One could learn a lot about the state of a fleet by just listening.

His next stop was to his rooms for a short break before dinner, long enough to find an errand for M'yikku and Maalash to keep the latter out of the way, so he could contact Azwokkus and get the explosive devices from him.

"You only need to plant three of these, four at most, to have a satisfying large explosion that will take out the station. Have at least one unit in the magazine area."

"They're very small," said Kusac, looking at a slim, dark package about one and a half inches by one inch by a quarter of an inch thick that he held in his hand.

"Bigger than usual," said the TeLaxaudin. "No time to completely microsize it. Master of nanotech weaponry we are. No need to be larger. Have way to detonate. You tell us when and we detonate for you from space. Signal travels farther as not going through atmosphere. Also you not at risk setting off charges."

"And not traceable? They can't find them?"

"Could but unlikely. You can easily place these out of sight on your inspection."

"Thank you, Azwokkus. I'll let you know how it goes."

Azwokkus vanished, leaving him alone in his room. He rejoined Cheelar, slipping him four of the explosive devices. "Keep them safe for tomorrow," he said. "I'm not leaving any in the room, but I don't want to carry them all myself."

"Aye, sir," said Cheelar. "M'yikku just called in, Niddoe has gotten us a table at the Officers' restaurant. They're waiting up there for us."

"Let's go meet them," said Kusac.

The restaurant was standard for all military stations. Just enough opulence to let the officer class relax, but not enough to make it as good as one in the private sector. They'd no sooner begun to eat than the station captain came to meet them.

"General Nayash, Captain Myazou at your service. I was waiting to hear from Lieutenant Niddoe that you were ready to eat, then I planned to invite you to dinner in my quarters."

"This is fine, Captain. Sit down, Niddoe. I'm sure the Captain doesn't expect you to jump to your feet! I like to get a feel for the people at each station, Captain Myazou. I'm not one for standing on formality. You're welcome to join us if you wish." Kusac waved the middle-aged M'zullian toward an empty seat.

"Thank you, General," he said, sitting down. "I'll join you but not to eat. I hear you're conducting a survey of security measures on each station. I've heard of all the raids back on M'zull, the Zsadhi ones. I hope we're not at risk out here."

"That's what this survey is about, Captain. To assess the risks at each of the three stations."

"I run a secure station here," he said, his voice tight with suppressed self-justification. "Any insurgents will find it next to impossible to get past my people and the security measures I've set up."

"I'm sure you're right, Captain Myazou, and this is just a formality. I'll be checking out the storage level after dinner as my time here is limited. By tomorrow morning, I'll be gone, but if I have any security recommendations, they'll be with you within the week."

"Can I escort you down to Level One after your meal?"

"Thank you, but no. We have Lieutenant Niddoe to act as our guide, I'm sure we'll be fine. Please, don't let us delay you from your own dinner any longer."

Obviously reluctant, Myazou got to his feet and, saluting, left them to finish their meal in peace.

"I do so hate interruptions when I am eating," said Kusac. "Even adequate food tastes better when eaten leisurely."

"Meals at your apartment in the Palace are certainly of a better quality, General Nayash," agreed Cheelar.

"Remind me to send ahead to Station Two tonight and tell them that I'll be berthed on my battleship for the duration of my visit and will expect to take my meals there. I hope my father had an adequate chef on the *Aggressor*."

The meal over, they made their way down to the first level in one of the central elevators. Security was tight—as the doors slid open, an armed detail demanded their IDs and clearance documents to access the area. Kusac handed the imperial order to Niddoe to show them, and they were passed immediately.

Niddoe led them to one of the service entrances to the fuel storage area where another set of guards again demanded IDs and authorizations from them.

"I haven't been down here myself," confessed Niddoe. "What is it you want to see? We may be better getting one of the workers to show us round."

"Do that, please," said Kusac. "I mainly want to check out the entrances and exits."

They waited while one of the guards called for a foreman on his radio. When he arrived, they stepped through into the bowels of the station where the giant fuel storage tanks held the fuel that was pumped all over the station to the various docking bays. To accommodate the tanks, this level was taller than two of the other levels combined, and though relatively clean, the smell of warm oil undercut with a harsh smell he didn't recognize filled the air.

"Each tank feeds a specific series of docking bays on a set level, though if a tank is empty and we need fuel to say a level three docking bay, we can divert it from one of the other ones. They do that at the pumping office up there." The foreman pointed upward and off to his left to a floor poised at mid-level among the giant containers. "Only way up there is a service elevator just below it. They have guards on it with stunners since they can't use energy weapons in here with all the fuel around. You might want to go see the office as it's the best view you'll get of the whole fuel depot."

"Sounds like a good idea," said Kusac, looking at the

rats' nest of pipes snaking vertically and horizontally all over not only the floor but the walls.

"Those pipes take the fuel between the tanks and correct the mix for each type of ship. We use a different fuel for the fighters than what the battleships use."

Kusac walked over to the pipes and put his hand against one, feeling it to see if it vibrated.

"Don't want to do that, General. We keep it pretty clean down here, but some fuel does get onto the pipes. It's pretty toxic if you get it on your skin,. Might want to ask to wash your hands up in the pump room," said the foreman.

"I'll do that, thank you," said Kusac following Niddoe and the foreman over to the pump room elevator.

CHAPTER 7

K'oish'ik, Zhal-Oeshi 9th (August)

THE visit to the Second Fleet, where his own people and ships were, and Telmaar's, began smoothly enough. He arrived punctually at their ninth hour of the morning. He'd spent the morning inspecting the ships, then retired to the *Aggressor*, his own command, for a late lunch, which proved to be as good as any served to him by Laazif.

After lunch, he headed down to inspect the lower levels and the fuel bays, as he had with the First Fleet. Again, the pumping station was mainly controlled from a raised platform with only a few maintenance folk carrying out essential checks on the ground level.

Wandering around on his own, looking for a likely spot to place the explosives, he was shocked to walk round to the back of a huge tank into Telmaar.

"What are you doing down here?" he demanded.

"I was about to ask you the same question," said Telmaar. "What's there to inspect down here, if you are doing an inspection for the Emperor, Long Life be His."

"Long Life," echoed Kusac—it had become second nature to utter the phrase every time he spoke about K'hedduk. "I think you are overstepping your position," he said frostily to the older male. "I am on official business and don't need to prove it to you, a junior officer! It's time you reported back to your ship!"

"I think you are up to something and am prepared to prove it," Telmaar said. "I followed you on the last station, as you wandered about the fuel depot, the same as you're doing here. It was as if you were looking for something, something a fellow conspirator might leave hidden down here!"

"Your imagination has gotten away with you," hissed Kusac, turning away from him. "I'll overlook your insubordination this time because of the friendship we've shared, but I won't give you a second chance."

"Friendship," sneered Telmaar, grasping him by the arm again. "I was never your friend. Inquisitor Ziosh ordered me to get close to you from the start, and that's what I did! I know you're involved in this Zsadhi movement, and I'll prove it!"

"You're going to do what?" laughed Kusac, grasping the other's wrist in a lock that painfully disengaged it and left him imprisoned. "I don't think so."

"Perhaps he won't, but we will," said another voice as two more M'zullians stepped out of the shadows to confront him. "Now let him go. The Inquisitor doesn't like his people being roughed up."

Still keeping his grip on Telmaar, Kusac sent a mental command to Cheelar, alerting him to the situation. Though Cheelar wasn't a telepath, it was possible for Kusac to at least send strong emotions to him and the other commandos.

At the same time, he twisted Telmaar's arm until the other was facing him and punched him square on the jaw, rendering him unconscious. He dropped Telmaar and turned his attention to the other two. They were junior officers that he'd seen acting as aides, the same way Cheelar and M'yikku did for him.

"Do you really want to mess with me?" he demanded. "Appointed by the Emperor to inspect these facilities?"

"He's not the real power on M'zull. Everyone knows it's Inquisitor Ziosh," sneered one of them, pulling out a firearm and aiming at him.

"Are you going to shoot me down here among tanks of volatile fuel that could blow us all up?" asked Kusac, moving fractionally nearer to his two assailants.

They glanced briefly at each other, allowing Kusac the opportunity to lunge forward and grab the forearm of the one with the gun. A quick tussle followed, during which the gun was dropped.

Kusac felt the pressure of a gun muzzle against the side of his head and froze.

"Stop right now. Let him go and stand up. We're taking you prisoner, and you can explain to the Inquisitor what you were doing here," said the second officer.

"I don't think so," said Kusac, letting him go and slowly standing up. "I have a job to finish, and I intend to do so."

He heard the pistol being cocked and the fallen gun being kicked away from him. "And we intend to stop you. You can come nice and easy, or you can come dead. We don't care much which way you choose."

Cheelar and M'yikku had been heading up to the service elevator to the pumping station when he sent his message for help. He could sense them close by now, close enough to hear them talking.

"You won't shoot me," he said. "You can smell the fumes for yourself; you know the slightest spark could blow us all up."

The gun moved from his head to his neck, pointing downward through his body. "Now it won't."

The officer he'd been tussling with regained his feet and aimed a low punch at his gut. Doubling up more than was necessary, Kusac groaned in pain. He felt the second draft of air as a knife spun past him to lodge in the throat of that officer while the one holding him suddenly released him with a brief exclamation of pain.

"You all right, General Nayash?" asked Cheelar, running forward to check on all three of the downed assailants.

Standing up wasn't as easy as he thought it would be, the blow to his stomach had hurt, but M'yikku's steadying arm was there to help him.

"We got your message, General," said M'yikku quietly. "Are you hurt?"

"Telmaar!" exclaimed Cheelar, looking up at Kusac. "Why would he attack you?"

"Seems he was an agent for Inquisitor Ziosh," said Kusac. "No, I'm not hurt. we just traded punches, but it could have gotten nasty very quickly."

"So we saw. Thanks for the heads up not to use our guns," Cheelar said wryly. "What do you plan to do with them? Telmaar's still alive, but the other two are dead."

"If he'd been alone, I had hoped to do a memory wipe on him and let him go, but he'd miss his two aides."

"You could still do that," said Cheelar thoughtfully. "All you need to do is suggest that these two have disappeared without leave, gone native or something. You can do that, can't you?"

"And Telmaar was a victim of your attackers," said M'yikku. "Perhaps you could make it that the two turned on both you and Telmaar? That would save the need to explain away the bodies."

"I think that idea's the best one," said Kusac. The pain in his gut having eased off, he walked over to where Telmaar lay on the ground and crouched down beside him, taking hold of his head with both hands.

It was more difficult when they were unconscious, and it took several tries to penetrate the other's natural mental barrier, but at last he was able to erase the real memories of their encounter and replace them with adapted ones from his own encounter with the two aides.

"Collect your knives. M'yikku, you go report the attack on me. Cheelar and I will wake Telmaar and make sure the false memories have taken."

"Aye, General," said M'yikku, heading off at a run.

"Here," said Kusac, passing Cheelar the small pack of explosives. "Find somewhere dark to plant this. I put the last one on the underside of a pipe at the back of one of the tanks."

Cheelar nodded and quickly vanished from sight. Moments later he was back. "Done. Shall we wake Telmaar now?"

"Yes, I want him awake before help arrives." He gently slapped Telmaar's cheeks and when that had no response, hit him harder across one side of his face. That got him waking up with a moan of pain.

He looked up blearily into Kusac's face. "What was that for?" he demanded, massaging his jaw. "And why am I lying down?"

"We were attacked, don't you remember? They knocked you out."

"Who?"

"I think they're your men," said Kusac. "They looked familiar. Yelled something about the Zsadhi and drew guns on us."

Telmaar sat up and peered over at the bodies. "It's my two aides," he said in a shocked voice. "Are you sure they attacked us?"

"You can see the guns on the floor, Telmaar. If they weren't attacking us, why would they have drawn them?"

He scrambled to his feet, swaying slightly. "My jaw hurts," he complained.

"It would. They punched you unconscious. Me, they were going to shoot."

"Down here, with the smell of fuel, and the fuel tanks not thirty feet away?" asked Telmaar.

"They weren't very bright, but they did yell something about the Zsadhi as I said. Guess they are starting to take out individuals now, rather than just damaging property and spreading leaflets."

"That's worrying," agreed Telmaar. "If two of my closest aides could be part of the Zsadhi movement, who is heading it up? It could be anyone."

"Well, we know it isn't the Emperor, but there's no love lost between him and the Inquisition. It could even be Inquisitor Ziosh who's behind all this."

"Impossible," snapped the other. "Inquisitor Ziosh is loyal . . ."

". . . to himself," said Kusac as a squad of soldiers bustled up, carrying stretchers and body bags. "You know there's no love lost between them."

"Agreed, but that's a far cry from what has been happening!"

"Lord General Nayash, sir. Hear that these males attacked you and Lord Lieutenant Telmaar," said the Sergeant in charge of the detail.

"That's right. I want them bagged up and sent back to M'zull with Lieutenant Telmaar as soon as possible today. He can give his Majesty, Health and Long Life be His, the report on how we were attacked down here. Personally, I think it was a suicide mission to explode the fuel tanks. I suggest you double your security from now on."

"Yessir! I'll see that the bodies are shipped out right away! Lord Lieutenant Telmaar, if you'd like to go topside to level 1, they'll order a shuttle immediately for you. We'll see to loading the bodies."

"General Nayash, you aren't going to leave it to me to tell the Emperor what happened, are you?" Telmaar asked.

"I'll send a transcript of the happenings directly to Lieutenant Zerdish. Have no worries about that," said Kusac smoothly as he began to turn away from the other and walk toward the elevator up to the pump room. "My inspection was cut short, so I need to carry on from where I was. I'm sure we'll meet again groundside, Telmaar."

Dismissed, Telmaar had no option but to accompany the Sergeant and the bodies up to the first level of the station.

"Telmaar's an agent for Ziosh," said Kusac quietly to Cheelar and M'yikku. "We'll have to find a way to distance ourselves from him, maybe even terminate him if it looks like he's becoming a liability. I did reinforce the idea that I am no threat to him or the Inquisitor, but I'm not sure how well that will hold, given all that's going on right now."

"We'll keep our eyes on him when he's around you," said Cheelar.

Kusac smiled briefly at him and M'yikku. "I have no doubt at all about that."

Zhal-Oeshi 11th (August)

The rest of Kusac's visit was uneventful, and when he'd finished inspecting the lower levels, he retired to the

Aggressor to send his report on the attack to the Emperor's office. The Generals of the Second Fleet were about the same for and against K'hedduk as those of the First Fleet.

His visit to the Third Fleet, however, had very different results. Decimated by the abortive attack on the Prime world in retaliation for Zhalmo's rescue, their morale was low as was their opinion of the Emperor. The trips had been successful in that all the explosives had been placed and he had a pretty accurate list of all the Generals for and against K'hedduk. A list he could now manipulate to suit his own ends.

Thankfully, with Telmaar back on M'zull, they were free to relax on the homeward shuttle trip. The final thing he did on his return was to get Cheelar to set explosives in the underground ship parking lot to prevent K'hedduk from leaving the planet the way he had left K'oish'ik as they retook it. Its detonation tied to those of the space stations, they would blow at the same command from the Touibans.

M'yikku had helped him compile the dossiers on each station as they traveled to the next one so that once they landed on M'zull, Kusac could submit the final report. He'd then be free to ostensibly head to his estate for a couple of days to see to business there, but, in reality, head to the mountain den and change back to his Sholan form. Already he was feeling the strain of keeping up the appearance of a Valtegan, and he knew from previous experience that if he didn't take the time out to recuperate now, he ran the risk of his body rebelling and forcing a physical change on him. Luckily, this had happened only once, at the mountain den where he was safe. Three days was the limit, then he had to change, and that time was up today.

His report handed into the Emperor's office, Kusac was headed to his apartment when a message came in on his comm unit from Laazif.

"M'Lord, it's Shazzuk. He asks that you come to the village as soon as you can."

"Tell him I'll be there later today, Laazif."

"Do you want me to join you at the villa, Lord Nayash? If there is a crisis at the village, you may be needed for longer than the one night you had planned."

"No, you remain here at the apartment. I'll be there in a few minutes to pick up your mistress. I'll keep you posted on how this affects my plans for the next day or two."

"As you wish, m'Lord."

"Dammit, I could have done without this today," muttered Kusac, cutting the connection and increasing his pace. "Let's get moving. The sooner I'm at the village, the sooner I'm done."

Nayash mountain village, same day

M'yikku got them there in record time. Parking in the main square, Kusac handed Mahzi out of the aircar first. Her family, and her new husband, were waiting anxiously for her and as they exchanged happy greetings, Kusac walked over to Shazzuk's house where the village leader was waiting for him.

"Lord Nayash," he said, ushering him into his office. "Thank you for bringing Mahzi with you. Her family have been anxious about her."

"She's only here until tomorrow, I'm afraid. What's so urgent, Shazzuk?" Kusac asked.

"There's been another change in the chapel wall painting," the village leader said, his tone reluctant. "Another part of the mural has disappeared."

"Excuse me?"

"The carving of Tashraka, the evil sister of the Zsadhi's wife, has vanished," said Shazzuk, face creased in a frown, part embarrassed and part worried.

"How can it have vanished?" asked Kusac. "It's a carving, part of a frieze, connected to the figures next to it!"

"The Zsadhi sword vanished," Shazzuk reminded him. "If it can vanish, then a carving is no different."

"It's very different. The sword was the real one, set into the wall, not a carving."

"Come and see," said Shazzuk, opening his office door.

"I knew you wouldn't believe me until you saw it for yourself. That's why I called you, even though your people in the mountain have seen it."

"They've been here recently?"

"They came yesterday with more leaflets for us for the Zsadhi raids."

Kusac grunted, and as they left the house, he called Cheelar and M'yikku over to join them. "Are you sure this isn't someone having a joke on us in very bad taste?" he asked. "It seems highly unlikely that not only do we have a magic sword, but also a magic carving."

"Call it what you will, but the carving is gone," said Shazzuk as they took the path to the chapel. "And, as I told you before, no one in the village would dream of defacing the chapel."

The day was getting on toward evening now, and sunset colored the sky in a myriad of vibrant reds, pinks, and oranges as the sun began to sink below the horizon. Rhassa had already lit the chapel lights and was waiting inside for them.

Kusac strode down the aisle to the front row of seats facing the bas-relief carvings of the story of the Zsadhi. There, near the center, was indeed a raw area that looked like the carving of the person there had been chipped out. Stopping a few feet from the wall, Kusac looked over to Rhassa.

"Tell me the story, Priestess," he said, pointing to the scene.

"You *are* the story. It happened in the ancient days when we females ruled K'oish'ik. This carving shows Zsadhi coming in from his years in the desert to challenge the false Queen," said Rhassa. "It's the carving of Tashraka that is missing. The legend is coming to life again."

"Why would that happen?" demanded Kusac. "There is no place in society for females, so where would she fit in?"

"As the false Emperor?" suggested Shazzuk.

"Wouldn't it be Captain of the guard in that case?" asked Kusac. "I just don't see it. I think someone defaced the carving, I don't for a minute believe that it pulled itself off the wall and walked into our present time." He got to his feet and turned toward the doorway of the chapel.

"Heed my warning, Zsadhi," said Rhassa in ringing tones. "Ignore Tashraka at your peril!"

"I'm warned, Rhassa," said Kusac before leaving the chapel and heading out into the twilight. Hearing the legend of Zsadhi always caused shivers to go up and down his spine, this time no less than the others. He knew personally just how real the Entities of Shola were, and though he didn't want to admit it, the Zsadhi, too. Could it be that Ishardia and Tashraka were also real, always fighting over the Zsadhi just as Kuushoi and Ghyakulla fought over Vartra? The thought was not comforting, and he tried to push it to the back of his mind.

Once back in the main village square, he pulled Azwokkus' vial from his pocket and let it drop unseen to the ground before crushing it underfoot, releasing the nanites that would protect the memories of not only himself and his team, but also the villagers, assuming Annuur and Azwokkus' plan went according to schedule.

He turned to talk to Shazzuk who had followed him out to the courtyard. "I have to leave now to meet up with my people in the mountains. I'll be back tomorrow afternoon for Mahzi, so make sure she's ready to leave. Is there anything else your insurgents need for their raids?"

"She'll be ready, m'Lord. The leaflets were what we needed, and thanks to you, we have them," said Shazzuk.

"Until tomorrow, then," said Kusac, getting back into the aircar.

The mountain den

The small cavern was bustling with activity when Kusac and his team finally arrived there. Kaid and Carrie stopped what they were doing long enough to greet them, then carried on as before. Kusac headed for the tent he and Carrie shared, getting out of his hated military uniform before morphing back into his natural Sholan form. He lay on the sleeping bags for a few minutes, waiting until the pain and the shaking that any change caused had subsided, then reached into his bag for a tunic.

Dressed in comfortable clothing, he folded the M'zullian clothes and sealed them into the protective cover kept there for that purpose. Finally ready to face the others, he clambered out of the tent again. Kushool was waiting by their central cooking fire with a hot drink for him.

"Coffee! I didn't think we'd have any left by now."

"We wouldn't if Annuur hadn't brought us some more," she grinned. "But we did keep some back specially for you and Rezac."

Squatting down by the heating unit, Kusac sipped the aromatic drink appreciatively.

"We're getting a package ready for Rezac's group," she said. "They have the next raid, as I'm sure you know. A factory for fighter craft this time."

"Sounds dangerous. I hope he's taking it carefully."

"Always," said Jo, coming over to join him. "He says stop worrying, he's not after the whole factory, just the area where the craft are painted because it's the most volatile process. He'll be coming to pick up the leaflets and explosives in an hour or two, after his dinner."

Kusac nodded. "I'll talk to him then. Any word from Annuur on how much longer until their nanites are ready?"

"The current estimate is two to three weeks left before they reach population saturation. Apparently, once the nanites have reached everyone, because they all communicate with each other, they'll alert Annuur and Azwokkus that they've achieved full coverage. The matter transformer will then activate itself for the last time, and turn on the nanites. After it's done that, it will destroy itself."

"I'll believe it when I see it," Kusac grunted. "Meanwhile, I was just up at all three of the space stations. They're now rigged to blow when I give the word to Annuur. I want this damned planet's ability to wage war utterly destroyed, and I want it isolated from any other planet. Its threat has to be gone forever this time."

"It will be," said Jo, reaching out to pat his arm.

Carrie came over and settled down beside him, leaning against him. "Well, that's done," she said. "It's good to have you back. How have things been with you, apart from setting explosives on the space stations?"

"Busy," he said, putting an arm around her shoulders and nuzzling her neck. "Mahzi is in the village with her real husband, you'll be pleased to know."

"I'm sure they're both happy with that arrangement. I was at the village earlier yesterday with Kaid—we used the morphing devices—to deliver them some leaflets."

"So I heard. I'm thinking that Shazzuk would make a good Governor for M'zull when the dust settles. His family's descended from the last governor, after all. I'm sure he'd be able to work with the Touibans and the rest of us."

"They'll certainly need a local contact who has his real memories. Have you treated them so they do?"

Kusac nodded. "I did it today; got us all, Cheelar, M'yikku, and myself as well."

"What about the other villages?"

"No, only this one. Rezac and I discussed this. These are the only people I trust. The fewer left with their memories, the fewer there are to deal with in case anything goes wrong. And their memories won't be genetic—they can't pass them on."

"Makes sense. How long are we staying after the nanites kick in and send everyone to sleep?" she asked.

"Assuming that's what happens, we wait until we've handed over command to the seniormost Touiban present, then we can get off here and head back to the Prime world with Toueesut on the *Couana*."

Carrie sighed. "I can't wait to get back to the cubs, and then back home to Shola! It seems forever since I've seen our little ones back home. The children will have grown so much!"

"They will. It'll be good to finally get home. And get our new cubs settled in their permanent home at last."

"I hate to ask you to move," said Kushool, "but I'm on cooking duty and it's time to start preparing dinner. You won't believe how much better the food is since Annuur began sending us fresh supplies!"

Kusac got to his feet, holding out his hand to help Carrie up. "We're going," he said. "Yes. It's been a lot easier all round since Annuur and the TeLaxaudin have been helping us. Just don't lose sight of what that help has cost us in past wrongs."

"I won't, Captain," said Kushool, all seriousness. "They still have to answer for what they did to us."

"No!" This time Carrie's cry brought her to wakefulness. Still groggy with sleep, she lay there trying to orient herself as to where and when she was.

She heard the closure on her tent being pulled open, then Kaid's head poked in to regard her in concern.

"You all right?" he asked, flicking his ears in her direction.

"Just a nightmare," she said, passing a hand across her sweating face.

"About what? Sometimes nightmares can be prophetic."

"The Zsadhi legend," she said, propping herself up on an elbow.

Kaid crawled into the tent, sitting down at the foot of her bed. "Worrying," he agreed. "I don't like all this Avatar thing. It's too mystical for me. Given the choices, I'll take Vartra any day."

"You haven't mentioned Him in a long time," Carrie said.

"He's been quiet for some time now," agreed Kaid. "I'm surprised He's taken such a backseat for so long. Not like Him at all. What part of the Zsadhi legend did you dream about?"

"The duel between Tashraka and Zsadhi. I saw it as if I was Tashraka. I'm afraid it means something. Don't say it," she added hurriedly as Kaid opened his mouth. "Even mentioning it could make it happen."

"Then we won't," said Kaid. "I can't see any reason it would if the nanites activate as planned. Annuur says they should have finished spreading within two weeks."

"The sooner the better," Carrie said.

"I'm sure it's only because you were given a replica of the Queen's crown that you had the dream," Kaid said, picking up the bronze crown and turning it around in his hands, admiring the workmanship.

"I'm sure it is," she agreed. "Thanks, Kaid. I'll be able to go back to sleep now"

Kaid put the crown back on the pile of clothing where it had rested. "I'll say good night, then," he said, getting up. "Kusac should be back soon, just a minor emergency in the village."

"That's Tashraka's crown," said Kusac an hour later as he flopped down on the bedding beside her. "How did you get it?" he asked, picking it up.

"One of the villagers, a female, gave it to me when we were there yesterday in Valtegan form. It's not the real crown; it's a replica."

"Looks real enough to me," he murmured, putting it down again. "Sends cold shivers down my spine."

"It definitely feels as if there's some of Tashraka in it, which is silly when it's not the original."

"I can sense what you mean," he said, reaching out to pull her close. "What do you plan to do with it?"

"Ask Connor to check it out and if it's okay, give it to King Zsurtul as a museum piece."

"Sounds good to me. Maybe we should pack it away rather than leave it here to trouble your sleep."

"Might be for the best. When I'm in the tent, I feel I have a connection to it," she said, resting her head on his chest.

Prime world, same day

"How on Shola did you get them to let us take the cubs out to one of the riverside work camps?" asked Jerenn as he slung the extra clothes and weapons' cleaning and sharpening kits into his large backpack.

"By pointing out that at one of the nearby camps we'd be close enough to call for help if needed, yet isolated enough that only those on the detail with us would know the cubs were there," said M'Nar, doing the same. He looked up at the other with a wide grin. "And I got N'Akoe on the detail with us."

Jerenn's ears flicked forward in interest even though he tried to cancel their involuntary movement.

"Aha! I knew that would interest you!"

"She's part of our detail now," he said, feigning mild indifference. "Of course she'd be on the docket to come with us to help deal with the young djanas, Gaylla and Vazih."

"Sure she would," M'Nar purred, fastening his backpack and picking it up. "Well, I'm done. Last one to the lounge is on latrine digging duty!"

N'Akoe, Jerenn, and M'Nar stood watching as Dzaka and Kitra herded the younglings into an aircar on the rooftop landing pad.

"They make it look so easy," said Jerenn as little Gaylla finally scampered up the ramp and allowed herself to be secured in the seat next to her brother Shaidan.

"It's pretty easy," said M'Nar pushing himself away from the wall and heading up the ramp. "You just have to keep emphasizing the fun things they'll get to do and not mention any rules."

"But we have to have rules or . . ." exclaimed Jerenn, following him.

"Yeah, but they don't need to be reminded of them every two minutes!"

"Brother Jerenn, sit with me!" squealed Gaylla as soon as she saw his gray pelt.

"No, me!" said Vazih. "You can't always sit with her. It's my turn today!"

"Now, Vazih, you know it's first come, first served. Brother M'Nar or N'Akoe would be happy to sit with you today."

"Sure I would," M'Nar said, mouth dropping in a wide grin as he took the seat beside her. "It would be my pleasure."

Vazih gave a small huff of annoyance, but as soon as M'Nar was beside her, she began to cuddle up against his side.

"Where are we going?" asked Dhyshac.

"Right now, we're headed for the shuttle port outside the city walls. Once there, we'll transfer to G Company's troop transporter and fly out to Base Camp Two. We'll be berthed there for two nights before returning to the Palace," said N'Akoe.

"G Company will provide security for you as well as carrying out their normal duties," said Jerenn as the whine from the aircar rose in pitch prior to takeoff.

He grabbed for a handhold as the cubs, in a flurry of excitement, leaned forward to try and look out the windows.

It took about an hour for the troop transporter to reach the base camp. The camp was basic in design, having half a dozen tents, a latrine, a fire pit, and a cooking area.

"What is a base camp?" asked Shaidan as the transporter landed just north of the fire pit.

"It's a camp where you base yourselves when working in an area. It's your main camp," said M'Nar. "From there you go out to where you are working and, if necessary, you can set up other campsites."

"Did your Aunt Kitra tell you what you'd be doing here?" asked N'Akoe.

"She said that we would be helping plant grasses and wildflowers by the side of the river," Shaidan replied.

"Why do we need to put plants in beside the river?"

"I know!" said Gaylla, bouncing up and down, her tail flicking excitedly from side to side. "They do it to stop the earth getting blown away in the storms."

"Exactly, well done, Gaylla," said N'Akoe, reaching out to ruffle the mop of hair that framed her face. "As Gaylla said, it stops the erosion caused by the wind and the river itself. Also, where there is grass, the herd beasts and the wild animals we've been releasing can graze."

"Not just wild animals and herds," said Jerenn, gesturing to them to release their seatbelts and line up behind the troopers to get out of the transporter. "Once an area is stabilized, then the Ch'almuthians in the town camp are able to occupy the area. Sometimes it's a ruined village, other times, the Ch'almuthians have to build themselves a new village. This one here was the remains of an older village, so they only had to repair the ruins."

"Why do they live in tents outside the city?" asked Dhyshac.

"Well, long ago, this world was the prime one for Valtegans . . ." began M'Nar.

"An' why we calls them Primes," said Gaylla.

"Yes, but then they had three worlds that belonged to them, one being M'zull where your papas are now."

"But long ago they found Shola, our world," said Jerenn, "and they fought a war with us which we lost. However," he said, smiling as the cubs all dipped their ears and looked sad, "we fought back and finally beat the bad Valtegans."

"We beat them so badly that all our worlds lost space travel and were set back hundreds of years," said M'Nar. "The Prime world was worst hit, being the leader, and because most of the people were in space, or on other worlds when they got stranded."

"I bet it saw the worst fighting, which is why there's ruins," said Shaidan.

"That's right," said M'Nar, patting him on the shoulder. "And when a world has very few people and loses all its technology, then it ends up like this." He waved an expansive hand out at the bare ground outside the window. "This is why we have to plant grass and other plants to make K'oish'ik green again."

The dozen Prime soldiers and the two Sholan Brothers with them began to file out to form a line outside.

"Ooh, tents!" said Gaylla excitedly, pointing. "Will we get to sleep in the tents?"

"Not this time," said Jerenn. "We're getting to live in this transport vehicle, but we will be eating our meals round the campfire."

Shaidan noticed the approving glanced M'Nar threw at the other Brother.

"The villagers here have arranged for a small feast for us," said M'Nar. "After we've eaten, it should be great fun sitting around the firc, toasting some of the special kind of soft candy the Ch'almuthians make."

"I think that they're roasting a young herd beast for us," said Jerenn, leading them off the transporter. "They'll already have begun cooking it in the village, and they'll just bring it down here later in the day to finish it off."

The troopers, under the orders of their Sholan officers, were already stowing their kits in their tents.

"Once the boxes of young plants have been unloaded, we'll have a snack and then start planting them," M'Nar said. "If you like, we can have a look around while we wait."

There was a loud chorus of "Yes, please!" and the three adults grinned at each other.

Their camp was in a dry area, a quarter of a mile from the river. Broad and fast flowing, the Nezoa wound its way down from the mountains a hundred miles to the north, to the small inland sea about forty miles south of the city.

As they approached the shallows at the side of the river, M'Nar called them all toward him. "I will only tell you once," he said. "The river Nezoa is the lifeblood of this area of K'oish'ik. It's deep and fast flowing. If you fall into it, we will be unable to save you. You'll drown and be swept away down to the sea."

Shaidan shivered slightly as he watched the Brother look at each one of them in turn.

"So you will *not* go near the river unless one of us is with you. Is that understood?"

"Yes, Brother M'Nar," Shaidan chorused along with the others.

"There is a small inlet where you can paddle in the water. Brother Jerenn and I will take you there for a play session if you're good."

"Stay back from the edges of the riverbank. They're just

wet soil and would give under your weight," said Jerenn. "All right, let's get moving! There's a lot to see before lunch."

As they began to get closer to the riverbank, Gaylla slipped her small hand into Shaidan's. "It sure is dangerous out here," she said, moving closer to him.

"It's only dangerous until we learn the rules," he replied. "Once we understand how things work, it won't seem so scary."

"Uh-huh," she said nervously, slowing right down and taking small, cautious steps.

"It's safe where we are," reassured Shaidan, giving her hand a gentle tug. "It's by the edge that we might have to be careful. Look," he pointed to the front of their line. "Brother Jerenn has only just stopped."

Gaylla nodded, clutching her doll more tightly in her other arm. "I see. So we's are safe where he is?"

"Yes, so long as we don't go any closer, we'll be fine."

This close, the river seemed so wide to Shaidan that he wondered if this was what the sea looked like.

Not far from the bank, the brown water churned and gurgled over rocks set into the side of the riverbed. M'Nar bent down and picked a small stick from a long-dead plant. He showed it to the cubs.

"When I throw this into the water, you'll get an idea of how strong the current is," he said. "You can come a little nearer." He gestured them closer.

They stopped about two feet from the edge.

"I'm going to throw this into the river, so keep your eyes on it." M'Nar carefully stepped nearer and threw the twig. A slight breeze caught it and whirled it farther out before unceremoniously dumping it into the water. There it was swept rapidly downstream toward the rocks.

"Now imagine that was you. We'd have no chance to reach you before you were swept onto the rocks, then away down to the sea, so pay attention to our warnings. We're not trying to spoil your fun, only keep you alive," M'Nar finished. "Now follow me to the safe inlet."

Here, the crystal-clear water gently lapped at a shore of

small tumbled pebbles and sand. It was shot with the silver glint of tiny fishes darting between the green-and-red water plants and the larger stones.

"Oh!" exclaimed Shaidan, kneeling down to better see them. "They're larger than the ones in the temple!"

"Different fish usually grow to different sizes," said Jerenn. "The temple ones are particularly small and chosen by the priests and priestesses for that reason."

"Back home on Shola, I take my cubs fishing every four weeks," said M'Nar, crouching beside Shaidan. "Of course, we're after bigger fish than these, ones large enough to eat. I'm sure we'll see some of those here if we're lucky."

Gaylla reached out to touch the fish nearest to her, disturbing the water and making them dart away in fright.

"If you disturb the water, they will swim away," said N'Akoe in answer to her exclamation of dismay.

"But the fishes are so pretty! I want to hold one," she said, shaking the water off her hand.

"Fish can't live out of water," said M'Nar sympathetically. "And you can't touch them like you can the young herd beasts."

"Perhaps we could ask for one of the glass cubes of fish and plants that the Primes have in their temple," suggested Jerenn. "You could have it in your bedroom. They are completely self-contained, so you wouldn't even need to feed them."

"Would you like us to ask for one for you?" asked N'Akoe, getting up.

"Yes, please!"

"Then I'll ask when we get back. Time to go see the village now."

The village was an eclectic arrangement of adobe huts that housed some forty villagers. The central area was crowded with people, all heading purposefully one way or another. Heads bobbed politely in their direction when they saw them.

A fire pit had been dug, and over it roasted a young herd beast. The smell of bread baking in the communal ovens mixed with the aroma of cooking meat, creating an irresistible scent that had all of their mouths watering.

The village headman came to greet them. As M'Nar ushered the cubs toward the central ovens and roasting pit, Jerenn took on the job of talking to him.

"So these are the Sholan young I was told about," said Mazul, watching as the cubs stood round the pit asking a million questions. "They seem very like our own young. Curious about everything."

"I think younglings are all the same no matter what species," said Jerenn. "We've seen a fair bit of Mayza, General Kezule's daughter, and—age aside—she's very like our cubs."

Mazul nodded. "Such closeness between our kinds is good for us all. As you see, the roast is almost done. I'll send four of our folk up to your base camp to get the fire started so we can move it over there to finish cooking."

Jerenn nodded. "I see you've even cooked fresh bread for us. Thank you for all this kind consideration. We really appreciate it."

"Compared to the new homes and help you've given us, a meal is nothing," said Mazul, shrugging aside Jerenn's concerns. "Just let us know tomorrow when you want help with planting, and we'll be there."

"I thought we'd start early in the morning to avoid the heat," said M'Nar. "Then we can take a long midday break and start up again midafternoon."

Mazul nodded. "Sounds like a good plan. We'll come for you at six in the morning."

"We'll look for you then," said Jerenn as he, M'Nar, and N'Akoe began to round up the cubs.

Third meal was accompanied by the villagers teaching everyone their Ch'almuthian folk songs. Later, when the beer was brought out, M'Nar and Jerenn escorted the cubs the few yards to the troop transporter to bed them down for the night.

"You carries me, Brother Jerenn," Gaylla said sleepily around the thumb she still sucked when overtired.

Jerenn picked her up and began walking to the transport as Gaylla snuggled up to him.

Shaidan walked beside them while N'Akoe took Vazih by the hand and followed close behind.

"You be a good papa. If I didn't have one, I'd choose you," Gaylla said. "You only a little broke inside."

Shocked, Jerenn almost stumbled. "What?"

"You's only a little broke," she said again. "Feelings there." She moved her thumb from her mouth to pat Jerenn on the chest. "Just need to unstick them." A huge yawn followed this pronouncement, then the thumb returned to her mouth.

Shaidan caught Jerenn glancing at him for clarification, but he schooled his face into the politely blank expression he had learned to use with Dr. K'hedduk.

By the time Shaidan and the other cubs were ushered into the transporter, the seats had been adjusted to form emergency bunkbeds. Tired and full of roasted meats and vegetables, the cubs queued up to brush their teeth, quickly groom each other, then fall into their beds.

Jerenn, M'Nar, and N'Akoe met in the forward area by the doors that they had reserved for themselves. The seating there only folded up against the bulkhead, but it left plenty of room for them to put down their bedrolls.

M'Nar quickly unrolled his and reached up to the overhead bin where their pillows were stored. "Incoming!" he said, throwing one to each of the others.

"We have pillows?" said N'Akoe happily. "I thought I'd have to use my backpack!"

"I made sure we had all the luxuries I could get," said M'Nar, flicking his ears conspiratorially. "I even managed to get us some real coffee!"

"Coffee right now would be really good," said Jerenn, plumping up his pillow before settling down on his bedding. "Did you bring a coffee pot to brew it in?"

"Better," said M'Nar, eyes twinkling as his tail flicked in pleasure. "I borrowed an electric brewer from the temple kitchen!"

"You didn't!" said Jerenn, sitting up. "They actually let you borrow it?"

"Well, not exactly," M'Nar temporized, wiggling his ears back and forth briefly. "But they will never know it was me by the time I put it back."

"You two are incorrigible," said N'Akoe with a laugh. "The coffee will go well with the bag of pastries I begged for us from the main kitchen." She reached for her backpack.

"Pastries and coffee," said M'Nar. "Just what we need after a hard day herding the cubs."

"Wait till we have had a full day of them," said Jerenn, making himself comfortable again. "We'll be exhausted."

M'Nar rifled through his pack, pulling out a bag of ground coffee and the coffee pot. Scrambling to his feet, he went forward into the main cabin, looking for a power outlet. "I'll be back in a few minutes. Just getting a large bottle of fresh water. The troops forgot to leave us one."

"All right," said Jerenn.

"See if you can get at least one plate for the pastries," N'Akoe called out.

"Large one?" M'Nar asked hopefully, standing in the hatchway.

She laughed. "Yes, large."

M'zull Palace, Zhal-Oeshi 12th (August)

It had been a stormy Council meeting, and when it was over, K'hedduk demanded that Kusac stay behind.

"You did a good job of inspecting the orbital stations, Nayash," said K'hedduk. "Your list of the Generals and their affiliations was most illuminating. I'll admit to some unwelcome surprises, but enough of that for now. I have another job for you. I want the Zsadhi, or whoever is fomenting this unrest, found and eliminated as soon as possible. You seem to have a knack for getting a difficult job done, so this is your next one."

Kusac suppressed his instant sense of panic. "Majesty, this Zsadhi could be anyone, or be concealed anywhere. Your best troops have been unable to find him in all these weeks, I can't see how I can be any more successful than they've been."

"You have a different way of looking at problems, an unconventional one. I trust that to guide you now."

At a loss to know how to answer K'hedduk, Kusac went with the first thought that came into his head. "It will mean going from door-to-door, Majesty, checking every business and residence in the city," he said. "It will be extremely disruptive of the normal running of the city, but it might be the best chance to catch those with a guilty conscience as well as those harboring publications like the Zsadhi leaflets."

"Then do it," said K'hedduk. "It's past time that these people were brought to justice! They must be getting their leaflets published somewhere. Start with the printing houses in the city. Search them, then close them down until this crisis is over!"

"Yes, Majesty, as you command." Kusac bowed and began backing out of the office.

Once in the courtyard with Cheelar, M'yikku, and Maalash, he revealed his plan. "K'hedduk wants us to do a door-to-door search for the Zsadhi," he said, "starting with the printers where the leaflets might be being produced. I need each of you to take two squads of soldiers and start doing that. Arrest any likely people who are either too loyal or obvious insurgents. We'll each take a compass point of the city. I'll take the North side, you the East, Cheelar, the South for you, M'yikku, and you the West, Maalash. Take your time and be thorough. Every house and business is what K'hedduk said, but start with any printers' outlets in your area and close them down after you're done. Take some workmen with planks of wood to nail up the doors. Meet back at the apartment at eighteen hundred tonight, and we'll go over what we found."

There was only one printer in his section of the city, so Kusac made his way there, ordering half his troops to guard the main delivery yard where the blank paper was delivered and the printed newspapers and publications were loaded onto trucks for distribution, while he took the rest in the front entrance.

"Gather your staff in the yard," he ordered the owner as the frightened male rushed out of his office to see him. "I have a message for you all from the Emperor."

As they began to file out under his squad's watchful eyes, Kusac, accompanied by four of his men, began going through the offices.

"Search everything," he said, standing at the doorway as they began turning over the desks and drawers. "Look for anything resembling the Zsadhi leaflets. You can't miss them. They are crudely made with the name Zsadhi and the sword symbol on them."

It was nothing but legalized vandalism, and Kusac was well-aware of that, but he had no option. He consoled himself with the knowledge that if Annuur's plan worked, none of this would matter in a couple of weeks.

After the first two offices had been dealt with, he left them to continue their search and went outside to join the workers in the delivery yard.

"His Majesty the Emperor, Long Life and Health be His, has decreed that all printers shall be shut down from now until the insurgent known as the Zsadhi has been found and captured," he said, raising his voice so everyone could hear. "Once our search of the premises has been completed, you will be released to return to your homes. You will be notified when the embargo on your business has been lifted."

A low growl of discontented muttering broke out, mainly from the manual workers. "How will we live in the meantime?" demanded one. "No work, no food!"

"See your Lord about that. It is not my concern, nor that

of the Emperor," said Kusac sharply. "The closure will only last as long as it takes to find this Zsadhi. If you have information that could lead to his capture, I suggest you tell me now."

There was more muttering, combined with angry looks, but it slowly subsided into a sullen silence until the rest of his squad came outside, their search concluded.

"Nothing, General Nayash," said the lieutenant, saluting him.

"Get the place boarded up," Kusac ordered before turning back to the workers. "You are dismissed. Do not return here until ordered to do so by the Emperor, May He Live Forever."

More grumbling and murmuring, but the crowd of workers turned and filed peacefully out of the yard, heading off into the town. Within a few minutes, Kusac and his platoon stood alone in the empty yard.

"Regroup outside at the vehicles," said Kusac. "House-to-house searches now. Three men per house. Look for any suspicious behavior, publications, or other items."

Later that evening

Back at the Palace apartment, Kusac headed for the library and, stripping off his jacket, helped himself to a drink from the sideboard.

Cheelar was already there. "How was your day?" he asked.

"An exercise in futility, obviously, and a great way to get the general population of the city riled up, irrespective of their caste. Help yourself to a drink. Are the others back yet?"

"No, but they shouldn't be long."

"Any problems? The mood nearly got ugly at the printers. Thank goodness for the caste scents that prevent them attacking us."

"Not to mention Annuur's booster," said Cheelar quietly, going over to the sideboard to pour himself a drink.

"Indeed," said Kusac.

"I had two printers. The first was a small one, more of a print shop for the needs of small groups and individuals. That place was fine. It was the larger one that nearly erupted. I left them in their offices as we searched them, which was a big mistake. Next time, I'll have them evicted first. I did feel guilty knowing I was depriving them of their livelihood."

"Not you, K'hedduk. He's the one wanting them shut down until the Zsadhi is caught. I suppose it makes sense."

There was a knock at the door, and it opened to admit M'yikku and Maalash. "General Nayash," said Maalash. "Reporting back. Only one printer in my section, and it is now closed down."

"At ease, Maalash and M'yikku. Help yourselves to a drink if you want one. Anything out of the usual happen?"

"Nothing, Lord Nayash," said Maalash.

"Just a lot of very pissed-off citizens," said M'yikku, heading for the sideboard. "Thank goodness for the castes! I'd certainly have been overwhelmed by angry print workers without it."

"I think we all felt that. The violence and anger is there, very close to the surface in the workers. The only thing keeping it in check right now is the caste scent prohibition. How did your door-to-door go? Anything found?"

"A few contraband items that workers shouldn't have, but apart from that, nothing out of the ordinary at all," said M'yikku.

"Anyone have any prisoners?"

"I arrested one man from the printers in my section," said Maalash. "He picked up a rock and threw it at one of my soldiers."

Kusac raised an eyeridge at Cheelar. "That shouldn't be possible."

"I figure maybe he's from one of the mountain tribes, not a worker."

"Did you talk to him?" asked Cheelar.

"Not yet. He'll be safe enough for tonight."

"What would bring a mountain dweller down to the city for work?" asked M'yikku.

"One of the insurgent groups?" asked Kusac.

"I hope not," said Maalash. "Stupid beyond belief to pick up a stone if he was trying to be undercover."

"I think we should question him tonight," said Kusac. "I don't want to risk anyone else getting their hands on him."

A knock sounded at the door and Laazif opened it. "Dinner is ready, Lord General," he said.

"Thank you, Laazif. After dinner, then," said Kusac, finishing his drink.

They'd barely started eating when a message was delivered from the office of the Inquisitor, thanking them for the captive, whom they had now transferred to their cells.

"Dammit!" swore Kusac. "I should have anticipated that! Are you sure he wasn't a known mountain villager, Maalash?"

"He's not one I've seen, Lord Nayash. Sometimes villagers do get a yearning for the city life and leave, but not often. Likely he is one of them."

"If he knows anything at all, the Inquisitors will get it out of him," said Cheelar. "Is there any way you can get him back?"

"None, not with Ziosh breathing down my neck already. The Inquisition cells are in a different place from the regular ones. We'll just have to hope there's nothing for him to tell them. In future, no prisoners to be sent to the cells; bring them directly to me. Meanwhile, we might as well eat since there's nothing else we can do right now."

After dinner, Kusac left the others in the library and headed for his office to contact Annuur.

"Ah, Kusac, good it is you contact me," said the hologram of the Cabbaran. "Urgent news I have for you. You must be on your guard. The Generals plan to assassinate you tomorrow. They believe you are too much a tool of the Emperor."

"What? How am I supposed to avoid that? I can't leave

the capital right now. I'm conducting this door-to-door search for the Zsadhi."

"The unrest this is causing is what triggered the planned attempt on your life and that of the Emperor."

"How did you find out? Do you have any details?"

"Checking in on that youth Telmaar were we. Nothing conclusive we find yet. Attempt will be after the Council meeting tomorrow morning. Suggest you miss meeting. Good news is the nanites have nearly reached saturation in the population. In two weeks we will be ready to trigger them."

"They told me that at the mountain den. I didn't think the Generals would be rash enough to act against the Emperor. Me missing the meeting wouldn't stop him from being assassinated."

"What you care about that? You want him dead anyway. This way, he gone and you alive."

"It's one thing to kill him myself, another to let him be assassinated. He's the only person that's keeping me alive right now in that case. All I need to do is avoid being arrested by Ziosh and keep me and the Emperor I hate alive for the next two weeks!"

Annuur spread his forelimbs in a gesture of helplessness. "More I cannot do right now. Perhaps you have a plan to divert the Generals? There is always the translocator. It will take you instantly to safety but will draw unwanted attention to you. Still, so close to final solution, perhaps is wiser you withdraw to safety, let what will happen to K'hedduk happen. Cannot risk losing you."

"I'll consider it," he said. "Let me see what we can come up with in the meantime."

"Be safe, friend Kusac."

The call over, Kusac pulled his comm unit out of his pocket to call Cheelar. "Come to the office, I have news."

When they were all settled round the table, Kusac updated them, glossing over the time before the Cabbaran plan took effect, and concentrating more on the threat of an assassin.

"Time to do that raid on the Palace Chapel," he said. "If

that doesn't divert the Generals from an assassination attempt, I don't know what will."

"What about the plan to take out General Geddash? Both together would ensure their attention was on themselves and not you," said M'yikku.

"I'd need a way to draw him out tonight. Not the easiest thing to do when planning a raid."

Cheelar checked his watch. "Twenty-one hundred. Isn't he at the Officer's club in the city now?"

Kusac nodded. "Yes, and he should be there for another couple of hours. We need something to make him leave the club, if not alone, then with only his aide with him."

"What about offering him information on the Zsadhi, information you refuse to consider?" suggested M'yikku. "Since he already has it in for you, anything you won't consider, he should want to hear."

"Get him to come to a meeting in a deserted spot nearby. Isn't there one of those print works we closed down in the area?" asked Cheelar, pulling the map of the city over and spreading it open. "Yes! There's one within a block of the club. Close enough for the General not to need more than his aide for backup."

"You'll be the contact, Maalash, since you're the newest of my aides. We'll get some local worker to go in with the note and you'll wait at the print shop for the General to approach you. While he's preoccupied with you, we'll take him out. Let's get moving on this now before it gets any later," said Kusac, grabbing a piece of paper for the note.

Inside the office of the print shop, Kusac maintained a light mental link with their worker messenger as he was told to wait in the club lobby for the General's aide. As instructed, he refused to hand the note to him, insisting it had to be given to the General personally. Finally, Geddash came, his aide in close attendance.

"What d'you want?" he demanded brusquely. "I'm General Geddash. Don't you know better than to come bothering me at this time of night?"

"Had to, m'Lord. The officer told me to give you this note." The worker held out a folded piece of paper.

"You could have given this to my aide," hissed Geddash, snatching it from him. "There was no need to disturb me!"

"He told me I had to give it only to you," he repeated before turning to leave.

"Wait! Who gave it to you?"

"I don't know him any more than I know you, m'Lord. He just paid me to give this to you, said it was urgent."

Geddash gestured him to leave and opened the note. He didn't recognize the writing, but what it said did catch his undivided attention. He hesitated, looking behind him into the depths of the club, then back at the note. It said he had to come now, the informant wouldn't wait for him. Mind made up, he crumpled the note and thrust it into his pocket, then turned to his aide.

"I have to go out for a short while. Someone has information on this Zsadhi person but is only willing to give it to me tonight if I meet him in person at the print shop in Third Street. I want you to follow me at a discreet distance. I don't expect trouble, but I intend to be prepared for it."

"Wouldn't you be better taking more backup than just me, General?" he asked. "If you wait ten minutes, we can get a squad of soldiers to accompany us."

"Too long, and too visible. No, we'll go now, Viszok. Keep your distance from me, but be close enough to come running if I call out for you."

"As you wish, General."

Kusac tracked them mentally from their hiding place inside the yard. The print shop was the one he'd dealt with earlier that day, so he knew the layout and had drawn plans for the others before they left the Palace. He'd told Geddash to meet inside the yard for privacy's sake.

"He's on his way," he said quietly to Maalash. "Get ready. Remember, we'll do the killing. Just act the part of the messenger and be alert to his aide arriving. And don't stand directly in front of him."

The young M'zullian nodded, then detached himself from Kusac's side to move deeper into the shadows that ran the length of the loading bays. Thankfully, it was an overcast night with no moonlight to throw everything into bright relief. The streetlight reflected from the low overhead clouds cast a pale orange light in the center of the yard.

Cheelar's soft breathing beside him was the only sound he could hear as his ears strained for the footsteps that he knew were growing closer. He was adjusting his grip on the knife for the umpteenth time when he heard the yard doors finally beginning to open.

He stiffened, readying his stance as the General, leaving the doors open, began to advance cautiously into the yard.

"Where are you? Show yourself!" Geddash called out, stopping some ten feet inside the yard and looking around.

Maalash stepped into the light. "Thank you for coming, General."

Geddash squinted at him. "Come closer, I want to see your face, get your scent. Your note said you had news to give me about the Zsadhi, news that Nayash wouldn't listen to."

Maalash began to walk slowly toward the older man.

"You're one of Nayash's people," said Geddash, eyes narrowing as the other drew closer.

"Yes, General. I recently entered his service."

"Well, what's this revelation you have? Let's be done with it!"

Maalash stopped about five feet from the General, keeping his hands in full view to show he was no threat. "The Zsadhi has to be one of our class, an officer."

"We know this," said Geddash. "This is nothing new!"

"I believe the Zsadhi is one of Nayash's people," he said quietly, taking another step closer to him.

"One of Nayash's people? What makes you think that?"

"When the attacks seem to happen, there is always one of his aides missing. In fact, that one has been missing for a week now and no one will tell me where he is."

"Do you suspect Nayash is involved in it?" he asked, losing his caution and moving closer to Maalash.

"I think it suspicious that he isn't concerned about where his missing aide went . . ."

Kusac raised his arm and taking careful aim, threw his knife. Cheelar's followed a hairsbreadth behind.

Through the air the knives tumbled, Kusac's striking Geddash in the chest as Cheelar's zipped past Maalash's ear and hit the General square in the forehead.

Without a sound, Geddash began to crumple, but Maalash leaped forward and grabbed him, hoisting him upward until it looked to an impartial observer like the two were in close conversation.

"Can you see his aide?" hissed Kusac running in the shadow's cover until he was close enough for Maalash to hear him.

Maalash looked quickly around. "No."

"Walk him over this way," said Kusac. "Let's get him into the shadows and get those knives out."

Struggling, Maalash put an arm around the General's waist and began to stagger over to Kusac and the shadows.

"Taking too long," muttered Cheelar, darting out of the shadows to Maalash's side to help him drag the General to cover.

In the safety of the loading bay, they let the General's body fall to the ground. Cheelar bent over him and pulled the knives free, being careful not to get any blood on himself.

"Check his pockets," said Kusac, pulling on gloves before reaching into his own pocket for the can of spray paint. "Get our note back if he still has it." He mentally scanned the area, finding the aide waiting patiently round the corner of the street, near the front door of the print firm.

"Got it," said Maalash, still rifling through the General's uniform pockets.

"Back off. Time to spray the sword on his body," ordered Kusac. "His aide is still waiting round the corner."

The other two backed away, keeping watch on the yard doors as Kusac began to spray the Zsadhi sword over the dead General's uniform. That done, he placed the can beside him. "Time to leave," he said. "We'll have to exit by the front door and take down the aide. I want him alive to find the body and call an alarm. Cheelar, can you do it? I'll link to the aide, so we'll know if you need help."

The young commando nodded. "No problem. Give me five." He turned and loped off into the darkness.

Viszok walked up to the corner of the street and carefully looked round it to see if the General had come out of the yard, but the street was empty. He turned and walked back to the doorway, stepping into the shadows there. He leaned against the doorjamb, folding his arms and wishing he were back at the club instead of waiting in this drafty street for the General.

The next thing he knew, he was lying on the ground with a massive headache. He groaned, putting his hand to the back of his head where he found a large and very tender lump. He struggled to sit up, moaning in pain, then the enormity of his situation hit him. If he'd been knocked out, what had happened to the General?

Lurching to his feet, he found he was still by the front door of the print works. Holding onto the wall, he made his way carefully round the corner to the double wooden doors of the yard. In the center, he could see a dark shape that with a cold feeling he suddenly knew was the General.

Fighting back the nausea, he staggered across the yard to what became increasingly obvious was the body of General Geddash. He slumped down beside it, feeling at the neck for a pulse, but the body was already cool to the touch. Reaching into his pocket, he pulled out his comm unit and called General M'zoesh's number. The head of Intelligence would know what to do.

"It's General Geddash," he blurted out when an aide answered the phone. "He's been murdered by the Zsadhi! He has that sword painted on his chest!"

Back in the Palace apartment, Kusac and his group tried to relax.

"That aide must have wakened by now," said Maalash, pacing up and down by Kusac's desk.

Cheelar reached out to grasp him by the arm. "Sit down," he said quietly. "We can't afford to have the staff here see us restless with no reason."

"Right," said Maalash, taking a deep breath. "You're right. I'll sit and wait like you."

"No need for that. Whatever else, we need to behave normally. I think we can afford to go out this evening to the club. We haven't been there for a few days," said Kusac.

"That's walking into the norrta's den," said Maalash, taken aback.

"Exactly. No one would expect us to do that if we were involved. Let's go. Remember to drink sparingly. We have a mission to do tonight."

"Still going ahead with that?" asked Cheelar as they began to gather their belongings.

"Yes," said Kusac, putting his uniform hat on. "That assassination attempt on me and the Emperor could still go ahead unless we have everyone here rushing about on high alert. The way to do that is to complete the mission as planned. Hitting their temple here and defacing it the same night their leading General is murdered will certainly do that. I can't guarantee either alone would be enough."

"Enough talk. We know what has to be done," said Cheelar. "If Maalash feels he cannot do this, I suggest he remain here and guard the house for you."

Kusac stopped, hand on the doorknob, and turned to look at Maalash. "Do you wish to stay, Maalash?" he asked quietly. "You're not trained as we've been. There is no dishonor to remaining behind this time."

Maalash stood taller and narrowed his eyes. "I'm with you, Zsadhi," he said firmly. "As you say, I don't have your training, so forgive me my doubts."

"Good man," said Kusac, reaching out to pat him on the shoulder. "You'll do fine as always. Just don't call me Zsadhi!"

The young soldier's face flushed a darker green. "Sorry, m'Lord Nayash," he muttered.

*   *   *

The club was like an ant's nest that had been kicked, with aides and staff running every which way. With an obviously puzzled look on his face, Kusac, flanked by his two aides, made his way to the bar area.

He saw Telmaar standing at the bar in deep conversation with General Shayazu, head of all the Palace soldiers.

"Get me a drink, Chcelar," he murmured, taking off his hat and tucking it under one arm. "I'm going to talk to Telmaar. Get yourselves a beer, too."

As Cheelar headed to the bar to get the drinks, Kusac caught Telmaar's eye and made his way over to him.

"Nayash, good to see you. Have you heard the news? Geddash has been assassinated by this Zsadhi fellow."

"That's dreadful. How did it happen?"

"His aide says he was lured to a print shop with the promise of information about the Zsadhi, then murdered. The Emperor is shocked at the news and has demanded that the area around the print shop be searched door-to-door," said Shayazu.

"This is taking it too far," said Kusac. "It's one thing to attack our breweries and whorehouses, but to actually attack and kill one of our top Generals . . ."

"This hits us hard and personally," agreed Telmaar. "No one is safe if they can reach someone like Geddash."

"He was a fool to let himself be lured out of the club to a lonely rendezvous," said Shayazu gruffly. "What?" he said, seeing Kusac's look. "I'm only saying what we all think! We must all be on our guard from now on. I've sent our soldiers in squads of eight men to a street to search the houses. Meanwhile, I've doubled the guards in the Palace and made sure that Lieutenant Zerdish has increased the Emperor's personal bodyguards."

"Sounds like you have everything in hand," said Kusac, nodding.

"As much as I can," he said. "I've Lord Telmaar's troops under me, and if you don't mind, I could do with yours as well to help with the door-to-door searches."

"Of course, take what men you need," said Kusac.

"Thank you. Now if you will excuse me, I've work to do."
He bowed to them both and hurried off.

"Bad business this," said Telmaar as Cheelar came up
with Kusac's beer and handed it to him.

"It is, indeed. Can I get you a drink, Telmaar? You look
like you need a refill."

"Thanks, the same as you, just another beer. Need to
keep our wits about us tonight, I think."

Prime world, same day

For the afternoon nap, M'Nar had arranged for a tarpaulin
to be laid on the ground by the troop's campsite, and an
awning to be erected over it. Before the second meal, he
had the cubs each fetch their own bedrolls and place them
there. He, Jerenn, and N'Akoe did likewise.

"A nap is always good," he said to Jerenn as they shepherded the now full and drowsy kitlings there.

"You're just giving into your hedonistic side," said
N'Akoe as she settled the two young females.

"Too right," he said, mouth dropping open in a grin. "If
you can't be good to yourself, you can't be good to others."

"You know, there's a weird kind of logic in what you
say," said Jerenn as he made sure all the cubs were settled.

N'Akoe was unsuccessfully trying to get Gaylla to go
back to her sister instead of joining Shaidan in the boys'
huddle of bodies.

"Don't bother trying to separate them," said Jerenn.
"She and Shaidan have an especially close sibling bond."

"But the djanas should sleep separately," she said, finally
giving up on Gaylla.

"Not nowadays. We always allow siblings to mix freely,"
said M'Nar. "Look, Vazih has joined her brothers while you
were seeing to Gaylla."

Sure enough, the cubs were all lying curled around each other in a large homogenous pile.

"But it isn't fitting," she objected, standing up. "In my t . . . town," she hastily recovered, ". . . we kept the males and females separated."

As inconspicuously as possible, M'Nar exchanged a glance with his sword-brother. "I think you'll find our way is better when it comes to the young djanas in their first season. Having known their brothers well, they're able to make better choices."

"Perhaps you're right," she said with a sigh before heading toward the transporter. "Back shortly, I need to pick something up."

"She's a Sleeper," M'Nar said very quietly to Jerenn as they straightened out their bedrolls. "I'd swear to it."

"I think you're right," Jerenn whispered back. "It explains a lot about her attitudes to many things."

"I wonder if she trusts herself and us enough to tell us about it," said M'Nar thoughtfully as he sat down on his bedroll and gave the cubs a last look over. As he did, he noticed Jerenn staring at Gaylla as she snuggled into her blanket with her doll tightly clutched in one arm.

"Something bothering you about Gaylla?" he asked quietly.

Jerenn turned his attention back to his sword-brother. "Just something that she said last night as I put her to bed."

"That you'd make a good papa? I know she's right," M'Nar grinned. "Once I've knocked a bit more of your stuffiness out of you, you'll make a great papa."

A small smile touched Jerenn's lips. "No, I was thinking more about the other thing she said. That I was a "little broke" inside."

M'Nar scrambled across the bedding to Jerenn, then settled down behind him. "Gaylla's a full telepath, and a powerful empath," he said, reaching up to massage Jerenn's neck and shoulders. "Gods, but you are tight there!" he exclaimed, beginning to knead the taut muscles. "I think she's aware of your past as a Terminator Brother, and is picking up on the cost of your last mission, before you became gene-altered like me. I can still sense the pain it caused you, so it's no surprise Gaylla is picking up on it as well."

"I thought I had gotten over that," he murmured, beginning to relax under his friend's hands. "I'm grateful to you for all the help you've given me over that incident."

"Obviously, it hurt you very deeply at the time, and it will take time to heal completely."

"How much more?" sighed Jerenn. "It seems to be taking forever. I still get the odd nightmare about her and how she manipulated my mind."

"I'm not a psychologist," said M'Nar, "but I can tell you that relaxing with the cubs and accepting the trust and love that they give you, especially young Gaylla, will go a long way to counteracting what you went through."

Jerenn gave a low chuckle. "Gods, listen to us, a former Terminator Brother and an undercover Consortia-trained one, both with their own share of missions that they'd rather forget, now helping form the minds and behavior of six very special cubs! Who would ever have thought this was a good choice for them or us?"

"It's the best one because we know how to avoid many of the mistakes we and the young people we've been sent to observe have made. Plus, we're both instructors, and I have cubs of my own," said M'Nar. "Who better than us to teach them to value each other and their family and friends, and to protect themselves from anyone wishing them harm?"

"Now you come to mention it, I see Vartra's hand in this," said Jerenn, finally relaxing into the massage. "At least this time we can actually see the benefits of what we're doing."

CHAPTER 8

M'NAR hadn't intended to fall asleep. Like the cubs, however, a full stomach in the hot sun soon had him almost cracking his jaw with yawns.

It was their quiet chattering that brought him back to wakefulness. He sat up, rubbing the sleep from his eyes.

"Good afternoon, Brother M'Nar," said Shaidan as Gaylla, grabbing her dolly by one leg, bounded over to see Jerenn.

"You's awake!" she said happily, bouncing onto his lap. "I helps with you this afternoon."

It was pronouncement, not a question.

"Uh," said Jerenn, one arm going round Gaylla, the other reaching out to steady himself.

N'Akoe emerged from the kitchen tent with the pitcher of cold water for them. "I see that all the sleepyheads are finally awake. Bring me your drinking bowls, kitlings, and have a drink before you start work again."

The cubs scrambled up, jostling their way over to N'Akoe. Their drinking bowls filled, they sat back down on their bedrolls.

"This morning, we planted grasses by the side of the river. This afternoon we're going to do something a little different. Some of you will be digging irrigation ditches, while the others will be planting a mixture of grasses and wildflowers. All these plants will fix the soil in place, and not only that, but the wildflowers will look beautiful among the grasses. After two hours, you'll switch places. That way everyone gets a turn digging ditches," said Jerenn.

"Dinner tonight will be a lovely stew the villagers are preparing for all of us," said M'Nar. "It's got a sauce made with real cream!" He licked his lips in anticipation.

"How long till dinnertime?" asked Dhyshac.

Jerenn consulted his watch. "About five hours," he said, "but trust me, it'll go faster than you can imagine. Now, if you've finished your water, go wash your bowls and put them to dry in the kitchen, then fill up your drinking bottles from the dispenser there, and finally put your bed rolls away."

Gaylla looked up from where she was using a hoe to dig part of a new irrigation trench. "N'Akoe, you come helps Brother Jerenn and me."

"I can't, cub," she replied, putting a friendly arm round the young female's shoulder. "I'm really sorry, but Dhyshac needs my help right now. Maybe later."

Gaylla huffed gently. "I s'pose so," she said, disappointed.

"She'll help you when she can," said Shaidan. "Remember, she has to look after us all."

"But she likes us best," she said, indicating herself, her brother, and Jerenn.

Jerenn coughed, avoiding N'Akoe's embarrassed look.

Gaylla turned her brightest smile on the Sister. "You wants to help us, don't you, Sister N'Akoe?"

For a moment, it looked to Shaidan as if the Sister's eyes glazed over as she hesitated before replying.

Shaidan dug Gaylla in the ribs. *You mustn't try to make her help us. You know it's very wrong,* he sent to his sister.

I's only helping them. They likes each other but won't say so, she sent back.

As he watched, N'Akoe's eyes unglazed and she seemed to mentally shake herself.

Shaidan reached out to smooth the transition so the Sister wouldn't know what Gaylla had done.

"I'll see if I can help you in a little while," N'Akoe said. "I have to help Zsayal and Dhyshac first."

"Okays," said Gaylla, her spirits already set to rights.

Shaidan looked at his sister's mud-streaked hands and feet, then ruefully looked at himself. "We'll need another swim in the inlet before dinner," he said to Jerenn.

The Brother glanced over to where M'Nar and his two cubs were working. "I think we'll all need a good wash," he agreed. "We're cleaner than Brother M'Nar and Vazih and Shaylor, though!"

Shaidan laughed as he straightened up to stretch his tired muscles. Looking round, he could see that they had covered a pretty large patch of land with the grasses and wildflowers. "It looks really good now, compared to the dry ground that was here before," he said.

Jerenn glanced up and quickly surveyed the area. "It does. It's nice to think we're making a positive effect on the landscape."

"Yes," agreed Shaidan, breathing in deeply to catch the rich scent of the damp soil, the grasses, and the pollen from the plants.

"Nothing like the smell that comes from sun-warmed soil. It feels like Ghyakulla herself is breathing," said Jerenn, flaring his nostrils.

Shaidan's mouth opened in a surprised and delighted smile. "Our earth Goddess? Yes! That's exactly what it's like!"

"You don't get that effect so often here unless you are by the grain fields or by the river because K'oish'ik is so dry."

"What's that?" Shaidan exclaimed, pointing into the near distance at a cloud of dust.

Jerenn looked. "I think it's the village herd beasts from Ch'almuth," he said, shading his eyes with his hand. "Looks like they're headed our way. We can't have that; they'll destroy all the young seedlings we just planted. The herd needs to be turned. M'Nar!" he called out. When his sword-brother looked up, he pointed to the dust cloud which was definitely moving closer.

Standing up, M'Nar ran over. "Herd beasts, heading our way."

"Agreed. N'Akoe," Jerenn called, gesturing her over.

"Take all the cubs to the transporter where they'll be safe. Herd beasts are headed this way and we need to turn them. Send word to the village too—we could do with all the help we can get."

"I'll go," said Shaidan, hopping from one foot to the other. "I'm the fastest runner."

"All right, you run ahead, Shaidan. Go by way of the base camp to warn anyone still there to load all the valuables into the transporter."

"Gaylla, do what the Brothers and Sisters tell you to do," said Shaidan.

Gaylla, sensing the air of concern and danger, nodded her head seriously. "I go with Sister N'Akoe," she said. "We safe in transporter."

"Go now, Shaidan," said M'Nar.

Shaidan nodded, then sprinted off for the base camp.

The ground he was running through was a kind of chaparral of clumps of scrub bushes interspersed with odd patches of the coarse wild grass endemic to K'oishi'k. It was well-suited to the herd beasts from Ch'almuth, which themselves had once roamed this planet.

A stray bush, tougher than the rest, snagged Shaidan's foot, sending him tumbling head over heels. With an "Oof!" of discomfort, he picked himself up and kept running.

Finally, he reached the base camp. A couple of the Prime soldiers were doing cleanup duty.

"Herd beasts coming this way," he panted, sliding to a stop in the dry soil. "Brother Jerenn says to load all valuables into the transporter."

The two Prime troopers glanced around.

"Can't see any cattle," one of them said.

"To the northwest," said Shaidan, pointing. "There." The herd was drawing noticeably closer now.

"I see them," said the taller of the two. "Put the valuables into the transporter, you said?"

"Yes," nodded Shaidan. "Gotta go. I have to warn the village."

The cattle were running faster now, sending up denser clouds of dirt into the air. He could sense M'Nar and Jerenn already there, on the edges of the herd, forcing them to turn away from the river. The plan was to get them to run between the river and the base camp.

"They're heading too far to the west!" shouted Jerenn as he and M'Nar, both on all fours, raced around the outer edges of the stampeding herd. "They'll go right through the village!"

"I know!" M'Nar shouted back. "I'll try to get ahead of them and drive them east!"

Jerenn suddenly found himself shadowed by two more Sholans, their shapes almost lost in the fine cloud of choking dust the beasts were kicking up.

"Where d'you want us?" shouted the younger one.

"One with M'Nar on the west side, the other with me. Drive them back to us. We need them to go between the camp and the river!"

"I'll send Shamgar there and stay with you."

The herd of forty beasts had other ideas and despite the presence of two large predators—M'Nar and Shamgar—they continued to head for the village.

Shaidan's danger sense suddenly kicked in at the same time he heard Jerenn trying to warn him.

Herd heading for you, Shaidan. Beware!

Glancing to his right, he saw the cloud of dust getting closer. He could even hear the lowing of the cattle.

Panic hit him like a shower of cold water and he almost stopped dead in fear. He reached out for the first adult mind he could find—M'Nar's.

Help me! he sent, forcing a link on the other Sholan. He felt the other's shock, then the contact firmed.

Where are you? asked M'Nar

In front of the herd!

Can you see them yet?

Just. There are two males with huge horns leading them.

Keep running, sent M'Nar while Shaidan heard him thinking, *Crap, crap, crap!*

*   *   *

M'Nar was thinking furiously about how to save Shaidan. He'd had a quick glimpse of the herd through the cub's eyes, and it didn't look good at all.

I can't outrun them, came Shaidan's thought. *I don't want to die, Brother M'Nar. What can I do?*

As M'Nar ran through half a dozen scenarios in his mind, he realized only one had any chance of success.

Do you remember what your father did when he got caught in a similar situation? You're going to have to do the same. It's your only chance.

Look after Gaylla, Shaidan sent, then there was silence.

Cursing, M'Nar forced himself to run faster. He couldn't let anything happen to the cub!

The thundering of hooves drowned out all other noises, and Shaidan had to force himself to push the sound away and face the oncoming stampede.

The two leading bulls were at least ten lengths ahead of the rest of the herd. If he was going to leap up onto the back of one of them, he would need all the help he could get.

At the back of his mind, he could hear a small yammering mental voice he recognized as Jerenn's. He reached out to touch the other's mind.

Shaidan you can't do this alone. You need a transfer of my hunting skills. Take what you need from me, kitling!

What Jerenn was offering was a desperate solution for a desperate situation.

Shaidan reached, letting all Jerenn's skills flood his child's mind—the skills of a Terminator Brother, one to whom the creed of *Observe, assess, recruit, or destroy,* was far more literal to him than the bulk of the Brotherhood. They were the top assassins, given the job of terminating rogue telepaths who tried to control or kill others.

There, too, were the hunting skills that Shaidan needed. They would give him the practical physical skills he needed, but they were literally those of an adult-sized person, not a ten-year-old. It was still better than nothing.

The pounding of the hooves drew closer. Shaidan could see the great muscles flexing on the shoulders and chest of the lead beast.

Swallowing the terror that he felt, he changed direction, running toward the bull, trying to think only of Jerenn's skills. He needed to jump onto the back of the beast, then hold on for dear life as he tried to slow this mad stampede.

There was no margin for error; he only had one chance. Reaching the bull, he heard its labored breathing, saw the flaring nostrils. It scented him and moved to one side, but Shaidan was there. He passed it, then did an about turn, now running parallel to it.

Snorting, the bull again began to veer, slowing slightly. The rest of the herd was catching up to it as Shaidan began to bunch his hind muscles, getting ready to leap.

The time had come. To delay was death, to miss was death. He pushed the negative thoughts aside and leaped. Claws extended, he only managed to latch onto the side of the bull. Bounced up and down by the motion of the terrified beast, he scrabbled to get his rear claws dug as deeply as possible into the heaving flesh beneath him.

The bull snorted and screamed its terror, beginning to turn to the left, heading away from the village.

Hand over hand, Shaidan pulled himself upward painfully until he was lying along the bull's back. Its terror of Shaidan now sent it dancing along, bucking and bellowing, threatening to unseat him.

Searching the memories, he stretched forward and fastened his jaws on the bull's shoulder, biting down just enough to make it stop bucking and continue running again.

Biting the beast's left shoulder had made it change direction toward the campsite. It was running flat out now, leaving the rest of the herd following at a greater and greater distance.

His skill transfer told him he needed to get it past the village, and far enough ahead of the herd that he could apply a choke bite to its neck and bring it tumbling to the ground.

Eyes smarting from the dust, he blinked, unable to see farther than the creature's neck. He had to risk releasing his jaws, or he couldn't lift his head and see where they were.

Letting go, he began to raise his head only to feel his

right-hand grip starting to slip. Thick-skinned as the bull was, Shaidan's claws were only those of a youngling, not an adult Sholan, and they barely penetrated the thick hide.

Terrified, he flexed his claws, tears springing to his eyes as he tried to hold on even more tightly. He risked a quick glance upward, seeing the adobe village coming into view on his right. He sank his teeth into the right side of the beast's shoulder, making it swerve to the left. Counting to ten, he risked another look, this time both forward and behind him. Instincts borrowed from Jerenn told him that the time for the choke hold was getting close.

Clinging on for dear life, hand over hand, he pulled himself upward till he could reach its neck. He made the mistake of glancing down, and all he could see was the ground speeding past as the sharp hooves pounded the dry soil into dust.

He pulled back as a wave of terror washed through him. Jerenn was right. He might know what he should do, but he was only ten years old; he was too small and weak to do it.

Think, he said to himself. *There must be something that you can do!* The point of biting the beast's throat was to cut off its air supply. There had to be another way to do that. How did the bulls breathe? Only through their noses, unlike his people who could also breathe through their mouths. What if he could press its nose closed? It was easier to reach than the underside of its neck.

He edged forward again until he could grasp the wide flaring horns, first with one hand, then with both. Flexing his hind claws, he dug in as deep as he could, eliciting a bellow of pain from the bull as its whole body seemed to twitch under him.

He let go of the right horn slowly, reaching his now free hand across the bull's head, until it was touching the top of the large, wet nose.

Lunging forward, he grasped the sides of the nose in his hand and squeezed, digging in his claws for good measure.

Bellowing its anger, the bull stopped dead in its tracks, and rearing up on its front legs, kicked its back ones high in the air.

Shaidan hung on like grim death as it continued to buck and bellow, his palms becoming slick with sweat. He felt his grip on the bull's horn loosening. Suddenly, he was sailing through the air to land on the ground in front of the bull. It snorted at him, lowering its head and bellowing its rage.

Shaidan looked around frantically for the rest of the herd. Meanwhile, the bull was staring directly at him.

Around him, the herd was gradually coming to a halt, as the other bull, a young one, had taken his lead from the herd leader and stopped.

The ground under him began to shudder. He looked back to the bull, saw him snorting loudly and pawing the ground in front of him, ready to charge at any moment.

Shaidan gulped. Slowly, he got up into a four-legged stance, gauging his distance from the bull. He rocked back on his feet, gathering himself to jump at the beast's face. If he could reach the nose again . . .

As he leaped, a blur of movement from either side of him resolved itself into a black and a gray Sholan, both hurling themselves at opposite sides of the bull's flanks. At the same time, his jaws closed on its nose.

With a bellow of sheer terror, the bull rocked back on his legs, stumbling to his knees. M'Nar released his hold, and with a snarl, leaped onto the bull's back.

"Well done, youngling," he said quietly, grasping the wickedly curved horns. "Let go now. We have it under control. Not many adults could have done what you just did."

Trembling, Shaidan let go and flopped back onto his haunches.

"Best move round to the side, Shaidan," growled M'Nar. "No point in keeping you in danger."

"Y . . . yes, M'Nar," he stammered, trying to get to his feet. For some reason, his legs refused to work.

"It's just a reaction from the danger," Jerenn reassured, letting the bull go and reaching out to help him to his feet.

"You saved the village and the lives of the villagers," said M'Nar. "If you hadn't rushed him, many could've died."

"Don't do this again, Shaidan," said Jerenn, putting a

hand on his shoulder. "Before you say it, we know that you didn't get cut off on purpose, but your life really was at risk back there."

Shaidan nodded his agreement. "I have never been so scared in my life. I know now that skill transfers aren't an answer for lack of training and age. I was too little to do what needed to be done."

"Good," said Jerenn flicking an ear at M'Nar's questioning look. "Nothing beats practice, young one, just remember that. You still did a remarkable job here, but maybe it would be better if we kept this to ourselves."

"Too late," said M'Nar as the villagers, chattering and shouting, ran up to them.

"You saved our herd!" the first one to arrive called out. "And without killing the alpha bull! We can't thank you enough!"

Two males ran up with leading ropes, which they efficiently fastened around the bull's neck.

"He's our prize bull," said the leading villager, tugging on his rope to make the beast stand."We'll corral them for the rest of today while we find out what made them stampede. They're usually very docile. Something must have spooked them."

"Probably a norrta," said the first male as the bull, snorting and puffing, stood. "It's their breeding season now, and they get very territorial at this time of year. We may have to change where we can graze them or go on a norrta hunting expedition."

"Sounds like something fun to do for a day or two," observed M'Nar, jumping off the beast now he was sure the villagers had the bull firmly under control.

"Captain Kusac only just killed one when he and his team met it in the tunnels under the city. It's no ordinary hunt," warned Jerenn.

"You're likely to meet a mating pair," agreed the villager. "No one has ever killed a mating pair. Usually, we resort to setting ground charges to blow them and the nest up."

"Where's the fun in that?" asked M'Nar. "We Sholans can do it! We have several advantages over you. We're used to hunting prey, not only with projectile weapons like guns, but also our natural claws and teeth. As long as we have explosives as a backup plan, we'd be glad to accompany you on such a hunt."

"We'll let you know tomorrow," said Jerenn. "Just now we have the youngsters to see to."

"Thank you again," said the villager as he began to lead the bull away. The rest of the herd, now docile, lowing and mooing, followed slowly.

Jerenn watched them for a moment or two. Then, as he heard a thump from behind him, he swung round to find Shaidan crumpled on the ground, eyes slightly glazed and trembling. Jerenn knelt down instantly, putting a reassuring hand round the youngster's shoulders.

"M . . . my legs just gave under me, and I started trembling, Brother Jerenn," Shaidan said shakily. "What's wrong with me?" he asked, turning a frightened face up to him.

Jerenn pulled him into a close embrace. "It's all right, Shaidan. It's just a reaction from being in such a dangerous situation. We all get it, but this is the first time for you, so it feels worse."

"Everyone gets it? Even you and Brother M'Nar?"

"Even us," he nodded, stroking the cub's head, watching as the flattened ears began to rise. "There's something you got from me that will help the fear pass more quickly," he said. "Look into my mind and you'll find it."

Shaidan began to speak, at first quietly, his voice trembling almost as much as he was.

"Fear is my adversary,
It brings the death of reason,
It clouds my senses and slows my actions."

Jerenn listened as the cub whispered the words that were second nature to him.

"I will face my fear,
I will embrace it,
Absorb and conquer it."

Shaidan's voice was growing stronger with every word.

*"I will use it against itself
To strengthen my resolve
And enhance my Gifts."*

It was the Brotherhood litany to banish fear.

*"Fear is my adversary,
But it is not my enemy,
For where it once was, there is my strength!"*

Now Shaidan took a deep breath and moved back a little from Jerenn, who instantly let him go.

"Thank you, Brother Jerenn. I should have remembered the Litanies. We've all been taught them, but I've never been able to relate them to real life till now. I won't forget this one again." He searched Jerenn's face carefully. "I didn't mean to take so much from you with the transfer," he said hesitantly. "It all just came at me in a rush, and I couldn't stop it."

"It's all right, cub. I offered it all to you; you didn't so much take it from me as accept it. However, I do think we should keep this between ourselves as I'd rather no one else know that you have access to all the Brotherhood secrets!"

Shaidan nodded slowly. "All?" he asked with a faint smile. "Don't worry, I won't know what those are unless it comes up in my daily life. That's how memory transfers work. I know that much from what we were taught by Dr. K'hedduk." He shivered briefly.

"Those days are long gone, youngling," said M'Nar quietly, holding his arms open when Shaidan turned to look at him. "Never again will that person get anywhere near you."

He accepted the embrace, returning it with feeling. "I miss Papa and Mama a lot, but I am so glad I have you two," he said.

M'Nar gave him a robust squeeze of affection. "We should be getting back to the others now. I know one small gray-furred person who is going to be most worried about you!"

"Gaylla! I almost forgot about her!" he said, pulling away

from M'Nar and dropping down into a four-legged stance. "She says she knows I'm all right but wants to see me right now," he said before racing off toward the transporter.

"He's a good lad," said M'Nar. "How're you? Any headache like you usually have when a telepath touches your mind?"

"Surprisingly, I am fine. He has a very gentle and light mental touch compared with even Brother Conner."

"Only the most powerful telepaths are that sensitive. I wonder just how powerful he is."

"Given whose son he is, I'd say very, and likely then some. I don't think anyone knows yet how powerful he or the others are," said Jerenn.

"And are they a threat? You must be assessing them, even on an unconscious level."

"Mmm. I don't see them being a threat to Shola if they are brought up properly. I'm hoping they'll keep them all together when they get back home."

"I'm sure they will. It would be cruel to separate them given that they've had only each other for so long in their lives. I know that like all the other clans, the Telepath ones have communal nurseries where cubs grow up together, yet their parents can take them out for several days at a time. I'm sure our new En'Shalla clan will have the same setup," said M'Nar.

"Knowing how much Shaidan means to the Captain, I'm sure the nursery will be in his house," said Jerenn, getting to his feet. "Enough of this. We'd better get back to our charges."

"Race you there," said M'Nar, sprinting off on all fours.

M'zull, same night, Lord Nayash's apartment

It was the small hours of the morning by the time the Palace had quieted down and those not out on patrols were in their beds.

Kusac had sent Laazif to bed and had gathered in his office with his commandos, M'yikku and Cheelar, and Maalash from the village. Moments later, two more figures appeared in the room—Kaid and Banner, their Sholan forms replaced by Valtegan ones thanks to Annuur's devices. Like the rest of them, they wore the regular green army fatigues.

Kusac nodded a welcome to his sword-brother and Banner, then addressed them all. "Has everyone got a translocator?" he asked, keeping his voice low.

A quiet chorus of affirmatives greeted his question.

"Good. The only rule, no matter what happens tonight, is do not get caught. At the first sign of trouble, trigger the translocator and leave. Do not wait for anyone else, not even me. We must not be taken captive, no matter what." He looked round them all, holding their gazes until they nodded agreement. Kaid was the last to reluctantly agree.

I won't put myself in danger either, Kusac sent to him. *You have my word.*

"You'll be returned here," he continued, "apart from Kaid and Banner. They will manifest back at the mountain den for their safety. As far as anyone else is concerned, we're doing a security sweep as we return from the city. We'll enter the corridor by the side of the Inquisition offices and make our way into the temple from that rear entrance. It should all be quiet at this time of night. Guarding the main doors into the temple will be M'yikku. Cheelar will scatter leaflets at the far side of the temple, where it's darkest. If you have time, put some in the prayer books there."

Cheelar nodded briefly.

"Maalash, you and Banner watch the back doors where K'hedduk and the priests make their entrance. Banner," he threw a can of silver spray paint at him. "Spray something suitable across the doors for me. Leave the can when you're done. Kaid, you'll help me defacing the statues and the font. Any questions?"

"Do we just stand and wait for the doors to open?" asked Maalash. "Seems like a . . ."

"No, one of you will have the door open a crack and be looking out," interrupted Kusac. "We all have throat mics, so make sure you signal us that someone is coming as you shut the door, then move the hell away from it as fast as you can. If it's only one person, let them enter and take them out—render them unconscious or kill them, whichever is better at the time, then go back to watching. Remember, use knives not guns to kill. If it's a group, shut the door, warn us, and leave immediately. We cannot win a pitched battle, so we don't want one. Better we leave the job half done and get out alive and free. Are we all clear now?"

There were no questions this time.

"Right. Move out in pairs," he said, gesturing to Maalash and Banner. "You first."

Fifteen minutes later, they had all reached the relative safety of the Temple, the doors being watched by Cheelar, Banner, and Maalash. Kaid and Kusac had taken up positions by the two giant diorite statues of the Emperor that flanked the rear entrance.

They looked up at the fifteen-foot–tall statue on their left.

"Too big to climb," said Kaid quietly. "What are you planning to do with it?"

Kusac reached out and put his hand on the plinth. It reached to about shoulder level on him. "I reckon a couple of Zsadhi swords on the bases should do," he said with a faint grin, putting his other hand on the plinth and beginning to concentrate on heating the volcanic stone.

Eyes closed, he concentrated on the rock, trying to create a raised bar the rough shape of the Zsadhi's sword in the middle of the front panel. It seemed to take forever, and all the while he could feel the energy leaving him to go into the rock.

Finally, Kaid's hand closed on his shoulder. "I think you've done the hard bit," he said quietly.

Opening his eyes, Kusac let his arms fall to his sides and took a couple of steps back to see what he'd wrought. Sure enough, the shape of the sword now stood proudly from the plinth. All that remained was for him to do the details.

Slowly he passed his hands over the shape, imagining the

details of the pommel, the quillons and the grip, before passing down to the blade itself.

"That's good enough," said Kaid, his voice rough with concern. "Have you enough energy to do the other one?"

Kusac nodded tiredly and turned away from that statue. Staggering slightly, he grasped Kaid's shoulder for support. "I've missed having you around," he said quietly as he steadied himself and moved over to the second statue.

"Not much longer now if Annuur is to be believed," his sword-brother said.

"I'll believe it when I see it," muttered Kusac, bracing himself against the plinth once more.

"Take some energy from me if you need it," Kaid said. "Don't risk being too weak to escape if need be."

"I may do that," Kusac said, starting again on the second sword.

Meanwhile, M'yikku was peering down the corridor through a crack in the door, listening for any sounds of people approaching. As Cheelar joined him, the night patrol came into view and he eased the door closed.

"Night patrol," he said in reply to his brother's questioning look.

"Close it and ask Kaid to sense if they come closer. They'll see if the door is partly open." Like a ghost, Cheelar faded back into the shadows.

"Kaid . . ."

"I heard," Kaid replied through the mic. "Checking."

The silence stretched forever until they heard "All clear," through their earpiece. "You can go back to watching."

"Leaflets done," said Cheelar quietly.

"Slogan painted," said Banner. "Assisting Maalash."

"Someone's coming!" Maalash hissed suddenly. "Inquisitor, heading for the door!"

"Close it," snapped Banner, grasping the villager by the arm and pulling him back to where Kaid and Kusac were still working on the plinth.

"Leave, we've done enough!" said Kaid, pulling Kusac away from the statue. "Stop now, Kusac. Time to go."

"Almost finished," he muttered, then Kaid was shaking him.

"Stop! Obey yourself and leave!" he hissed, pressing Kusac's translocator, then his own.

Exhausted, as the door only feet away from him began to open, Kusac felt the room about him start to fade. Then he was tumbling to the floor in his office as Cheelar, M'yikku and Maalash appeared around him. As they bent to help him to his feet, Kaid appeared.

"He needs food and rest. Get him to bed and make him eat some soup. I'm sure Laazif can get something together even at this time of night. He's still up, waiting to hear you all head off to bed." Then he was gone.

"Maalash, you head to your room. M'yikku and I will see to this," said Cheelar, helping Kusac to walk to the door. "You get the food, M'yikku, I'll get the Captain to bed. I expect there to be a general outcry very soon."

"Tell me again why we're doing this if the Cabbarans have nanites that will solve all our problems," Kusac asked tiredly.

Maalash stopped and turned back to face him. "Because the Zsadhi legend must be played out again, this time for the last time," he said. "Only then can we be sure that the old empire will truly die."

K'hedduk was incandescent with rage. "My own temple! This is an insult to me personally! Where is Nayash? I told him to find this Zsadhi person and he manifestly hasn't done so! Where are the guards supposedly on duty tonight? I'll have them flogged for letting this person past them to deface my temple! Zerdish, fetch Nayash immediately!"

Zerdish signed to one of the guards to approach him and gave the order to bring Lord Nayash to the temple.

The guard returned some few minutes later without him.

"Where is he?" demanded K'hedduk, pacing up and down in front of the two massive statues as he waited for the head stonemason to arrive.

"Majesty, Lord Nayash is ill in bed," said the guard, bowing fearfully. "A sudden fever that struck when he came off duty earlier this evening, so his steward told me."

K'hedduk stopped his pacing and swung round on the hapless guard. "He's lying! He's not even in the apartment! Did you demand to see him?"

"Yes, Majesty! I saw him lying in bed, pale and sweating. I didn't get too close lest I caught what he had."

He was dismissed with an imperious sweep of K'hedduk's arm. "Where is that damned mason?" he demanded. "I want to know how the statues have been defaced. It's enough to think that a person sneaked past my guards, but that he carried a large stone melter as well is beyond comprehension!"

"I'm here, Majesty!" came the voice of the stonemason as he hurried across the temple to where the Emperor stood. He bowed low. "My apologies, Majesty, but I was asleep and had to dress before I could present myself in front of you."

"How was that done, Khoobu?" demanded K'hedduk, pointing to the raised sword-shaped mass that disfigured the highly polished surface of the stone plinth.

Khoobu stepped closer, reaching out tentatively to touch the raised surface. "Oh, my. I have no idea how this was done," he said, examining it more closely. "It looks as if the very stone has been melted. See how porous it is. That can only happen at extremes of temperatures that we cannot duplicate."

"Are you saying we don't have the technology to do this?"

"Yes, Majesty, that's what I am saying. I don't know who did this, or how, but it was not one of us." He stopped, aware of what he had said. "Oh, goodness me! Does this mean that we have people not of our world here?"

"Get out of here, and fetch your tools! I want all traces of this removed by tomorrow morning! And fetch decorators, I want those sword symbols painted over as well," hissed K'hedduk. He turned on Zerdish. "Didn't I tell you that they had left someone behind when they took that damned female? Perhaps you will search more assiduously for him now! I want every apartment, every room inside the Palace searched! I don't care who is disturbed. Do it!"

"It shall be as you command, Majesty," said Zerdish, turning away to issue orders to his men.

K'hedduk began striding toward the south entrance, making Zerdish run to catch up. "Send for Dr. Valger and his team to meet me in lab six," he said. "I want to know what, if any, progress he's made with that damned alien machine!"

The lab was dwarfed by the size of the object that sat in the middle of the floor. Huge power cables looped across the room, connected to banks of control desks and screens. These all faced inward in an octagonal arrangement with wide passageways left between them. It was in the center of this that the alien artifact squatted.

Over seven feet tall, it looked like it had grown out of the floor rather than having been manufactured. Its shape resembled some giant insect with two spindly legs for each of its six sides. Greenish black in color, all its lines curved into each other in ways that defied the eye's ability to follow. Its various parts were linked by webs of filaments that had once glowed with light and life, but now lay dark and dead.

"What d'you mean you can't get the device to work?" K'hedduk demanded of the two scientists and the engineer facing him. "You've been working on it for over two weeks now!"

"It's like nothing we've ever seen, Majesty," said Dr. Valger, leader of the group. "We've been unable to open it up and see how it works. Unless we can get it opened . . ." He shrugged, leaving his sentence unfinished.

"Have you tried to force a way into it? Have you done anything other than complain that you don't know what it is or how it works?" asked K'hedduk.

"We tried to take readings of it with our instruments, but we couldn't find anything. No power source, no activity of any kind," said the other scientist. "We can't get it to manufacture the flowing metal nanites. It's as if it is dead. Maybe because we lost part of it out by J'kirtikk."

"We did try to force our way into it, but we couldn't even scratch the surface," said the engineer. "As far as we're concerned, it's dead, Majesty, and nothing we can do will activate it."

"Then it's a giant paperweight," hissed K'hedduk. "Get it taken up topside to the outer courtyard where you can at least try to blow your way into it with small charges!"

"How can we do that? It's so heavy?"

"That's your job, not mine! My brother's scientists got it down here somehow, so you can get it out. I want it moved within two days," he snarled, storming out of the lab, leaving the three males looking hopelessly at each other.

"We could call General Shayazu and get his soldiers to haul it topside," said the engineer.

The other two nodded their agreement enthusiastically. "That's the best solution," agreed Dr. Valger. "His people were in charge of cleaning up after the attack, after all. They have the facilities to do heavy moving."

"It's on a plinth at least," said the engineer. "That should make it easier for them to move it."

Palace of Light, K'oish'ik, Zhal-Oeshi 13th (August)

"So you're going to examine the cubs today?" asked Conner as he finished his breakfast.

"I thought I would talk to them, and to the Brothers and Sister working with them," Noni replied, sipping her bowl of c'shar. "I wish they would get us some real mugs," she grumbled. "I really don't like these wide-rimmed bowls at all."

Conner laughed gently. "I'll ask for some to be sent

down for us from the *Khalossa*," he said, reaching across the table to pat her hand.

"Well, I'd better get going before the adults all head out. I know the cubs are in today with their lessons," she said, patting his hand in return and getting to her feet.

Noni made her way upstairs to the fourth floor, being passed through seamlessly by Security. She stopped, not at the nursery door, but at the open one leading into the central common room that Jerenn and M'Nar had arranged for themselves and N'Akoe.

She stood there watching the two males, scrambling about turning cushions over and looking under chairs until one of them noticed her.

"Um, Noni!" said M'Nar, standing almost to attention. "Sorry, didn't see you standing there. What can we do for you?"

"You haven't found your brush yet, have you?" she said, entering the room. "It's in the bottom of the wardrobe where you dropped it last night. Go get it, or you'll never concentrate on what I want to know," she said, gesturing to the piece of furniture that stood in the far corner of the room.

"Noni," said Jerenn. "May the sun shine upon you."

"And you, youngster. It's you I want to talk to first. Now that M'Nar's found his favorite brush, clear that sofa so I can sit down," she said, leaning on her cane as she made her way into the room.

"What can I do for you, Noni?" asked Jerenn as he watched M'Nar beginning to back out of the room in what he thought was an inconspicuous way.

"Oh, no, you don't, youngling!" said Noni, grasping him firmly by the arm. "You can go fetch us a cup of coffee. And I do mean a cup not a bowl," she added. "Ask the kitchen for a couple of their sweet pastries while you're at it."

"I don't know that . . ."

"This is me you're talking to, young M'Nar! I know you wouldn't have been here five minutes before you knew the name of every cook and chef in the Palace, and how to get into their good graces! So off you go and don't hurry back. Take about ten minutes at least."

"Yes, Noni," he said, hurrying off as soon as the older female let him go.

"You, Jerenn, can sit and talk to me," said Noni, taking a seat on the sofa and waiting expectantly for Jerenn to sit down opposite her.

"I never saw much of you when you were at Stronghold," she said when he'd settled himself. "Was there a reason for that?"

"Not really. I just never had the need to come to see you. Most of my aches and pains were settled at Stronghold or I worked through them. I was away for long periods of time," he added.

"What about that incident on your last termination? You got involved with your target and almost became a victim, didn't you? Who did you go to for help over that?"

"It was classified," he said stiffly. "I wasn't able to go to anyone outside the Brotherhood."

Noni waved her hand dismissively. "It isn't about that that I want to talk. Now you are working with potentially one of the biggest threats to Shola. Have you been given instructions to assess the cubs?"

"If I had, you know I couldn't tell you, Noni," he said.

"Then I'll ask you about your personal assessment of them. Do you see them as dangerous?"

"Dangerous? Yes, they have the potential to be a devastating weapon in the wrong hands—if anyone could make them act against their natures."

"How do you mean?"

"They were made to be a weapon for K'hedduk, now the Emperor of M'zull, but even then they had other ideas. If not for Shaidan, they would have become his creatures, but he held them together as a group and fostered independence of thought where he could. He fought his conditioning."

"With Vartra's help," Noni murmured.

"With Vartra's help," Jerenn agreed. "But he had the strength of mind to listen to Vartra and strive to be free."

"So Shaidan is their natural leader. Does he exercise his control over them?"

"No, the only one he looks to influence is Gaylla, and that only because she is so simplistic in her outlook on life."

"Simplistic, eh?"

Jerenn hesitated. "The general feeling about Gaylla is that she's a little slower than the other cubs. Something certainly affected her when she was born. Rumor has it that if General Kezule hadn't personally asked for Gaylla as a 'pet,' then K'hedduk planned to terminate her. That would have been despicable. She's perfectly able to live a long and meaningful life."

Noni heard the hint of anger in his voice as he spoke of K'hedduk and what had nearly been Gaylla's fate.

"Are they a danger to Shola?" she asked. "How do you assess their potentialities?"

"Firstly, they aren't weapons; they are cubs, and individuals. Once you get to know them, you can see they each have their own personalities, their own likes and dislikes. Every day their development becomes more and more like that of normal ten-year-old cubs." He stopped for a moment, obviously gathering his thoughts.

"Could they be used as weapons against us?" he continued. "Yes, the same way any telepathic cub could be used against us—they are no different in this than any youngling would be. Are they special? Well, they started out special because of their early training with sleep tapes as telepaths. Now, however, all they care about is the next outing to the river, or to the farm, or their next sugary treat! They are becoming more and more normalized as time goes on, and it's down to good parenting by all of us involved in their education and training."

"You speak like one too invested in their continuation to be impartial, Jerenn."

He looked Noni straight in the eyes, setting aside all the stories about her and how she could manipulate people. "I dare you to get to know them and remain impartial," he said. "They are cubs who want to be looked after and loved, not impassive, soulless little people, forged by some mad doctor to be weapons against us."

Noni smiled and nodded, sitting back in her seat. "So if I ordered you to terminate them, what would you do?"

Jerenn looked aghast at her, mouth opening in shock. "First, I wouldn't believe you because you haven't the authority to do that. Second, I would protect them with my life. They are innocents and don't deserve termination just for the circumstances surrounding their genesis."

"And going against what you have been ordered to do wouldn't bother you?"

"Once again, you don't have the right to order me to do that. I am of the En'Shalla Clan, beyond the rules of others, as are they. Neither you nor Commander Rhyaz has dominion over me or the cubs. Djana Kitra Aldatan has entrusted these cubs to me, and I will ensure they remain safe," he said firmly.

"Well, well, they have gained your loyalty," she said. "Not an easy thing to do, I am told. It seems I must meet these cubs for myself, and make my own mind up about them."

Jerenn gave her a long look. "You were testing me," he said. "You have no intention of ordering me to terminate them, have you?"

"As you said, I have no jurisdiction over you—or them. You can come back in now, M'Nar," she said, raising her voice. "I know you've been standing there listening."

M'Nar came in carrying a tray of drinks and pastries, a stubborn look on his face. "I'd protect them with my life, too," he said, putting down the tray with its three mugs between Jerenn and Noni. "They're no different from my own berrans, Noni, and I defy anyone to say otherwise!"

"Peace, M'Nar! I pose no threat to the cubs," said Noni, holding up her hand. "I had to know how you felt about them, and how deep that feeling went, that's all. Sit. Pour the coffee and tell me why you are secretly training Shaidan in the use of weapons and combat skills."

Jerenn's ears flattened as did M'Nar's, but only momentarily.

"We're teaching them all combat skills, Noni," said

M'Nar smoothly as he lifted the coffee jug to pour it into the mugs. "Brother Dzaka gave us permission to do so. After all, he was raised in the Brotherhood and was practicing the skills we're teaching the cubs at the same age they are now."

Noni waited till he put the jug down, then reached out to rap his knuckles with the head of her cane. "Don't treat me like an idiot, boy! You are teaching Shaidan special skills! Why?"

"He has a premonition of danger, Noni," sighed Jerenn. "If we didn't teach him in a controlled situation, he might sneak out and try to get someone with less morals than us to teach him what he wants to know. At least he is learning the correct way to use weapons and martial arts, along with the knowledge of when it's right to do so."

"Hmm. What's so special about Shaidan? Gaylla I can see; with her huge eyes and that smile, she would touch a stone heart. But Shaidan?"

"He's so serious, and cares so much for his little sister and the others," said M'Nar. "He's put himself in the firing line to save them many a time, whether it be to face down an adult's anger with one of them, or . . ."

". . . to push them aside and face a herd of stampeding cattle," said Noni drily. "Let's keep the knowledge of *that* escapade between us, shall we?"

Jerenn hissed in a breath, ears flattening briefly.

"Think I can't pluck information from you without you knowing it?" she asked. "It was at the front of your mind, that's how I knew. I don't go poking about in your mind without an invitation, or a damned good reason!"

Put in his place, Jerenn focused on adding creamer and sweetener to his coffee.

"Shaidan's not always serious," said M'Nar, handing a mug to Noni. "You should see him when he's just being a ten-year-old cub, playing in the pool, splashing his brothers and sisters with water. It changes his whole personality. We like to think that as well as helping him face this sense of danger with practical training, we've helped them all to just have fun."

"I can think of no one better than you to teach them

about fun," said Noni, accepting her drink and adding her
own creamer and sweetener.

"Thank you, I think," grinned M'Nar, holding the plate
of pastries out to her. They were small, bite-sized ones. "The
pastries were for an official meeting this afternoon between
the King and some of the town leaders from farther away. I
was able to persuade the cook we needed them now."

"And so we do," said Noni, resting her cane against the
sofa and taking one of the delicate pastries. "Now, tell me
about the other berrans."

Noni left the two Brothers and headed down to the library where she knew the cubs were either sitting reading
or choosing books. It had been decided to keep them fluent
in both Sholan and Valtegan, the latter having been their
first language under K'hedduk.

She was met at the door by a rather frazzled Kitra, with
Dzaka hovering just behind her.

"You're not to do anything to the cubs that my brother
wouldn't approve of," she said defensively. "They're family,
En'Shalla clan cubs, and responsible only to us and Father
Lijou."

"I know, child," said Noni, patting her on the shoulder
and sending soothing thoughts her way. "I just want to meet
them, nothing more. Come, introduce me to them one at a
time. Leave Shaidan and Gaylla for last. You're welcome to
stay, you know."

Reluctantly, she went to fetch Vazih first, telling the
young female to sit on the floor cushion beside Noni as she
wanted to talk to her.

As Noni chatted to the cubs, she kept her eyes on
Shaidan and Gaylla, watching how their demeanor echoed
how the conversations with the others went. At first nervous, then gradually gaining in confidence, the other cubs
quickly chattered away quite freely with her. In fact, she
realized, it wasn't just Gaylla and Shaidan who were aware
of the feelings of the others, they were all aware of each
other, echoing all their fears and finally their confidence.
Although definitely distinct individuals, there was a unity

about them that had them always aware of each other, at least when they were in close company like this.

At last it was Gaylla's turn.

"Would you like to ask your brother Shaidan to come over, too?" Noni said.

"Yes, I'd like Shaidan to be wif me," she said, taking her thumb out of her mouth and looking over to him. Without being asked, he joined them, sitting on the floor with his sister at Noni's feet.

"So, Gaylla, what's the name of your doll?"

"Shishu," she said, putting it on her lap and patting down the dress so she was tidy.

"Why Shishu?"

"Cos she's a Prime like Shishu," she said, "not Sholan like me 'n Shaidan."

"Why's she a Prime?"

"Doctor Zayshul gave her to me when we first left the bad man. We didn't have toys with him, only with Doctor Zayshul and the Gen'ral."

"What did you and Shishu think of that?"

Gaylla gave her an old-fashioned look. "If you mean Shishu the person, I dunno, but my Shishu is only a doll. She finks what I tell her to fink."

Noni smiled. "Of course she does. So what did you think of Doctor Zayshul?"

"She's nice, so is the Gen'ral. He says he's strict, but he isn't really, at least wif me an' Shaidan. He likes us."

"He kept me close because I got hurt badly when he rescued us," said Shaidan. "It got . . . complicated when my papa came to get us. He was allowed to take the others away but not me as the General wanted him to come back and help him."

"What did you think of that time?"

Shaidan shrugged. "Papa says I was programmed by Dr. K'hedduk and no one could undo it until Vartra helped me. And I was where my papa was, which was what he wanted."

Noni nodded. She had heard the story of how the Entity had helped to free the cub from his programming.

"What did you think of Vartra?"

"He was strange. He could come and go unlike me and Papa, but I liked him. Where is he? I haven't seen him in a long time."

"Where, indeed?" murmured Noni. "I hear you are a bit different from the other cubs, Shaidan."

Shaidan stuck his chin up and looked her squarely in the eyes. "Papa says I am part Valtegan as well as Human and Sholan, and that I should be proud of that."

"As you should be," Noni agreed with him. "When do you notice your Valtegan self?"

"I don't, really," he said. "Lieutenant M'kou has shown me how to use that part of me to go into a healing trance if I need it, but I haven't needed to do that yet."

"I'm glad to hear that," said Noni. "What about you, Gaylla? Do you have anything special you can do?"

She thought for a moment then smiled up at Noni, her whole face lighting up. "Aunty Kitra says I's good at giving hugs!"

"That's a very important thing to be able to do," agreed Noni seriously. "And what is Shaidan good at?"

Gaylla turned to look at her brother, tail flicking happily beside her. "Looking after me," she said, leaning against his side. "He looks after us all, but 'specially me."

Noni leaned forward to stroke Gaylla along the jaw, then to pat Shaidan's cheek. "Thank you for talking to me," she said. "Run along and play now, before it's time to pack up for second meal."

She watched as they scrambled to their feet, Shaidan helping his sister until she ran off on her own. He began to walk away, then turned back to look at her, a look that reminded her vividly of his father, Kusac.

"Did you find out what you wanted?" he asked. "Papa promised me we'd never be used as weapons. We just want to be kids." Then he turned and walked over to Kitra, leaning up against her.

Noni felt a sense of desolation come briefly from him before it was firmly suppressed and Shaidan began to smile up at his aunt and answer some question as Kitra looked anxiously over at her.

"Time for me to go, Kitra," she said, getting to her feet and leaning on her cane. "Conner will think I've got lost! You're all doing a grand job with these younglings, keep it up. I'm more than happy with what you've all accomplished in such a short time."

Kitra wrapped an arm around Shaidan's shoulders. "I'm glad to hear that, Noni. These cubs are just so special. They've been through a lot, but now they're home with us."

"Indeed, they are," said Noni. "Just keep doing what you're doing and I'll see you all when you're next in the temple."

As she left, Noni had much to think about. Of them all, at the two opposites were Gaylla and Shaidan. If Gaylla was slower than the other cubs, then Shaidan was far more mature. He knew exactly their worth to the Sholans, and to their enemies, and he wanted none of it. That was to the good. It meant he'd always be on his guard, not a bad thing for a cub so spectacularly as hybrid as he was.

As for bringing them back to Shola, well, that was purely a clan matter as far as she was concerned. They should be taken to their home as quietly as possible. There was no need for a big reveal to the authorities. Those that knew about the cubs could find out about them from her as she intended to keep her eye on them. Not because she distrusted them, but just to see how they matured compared to cubs born normally.

Satisfied they were no threat at this time, she made her way back down to Conner in the temple.

Palace of Light, Zhal-Oeshi 14th (August)

Shaidan stopped at the open door to Jerenn, M'Nar, and N'Akoe's common room and rapped his knuckles on the door frame. Only M'Nar was in.

He looked up from the booklet he was reading. "Hello,

Shaidan. We're not ready for you yet. We've got something new to try out on you! Jerenn's down at the indoor training room checking it out. Give us about another half an hour."

"It was you I wanted to talk to," he said. "Can I come in?"

"Sure thing. What's up?"

"I just wanted to let you know that I keep a journal," Shaidan said, walking into the room. "If anything should happen to me, I want you to know where I keep it. Maybe something I've written in there will help you find me if I go missing."

"This is an awfully serious topic for a youngster," said M'Nar, putting the booklet down on the coffee table. "What on earth is happening that could make you talk like this? Is everything all right?"

"Everything is fine right now. I just have a feeling, that's all."

"What kind of things are you putting in your journal? Just day-to-day stuff, or more?"

"All sorts of things I think are important," he said. "Right now, they don't matter, but some day they might."

"If you think your writings might be important one day, perhaps you should show them to me now," said M'Nar. "Some things are not for young people to worry about; they're for the grown-ups. I know you've had to deal with more than your share of grown-up things in your life, but now you don't have to. Now there's lots of us all happy to look out for you, take the worries away from you."

Shaidan backed off a little, concerned that he'd said too much. "It's nothing like that," he said. "I just have a feeling at the back of my mind that something isn't quite right, that's all."

"So where do you hide this journal?" asked M'Nar.

"There's a secret passage in the library," he began, then the sound of running feet disturbed him.

Gaylla burst into the room. "We's ready!" she exclaimed, rushing over to M'Nar. "You take us now to see the surprise!"

Shaidan took advantage of the distraction to leave the

room and head back to the nursery where the rest of his brothers and sisters were still cleaning up after second meal. Brother M'Nar had gotten just a little too interested in his journal. He'd told him no lies. Right now, it wouldn't make all that much sense to anyone, though he had written about his times with Unity and what Unity was. It was all anecdotal, though, as Brother Jerenn would say, since he had no way to back up what he was saying.

"Hey, Shaidan, look what I found," said Vazih, holding out an elaborately crafted bracelet.

"Can I see it?" he asked, holding out his hand.

"Here. I found it among the plants in the garden by the elevator."

He turned it over in his palm. It was made of silver-colored metal, for a wrist smaller than his own. There were points on it, four of them, only on one side. Each one had a different shape carved into it, like a letter, but in a language he didn't know. He felt a cold shiver pass down his spine. There was something about the piece of jewelry that just didn't feel right. "You should give it to Shishu," he said, passing it back to her. "It belongs to someone, and she'll be able to find the owner."

"I might just keep it," she said, trying to fit it round her wrist.

"Don't!" exclaimed Shaidan, reaching out to stop her.

The lights in the nursery dimmed, then brightened until all he could see was the glare of them washing out everything else in the room. He shut his eyes tightly, trying to turn his head away from the glare, but he couldn't. Tiredness flooded through him, making his limbs feel leaden. He fought against it, trying to stay awake, to open his eyes.

Shaidan, it's safe, came a mental voice he had grown used to. *Let the tiredness fill you, it's only for a moment and won't harm you. Rest.*

He came to, standing beside Vazih, but her hand was empty now. She blinked slowly at him.

"Let's hurry to the Brother's room," she said. "I sensed they have a surprise for us."

"Yes," said Shaidan, looking round the room. Everything

was the same, but it wasn't. Vazih had been holding something that was now gone.

Unity, what happened? he demanded. *I need to know! There were lights, bright lights!* But Unity didn't respond to him, and he knew it wouldn't.

He stood there, trying to work out what had happened as his brothers and sister left the room, going to M'Nar and Jerenn's common room. There was a familiarity about what had happened, an awful familiarity. It was something his papa had experienced as well, something that for him had not been good. He shivered and suddenly ran from the room to where he knew M'Nar still was. There, he flung himself into M'nar's arms, still shaking with fear.

N'Akoe was there now, and as M'Nar clasped him close, he knew the Brother signaled her to take the others down to the barracks training room where Jerenn was waiting.

When the room was empty, M'Nar picked him up and just held him, making soothing noises until he stopped shaking.

"What is it, Shaidan?" he asked quietly. "What has gotten you so frightened?"

"The lights," he said, burying his head deep into the Brother's shoulder. "There were bright lights trying to make me sleep and forget something."

"What? Where were the bright lights? When was this?" demanded M'Nar.

Shaidan could sense the other's concern. "Now. It happened now, in the nursery," he said. "You must have seen them. All the lights have to be connected."

"Are you sure? I saw nothing, and if the lights had suddenly gone bright like that, surely the others would have seen it, too?"

"It made them sleep, M'Nar. It made them sleep! This happened to my papa, too. I remembered it from his memories. Bad things happened to him when the lights went bright!"

"Hang on, Shaidan," he said, turning him so he was looking him in the face. "What bad things happened to you just now?"

"Vazih was showing me something, but it had vanished when the lights went back to normal," he said.

"Does Vazih remember showing you something?"

"No," he said, "but I told you, the lights made them forget, only I remember. They took it!"

"Who took what?" asked M'Nar, his voice remaining reasonable.

"The ones who made the lights bright. You have to believe me, Brother M'Nar, you have to!"

"I believe you think something happened," temporized M'Nar, "but how could something like that happen and no one but you be aware of it? I didn't even notice anything,"

"It happened! Ask ZSADHI!"

"ZSADHI, did something happen to the lights just now?"

"Yes, Brother M'Nar. Ten minutes ago the lights dimmed and flared."

M'Nar looked at Shaidan. "What caused that, ZSADHI?"

"I cannot tell you, Brother M'Nar."

"Did anyone enter the nursery during that time?" he asked slowly as Shaidan's arms tightened round his neck.

"I cannot tell you, Brother M'Nar."

"Well, it seems the lights did flare, Shaidan, but no one came into your nursery. If they had, then ZSADHI would have known."

Shaidan looked at him. "Perhaps ZSADHI is refusing to tell you," he said. "AIs can keep things to themselves."

"Not this one; it's bound and unable to do or say anything that it isn't programmed to do. I think you've certainly had a fright, and the lights did indeed flare up, but that's all. Come on, I think we should get down to the barracks now and see what Brother Jerenn's got for us, don't you?"

Slowly, he nodded. "Yes, but I know another AI that can think for itself," he said, as M'Nar put him down onto the ground and took his hand.

"You do? Was there one at the General's home when you were with him on the asteroid base?"

"No. It lives far from here, but it has nodes here that I can access. It talks to me."

"It does?" said M'Nar as they walked down the corridor to the elevator. "Does it have a name?"

"Unity. It's told me lots of things about the Cabbarans and the U'Churians."

"Are these the things you write about in your journal?"

"Yes, stuff like that, and other things."

"You said you keep your journal in a secret passage."

"Yes. Not the one in the banquet hall. The one I use is in the library. It leads down to the first floor. I used it to go outside when I wasn't supposed to," he said with a guilty look on his face.

"How do you open it?" M'Nar asked as he pressed the call button for the elevator.

"You press the carvings of one of the giant dragonlike creatures," said Shaidan. "What is the surprise Jerenn has for us?"

"You sure you want to know? Wouldn't you rather wait until we get there and he can tell you?"

"No, because the others will be there already and they'll know before me."

"It's special reactive armor made for you by the Touibans. When used with their special training guns, if you get hit, your armor lights up in the area where you were hit and you can't move that body part, like an arm or a leg. If you get hit by a kill shot, then your armor freezes you and you fall over and can't move at all. The adult version also hurts if you get hit. The idea is it teaches you how to avoid getting hit in a fight and how to use your guns safely. For you, it will be more of a game than anything right now, but it will give you the basics of good weapons control."

"Ooh, that sounds like fun," said Shaidan, cheering up. "Let's hurry and catch up to the others."

Ghioass, same day

Annuur handed the TeLaxaudin bracelet to Azshuss. "How long this has been there is not known," he said. "Lucky it was I monitoring the cub and saw what had been found."

"Whose arsenal is this from? Why it there?"

"Why ask me? I only know it dangerous! Cubs could have triggered it and died, had to act. Hunter cub kept awareness. Problematic like father," he sighed. "Hope none believe him."

"I see to safe disposal of bracelet. Thanks to you for fast action," said Azshuss. "Dropped during the evacuation when K'hedduk was here is likely."

Prime world, later the same afternoon

"So what you're telling me is that the lights did flare up in the nursery," said Jerenn.

"Yes, ZSADHI confirmed it. But he said he couldn't confirm that anyone else had entered the nursery during that time."

"Couldn't, or wouldn't because of its programming," said Jerenn. "Is there any way we can check this out? I know it sounds far-fetched, but from what you said, Shaidan was very clearly afraid and has in his memories something of a similar nature happening to his father."

"ZSADHI, when the lights flared in the nursery, did anyone else enter that room?" asked M'Nar.

"You already asked me that, Brother M'Nar. I told you then that I couldn't answer that question."

"Are you saying you couldn't answer me, or are you unable to do so because of your programming?" persisted M'Nar.

"If I was unable to answer you because of my programming, I would be unable to tell you that." There was a note of censure in the electronic voice.

"Have the lights flared up like this before?"

"From time to time, the lights do flare," agreed ZSADHI.

"What is the reason for these flares?" asked Jerenn.

"Fluctuations in the levels of power to the lighting relays."

"Is there ever an outside reason for this to happen?"

"I couldn't say, Brother Jerenn. It is not my function to monitor power to the lighting units. My function is to handle internal security and to answer the needs of the people living within the Palace of Light."

"Not exactly helpful, is it? Who else would know about the lights flaring and people forgetting things? All the people who were working with the Captain are away on this mission on M'zull with him."

"Not all," said Jerenn. "Jurrel is here."

"Jurrel wasn't with him for most of his time here. There are two people who were, though. Doctor Zayshul and General Kezule," said M'Nar.

"I am not going to talk to the General about this," said Jerenn firmly. "He'd likely want our hides as floor coverings for even broaching a topic the rawest recruit would dismiss as nonsense!"

"The Doctor, then. She's more approachable. You're missing something important here, Jerenn. It not only happened to the cubs and everyone on this floor, it also happened while I was here in our rooms!"

"You have a point," said Jerenn. "What do we say to her? You don't just sashay up to someone and ask if they saw bright lights and found themselves having forgotten something! If they forgot it, they probably forgot they forgot . . . if you see what I mean."

"We say Shaidan had a nightmare and ask if she's ever come across something like this," said M'Nar, getting up. "Let's go now."

CHAPTER 9

RELUCTANTLY trailing after him, Jerenn followed M'Nar to the security checkpoint outside the hospital.

"We'd like to talk to Doctor Zayshul," his sword-brother said to the guard on duty. "Please say it's Brother M'Nar and Brother Jerenn, and that we work with the Sholan cubs."

The guard looked them up and down, then nodded to his seated colleague. "Tell the Doctor she has two visitors from the nursery," he said.

"That's not what I said," M'Nar muttered to no one in particular.

Minutes later, Doctor Zayshul came bustling up to them. "Good afternoon, Brothers. How can I help you? Nothing is wrong with the cubs, I hope?"

"The cubs are fine, Doctor Zayshul," said M'Nar, exuding a confidence he didn't actually feel. "We, Brother Jerenn and I—were wondering if we could have a private word with you."

A puzzled look crossed her face, but then she nodded and gestured to the room opposite. "Certainly. Let's use the lounge. It should be empty at this time of day."

The lounge was a pleasant room, with wide windows in the west wall that overlooked the barracks exercise yard.

Doctor Zayshul took one of the easy chairs near the door and gestured to two opposite her. "Please, be seated. Can I get you a maush or a coffee?"

"No, thank you, Doctor. We wanted to ask you what seems like an unusual question, if we may."

"By all means," she replied, looking intrigued.

"When Captain Aldatan was still here in the Palace, did you and he ever experience flickering lights and a memory loss?" asked M'Nar.

Neither of them were prepared for her reaction. The color drained from her face, leaving her features a pallid, almost deathly pale green.

"Why do you ask?" she demanded in a faint voice. "Has it happened again? Please tell me that it hasn't."

M'Nar glanced briefly at Jerenn. "I'm sorry, Doctor. We didn't mean to stir up bad memories," he said quietly. "Yes. It happened this afternoon to two of the cubs—Vazih and Shaidan, but only Shaidan was aware of it happening."

"What happened? What does he remember?" she asked leaning forward. "His father was aware of it happening at times. They are so alike."

"Shaidan says Vazih found something that she was showing to him and then the lights flared and the item was gone. ZSADHI sensed nothing. It says no one else entered the nursery during this time."

Doctor Zayshul got to her feet and began to pace, wringing her hands in distress. "We never thought to ask ZSADHI if it sensed anything," she admitted, "but I would believe Shaidan. If he tells you that something was taken, then it was."

"What do you know about the lights flickering, Doctor?" asked Jerenn. "Can you tell us anything about it?"

"Only that it happened frequently here in the Palace at one time." She stopped, holding onto the back of the easy chair. "Captain Aldatan—Kusac—believed it had something to do with the TeLaxaudin and the Cabbarans. According to Kaid, it happened to them when they were on the *Kz'adul,* and when it happened to us, there were TeLaxaudin in the Palace."

"As there are now," said Jerenn thoughtfully.

"Please let us not be returning to those times," she moaned, clutching the back of the chair so tightly her knuckles showed white. "I couldn't remember it happening, but Kusac, he wrote it down, hid it so he could remember what he'd been made to forget. He never knew when it would hit us, when we would have our memories of events altered."

"It sounds to me like this was a one of a kind happening, Doctor," said M'Nar reassuringly. "I think Vazih did find something, something left behind by the TeLaxaudin. Maybe they dropped it during their mass eviction when K'hedduk was in charge of the planet. It was overlooked until now. If it was something dangerous, then they would act quickly to remove it for the cubs safety."

"It also means they are still watching us," said Jerenn quietly, getting a dark look from M'Nar as the Doctor moaned and sat down in her chair again.

"What are the TeLaxaudin working on?" asked Jerenn. "They're in the labs over on the north side, aren't they?"

"That's classified," she said, regaining some of her color. "Let's just say it has to do with Prime fertility. Do you really think it is a one of a kind incident?" she asked hopefully.

"I really do," said M'Nar, getting to his feet. Jerenn following his lead. "We just wanted to see if what Shaidan thought had happened, had indeed happened."

Jerenn held out his hand to the Doctor. "Thank you for sparing us some of your time, Doctor. We're sure there is no further threat to the Palace security. ZSADHI itself perceives none."

Doctor Zayshul shook his hand. "You will keep me informed, won't you?" she asked anxiously.

"We give you our word," said M'Nar as they took their leave.

Once back in their own room, M'Nar shut the door. "You realize we can't report this to Brother Dzaka, don't you? How can we tell him that nobody used a flashing light in the dormitory to wipe Shaidan's and Vazih's memories of her finding something, a something that this nobody also took from her. ZSADHI has no records of anyone entering the nursery during that time, and Shaidan has no one to confirm his version of events."

"We have Doctor Zayshul to confirm that similar losses

of memory connected to flashing lights affected her and Captain Kusac," said Jerenn.

"And I have the feeling she'd rather not be called upon to confirm that."

"So what do you suggest we do?" asked Jerenn.

"Look into it more closely, of course."

"How? No one who experienced it in the past except the Doctor was here when it happened. Do you suggest we go ask the TeLaxaudin if they have ever used flashing lights to rearrange folks' memories?" asked Jerenn, a trifle sarcastically.

M'Nar shook his head. "Nope. Those guys really give me the creeps." He shrugged. "I don't think there is anything we can do except be on our guard for any similar happenings around us. It really comes down to do we believe that this happened to Shaidan or not? I believed it did, even before we heard what the good Doctor had to say. Call it a parent's extra sense if you like. Besides, what could Shaidan possibly gain from lying to us about this?"

"Nothing," said Jerenn with a sigh. "I have to agree with you that in light of what Doctor Zayshul said, it seems Shaidan is telling us the truth."

"ZSADHI, from now on, you will let me know if the lights flare unexpectedly around us or the cubs," said M'Nar. "And if the lights do flare, you will watch for any intruders in the same area. Do you understand?"

"I understand, Brother M'Nar, and will do my best to follow your instructions."

"Good," said M'Nar. He had considered telling Jerenn what Shaidan had said about this other AI called Unity, but he was keeping his own counsel on that for now. He knew instinctively if he told Jerenn, Shaidan would know and would consider it a betrayal of trust. For whatever reason, he'd chosen to take him into his confidence, and M'Nar intended to keep that trust until Shaidan himself chose to share it with others.

Ghioass, Zhal-Oeshi 15th (August)

Giyarishis gathered his data crystals and prepared himself to use the translocator. It was time he presented his reports not only on the Hunter cub, but on the discovery of the morphing device that had enabled the Isolationists to assume the likeness of Kuvaa and to fool him into taking false orders from their agent instead of the real ones from his real handler.

Some of this information wouldn't be new to Kuvaa, but some of the background information he had acquired was, and it was this he didn't trust anyone but himself to deliver. He dialed in the location, then pressed the translocator button. As the world around him began to fade, and his destination began to solidify, he realized he was not where he expected to be. He scrabbled at his side for the translocator, but his hand was firmly grasped by Zaimiss.

"Here we need you, not in Reformist offices," said the other TeLaxaudin as the hoofed hands of Sivaar and Tinzaa grasped hold of his arms and removed his translocator.

"Information you have and we are needing it," said Zaimiss. "Strip him of his arsenal, Shumass," he ordered a fellow TeLaxaudin. "He will not be needing it in our interrogation room."

Efficiently, Shumass and the two Cabbarans removed his rings, bracelets, and belt.

"We not be forgetting this brooch," said Tinzaa, plucking the ornament free. "Tyakar, you and Naisha take him for interrogation."

"As you order, Master Tinzaa," saluted the U'Churian guard before he and his colleague dragged off the unfortunate TeLaxaudin between them.

Zaimiss was standing watching the colors of sunset spread across the mountains that surrounded this safe house of theirs when Naisha entered.

"Sunrise and sunset are loveliest times of day, Naisha," he said. "Sky so alive with color, and possibilities. Have you news for me?" He turned, his draperies, echoing the sunset, swirling round his spindly bronze legs.

"Yes, Master Zaimiss. The encryption on the files was rudimentary as you suspected. Tyakar's interrogation of him only confirmed what Shumass' decryption gave us. The other factions are aware of how we Isolationists were able to duplicate Kuvaa to mislead Giyarishis himself. They have indeed had a protocol installed in Unity preventing us, or anyone, from using that subterfuge again."

"That was as we suspected. What else did you discover that was so important that Giyarishis didn't trust Unity to deliver it to his people?"

"He has been watching the Hunter cub called Shaidan. It seems he can disappear from the surveillance equipment that Giyarishis was using. That made it important that both the Reformists and the Moderates be informed."

"The Hunter cub is a small nexus in his own right," murmured Zaimiss. "How can he hide from our surveillance equipment? Should be impossible! What of our projection of the potentialities? Is he absent from them because he wishes, or because he just isn't involved?"

"I couldn't say, Master Zaimiss," said Naisha.

"Of course, you couldn't," snapped the other. "Go, find out the answer to my question from Giyarishis—does the Hunter cub conceal himself from the potentialities as well as the surveillance program?"

"Do as Skepp Lord Zaimiss says," said Sivaar.

"As you wish, Master Sivaar." Naisha bowed and left.

Naisha had no stomach for interrogation like Tyakar had. He seemed to relish eking out every last secret from their unfortunate captives. Thankfully, they rarely had any. This one, Giyarishis, like all TeLaxaudin, had a habit of spilling their secrets if you looked sternly at them. Fragile and spindly beings, it took very little "persuasion" to get them to reveal all their secrets. It was why they relied on them, the U'Churians, to be their protectors and the muscle for any task that needed strength.

He pushed open the door into the interrogation room. Tyakar had obviously been busy while he'd been giving the report to Zaimiss as Giyarishis was sporting several deep bruises, one on his oval face, just under one of his huge multifaceted eyes, and others on his arms where they lay strapped down to the chair.

"Master Zaimiss wants to know if the Hunter cub can choose to remain unseen in the potentialities," he said brusquely from the doorway.

"Our guest doesn't know," said Tyakar regretfully, stepping back from their captive who was moaning softly. "Nothing I've done has been able to give me any other answer."

"You go tell him," said Naisha, coming into the room and letting the door close behind him. "I'll see to transferring our guest to his cell."

"I should refuse," said Tyakar. "You're too soft on them, but there's nothing more to be had from this one, so you might as well do the transfer." He laughed and gave the chair a kick that sent vibrations shaking through Giyarishis who moaned more loudly.

Naisha held the door open for his colleague and, when he was gone, went over to the chair and began to release the trembling TeLaxaudin.

"Please, no more pain." Giyarishis moaned as he was helped to his feet. "I have said all I know."

"No more pain," agreed Naisha, leading him toward the door. "I'm taking you to your cell now. It isn't much, but it has a bed and blankets. Just try to relax. They should feed you in a few hours."

"Why you do this? You not like the other one," asked Giyarishis as they walked slowly down the corridor to the room they were using as a cell.

"I go where the work is," he said. "The Isolationists hold our family's contract, so we all work for them as soon as we're old enough to be trained. You know that; you likely have your own indentured families."

"My family has, but I work on K'oish'ik, the Prime world, and we have no U'Churian servants there. We cannot give our relationship to you away. It would make you wonder about those not on Ghioass."

Naisha stopped dead. "There are more of our kind, ones who don't live on this world?"

"Shh!" said Giyarishis, stumbling. "Maybe they watching us! This world not yours, you have your own world. Many, many years ago, some of you brought here to live and serve us."

"How long ago?" demanded Naisha, starting to walk again.

"So long your people think this is their home. It isn't, is the TeLaxaudin home world."

"But the Cabbarans live here, too!"

"They live here because the Camarilla meets here. You must have heard of it?"

"I have, but didn't think much of it since it doesn't concern us."

"It does—oh, it does—but you not know how."

Stopping at a closed door, Naisha opened it, drawing the small alien into the room with its single bed, suitable sanitary facilities, and washbasin with a wide-mouthed cup.

"Here," he said, reaching into his pocket for a small vial which he handed to Giyarishis. "Some of that oil you use for your wounds. Hide it. Don't let them know I gave you it."

"Thank you for your kindness," the TeLaxaudin said tiredly, staggering over to sit on the narrow bed. "You can always go to the Moderates or Reformists and ask for sanctuary with them."

"My whole family would suffer for my actions if I did that," Naisha said quietly. "I have no choice but to stay with what I know."

Giyarishis' eyes swirled as he focused on the young U'Churian. "But now you know so much more, don't you?" he said, equally quietly.

Phratry leader Kuvaa, said Unity. *Agent Giyarishis left the Prime world to come here and did not arrive. I suspect he has been intercepted by your rivals, the Isolationists.*

"What? Giyarishis is missing? For how long?" demanded Kuvaa, her nimble front hooves flying over the keyboard that was ancillary to Unity's controls as she attempted to raise her colleagues in the Reformist party.

At least thirty minutes now. You should know they are watching the Hunter cub.

Thirty minutes in what was an instantaneous form of travel? Something was very wrong. As for the Hunter cub . . . "Leave him to me," she said. Finally, Azwokkus, leader of her party, responded.

"Urgent news," she said, accessing their pseudo-mental link and instantly apprising him of the situation.

Seconds later, Unity warned her that Azwokkus was incoming to her location at its primary access room.

"Privacy protocol, Unity," she ordered before the other could speak.

Privacy initiated, Phratry Leader.

"When was Unity warning you?" demanded Azwokkus.

"Has only just given me the news," she said.

"Is unconscionable. Lockdown protocol for such an occurrence, isn't there? Implement it now, we should."

"Would alert them to our plans and knowledge of theirs. Better we only retaliate in kind. Planning we are to imprison those guilty of manipulating the Hunters and their allies. All those aiding the renegade sand-dweller K'hedduk are our legitimate targets," she said.

Azwokkus sighed. "Tempting it is to act once and for all right now. As you say, need is to be circumspect. Kouansishus is in Palace, as is Ayziss. I see Kouansishus as greater threat. Unity, send to Phratry leader Shvosi, and Agent Annuur. Have Shvosi report instantly to Annuur, then go to sand-dweller Palace and arrest Kouansishus. Use drugs to subdue him. Transport him to safe house in Tharash and imprison him in basement room."

It shall be done as you command, Skepp Lord Azwokkus.

Annuur's home, Ghioass

"About time," muttered Annuur, rifling through his kit bag till he found the tranquilizer gun he was looking for. "Tirak, come with us, and take this," he said, thrusting the gun and a pack of five ampules at him. "Giyarishis been abducted by Isolationists. We now going to take one of theirs from Prime Palace labs, without alerting anyone else."

Tirak raised an eye ridge at him as he checked the gun's action and loaded up the two chambers with ampules. "And how we going to do that? A party of two Cabbarans and a U'Churian when there are none of our species in the Palace?"

"Carefully and quietly," said Annuur, picking up a second tranquilizer gun and ammo and going through the same routine. "I know the labs in Palace, so we can go direct to his. We arrive, I shoot him. In an ideal world he falls over, you pick him up, and we leave. If this not happen, you also there to handle any resistance to us. Hand me your translocators. I synch them to mine so that we arrive and leave simultaneously. Any questions?"

"Yes, why I here?" demanded Shvosi. "I not needed for this. Better I go to the safe house and get room ready for prisoner."

Annuur looked Shvosi up and down, then nodded. "We two enough to handle Kouansishus. Go, make room ready. Plenty drinking water there, he will need it when wakens. We transport him direct to basement."

Relieved, Shvosi winked out of the room to rematerialize in the safe house many miles away.

"What if there are others in the room?" asked Tirak.

"Shoot them, then concentrate on target. Drug works well on all our species. Side effect is memory loss of about an hour so they forget what happened. Better just us going," said Annuur, handing Tirak back his translocator. "Shvosi not military like us, not fighter. You ready?"

"Ready," Tirak confirmed, loosening his blaster in his holster, just in case.

With a suddenness that he still wasn't used to, Tirak materialized in the lab on K'oish'ik, the Prime world. There were two figures already there, both turning slowly to look at them.

Without waiting for instruction, Tirak said, "Right," and immediately shot the one on his right. Annuur took the one on the left and both went tumbling down at almost the same time.

"Secure the door," snapped Annuur, putting his gun away and dropping down to all fours.

Tirak ran for the door, making sure it was shut as Annuur scampered over to the two fallen TeLaxaudin.

"That one is Ayziss." He pointed to the tumbled pile of green draperies. "This Kouansishus," he said, indicating the one in the blue draperies lying with his limbs bent like some discarded child's toy. "Pick him up and we leave now. If he wakes, render him unconscious. Must not use his weapons."

"Aye," said Tirak, heading back to the two fallen aliens and picking up the one Annuur indicated.

Kouansishus weighed hardly anything; it was like picking up a bundle of twigs with more awkward angular parts than actual weight. "Ready, but I can't see any weapons."

"Weapons are his jewelry," said Annuur. "TeLaxaudin are techs, miniaturized weapons they have in rings and bracelets. Just keep him unconscious."

The room around them winked out to be replaced with a brightly lit corridor that from the lack of any windows and natural lighting, was obviously underground.

"In here," said Shvosi, standing in an open doorway.

Tirak carried his burden into the room, going over to the basic cot bed and placing him down on it. He straightened the limbs, then looked over to Annuur for further orders.

"Wait with us, trank gun ready," said Annuur. "Shoot him again if he wakes, or we all be dead. Have to remove his arsenal now. Shvosi, you help. Here," he said, pulling a small sack out of one of his belt pouches and handing it to her while Tirak moved so he had a clear shot at the supine figure.

They worked quickly and efficiently and within a few minutes had stripped Kouansishus of everything but his blue draperies.

"Leave now," said Annuur. "He should sleep for an hour, then waken."

They filed out of the cell, Shvosi locking the door behind them.

"Tirak, you remain here for now," said Annuur. "Guard the cell till Azwokkus sets up security. I talk to him now about it. Will get his homekeeper to bring you food and drink while you wait."

"Chair in here," said Shvosi, trotting into an adjacent room to start dragging a chair out for him.

Tirak went to her aid. "I'll get it," he said, picking it up and carrying it out into the hallway. "You aren't exactly designed to go carrying chairs."

Annuur laughed and rose up on his hind legs to pat him on the lower chest. "That, friend Tirak, is why we are Family," he said. "You do the jobs we cannot."

Ghioass, Camarilla chamber, later that day

Azwokkus sat on his cushions in the Reformist area of the Camarilla's main hall. It was still daylight and the windows were tinted to protect those inside from the glare of the sun. He sat quietly, watching the literal hum of activity from among those in the Isolationists' camp.

"It will be amusing, will it not, to see if they say anything," said Aizshuss.

"I think they will not be so bold," murmured Azwokkus as Kuvaa came trotting over to take her place among them.

"All has been arranged as you wished," she said quietly, making herself comfortable on her sloping padded seat. "Ayziss was with Kouansishus when we took him. He had to be knocked out. Likely he be conscious now and has returned to Ghioass."

"So we start winnowing out the bad," said Azwokkus. "When the Hunter comes, must be ready to answer to him."

"Do you think our answer be good enough?" asked Kuvaa.

"It better be," said Aizshuss, eyes swirling as he looked into the distance to better see Shvosi and Annuur approaching. He glanced from them toward the podium and the huge screen that displayed the current potentialities.

"Something is happening," he said abruptly. "Look at potentialities—new nexus occurring. Who Speaker today?" He looked round, seeing Needaar, the Cabbaran Elder, moving forward to take the podium as one of the circle of U'Churian guards ringing the chamber brought forward a special padded seat for her.

"Silence," said Needaar, once she had arranged herself facing the hall, her voice ringing out both in her native language, and translated into the humming and clicking tones of the TeLaxaudin. "A new nexus we have suddenly, unlike any other. Must examine the potentialities, see what occurs because of this. Questions I take," she said.

Shumass, a TeLaxaudin of the Isolationist party, raised his arm. When he received permission to speak, he asked, "On which world is this?"

Needaar peered at the screen, adjusting it with the controls at the podium so the small roiling mass of color that was the new nexus was centralized in the view. "Difficult to tell. Could be on either of sand-dweller worlds, M'zull or K'oish'ik," she said. "Nkuno, your question."

"The identity of the nexus, can we tell it?" the Cabbaran Elder in the Reformists asked.

"Not at this time," she replied. "Elder Khassis."

The TeLaxaudin Elder got to her feet. "Can we make educated guess? Or at least know race of new nexus?"

"Welcome you are to come and examine potentialities," said Needaar, "but from what showing here, I cannot tell more than there is new player in this volatile situation."

"More information we need," demanded Shumass, standing up, spindly arms waving in emphasis. "Someone should go to observe!"

"Speaking out of turn are you, Shumass!" said Needaar. "You, an Isolationist, want to interfere? Who do you suggest we send to planet full of sand-dwellers? None of our races do they know, apart from their Emperor! As always, we wait for potentialities to become more clear, then we can act."

"Waiting is for . . ."

"Remove the member," said Needaar loudly, drowning out the rest of what Shumass had to say as she gestured to the nearest U'Churian guards. "Warned before you have been about outbursts! Not to be admitted until apologies can he offer!"

Htomshu, the Elder in the Moderate party lifted her arm, waiting patiently to be noticed. Needaar nodded in her direction as the central air strove to wipe the hall of the outraged scents that Shumass was emitting as he was unceremoniously taken out.

"Can examination of the potentialities be had?" she asked, resting back down on her cushions.

"Certainly, Elder Htomshu. Can come up here and look now, or in own quarters examine them on a replica of this screen."

"Seeing now would be preferable," said Htomshu as she pushed herself up from her nest of cushions.

As the Elder made her way up to the podium, Zaimiss, leader of the Isolationist party entered the hall, his hand raised as his blue-and-purple draperies swirled gently around his spindly legs.

"Leader Zaimiss, you may speak," said Needaar, pointing to him.

"I wish to examine potentialities, too. Not for one party this should be but all."

"As you say. Leader Azwokkus, would you be wanting to come up, too?"

"Most assuredly. Intrigued we are as to new player in midst of turmoil already happening there," said Azwokkus as he got to his feet and began to approach the podium.

Before any of the three leaders reached the podium and the huge screen, Needaar called on Unity.

"Unity, raise protective screen."

"What protective screen is this?" demanded Zaimiss as he stepped up to the podium. "Why I not hear of it before now?"

Screen raised, Speaker Elder Needaar, said Unity as a faint glow seemed to suddenly place itself between the screen and the rest of the room.

"You hearing now," said Needaar. "Screen ordered by Unity's security. It prevent any interference with potentialities while we wait for resolution on M'zull to play out as per will of Camarilla."

"I hear of it only now, too," said Htomshu, "but I applaud foresight of member who ordered this."

Kuvaa raised herself on her forelimbs before sitting back on her haunches and stepping off her chair. "I, security agent for Unity, ordered this. Vital no one interfere with potentialities at this time. When crisis over, protective screen will be removed so changes to potentialities can be made."

"I object!" said Zaimiss. "Who you to decide when potentialities can be altered?"

"I am will of Camarilla, Security for Unity. Camarilla voted on outcome on M'zull. Now, only days away from resolution, no one can be allowed to interfere. I see Camarilla's will be done," she said, bowing her head to the assembly.

"Decision taken with quorum of Elders," said Needaar. "Has precedence, happened in past when waiting for Camarilla decision to play out. Matter is now closed. If you wish to examine screen and potentialities, Elder Leader Htomshu, Leader Zaimiss, and Leader Azwokkus, please step forward and do so. If not, return to seats."

All three leaders stepped up to the screen and peered carefully at the swirling nexus of colors.

"It's growing," said Azwokkus, tapping the protective screen. "Not fast, but it is growing."

"Wasn't there a secondary nexus before today?" asked Htomshu. "Smaller than this one?"

"Kuvaa, you know this better than the rest of us," said Needaar. "Come to podium."

Kuvaa made her way along the plant-lined path up to the podium, her small hooves tapping out the rhythm of her steps. Once there, she sat down on her haunches by the screen.

"Beginnings of this one I think it was," she said. "Difficult to tell as not always there. Came and went."

"Surely that is impossible," said Htomshu.

"Unlikely, not impossible," corrected Kuvaa. "Yet it happened. Potentiality building in nexus person, then dissipates as they take no action. Builds again till we have situation like this."

"How we know this is same one?" demanded Zaimiss.

"We don't," said Kuvaa. "This is all potentialities, what most likely to happen, not what will, or must happen. You know we deal not in probabilities, but in possibilities of the future."

Needaar nodded. "Kuvaa speaks the truth. We all know we look at possibilities of how future will unfold, and adjust it to get best possible outcome. Nothing, even what we arrange, is definitive, only prospective."

"Then all we can do is monitor the situation," said Htomshu, turning to walk back to her seat.

"This is so," agreed Needaar. "If there is any further change to this or the main nexus, then you will all be notified and we will convene again here."

"I expect to be informed immediately," stated Zaimiss, exuding the scent of imperiousness.

"Then best you set one of your people to keep watch on the potentialities!" snapped back Azwokkus. "Phratry Leader Kuvaa has much to do, more than just sitting watching screens for us!"

"Phratry Leader Kuvaa will report what she sees when she has time to do so among her other duties. This meeting convened by her contacting me with changes in nexus. I remain Speaker for the next several weeks should you need to call for a meeting to be convened. Any other business to be discussed?" She looked round the hall, but despite some low muttering from the Isolationist enclave there was no one claiming her attention. "Then meeting is closed," she said.

M'zull Palace, same day

"I'm sick of pretending to be ill," Kusac hissed, pacing back and forth in his bedroom. "Enough is enough! I can't even go to see Carrie and Kaid in the mountains in case someone comes from K'hedduk to inquire about my health! Today I am well, even if it means I am at risk again. Has Rezac closed down his mission as Lord Lorishuk? Is he back at the mountain?"

"You know he is, Captain," said Cheelar soothingly. "He's ready to come here with Noolgoi and Noi'kkah as soon as you are ready to discuss the details of the next raids."

"Besides, you were ill," said M'yikku. "You did have a fever."

"Only for one day! I just overdid it on the last mission. I need to get out and see what has happened in my absence from the Court."

"We have kept you posted," said Cheelar. "The main thing that's happened is that K'hedduk has had that device dragged up out from the labs to the main courtyard above ground."

"I want to know why he did that."

"Best I could find out is so he can destroy it," said M'yikku.

"We can't let him do that! We need it to accept the Ready signal from the nanites, then to switch them on!"

"How robust is it?" asked Cheelar.

"Pretty strong. According to Annuur, this is a machine that got lost thousands of years ago in hyperspace. It was finally found and given to the M'zullians to help their war effort," said Kusac.

Cheelar grinned. "Then hopefully it can't be blown up and the TeLaxaudin can come get their missing matter transformer back. Or the Touibans can claim it as war plunder. I bet they are itching to get their hands on it."

"That's a certainty," nodded M'yikku.

"I need to try and persuade K'hedduk not to blow it up," said Kusac. "You're missing the point here — any damage to it and the Cabbarans' plan goes up in smoke with the matter transformer!"

There was silence. "How do we do that?" asked a chastened Cheelar quietly.

"I have no idea right now because I've been stuck in this room for the last two days! Now let's get out of here and see what we can find out," said Kusac, opening his bedroom door and stepping out into the hallway.

"Can you at least stop for breakfast first?" asked M'yikku, hurrying after him.

"Yes! Maalash, tell Laazif we want breakfast served in the dining room now," he said, heading left at the junction down to the dining room and the main door.

As they were eating, a message came in from the Emperor, demanding his presence. "Time I reported in to him," said Kusac. "Tell the messenger I'll be there in ten minutes."

Laazif nodded and withdrew to deliver the message.

Kusac pushed his chair back and checked to make sure he was presentable. As they headed out of the dining room, Cheelar grabbed Kusac's cap along with his own and handed it to him.

"Thanks," said Kusac as they swept down the corridor then out into the main passageway for the Palace.

"Well, at last you are back to duty," said K'hedduk, his tone irritable. "I expected you to be up and about before this!"

"Majesty, I apologize for my illness, but it was unavoidable. I am fit and well again, and at your service." He bowed deeply, tucking his cap under one arm.

"You know this Zsadhi struck my temple, don't you?"

"Yes, Majesty. My aides informed me of that once I was well enough. May I see what he did?"

"The damage has been reversed, and there is nothing left to see now," said K'hedduk harshly. "More than ever, I'm sure it isn't one person. It must be a group of people."

"I'm sure you're correct, Majesty. There's been just too much damage on each raid for one person to achieve in such a short time."

"It's also a question of how the damage is being done," said K'hedduk, getting up and resting his hands on his desk. He glanced at Zerdish, standing behind and to the side of him. "If I was a superstitious person, like the vast majority of M'zullian workers and soldiers, I would suspect that there were supernatural powers at work here. Even we cannot melt stone the way they can, and diorite is one of the hardest stones to carve!"

"I doubt there are supernatural powers at work, Majesty . . ." began Kusac.

"Then there is the fire at your father's funeral, with flames reaching high into the sky. Another almost supernatural act!"

Kusac waved his free hand helplessly. "I really don't know what to say, Majesty. I am sure there is a rational explanation for these events. We just need to find it."

"No! You just need to find it," said K'hedduk. "I tasked you with finding this Zsadhi person, or group. What progress have you made?"

"We closed down all the print shops before I took ill, Majesty. Have there been any other attacks or desecrations since I've been ill?"

"You should know the answer to that question, not me!" K'hedduk hissed angrily.

"Apologies, Majesty. I meant to say there have been no incursions since then, have there?"

"One," said Zerdish. "Three days ago. A paint factory for fighter craft. The damage was substantial."

"Ah, I hadn't yet been informed of that," Kusac said apologetically. "I hear that there is a piece of equipment you found in one of the labs that has been taken to the surface?"

"Yes. What of it?"

"It might be connected to the people doing the Zsadhi attacks. I'd like to have a look at it."

"How could it possibly be connected to that?" demanded K'hedduk angrily.

"I don't know. That's why I want to look."

"My best scientists have tried to make the damned thing

work to no avail! What makes you think you can have any effect on it?"

"Were they looking to see if there was any way it could be responsible for the melting stone?"

"No." There was just a note of hesitation in K'hedduk's voice now.

"It wouldn't take long for me to look at it. Perhaps there was a detachable part of it that someone in the Palace knows how to use. A quick study of it could tell me that. Now that it's out in the open, having it guarded by security cameras might be a good idea, to see if anyone comes up to examine it in the night."

K'hedduk straightened up and placed his hands behind his back. Kusac could sense a newfound confidence seeping into the M'zullian's mind. He was thinking that he knew it was an alien device, and just perhaps the alien left behind after the raid knew something about it that he didn't.

"It's possible there is more to be learned from that object. I'll give you two days to come up with some answers before I decide whether or not to dispose of it."

"Thank you, Majesty. I'll get right on it," said Kusac, bowing and backing his way out of the Emperor's office.

I got two days, Kusac sent to Rezac and Kaid.

L'Shoh's realm

L'Shoh met Ghyakulla and Vartra by his throne and led them to the suite of rooms he had beyond it. A fire blazed cheerily in the hearth, and heavy crimson drapes shut out the perpetual howling of the wind.

He gestured to them to be seated, then offered them a drink from a tray.

"Fruit juice for you, Ghyakulla," he smiled. "I haven't forgotten your preferences, and a good red wine for you,

Vartra. One from the Western Isles, I believe. I think you'll like it."

Vartra accepted the glass with a nod and tasted the wine. He wasn't a connoisseur, but it was pleasantly rich and fruity.

"Why are we here?" he asked L'Shoh.

"We," L'Shoh indicated himself and Ghyakulla, "need your help. It's time you took a hand again in the affairs of our people."

"Who this time?" he asked sardonically. "Kusac or his children?"

"Both. We almost lost control of him during his last mission in the temple. He suffered a high fever caused by pitting his mental will against ours. I don't know if we can maintain our influence much longer."

"So you want me to do what exactly?"

"Be with him, ease the way on this mission to the harem. It's essential we have him hit the harem to further destabilize K'hedduk. He will see it as another personal insult to him. We need Kusac to phase in and out of almost Sholan form so he appears as a black-skinned Valtegan to the females of the harem."

"So you want Kusac's Lord Nayash seen as the Zsadhi?"

Ghyakulla, quietly sipping her fruit juice, nodded her head and sent him an image of Kusac morphing into the shape of a black-skinned Valtegan.

"K'hedduk must believe the Zsadhi is real," said L'Shoh. "You must help Kusac become him."

"And how do I do that?"

"You push him to reveal that side."

Vartra looked at L'Shoh over the top of his glass. "You realize this could affect your influence over him after this event, don't you?"

"This mission will be his last. After that, he will need to call K'hedduk out for a duel."

"Why can't you just play with K'hedduk's mind instead of Kusac's?" asked Vartra. "That way you could be more sure of getting what you want."

"We can only affect our own."

"When will you stop influencing them?" Vartra demanded, putting down the wineglass on the low table in front of him. "When will this be over?"

"As soon as the M'zullians forget their warlike ways," said L'Shoh. "Then your geas will be over and your life will resume, when you have chosen between Ghyakulla and Kuushoi."

Vartra got to his feet angrily. "You ask me to manipulate good people almost beyond their limits, then tell me that I have to decide which of two Goddesses to choose? You are stretching even *me* beyond *my* limit!"

He sketched an opening in front of him and instantly a portal formed, leading into a summer woodland. A thatched-roof house with a lean-to smithy stood in the center of the clearing there. Stepping through the opening, he left L'Shoh's realm and the two Gods behind.

L'Shoh looked at Ghyakulla. "Well, that could have gone better," he said as the portal closed.

"We are pushing them all too hard," she said, pronouncing the words slowly as she put down her fruit juice. With a sad smile, she sketched a portal to her own realm and stepped through, leaving the lord of Hell's realm behind.

Kuushoi's realm

Kuushoi reached out a languid finger and stirred her viewing pool, banishing the image of L'Shoh's comfortable living room with its fire. Instead, as the water stilled and froze, it reflected the soaring pillars and soft white draperies of her realm of ice and snow.

Beside her stood her Dzinae of dreams, Gihaf, in male form for the present.

"I have need of you, Gihaf," she said, turning to him.

"Your will, as always, is mine," he said. Deep blue eyes regarded her from a face of pale gray fur.

"Good. I need you to visit our little human dreamer in her caves of ice on that M'zull world," she said. "It's time you wove a dream of good Queens defeated by evil sisters."

"The dream of the crown forged with the eggshells of the innocent?" he asked. "The crown that . . ."

". . . lies in the mountain cave, kept close by the human female. Yes, that crown," she purred, stroking his cheek gently. "Go in your female form, though, Gihaf. She will relate better to a female showing her visions of a lost past than a male."

"As you wish, Lady," said Gihaf, the planes of its face already beginning to lose their masculine edges and soften to curves that were echoed in the lithe body. Slowly, Gihaf shrank in height till her head reached the Goddess' shoulder.

There had been a tinge of regret in the voice that Kuushoi had noticed.

"Worry not, Dzinae, when you have woven this marvelous dream of stolen crowns, murdered sisters and banished males, you can return to my side in your male form."

"I exist to please you, Lady," came her soft voice as her mischievous blue eyes twinkled up at Kuushoi.

"See you spin your dream well, Gihaf. She must know that this false male is no more an Emperor than the Captain of Ishardia's guard was. Without her aid as a sorceress, he cannot prevail. There are always two sides to a legend, are there not?" She smiled slowly, continuing to stroke Gihaf's cheek.

"Is it your wish that the false Emperor should win, Lady?" she asked.

"No, let the better fighter win this time," she said, letting her hand fall to her side. "Go now, and spin your tale of deceit and power."

"As you will, Lady," curtsied Gihaf. With a coquettish flick of her tail, she turned and sashayed her way along the corridor to her own rooms.

M'zull, outer Great Courtyard, same afternoon

The outer courtyard was similar to the one on the Prime world, except that there were no stores and restaurants ringing it, nor entrances to the public buildings. Those had been blocked off eons ago. Instead, it was a giant turntable entrance for ships to be lowered down to the Palace parking and debarkation areas.

Kusac, flanked by Cheelar, M'yikku, and Maalash, made his way over to the far edge of the courtyard where the giant turntable ended and the regular solid ground began. There, the alien matter transformer, supported by its spindly collection of legs, sat on its transportation dais.

"Check for microphones or hidden cameras, M'yikku," said Kusac quietly.

"Aye."

"Does it make your eyes go all funny?" asked Maalash, trying not to look at it.

"Not so much," said Kusac, pacing up to it. "It can distort reality if you stare directly at it. I try to look at it kind of sideways."

"It's clean, best as I can tell," said M'yikku, palming his scanner.

Kusac mounted the dais and walked around the transformer. "This is only half of it. The other half was destroyed at J'kirtikk by a Watcher ship. Annuur's ship, if memory serves. This part only duplicates nanites and lets them go. It doesn't disperse them properly the way the upper portion would. We need this to be undamaged for the next week at least until the nanites have finished dispersing and have been able to update this device as to their status. It will then initiate the on switch, and within minutes all the nanites will be active and will carry out their appointed task."

"So we have to keep this unharmed till then," said Cheelar. "Looks like it is pretty robust. From the darkened areas, it appears that someone has already tried to use a blaster on it."

"The tech is centuries ahead of what even we have," said Kusac, reaching out carefully to touch it. He gave a sigh of relief as nothing suddenly hummed into life under his fingers. "It's dead to us right now, waiting for the signal from the dispersed nanites to waken it up."

"How long till that happens?" asked M'yikku.

"A week, two at the most."

"We need more time," said Maalash. "I may not understand most of what you're talking about, but I understand that."

Kusac nodded and began to walk round the device, examining it properly this time. Last time he'd seen it, it was humming with life and had overwhelmed him by its alienness. Now, it was just an interesting greenish black, semi-organic artifact, devoid of life.

"The webbed areas look the most vulnerable," said Cheelar, pointing. "I don't know if they are."

"Neither do I," said Kusac. "Maybe we can ask our friends about that, but I agree with you. There's less mass to absorb damage, so they are most likely to be damaged first."

"Why are we looking at this now?" asked Maalash.

"Trying to see if a bit could have been detached from it to form a weapon that melts stone," said Cheelar.

"Since it is organic, then a piece could have budded off anywhere," said Kusac. "When I first saw it, it opened up a hatch that grasped hold of my hand."

"Why did it do that?" asked M'yikku.

"Long story," he muttered. "No time to tell you now. Well, I can see places where it looks like pieces could have been taken from it, but how do we prove that without providing a piece made of the same substance?"

"Can our allies get us something made of the same material?" asked Cheelar.

"Again, that's something I'll have to ask them. If they are even still using the same fabrication method. It is an extremely old device."

"Let's get us some scientific measuring devices. You know, radiation counters, electrical current readers—that kind of thing—and crawl over it some more after I have asked Annuur for what information we can get about this thing," said Kusac, moving back from it and turning to step off the dais onto the ground again. "Let's at least look busy in the meantime."

Prime world, that evening

It was getting late, but the lighting had not yet come on in the library where Gaylla was sitting behind one of the easy chairs at the back of the room, a book open on her lap. She was humming a tuneless little song to herself as she cuddled her doll and read the book. Suddenly she stopped, peering into one of the shadows where the floor-length curtains hung on either side of the windows.

"I know you's there," she said. "Why you watching me?"

The shadow resolved itself into the figure of a Sholan male, wearing a dark shawl around his black tunic. He held it as if he was carrying something in it.

"I didn't want to disturb you, little one," he said, coming closer. "Are you enjoying your book?"

"Uh-huh. Better since they gots more books from the other towns nearby, and from Shola," she said, staring at the shawl. "Not many for us to read at first, now there is."

"I'm glad to hear it," he said. "You need to have books you can read."

"It moved!" she said, pointing to his shawl. "What you got in it?"

"Me?" he asked, smiling. "Who says I have anything in my shawl?"

"I do!" she said excitedly, her still pointing hand bobbing up and down now. "It moves again!"

"Shh," he said, putting a finger up to his lips. "You're making too much noise, you might frighten it."

"Show me, show me!" she insisted, doll and book both forgotten as she got to her knees to be on an eye level with the bundle that the stranger was carrying.

"Careful, you'll damage the book, and you wouldn't want to do that," he said.

Hastily, she closed the book and moved it to one side. "What have you got?" she demanded, reaching out to touch the slightly moving bundle he was carrying.

"Gaylla," came Shaidan's warning voice from just behind her. "Don't talk to strangers," he said, stepping up to stand beside her.

"He has something for me!" she said.

"He's a stranger, Gaylla. We don't know him."

The stranger lifted his head up from the pool of shadow it had been in, revealing to Shaidan a familiar face.

"Not quite a stranger, Shaidan," Vartra said softly. "It's just been a long time since we last met."

"What happened to you?" asked Shaidan. "I looked everywhere for you."

"Forces beyond my control prevented me from coming to see you," he said apologetically. "It won't happen again, I promise."

"You knows him, so he's not a stranger," said Gaylla, turning round to tug on her brother's arm. "Can I see what he brought me now? Can I? Can I?"

Shaidan looked down at her anxious face. "Yes," he said. "Vartra isn't a stranger. He was a good friend to me when I needed one."

"What has you got?" she asked, all decorum gone now as she leaped to her feet and bounced up and down excitedly. "Show me!"

Vartra slowly pulled back the shawl to reveal a small white furry bundle curled up on his arm. It squirmed, and a little pointed snout and a pair of dark eyes peeped out at her. Small pink ears twitched as it let out a quiet chittering sound.

"Ooh!" breathed Gaylla, leaning against Vartra for a closer look. "What is it?"

"It's a jegget, one of the little creatures special to our Sholan Nature Goddess, Ghyakulla."

She reached out a tentative finger and looked up into Vartra's face. "Can I touch it?"

"Yes, but very gently," he said.

"Ooh, it's so soft," she whispered, stroking it with one finger, then her whole hand. "It's warm!"

The jegget snuggled its face into her hand.

Gaylla laughed delightedly. "It's got a wet nose," she said, grinning up at Vartra, then Shaidan.

"I brought it for you," Vartra said. "But you have to be very careful of her. She needs to be fed every day, and to be given clean water. You can't always carry her around like I am doing," he added, "but you can walk her once a day on a leash like this one. Do you want to hold her now?"

"Yes, please," she said, holding out both arms as Vartra carefully passed the young jegget over to her, giving her the end of the leash to hold.

"She's mine to keep?" asked Gaylla, gently cuddling her new pet.

"She's yours to keep," agreed Vartra, gently stroking Gaylla's hair. "You'll have to pick out a nice name for her, so she'll come when you call her."

"I will, I promise I will!" Gaylla lowered her cheek till it rested against the white fur of the jegget and began quietly crooning the tuneless song she had been humming earlier.

Vartra's eyes caught Shaidan's as he rose to his feet. "You'll need to keep her in a cage for a few weeks till she learns to stay with Gaylla," he said. "Feed her meat twice a day. Oh, and she's telepathic, like you." He laughed faintly. "No, not like you, but jeggets are the only other telepathic beings on Shola."

"I'll tell them how to look after her," said Shaidan. "But why are you here? It wasn't just to give Gaylla a pet, was it?"

"It was to let you know I am back," he said. "Beyond that, don't ask." He took a step back, blending again into the shadows of the curtains.

"Vartra," began Shaidan, stepping forward as the lights came on, but there was no one where the shadow had been. He sighed, knowing the enigmatic Sholan had disappeared again. Turning to his sister, he took her by the arm.

"We better go and tell Aunt Kitra about your jegget," he said.

"She says she's called Snow," said Gaylla, lifting a face wreathed in smiles to him.

"A good name," he nodded. "Snow is white stuff that falls from the sky in winter, and she's white. Let's take Snow to Aunt Kitra and Uncle Dzaka and see about getting a cage for her."

"She doesn't need a cage," said Gaylla as they walked out of the library. "She says she'll be good."

"I think we should do what Vartra said with her," said Shaidan. "It's all new to her, she's only a baby . . ."

Gaylla tutted. "Well, all right, so long as she sleeps with me at night!"

M'zull, mountain den that evening

"Yes, can get you a piece of similar construction," said Annuur. "What you need it to do?"

"I need it to be seen as if it has been extruded from the main part of the artifact and is actually a weak blaster. You know, press a depression or button, and a spluttering stream of low energy comes out of it. If it looks like a piece is missing, so much the better. I can then say it is probably missing a power unit."

"I can do this. When you need it?"

"Later tonight?" Kusac asked hopefully. "I need to decide where to find it tomorrow. By the way, don't go near the matter transformer as it is being monitored by security cameras."

"Pft, that is nothing to us. What if you find the piece loose on the transformer when you go to look at it tomorrow morning? They will maybe think your poking and prodding after their people have done the same has driven this piece loose."

"That would work," said Kusac, with a very human grin. "Now just assure me that the transformer is still working despite its appearance and I'll be happy."

"Is working," confirmed Annuur, "but must prevent K'hedduk from trying to explode it, or it may become impaired. Most is very strong, but some parts are more sensitive, weaker than others. Yes, it could become damaged."

"What? There is a real risk?" groaned Kusac. "Why hasn't it a built-in force field?"

"Because then no one trying to blow it up! Do what you can, we will monitor it and if any damage happens, will try to rectify it."

"It's not going to be easy to stop him from trying to destroy it," Kusac warned. "He's still angry about how he thinks Lassimiss walked out on him."

"Do your best. Only have to keep it protected for two maybe three days, then all will be fine."

"This job gets harder by the day," he groaned.

Annuur reached up to pat his chest. "Well you are doing, friend Kusac, very well indeed. So soon now we be done forever with these sand-dwellers on this world!"

"I'll look for the part tomorrow, then," he said.

Annuur nodded and winked out of existence.

"Where's Carrie?" he asked Jo as he made his way into the main chamber. "I can't stay for long, I just wanted to see she was all right."

"I don't know, now you come to mention it," she said, looking around. "Have you tried your tent? She's been a bit withdrawn the last day or so."

"That's not like her," he said, frowning. "What caused that, I wonder?"

"It happened after we went to the village the other day. You know, the day she got that headdress from them."

Carrie was dreaming of a world that existed light-years away and thousands of years ago. She was both the participant and the observer as she watched the scenes unfold before her eyes.

Someone had had the effrontery to demand her presence outside the comfort and safety of her Palace. As the people had gathered in the courtyard, she had to show herself to them, show she was unafraid!

She dressed with care. Her robe was short, made of the softest fabric spun by insects kept exclusively in the Palace gardens for that purpose. A deep emerald green, it contrasted perfectly with the bronze body armor she always wore during any public appearance.

Greaves were clasped on her lower legs, covering the brown leather boots. Bronze armguards covered her wrists and forearms, and on her hands she wore mail gloves, each link smaller than the nail of her tiniest finger.

But it was the helmet that caught the eye. Resembling the Prime royal crown, it featured the body of one of the raptors that soared in the skies around her capital. This one, the Queen's crown, was the only feathered bird on K'oish'ik. She'd heard them called L'shol's crows by the soldiers for their preference to feast on the bodies of the fallen. A fitting crown for an absolute ruler like herself.

The head of the bird reared threateningly over her brow, emerald eyes glittering, ready to attack any who would wish her harm. Open wings dipped down, cupping her head, protecting her skull, the tips of the blue-and-gold wings almost touching her shoulders. The spread blue tail feathers were angled down to protect the vulnerable back of her neck. It truly was a crown worthy of the Queen of K'oish'ik!

As soon as she lowered it onto her head, she felt its magic surround her like an all-enveloping cloak. She knew what none suspected, that using the shards of the shell of her firstborn that she'd sacrificed to the mage woman, her crowning helmet was imbued with the magic to turn aside any edged blade wielded against her. The cost of this magic had been great, and the protective fields only extended a hand's breadth from her body.

Her servant attached a flowing cloak of the same emerald green, then stood back to allow the Royal armorer to approach and fasten her sword belt. On bended knee, head bowed, he presented her with the royal sword.

Made of bronze, the hilt was long and decorated with alternating rings of brightly colored enamels and semiprecious stones—turquoise, lapis lazuli, gold, and ivory inlays showed off the bronze blade to perfection.

She spared a moment to enjoy its beauty before placing it in its scabbard.

"Majesty, he is calling for you," bowed Nezaabe, head of her guards and her lover.

"I am ready," she said, turning away from the polished bronze mirror. Around her ankles, the cloak swirled like a sea of green.

"Don't go, Majesty. It's a trap," said Nezaabe. "He's planning to kill you."

"Nonsense," she said, her boots echoing on the tiled floor as she strode toward the central staircase down to the courtyard. "He can only hurt me if I agree to fight him, and I don't intend to do that."

Nezaabe scrambled to his feet and followed her down to the grand courtyard.

The crowd was sullen when she emerged, only breaking into half-hearted cheering when forced to do so by the army standing among them and lining the courtyard.

Carrie moaned uneasily in her sleep, aware she didn't want to continue her journey into the Prime past.

Flanked by her bodyguard, Tashraka marched across to the carved stone throne and sat down.

Until now, she had ignored the male standing facing her from the far side of the courtyard. Now she looked at him. Skin burned almost black by the desert sun, the male Prime was carrying a sword that she, Carrie, recognized only too well.

"Zsadhi," she muttered in her sleep, beginning to make small restless movements. "Not the Zsadhi."

"You were banished from here," she heard Tashraka say. "Returning will cost you your life, Zsadhi."

"I haven't come to bandy words with you, Tashraka, I've come to challenge you to a duel, one-on-one." Zsadhi's voice rang out, filling the courtyard. "Too long have you abused the people of K'oish'ik with your harsh rule. It's time it was ended, along with you!"

"I'm not Tashraka, I'm Ishardia, Zsadhi. Your time in the desert has done more than tan your hide black; it's damaged your eyesight," said Tashraka.

"I know all about your foul pact with the sorceress! You traded your first egg for the transformation spell so you could swap bodies with your sister—my wife! You then denounced us as assassins, burning your sister to death and banishing me to the desert. You may have fooled the people, Tashraka, but not me. Now face me in honorable combat!"

"No! Not that," moaned Carrie, deep in her nightmare vision.

The murmuring of the crowd began to resolve itself into a chant, a chant for the Zsadhi. Slowly at first, it quickly gathered momentum until their voices filled the courtyard.

"Zsadhi! Zsadhi! Zsadhi!" they chanted.

"Silence!" yelled Tashraka, pushing herself to her feet. "I will not tolerate such insubordination!"

"Face me in honorable combat, Tashraka," said Zsadhi, pacing back and forth, swinging his sword to loosen up. "You can't be afraid of me, I'm only a male, not permitted to fight. What is there to fear?"

"You shouldn't even have a sword," she hissed. "You are an abomination! You were granted too much freedom, and you misused it! I will personally see that you are punished for your presumption! Guards, take him!"

The chanting grew louder as the people linked arms and prevented the Royal guards from entering the courtyard. The chant changed to one of "Fight! Fight! Fight!"

Incensed, Tashraka turned to Nezaabe for a brief and intense exchange that ended in her making a cutting motion with her hand and walking angrily away from him and toward the open courtyard.

Loudly invoking the Goddess of Battle, she drew her sword and held it up at arm's length, letting the sun's rays glint golden off the bronze.

Carrie woke with a jolt and a cry of distress.

Kusac ran to the tent and pulled the entrance open. "Carrie! What's the matter? I was worried about you," he said, going to her side.

"Just a dream, no need to be concerned," she said, sitting up and rubbing her eyes. "I'm fine. A cup of coffee will set me to rights." She pushed back her sleeping bag and scrambled to her feet. "You worry too much."

Kusac followed her out and watched as she headed to the camp kitchen for a hot drink.

"Something's up with her," he said to Kaid. "What's happened to put her so out of sorts?"

"I have no idea beyond it's been a very intense mission for all of us. Maybe it's getting to her at last," said Kaid. "Just say good-bye to her and leave it to me to see how she is. Keep it simple between you both right now. You don't need complications so close to the end of the mission."

Kusac nodded, grasping his sword-brother by the shoulder. "Thank you," he said before heading over to his mate.

"I have to go now," he said. "I just came to say good-bye."

She turned to look at him, offering a cheek for a kiss. "This should all be over soon, I hope."

"I hope so, too," he said. Her cheek felt cold to his lips. "Good night, love."

"Good-bye."

Disturbed at her behavior, he still took Kaid's advice and walked away. Once in the outer cavern, he activated his translocator and was instantly back in his bedroom where Cheelar and M'yikku waited for him.

"They'll have a piece acting like a blaster for us to find on the artifact tomorrow," he said. "We need to keep them from blowing it up as I found out they really could damage some of the weaker parts. I'm betting you're right and that it's the webbing that is more fragile."

"I think you're right," agreed Cheelar.

"I also found out we need several more days' grace before K'hedduk decides to blow the damned thing up. A week would be best, but I have no idea how we are going to do that."

"Would another mission help?" asked Cheelar. "It would give him something else to obsess over. But what could we do that could top the temple?"

"The harem," Kusac heard himself saying. "We'll hit the harem, leave Zsadhi symbols on the walls, and on the door of his wife's room. What better way to anger him than to strike at what the people see as his masculinity?"

M'yikku nodded his head vigorously. "Perfect! Trust me, nothing could cause him more embarrassment! But how do we get in and out without being seen?"

"Annuur and his flickering lights," said Kusac without even thinking. "It will render them deeply asleep, and when they wake, they'll have no memory of what happened."

"You really hate K'hedduk, don't you?" said Cheelar quietly.

"Yes, for what he did to me, to my wife Carrie, and to all the cubs," said Kusac, his voice as cold as ice.

"Why don't you use the flickering lights to take your revenge? Either take him prisoner, or kill him?"

"Because this is personal," he said, looking at Cheelar. "Up close and very personal. I will face him when I kill him, so he knows it is me taking my revenge, and no other."

He watched Cheelar shiver slightly and smiled, reaching out to squeeze his arm reassuringly. "Don't worry, Cheelar. My feelings are reserved for K'hedduk alone."

CHAPTER 10

M'zull Palace, later that evening

ANNUUR sat in Kusac's reception room, listening to his plan. "It can be done," he said slowly. "We need Azwokkus to do as you know this is TeLaxaudin skill, not one we have. Will need affect whole Palace to enable you to get there and away unseen. I go check and be back." Annuur disappeared. Kusac, Cheelar, M'yikku, and Maalash waited with varying degrees of impatience for the Cabbaran to return.

When he did, it was with Azwokkus. "Can be done, but timing must be specific. Half an hour you have, no more as effect over large area. If area smaller, time longer."

"Understood," said Kusac.

"Why you do another mission? Thought you were finished."

Why was he doing this one? He frowned, trying to remember his reasoning, but he couldn't. "It seemed right," he said lamely. "All we have to do is spray the Zsadhi sword and name in the harem, and have me put one stone sword on the wall. In and out."

"Be sure you keep it simple," said Azwokkus. "More complex, more time."

"You have transporters," reminded Annuur. "You can return direct to your rooms rather than have to run through Palace."

"Good point," said Kusac. "I forgot that. We'll have plenty of time, then."

"When you want to go?" asked Annuur.

"As soon as possible," said Kusac. "I just need Cheelar to fetch our paints from the mountain den first. Can't keep any here in case we get searched."

"Good thinking," nodded Azwokkus, head bobbing on his spindly neck. "Go for paints and I get ready to release energy pulse for lighting."

Ten minutes later, the lights in the room flickered then flared brightly into incandescence, before falling back to a normal level.

"Is done," said Azwokkus as the others behind their darkened glasses all blinked their eyes rapidly, trying to rid themselves of the afterimage. "Set timers and go now."

"On our way," said Kusac, stepping out into the corridor and from there into the underground concourse.

They made their way hurriedly along the thoroughfare until they reached the Security station. At this time of night, there was only one soldier on duty and he sat frozen in his seat, eyes closed.

Kusac approached him alone and waved his hand in front of the unconscious male's face, then gently pushed his arm. Getting no response, he gestured the other three to follow him. They hurried past him and into the large room where supplicants to the Emperor waited on his pleasure before being escorted to the Throne Room.

Across the main cavern courtyard they went, till they reached the corridor on the northeastern side. This led them to a locked anteroom. A quick kick had the door swinging open. As expected, the room was empty at that time of night. Ahead was another corridor off which was the door to the Emperor's harem.

"Twenty minutes," whispered Cheelar.

"Noted," said Kusac. "Through there," he said, pointing to the heavy door.

Cheelar was there first. "It's locked, and a kick won't open it this time."

"Stand back," ordered Kusac, pulling his blaster and shooting the lock. It disintegrated in a shower of sparks and chips of wood. "We haven't the time for subtlety," he said, pushing the door open.

They found themselves in what appeared to be a communal bedroom, Beds, with mounds where sleepers lay, were set against the wall, the space between each divided by a gauzy curtain. They could see four such beds where they were, but the room, appearing more like a corridor than anything else, extended on either side of where they stood, and they could see more beds at the two junctions. A door ahead of them was partially open, and it was through this that Kusac led them. The air was moist and warm, courtesy of the large pool that dominated this room. Round it, piles of cushions were arranged so that the Emperor's concubines would be able to bathe at their leisure, then take their ease on them.

"Fifteen minutes," said Cheelar.

"Get moving," said Kusac. "I want us out in ten!"

They split up, the other three each taking a wall to spray with the sword symbols and the name Zsadhi.

Kusac headed to the fourth wall, the eastern one, and placing his hand on it, began to feel for the nature of the stone beneath the plaster. Finding it, he began to manipulate it, turn it plastic so he could shape it into the form of the Zsadhi's sword.

It took more effort than he realized, and sweat was beginning to form on his face by the time he had the basic sword shape. He felt drained this time.

"Five minutes," said Cheelar coming up beside him. "Leave it like this, Captain. No one will care that it isn't as smooth as the others."

Kusac nodded, taking his hand away from the wall and shrugging his shoulders to loosen them up. He could swear his right shoulder felt as if a weight had been placed on it. Taking a step, he stumbled and cursed as he clutched at the wall to steady himself. Cheelar reached out to help him and he accepted the supportive hand on his arm gratefully.

"Go," he said to M'yikku and Maalash. "We're coming."

The two winked out of existence as they heard a stirring from the bedroom beyond. Fear of capture flooded through him as he was suddenly bent double with a pain that racked his whole body. He saw his hand change, start to turn black and morph into his Sholan self.

"No! I can't change," he muttered as Cheelar fought to keep hold of him. Another spasm rippled through him as he again began to change. This time, it wasn't just his hand, he could feel his whole body stretched to its limit as the bones and muscles began to reform. He stifled a cry of pain and gripped Cheelar's arm hard.

"Leave, now," he gasped. "I will follow if I can!"

"I can't leave you, you're changing into your Sholan self," said Cheelar, trying to get him to stand upright. "Your clothes, they're splitting, falling off you! I need to activate your translocator!"

Cheelar bent down to pick up the shredded clothing and the belt with its translocator still attached. Thrusting it into Kusac's trembling hand, he heard a high-pitched scream as he simultaneously pressed Kusac's device and his own. The scream was abruptly cut short as the pool room winked out to be replaced by Kusac's bedroom where the other two were already standing waiting for them.

Kusac fell to his hands and knees, remaining in that crouched position while the change flowed excruciatingly through him. When it was done, he looked blearily up at the others and sat back on his haunches.

"Well, I was seen," he said, his voice hoarse. "They have their bloody Zsadhi sighting tonight, dammit! This shouldn't have happened. I should have had another full day before I needed to worry about morphing into my real self!"

"I think creating the sword just wore you out," said Maalash. "It would tire anyone."

"It shouldn't have; that's the point. There's no reason for me to be so drained, unless . . ." He raised his head. "It can't be," he whispered. "I didn't plan this mission, I was made to do it! Made to let myself be seen mid-change so I looked like their Zsadhi. I thought I felt a hand on my shoulder tonight, draining me of my energy so I would change! Dammit, Vartra! How dare you manipulate me to your own ends! I am not Kaid!" he snarled, standing up and initiating the change back to his Valtegan self.

It hurt like hell, but it was the only safe form for him right now. Bending down, he picked up the shredded clothing that Cheelar had brought with him. "Get rid of this," he said, shoving it at him. "Go to the den and give it to them; we can't risk anything being found here. M'yikku, fetch me a clean uniform. Maalash, get Laazif to serve supper for us all in the family dining room."

When they hesitated, he glared at them. "Well, jump to it! We could have a visitation by security at any time!"

M'yikku ran over to his wardrobe and pulled out a fresh shirt, uniform pants, and jacket which he handed to Kusac. While he was dressing, Cheelar returned, bringing with him a small blast of cold air.

"Kaid . . ." Cheelar began.

"Already talking to him," said Kusac as he continued putting on the clothes.

What the hell happened? demanded Kaid. *What makes you think Vartra was involved? We've heard nothing from him for months now.*

I know, but I've felt him before, like a hand on my shoulder when he's standing right behind me.

Yep, that's one of the ways he influences you. This last raid is not your usual style, I have to admit. A bit high profile for you, but it's right up the street of someone wanting the Zsadhi to be seen!

Cheelar was with me, I hope he wasn't seen.

He told me. I think the fact he was bending down at the time, and that you would have certainly looked like a legend come to life will ensure that all she saw was you.

Let's hope so, he sighed. *I'm getting some supper. I need it after being drained so badly and doing two morphs in such quick succession. Let's hope it doesn't throw me into a fever like it did the other day.*

Keep me updated, sent Kaid. *Be safe tonight.*

You, too.

He turned to look at Cheelar and M'yikku. "Food," he said succinctly.

Vartra's realm

"I've done your will, L'Shoh," Vartra said as he returned to his own realm of the woodland forge. "And I know you can hear me! I arranged to have him seen by two of the harem favorites, so you have your sighting of him as the Zsadhi. Now I will do what I see right by them all!"

Early on Zhal-Oeshi 15th (August)

"My harem they hit this time!" fumed K'hedduk to Zerdish. "This will be kept as quiet as possible, I will not be made a laughing stock! And two of the females said they saw the Zsadhi! Can you believe it? A black-skinned Valtegan, no less! I don't know whether to believe them or have them whipped for lying!"

"I don't think they were lying, Majesty," said Zerdish carefully. "I think they genuinely believe that is what they saw. It's possible that one of this team of raiders is using something to darken his skin to make him appear to be the Zsadhi of legend."

"Sounds more believable than that the actual Zsadhi is visiting the city like this," grumbled K'hedduk angrily. "I want to know how they got in here unseen by any of my security!"

"I'd like to know that, too," said Zerdish. "I wonder if there is any collusion between them and the security people on duty tonight."

"Have them arrested for incompetence," fumed K'hedduk, clutching his dressing gown closed around himself. "Give them to Ziosh to interrogate!"

"Already done, Majesty. We should have some news by morning."

"Have you got a clean-up crew in there? I want the suite back to normal as soon as possible! And cancel any visits by the Court wives in the meantime, I will not have word of this incursion known outside this room!"

Zerdish bowed. "Is there anything else you want, Majesty?"

"Yes, get Nayash here and have the kitchen prepare some hot food for two at once! I'm not going to get any more sleep tonight, so I don't see why anyone else should. I'll be in my room dressing if Nayash arrives before I'm ready."

"Yes, Majesty," said Zerdish, bowing again as K'hedduk swept out of the room to get dressed.

By the time Kusac arrived at the Emperor's dining room, K'hedduk was a lot calmer and was sitting at a side table eating. Another chair waited there, with a place set and a meal waiting under a warming lid.

"Sit, eat," said K'hedduk, pointing to the place at his table. "I have a job for you to do tonight," he said. "I need you to rid me of those Generals you labeled as untrustworthy, and Inquisitor Ziosh. Make it look like this Zsadhi is responsible for it. Might as well get some positive use out of him."

"Rid you of them?" asked Kusac, taking the lid off a plate of scrambled eggs and some streaky, narrow, fried breakfast meat. He put the lid on a mat left on the table for that purpose.

"You want me to kill them?" he asked carefully, lifting up a fork and scooping up some of the eggs. Having only recently eaten himself, he really wasn't hungry, yet he had to appear to be.

"Don't be dense," snapped K'hedduk, concentrating on eating. "Yes, I mean kill them. The Zsadhi hit again tonight.

This time, though, he was seen. I want these murders put down to the Zsadhi's doing."

"He was seen?"

K'hedduk looked up at him. "Yes, he was seen, by two of the females in my harem. Somehow this person pretending to be the Zsadhi got into my harem, and he and his gang left scrawled images of the sword over the walls and another one melted into the stone. Obviously," he said, looking back down at his plate, "I don't want that news known, but if there are several deaths in the Palace caused by this Zsadhi, then word of a sighting will not be untoward."

"If I'm to make it look like the Zsadhi has killed all these people, then I'll need supplies of paints like those they use," said Kusac.

K'hedduk snapped his fingers, and Zerdish brought over a backpack filled with cans of spray paints in red and blue, the colors that had been used for the Zsadhi raids.

"Use them," he said, pushing his plate away and getting to his feet. He threw his napkin on the table as Kusac leaped up to his feet.

"Finish eating, then gather your men and go forth now in the dark of the night, to kill these threats to my rule of law," he said. "Return when you're done. In the meantime, I intend to see to destroying that alien device sitting up in the outer courtyard once and for all!"

He was gone before Kusac could remind him he still had another day to examine it.

"The Emperor will be displeased if you leave the food," said Zerdish before following his master out.

He sat down again, looking at the food before slowly starting to fork it into his mouth and forcing himself to swallow it. This was going to take some planning. There were only three of the Generals he had labeled as untrustworthy on M'zull at this time; the other two were on the space stations with their fleets. And in the meantime, he could do nothing to stop K'hedduk from blowing up the transformer!

He sent to Kaid, alerting him to what was happening and asking him to pass it on to Annuur in the faint hope there was something they could do to prevent the artifact from being disabled.

Finishing the meal, he picked up the backpack and left, heading for his own quarters, and sending ahead mentally to meet Rezac there in Valtegan form and his two commandos, Noolgoi and Noi'kkah.

They were all waiting for him in his large public lounge area.

"I've checked the room," said M'yikku. "It's clean."

"K'hedduk has issued orders for me to kill the three Generals currently on M'zull that he believes are disloyal to him," he said quietly. "As you know they are Generals Lezhu, Shayaza, and Chaikul. As well as that, he wants Inquisitor Ziosh killed." He looked round the group. "He wants the Zsadhi, who was sighted tonight, to be held responsible for these executions and has given me paints so we can paint Zsadhi symbols on the walls and doors of our targets. That's the good news," he sighed. "The bad news is he is going to the transformer now to blow it up." He held up a hand for silence as the expected outburst came from his team.

"I have told Kaid and he will have alerted Annuur. As of right now, I don't know if there is anything they can do to prevent it from being damaged. However, that is not our concern right now. Carrying out the executions is."

"Two teams?" asked Rezac.

"Two teams," Kusac confirmed. "You will lead the team taking out the Generals. I will lead the team targeting the Head Inquisitor. Keep it simple, just knock on each door, gain entry to the house and the General, and kill him. Kill anyone who sees you, and decorate the place with Zsadhi swords. It's night; that and the darkness will be our friend. I'll take Cheelar and M'yikku with me. Maalash, go with Rezac. He'll need your help tonight. Noolgoi and Noi'kkah, with Rezac as usual. Can you manage with four of you?" he asked.

Rezac nodded. "We'll manage. Can you?"

"I should be able to. After all, he isn't a soldier like the Generals you're dealing with."

"But he does have a lot of underlings close at hand," said Rezac quietly. "My advice? Have Kaid and as many as he can get together ready to transport in at a moment's notice in case anything goes wrong."

"You might be right," he said. "This is another fight that has been coming for some time. Let's get going. Don't forget your paint cans," he said, holding out the backpack for each of them to take a can.

"Have you formulated any plans on what you're going to do?" asked Cheelar.

"Not yet. Get him alone and keep him isolated from his priests for a start," said Kusac, rubbing a hand over his head, thinking how much more comforting it felt when he had ears and fur.

"Can we get him into a place of our choosing, like the Throne Room?" asked M'yikku. "In his office, he's at the heart of his little kingdom of priests. Too much chance of one or more of them coming into the office when we're there."

"To do that I'm going to need a pretext to get him out of his office," said Kusac. "He's been after me to give him information on what K'hedduk is planning for some time now, but I've always managed to avoid him. I'm not sure how convenient it would seem if I suddenly turn up wanting to do just that."

"It may seem convenient, but he can't afford to miss an opportunity to get information on his rival," said Cheelar. "You could send one of us with a message for him to meet you in the Throne Room."

"And he won't come and will demand I go to him. Then he'll be on his guard. Dammit, I'm just going to go into his office and shoot him and anyone else who gets in my way," said Kusac, throwing the backpack to M'yikku and striding out of the room. "I need to try and stop K'hedduk from destroying the transformer!"

The other two were almost running to keep up with him as he made his way down the final corridor between the temple and the priests' offices, then stopped at Inquisitor Ziosh's room. He already knew the head priest was there and alone. Reaching out mentally to silence him, he yanked the door open and entered, the other two filing in after him.

Ziosh sat there, eyes following him as he pulled out his gun.

"You have no idea how pleased I am to end your reign of terror, Ziosh," he said quietly, aiming at the other. Two short "pops" of sound and the Inquisitor slumped to the desk, most of his head decorating the wall behind him.

"Paint the Zsadhi symbols now," ordered Kusac. "I'll keep watch for any of his priests." He leaned against the door, gun ready, his eyes taking on a slightly distant look.

"Done," said Cheelar, a few minutes later.

"A group of priests in the Throne Room heading here," said Kusac. "We'll take them out and desecrate the room."

"What about preventing K'hedduk from blowing up the transformer?" asked M'yikku.

"I can't reach him in time," he said, opening the door. "We'll have to hope that Annuur has a fix for it. Let's do what we can for now."

"Why's he hitting out like this at all these people and the artifact, getting it to look like the Zsadhi did it?" asked M'yikku. "I thought he wanted the Zsadhi caught and his exploits suppressed. Now suddenly he wants very public deaths blamed on him? Is he losing it or what?"

"I think our destabilizing plan is working well," said Kusac with a feral grin, running down the corridor to the Throne Room entrance. As he did, he had a niggling feeling that this was not the wisest thing to do right now. He should be getting back to his apartment and meeting up with Rezac . . .

He shrugged his shoulders, feeling the weight on them vanish as he did. "No," he muttered. "You do not control me, Vartra! I'll damned well do it my way from now on!"

Throwing open the heavy Throne Room door, he dived inside, followed by the other two. Several feet away a group of five priests stopped suddenly and began to turn to run the opposite way. It was too late as the beams from the three energy pistols cut them down and finished them off.

"Paint it," ordered Kusac, getting up from the crouch he'd assumed and heading over to the throne at a run.

It was stone, with a high back decorated with creatures he knew Carrie would call griffins. Kusac put his hand on it, reaching for the nature of the stone. It was softer than the diorite he'd been dealing with and would only take moments to form a Zsadhi sword out of it. "No, I'll not do it, Vartra," he hissed, snatching his hand back. "Hit the translocators now," he ordered. "Time to leave!"

Mountain village, same morning

Carrie had gone to the village with Kaid, T'Chebbi, Banner, and Jo, all of them using the Cabbaran-gifted morphing suits to appear as M'zullians. They were there to talk to Shazzuk about the future they hoped he would be involved in with them.

Leaving the males to chat, Carrie wandered off to the chapel, a bundle wrapped in a piece of blanket under her arm. She was looking for Rhassa, the priestess.

"Greetings, Carrie," said Rhassa, looking up from where she was arranging flowers on the altar. "What brings you in here today?"

"I wondered if you could tell me anything about this," she said, unwrapping her bundle to reveal the glittering headdress.

"Ah!" exclaimed Rhassa, dropping the flowers and taking a step back from her. "Where did you come by that?" she asked.

"One of the village females gave it to me the last time I was here. She said it was a replica of Queen Ishardia's crown." Carrie held it out toward the elderly female, but she refused to touch it, backing away until she knocked the vase off the altar.

"Burn it! That's the second vase this month," Rhassa lamented, bending down to pick up the flowers and the broken pieces of glass. One of the village women came running forward with a cloth to mop up the spilled water from the altar and the floor.

"Bad omen, and today of all days!" the woman exclaimed. "It's one of the inauspicious days of this month, bad things happen on such a day. This is only the beginning, mark my words!"

"Enough! You let your tongue do your thinking instead of your brain." chided Rhassa, flicking the blanket over the crown before throwing the broken pieces of the vase into a waste bin. "Go back to your children and leave us to the chapel," she ordered.

Sniffing and complaining, the other female left.

"What can you tell me about this crown?" asked Carrie, uncovering it again.

"We have no such replica of the crown in our village," Rhassa said quietly. "Let me show you something else," she said, reaching out to take Carrie by the arm and lead her to where the wall frieze was missing a figure.

"Until the day you last came, there was a figure in this space—the figure of a female wearing that crown. But she wasn't Queen Ishardia the Gentle; she was her evil sister, Tashraka."

Carrie's face paled as she reached out a hand to touch the rough stone of the frieze. Beneath her fingers, it felt so cold it almost burned. She looked up suddenly, eyes blazing. "You lie!" she hissed. "It was Ishardia that was there on the wall, not Tashraka!"

"I speak the truth," said Rhassa, folding her shawl more closely over her chest. "Until you left that day, the carving of Tashraka wearing that crown was there."

"I will not consort any longer with liars," Carrie said coldly. "You are not fit to be a priestess when you cannot tell the truth from a lie! Leave this chapel and never darken its doors again!"

Rhassa stared at her, mouth open in shock until Carrie took a threatening step toward to her. "Leave!" she shouted, placing the crown slowly on her head. The fit was loose at first, then like that night in her dream, she felt the wings tighten protectively around her. A feeling of power suffused her body.

She looked to where the priestess had stood, but she was no longer there. Good, she had much to do and not much time to do it in. First, she needed to reach the Palace. Once there, she would find this K'hedduk and make him Captain of her Guard. It was time that the proper order of things was restored to this world. Males were not fit to rule.

She left the chapel, drawing the shadows of the afternoon around her so that none saw her leave.

M'zull Palace, Kusac's apartment

Kusac had just materialized in his bedroom with his two aides when suddenly his link to Carrie changed radically. No longer was there the closeness; now there was only a coldness and disdain, and a sense of distance.

He staggered, catching hold of Cheelar to steady himself, and reached mentally for her. Anger and hatred flooded back along their link to the point he had to drop it.

"What is it?" demanded Cheelar as Kusac pushed himself to his feet.

"Something is wrong at the den," he said. "Keep a watch for me, I'll be back." With that, he tuned his translocator to their mountain base and vanished.

Materializing in the main cavern, he discovered they were all at the village. He reached out for Kaid, sending a wordless request for an update.

It came back instantly. *Carrie's vanished. She was carrying the crown of Tashraka and went to the chapel to ask about it. Said she got it from a female on her last visit, but that's impossible. There is no crown and there was no female. What there is you won't believe—a missing figure on that damned frieze—that of Tashraka wearing her armor and that crown.*

I know about the missing figure. My link to her has gone,

e sent back. *I can only sense anger and her hate of me. She
sees me as her enemy.*

She would—you're the Zsadhi to her Tashraka, sent Kaid.
*The villagers are convinced she is heading to the city to help
K'hedduk, and that she'll tell him all about you and about
the village helping you. We have to stop her.*

*We've more problems. K'hedduk has blown up the matter
transformer. Annuur says it can't receive the signals from the
nanites or activate them when they are ready.*

Crap, sent Kaid. *You get back to the city, I'll tell Annuur
and start a hunting pack to find Carrie. Be careful of her, by
the way. Apparently, she was some kind of a sorceress in her
time. And before you rubbish that, she put on that crown and
it changed her utterly, even down to her looks—she now* is
*Tashraka to all intents and purposes according to Rhassa,
who saw it happen.*

Has she any advice?

*Beyond saying she told you so? None. She says we have
to let the legend play itself out one final time.*

*Kaid! The Zsadhi killed Tashraka! Gods, I am not going
to even fight her, let alone kill her!*

You may have no choice, sent Kaid his mental tone heavy
with sorrow. *We cannot let the M'zullians continue in their
desire to reconquer the known galaxy. They have to be
stopped once and for all. There's more at stake than just us.
I'm sure we'll be able to stop her,*

Kaid heard his mental howl of desperation as if he was
in the cave with him. There was nothing he could say or do,
no more comfort he could offer.

Abruptly Kusac's presence vanished as he returned to
the city.

Mountain village

"Shazzuk, we need to mobilize every male who can hold a
weapon to find Carrie," Kaid said. "It may mean going to
the city because we believe she is headed there to see the
Emperor."

"Of course, we'll help. I personally think this business of legends coming to life is all very questionable. There is no reason why Tashraka should be here now, even if your friend is the Zsadhi."

"To stop us from beating the Emperor," said Kaid. "The plan we have is bigger than you can imagine. Yes, we are running raids and leaving Zsadhi leaflets and graffiti all over the places we hit, but more is happening."

"What more is happening?" Shazzuk gave him a perplexed look and waited to hear what he had to say.

"We need to talk in private," he said.

Shazzuk searched his face, then nodded and led him back into his house where the other villagers couldn't see or hear them.

"You know about alien races, don't you?" asked Kaid. "I mean, that they exist? That there is a Prime world where your species originated from?"

"We know this, and about the slave races."

"Well, today those slave races and some others are hell bent on stopping your world from reforming the old Valtegan Empire."

"I can understand this. What is your point?"

Kaid took a deep breath and turned off his chameleon suit, revealing himself as a Sholan. "I'm not a Valtegan, Shazzuk, I'm a Sholan. We were the last slave race, and the one that caused the Valtegan Empire to fall."

With an exclamation of shock, Shazzuk backed away from him until he hit the wall. "How many of you are there here?" he asked. "Are you all Sholans? I know Nayash is one."

"Not all of us, and we're not your enemies. We need to stop the M'zullians who are the warrior and officer castes. We're trying to bring about a situation where all your people can be like you in the mountains—one caste, not three."

Shazzuk put his hand up to his forehead, rubbing it as a frown creased his face. "How can you possibly do this?"

"Let me turn my camouflage suit back on," he said, activating it again. "I can't deal with the whole village suddenly knowing what we are right now. We have allies who will help us by taking the warlike natures away from the warrior and

e officer castes, and by allowing the females to move freely
gain in your society." Kaid could feel and see some of the fear
and tension leave the other's body as he continued to talk.

"How?"

"I don't know the details, but you will be able to ask
them for yourself. Nayash wants you to take on the role
your ancient forefather had, that of Governor. Your world
will need wise rulers to replace the folk like K'hedduk, your
current Emperor."

Shazzuk looked behind him for a chair and moved to the
nearest one, sitting down heavily. "I can't take this in at the
moment, Kaid," he said, his voice strained as he shook his
head. "We have to find Carrie right now. If she reaches the
city first, and tells K'hedduk about us, we're as good as
dead. You're as much at risk as we are. Let's leave the rest
until after this is over."

Kaid nodded. "As you wish. Let's get moving."

M'zull Palace, Kusac's apartment

Back at the apartment, Kusac tried to calm himself. He'd
been without his link to Carrie before. He could cope with
that side of things. What he refused to cope with was reliv-
ing some Valtegan legend that meant he had to fight his
wife to the death! Dammit, Tashraka hadn't been Zsadhi's
wife, the good sister Ishardia had been. She'd been the one
burned at the stake.

If he could get the damned matter transformer working
now, then perhaps with all the M'zullians unconscious,
whatever had Carrie in its grip would loosen it once there
was no clear enemy and all memories were wiped out. It
was all he had that he could try.

Despite the fact that Kaid had said he'd contact him, Kusac called Annuur on the translocator.

"Have you heard from Kaid?" he asked.

"Yes. Sorry I am to hear of your predicament. Nanit‗ now ready as far as can tell from last update. Need matte‗ transformer working to be able to signal them. Working on fix we are."

"Work faster, dammit!" he snapped at the hologram. "I will not fight my wife, Annuur!"

"Then do not. Keep distance from K'hedduk till nanites work and all are unconscious."

"Not possible. If she goes to K'hedduk, then my life and those of my team are all at risk. We have to fight back or die."

"Will work on it," assured Annuur before vanishing.

Outside in the concourse leading to the inner grand courtyard, all was chaos as priests came running out of the Throne Room yelling about the deaths of not just their fellow priests, but also of their Head Inquisitor.

As Kusac stood in the courtyard flanked by his aides, he was mobbed by the terrified males, all demanding he do something about the deaths.

He tried to extract himself, saying he would report the matter to Security, but they weren't listening. Each one yelled louder than his neighbor until one of them finally grasped hold of him.

Kusac's temper broke and with a loud hiss of anger, he backhanded the male so hard he flew across the courtyard to tumble against another passerby.

"Go see to your dead!" he yelled at the shocked group. "They must need preparing for their funerals! I have said I will report the matter to Security and I will. Now get out of my way!" He stormed back to the large waiting room, and from there to the security post where he reported the deaths of a number of priests and Inquisitor Ziosh.

Heading back to his own apartment again, he told Annuur to tell Toueesut to trigger the explosions at the fleets and in the underground ship parking area. He then headed for the surface to try and find Carrie before she reached K'hedduk.

The explosion from the outer grand courtyard was all he

uld have wished for. The ground trembled and shook for several minutes. Flames and clouds of smoke and debris were blasted high into the sky.

Screaming pedestrians ran in the opposite direction or stopped to stare in horror at the chaos and damage as the dust and debris from the explosion began to fall back down on the city. Suddenly, in the middle of all this, the large view screens came to life with the broadcast Kusac had made as the Zsadhi, telling the people that the false Emperor K'hedduk would be brought down and they should turn now and fight for their own freedom from his repressive rule.

The broadcast seemed to be on an ever-repeating loop and no matter where in the city he went, all he could see was himself as the Zsadhi telling them that their war fleets had been destroyed and exhorting the population to riot. And they were—worker rioters were everywhere, breaking into the government-owned stores and taking what they needed, causing fist fights with each other, grabbing all the food they could carry from the grocery stores.

"Captain, it isn't safe out here," said Cheelar. "I know we've had our scents augmented so that they won't attack us, but outside the Throne Room, they grabbed hold of you. If enough of them did that, they could have killed you! We should get under cover somewhere we'll be safe."

"Where's that?" asked Kusac tiredly, leaning against a building at the corner of the street they were on. "If Carrie reaches K'hedduk, then our lives aren't worth anything if we go back underground. We're safer out here, plus there's a chance we'll see her." The stress was making him feel lightheaded, giving him a pain in his chest and making it difficult for him to keep a grip on his M'zullian form.

"The chance is slim, Captain," said M'yikku. "Let's at least head back to the outer courtyard where we've a better chance of seeing her."

"Lead on," agreed Kusac.

CIRCLE'S END

M'zullian Palace, K'hedduk's office

"What the hell's going on outside my office?" demanded K'hedduk as the sound of raised voices and crashes penetrated his heavy door. "Zerdish, go and see!"

Before Zerdish could reach the door, it was flung open with such force that it bounced off the wall. Standing framed in the doorway was a sight that K'hedduk found hard to believe. A Valtegan female, dressed from head to foot in archaic bronze armor—the mail shirt glinted like a second skin in the artificial light, contrasting with the solid embossed greaves and arm guards. On her head she wore a royal crown of pure gold in the form of a blue-feathered raptor. Wings cradled her skull with the tail feathers covering the back of her neck. At the front was a rearing long-necked bird's head. In her right hand she carried a sword such as he'd only seen in history books—a bronze blade with the grip made of alternating rings of gold, turquoise, and lapis lazuli. A sword, like the armor, from his world's far past, and one that was slowly dripping blood on his pale carpeting.

"Which one of you claims to be the Emperor?" she demanded in a harsh voice.

"I am," said K'hedduk, getting to his feet. "Who in all the hells are you?"

"I am Tashraka, the true Queen of this benighted planet," she said. "Your people are rioting because of the raids carried out by the Zsadhi. Your Lord Nayash is the traitorous Zsadhi. He planned to destabilize your world by attacking prominent people and businesses, and creating fear and havoc everywhere. This he has succeeded in doing. His next stage is to call on his alien allies to land and take over here. Unless you leave now, you will be captured by them."

"How do I know you're telling the truth?" demanded K'hedduk, looking briefly at Zerdish who was moving to his side. "Nayash is no traitor! You could be working for my enemies!"

"You've seen the broadcasts," she said, pointing to a

wing screen set against the wall. "You know he's de-
oyed your three fleets and the space stations, as well as the
hips stored underground here. He ensured you killed only
the Generals loyal to you, not those who were traitors. I tell
you again, there is no escape unless you come with me."

"She's only a female," scoffed Zerdish. "She knows nothing. How did she get free of her master?"

Carrie took several paces into the room and pointed her
sword at the other's face. With a gesture, her blade began to
glow an ominous dark pulsating red. She spun it in the air,
drawing a figure eight that continued to glow after her
blade was still.

"Don't make the mistake of underestimating me," she
hissed quietly. "I am a sorceress as well as a warrior. Those
outside miscalculated and they no longer breathe. Their
blood pools on the floor. Will yours join it?"

Zerdish sneered and reached for his gun. Before his
hand was anywhere near it, a knife blade was sprouting
from his shoulder. He hissed in pain, hand going instantly
to the wound.

"The next one will be in your throat," she said quietly.
"Now, K'hedduk, shall we leave this place for one that is
safer, or will you wait here for Nayash to come and kill you?"

"Lead the way," he said, coming out from behind his desk.

Prime Palace, same day

Shaidan knew something wasn't right. He could feel it in
every atom of his body. It was his mama this time; he was
sure of it. Something was very wrong indeed with her. He
had to talk to Unity, find out what was happening, and help
if he could.

Luckily, it was their morning break time when they could
do what they wanted for fifteen minutes. After checking
that his sister Gaylla was settled with her jegget, Shaidan

headed for the library. He went straight for the secret
nel and locked himself inside it.

Unity, he sent, consciously using the little metal tran
ceiver woven into his hair. *I need to talk to you!*

Welcome, Shaidan. How can I help you?

*Something is wrong with my parents! Mama doesn't feel
like herself. I can sense something really wrong with her, and
it's upsetting Papa.*

How can you sense them from that far away?

With my help, interrupted a mental voice Shaidan knew
well.

Vartra! I must go help my mama and papa!

*Indeed, you must, youngling. Unity, make it happen if you
please, but protect him from the nanites or, because of his
Valtegan side, he will risk being memory wiped.*

I can protect him, said Unity. *What's happening to your
mama is complicated, Shaidan. An evil spirit is affecting your
mother, and she is indeed threatening your father's safety. As
well as that, a device that could end this trouble has been
damaged and no longer works.*

How can I help? he demanded. *Send me there. There has
to be something I can do to help!* Tears began to form, which
he brushed away with his forearm. His pelt began to bush
out, and he had to fight to make it lie flat again. If he was
going to help his parents, no one could know what he
planned to do.

*The machine needs a bypass, something that will connect
two parts of it that are working to make up for the damaged
part. I can send you there to apply that bypass.*

Yes! Send me there, Unity!

*As for your mother, perhaps seeing you will be enough to
dispel the evil presence.*

*Trying something is better than sitting here feeling the
wrongness*, he sent. *Let me get my knife, then you can send
me to my papa and mama.*

*I will have to bring you here first to get the bypass instru-
ment and tell you what to do. I'll also charge you with the
same nanites as your father has, so you'll not be affected.*

Let me get my knife, he repeated.

M'zull, outer courtyard, west side

Shaidan materialized right beside the alien matter transformer. "Thank you, Vartra and Unity!" he whispered,
clutching the rod that would help fix the machine. Looking
round, he saw the chaos that the underground explosion
had wrought. The artifact squatted to one side of what was
left of the courtyard, the very center of which had been
blown to smithereens. In the distance, he could see a group
of people emerging from one of the buildings that ringed
the courtyard. He knew that one of them was his mama, but
he had a job to do before anything else. Everything de-
pended on him performing this bypass.

He walked round the device quickly, finding a place where
he could start to climb it. Near the bottom, where the plinth
on which it stood had been destroyed, he saw the black marks
left by the explosives. Down by the ground level, he could see
the web there had been broken by the explosion. He needed
to get up onto the top of the device and find the nearest two
webs. Once there, he had to expand the small pole they had
given him until it was long enough to link them together.
When it was in place, the last thing he had to do was to press
a switch placed on the middle of the pole to activate it.

Finding a foothold, he began to climb slowly up the artifact. It wasn't easy because it was so rounded that his fingers
and feet kept slipping off—it was difficult to get a good grip
even with his claws. Finally, he made it to the top. He
reached for the pole where it was clipped to his belt. Tugging it free, he fastened one end of it over the nearest web,
then began expanding it until it reached the other web
some two feet away.

A stone bounced off the artifact, startling him and making him look up. A crowd of angry looking people were
standing not far from him, yelling and shouting. Another

rock came sailing through the air. Shaidan ducked just in time, so it missed him. He pressed the button on the pole, then rummaged in his pocket for the translocator. Pressing it against the artifact, he slid back down until he was on the ground again.

The transformer began to hum into life, lights glowing and flickering on the webs where he'd placed the bypass.

Looking round, he got his bearings again. Slipping under an extruded limb section of the artifact, which was now warm to his touch, he found himself facing the group of people which contained his mother. Then he saw who she was with—it was Dr. K'hedduk who had birthed them from the tanks and had kept them prisoners in his lab!

He shuddered, looking away as fear coursed through him. Fighting it, he glanced back to see that the group had stopped and were staring at him.

Kusac let Cheelar and M'yikku lead him back to the Palace. Their route brought them out on the western side of the open air grand courtyard, near groups of workers quarreling among themselves and pelting the now glowing matter transformer with stones.

"Someone's managed to bypass the damage," said Cheelar in surprise.

Kusac saw a small black figure sliding down the side to crouch on the ground at its feet. "Shaidan!" he exclaimed. Then, as Cheelar looked at him in surprise, he said it louder, pointing. "Shaidan's there! Over by the transmitter!"

"I don't see him. Are you sure?"

"He's round the other side of it now. He didn't see me." He reached out with his mind, but the cub was focused on his task and didn't respond.

"Over there, look," said M'yikku, grasping his arm. "Isn't that . . ."

"Carrie," he said, looking. "With K'hedduk." He clutched his chest. The pain was like a knife cutting at him now, making his breath come in short, agonizing bursts. He could feel his consciousness beginning to fade in and out.

"Captain!" hissed Cheelar. "You're doing it again, almost changing into your Sholan self!"

"I can't control it!" he said, falling to his knees as the change dominated his senses. He crouched there on his hands and knees, his clothing splitting and falling away as his muscles changed, grew larger, and his skin went from green to black. He tried to howl his pain, but all that emerged was a hiss of anguish.

Lifting his head, he saw his hands and arms—they were still Valtegan, but the skin, the skin was as black as night, as his fur would have been.

"No, damn you all!" he yelled. "I will *not* be your puppet!" He sat back on his haunches and glared around him. "I am not your Zsadhi!"

M'yikku was trying to back away, but Cheelar was holding onto him. "Captain! Like it or not, you are the Zsadhi now. You have to stop them!"

"Stop who? I will not fight my wife, I've told you that!"

"Shaidan is running over to them! She's coming toward him, sword drawn!"

Kusac looked. The small figure of his son was running toward the battle-clad Valtegan warrior his wife had become. Hissing his anger, he got to his feet, doubling over as the change took hold of him again, coating his limbs with black fur that, as quickly as it appeared, vanished again. He staggered, trying to get his balance. "I can't do anything in this state," he hissed at Cheelar.

"You have to decide who you are," said a voice he'd come to hate hearing as much as Kaid had. "You need a weapon. This will serve you well." Vartra thrust a double-handed sword at him, waiting for him to take it.

"No!" he hissed, even as his hand automatically went up to receive it. "Not the Zsadhi's sword! I swore I wouldn't be your puppet!"

"Then do it to save your son—and your wife," Vartra said before vanishing.

"Mama!" As he ran over to her, Shaidan reached out mentally for his mother, but something hard and angry met him instead. Shocked, he slowed down, walking now. "Mama, it's me, Shaidan!" he called out.

"Demon! I don't know you! Call me not mother, I never birthed such as you!" she hissed back, pacing up and down in front of K'hedduk, spinning her sword round in her hand.

Shaidan crept slowly closer, stopping almost within arm's reach. "You didn't birth me, but you are my mother," he said. "He birthed us from containers." He pointed to K'hedduk, behind her.

She looked round, momentarily confused at what he said, then turned back to him. "It matters not. You are no child of mine. Come no closer, or I will attack you!"

He felt her confusion and pushed harder with his mind, sending her images of them going swimming at the pool and playing in the nursery.

"Stop that!" she said, shaking her head. "Mind stealer!"

Again he edged closer, pushing his mental advantage, making her relive the day she and his father had left on their mission to M'zull.

She let out a wail and clapped her hands to the blue-and-gold wings of the crown, pressing them even more tightly to her head.

This time he barreled into her, flinging his arms around her waist. "Mama! It's really me, Shaidan! Please come back to me!"

Touching her created an even closer bond, allowing him to see past the harshness of this Tashraka person she had become, to the mother he knew underneath the crown. Next thing he knew, she'd torn his arms free and flung him violently aside. He sailed through the air to land hard some ten feet away. As she dropped into a crouch and began to move toward him, he struggled to his feet and began to back off.

Tears he didn't mean to shed began to gather. The fall had hurt him, not badly, but enough.

"Mama, please," he pleaded. "You know it's me. Look inside and you'll find the memories. Please, Mama!"

A black figure suddenly ran past him, tackling her, sending her sprawling onto the ground. "Leave our son out of this," hissed the dark-skinned male, standing over her. "If you need someone to fight, fight me!"

"No! It's not her, Papa, it's something evil, something in the crown!" Shaidan ran toward the fallen female as she scrambled to her feet, but with a backhanded blow, she sent him spinning into Kusac and danced back to a safe distance.

"So you're the Zsadhi," she said, looking him up and down. "No armor, you'll be no match for me." She circled him, swinging her sword in front of her, doing figures of eight to keep him at a distance. "Come on, then, great savior of the people, attack me!"

Ignored now, Shaidan sat up slowly. His mouth felt swollen, and he could taste something metallic. He rubbed at it with his hand, wincing as it hurt, seeing the blood darkening his palm.

She suddenly lashed out at his papa who miraculously had his blade there just in time to block it.

"I won't fight you, Carrie," he said, his sword at the ready position as he followed her body movements. "You aren't Tashraka, or Ishardia—you're my wife. Stand down, I want K'hedduk, not you."

She lashed out at him again, a flurry of blows he was hard-pressed to avoid. Several found their mark, leaving shallow, bleeding slashes on his right arm and left thigh.

Shaidan used the opportunity to creep up behind her.

No! It's too dangerous! sent Kusac.

You can't fight her, Papa, I have to do this.

Shaidan reached inside himself, looking for ways to combat his mother's belief that she was this ancient warrior. Finding several, he gathered his mental strength and lashed out at her mind, stunning her and bringing her to her knees almost insensible with pain as simultaneously he launched himself at her back.

He scrabbled to hold on as she fell, but his grip was enough. With one hand, he grasped the rearing head of the raptor at the front of the crown and pulled the whole thing free of her head. Flinging it aside, he let go of her and fell to the ground in a small, exhausted heap.

Ghioass, Isolationist party HQ

"So they fight with the mother," said Zaimiss. "Keep watching, soon we will get a chance."

"Surely you don't want to take him in front of the Hunter?" said Tinzaa.

"You Cabbarans have no stomach for this fight. What can he do? No knowledge he has of who takes son! Unity, be ready to transport him here."

I cannot do that, Leader Zaimiss. I have no authorization to do this. It needs the order of two people, one being an Elder.

"I give authorization!" said Tinzaa. "Bring the Hunter cub here at once!"

As you wish, Elder Tinzaa.

M'zull, outer grand courtyard

Kusac stood there, hardly able to believe what had happened. One moment Shaidan had been sitting on the ground just behind Carrie, who was now unconscious and had reverted to her normal human form, the next, he had gone—just winked out of existence.

"Shaidan!" Kusac shouted at the top of his voice and his mind, but there was nothing. Not a trace of his son remained.

A movement to his right instantly drew his attention. It was K'hedduk, in the company of the injured Zerdish and several others of his bodyguards.

"You stay there," said Kusac, pointing his sword at him. "I want you. I have waited a long time to face you one-on-one, and you will not deprive me of it now!" Keeping his eyes on the whole group of six, he began to move to his left to where the crown lay on the pitted surface of the courtyard. Reaching it, he stamped on it hard, smashing the wings together, breaking the inlaid lapis so that never again could it be worn.

"Take him!" ordered K'hedduk, pointing at Kusac. "He's threatening my person. I want him dead!"

"Cheelar, M'yikku!" called Kusac. "To me!"

"Always, Captain," came Cheelar's quiet voice from beside him.

"If they move, shoot them. If they pull a weapon, shoot to kill. Leave K'hedduk for me. Understood?"

"Yes, Captain," Cheelar said, moving out to cover the bodyguards.

Zerdish moved to step in front of K'hedduk, but as a blaster shot sent chips of concrete up into his face, he pulled back.

"I don't advise it," said M'yikku quietly.

Three of the bodyguards began to slowly shuffle backward until Cheelar let off a couple of warning shots.

"Look, this doesn't involve us," said one. "You want the Emperor, you have him, we're not going to interfere!"

"You can move away," said Cheelar, "but carefully!"

Kusac, we're here! sent Kaid. *Have you got Carrie?*

She's unconscious. It was that crown that changed her. Come and take her to safety!

K'hedduk?

I have him, but Shaidan was here. He bypassed the transformer for us, managed to knock his mother out, then suddenly vanished!

Silence for a long minute, then: *He's not here, Kusac,* sent Kaid quietly. *I have no idea how he got here, or how he left. I asked Annuur and he said he isn't on the Prime world either.*

I have to see to K'hedduk now. If anything happens to me . . .

I'll see to Carrie and Shaidan.

"You traitors," sneered K'hedduk. "You'd sell yourself to a killer like this?"

"We didn't agree to fight legends," said their spokesman, speaking again.

"Give me her sword, Kaid," Kusac said, holding out his hand for it. Kaid threw it over to him, pommel first. He caught, it then turned to K'hedduk.

"You're good at getting others to do your dirty work for you," he said. "This time, take this sword and face me yourself."

"How can I face you?" asked K'hedduk. "You're a legend, not a person!"

"Oh, I'm a person, all right. I'm Kusac, the Sholan on whom you implanted a control device on the *Kz'adul*. You took my wife prisoner, too." He pointed to where Kaid was carefully lifting Carrie up. "Remember her? The Human female? We were all on the *Kz'adul* about two years ago."

"You're not Sholan! I know a Sholan when I see one. You're a M'zullian like me. You've just stained your skin black!"

Kusac threw Tashraka's sword at him and, reflexively, the other caught it.

"You'll fight me, or I'll execute you. I don't care which," said Kusac. "You have to answer for your crimes against me and my clan. This way, you have at least a chance of beating me."

K'hedduk turned to Zerdish, handing him the sword while he pulled off his jacket. Throwing the garment at him, he took the sword back.

Kusac watched as K'hedduk swung the blade a few times, adjusting his hands on it till his grip felt comfortable. All the while, though, his mind was still searching for any trace of his son.

The villagers, along with Kaid, Rezac, and the others, formed a circle around the two combatants with only Zerdish and one of the other black-clad bodyguards inside it. Weapons raised, some looked outward to the civilians gathering to see the fight, and others faced inward to the combat about to take place.

Keep him busy for about fifteen minutes. Then the nanites should kick in, Annuur says, sent Kaid.

He'll be dead by then, Kusac replied. *Get Annuur onto finding my son!*

The pain in his chest hit him again as he paced toward the middle of their impromptu circle.

If you want to survive to find your son, you have to embrace the legend, Vartra's voice sounded in his mind.

Never! he replied, brought to his knees again as the

change took him, turning him into a full Sholan just long enough for K'hedduk to see him and recognize him.

"I do know you," said K'hedduk, as he rushed at Kusac. "You were in that stasis pod the *Kz'adul* found. You had a mental link to a Human female."

The sword was descending toward his head, but Kusac threw off the pain at the last moment and got his sword up to block it. Pushing hard, he threw the M'zullian back and scrambled to his feet.

K'hedduk recovered his balance and came at him again. "Yes, I learned a lot about you and your mental link," he said, circling him. "Pain given to one of you was felt by you both. I had fun discovering that. Even the slightest application of it gave me a response from both of you!"

Kusac knew K'hedduk was trying to enrage him to lose his self-control, but knowing didn't stop it from being effective. He circled, blocking the blows as they came in, conserving his strength. K'hedduk would make his mistake and then he would strike. Till then, let him wear himself out.

"The female, such a low pain threshold she has. Perhaps I can experiment on her some more!"

A flurry of blows rained down on him this time, some of them just nicking him as his anger and the pain in his chest slowed him down. This time, he met them with big sweeping blows, each one knocking Khedduk's sword aside and driving him back.

"You talk too much," snarled Kusac, finally remaining in his true Sholan form.

K'hedduk hissed his rage, redoubling his efforts.

Kusac lashed out with his foot when he got close enough to him, and when K'hedduk went flying backward, followed it up with a sword blow at his side that just contacted.

Staggering and hissing in pain, K'hedduk clapped his left hand to his side and backed away from Kusac. He risked a glance at the wound. It was deep, but not life threatening.

"I see you found the brats alive," said K'hedduk, keeping his distance. "Pity. I intended them to die when I had no further use for them."

"They aren't brats. They are children, our children," snarled Kusac, ignoring the pain in his chest as he rushed forward and ducked under the other's blade to close with him. Face-to-face, Kusac smiled a human smile, showing his teeth. "And you will never threaten them or us again when I am done with you!"

"Words!" hissed K'hedduk, struggling to push him aside as their blades remained locked above their heads. "You'll need more than words to beat me!" His knee came up to hit Kusac in the gut, making him double over at the shock of it.

As he staggered back, K'hedduk's left hand came round for a punch to his face, but Kusac's hand was there first to catch it. He squeezed hard, eliciting a cry of pain from the other, then he shifted his grip to bend the fingers back. There was an audible snap, followed by a hiss of agony from the M'zullian.

Kusac released him, straightening up as K'hedduk's other hand brought his sword down hard, trying to pommel punch Kusac on the head. He missed and with a cry of rage, the bodyguard Zerdish charged at them, knife held out to stab Kusac. Three guns blasted him, but he made it far enough to push Kusac away from K'hedduk and stab him in the leg with his last dying lunge.

"Dammit, Kusac! The nanites go live in minutes now! Hang in there!" shouted Kaid.

It might as well have been hours. Kusac limped back, reaching for the knife stuck into his left leg. K'hedduk came barreling in toward him, sword held in one hand, his other useless hand dangling at his side.

With a roar of anger, Kusac pulled the knife free and threw it at him. It struck the M'zullian square in the chest. With his free hand, Kusac reached out physically as well as mentally and raised K'hedduk high into the air.

"You will not live to threaten us another minute!" began Kusac, then suddenly time seemed to slow down and a slight figure materialized in front of him.

"He is mine now," said a feminine voice as control of K'hedduk's body was taken from him. "For his crimes against my people and yours, he will burn for all time!"

Kusac blinked as his arm fell to his side and he got a clearer look at the Valtegan female in front of him. Her form blurred slightly, overlaid with the golden fur of Ghyakulla, then it faded to be replaced with the golden-scaled form of La'shol.

Her hand was wreathed in flames, flames that spread toward where K'hedduk dangled in midair. Within moments, he was surrounded by them, flickering in shades of orange and red and yellow.

"Burn, damn you, burn for all time!" snarled Kusac as he watched the flames burn fiercely and leap twenty feet into the air.

A terrible cry of anguish came from the center of the conflagration as clouds of thick smoke began to form. Sickened, Kusac backed away from the heat even he could feel. As he did so, the burning mass that had once been K'hedduk, Emperor of M'zull, fell to the ground.

"Justice has been done," said a voice that now sounded male. For a brief moment, the vision of the Nature Entity of the Valtegans became that of the Sholan Lord of justice, L'Shoh. Then the Entities were gone, leaving him alone beside the still smoking corpse.

Kaid was suddenly at his side, as was Shazzuk. The last of K'hedduk's bodyguards suddenly cried out and fell to the ground.

"Did you see that?" he asked, turning to them. "The Entities?"

"We did. He's in L'Shoh's hell now," growled Kaid.

Kusac nodded. "Finally."

"The nanites have kicked in," said Kaid, taking the first aid kit from Shazzuk.

"I need to find my son," Kusac said.

"We have to wait till the Touibans arrive and we can hand over this world to Shazzuk."

"You really are all Sholans," said Shazzuk in disbelief as around him, one by one, the others dropped their camouflage or transformed back into their natural form.

Kaid looked at the M'zullian in amusement. "I told you we were, but some of us are Primes from K'iosh'ik."

"But these people, they're all dead," said Shazzuk, look
ing round the courtyard at the bodies all lying on the groun
"What have you done to my people?" he demanded.

"No, they're not dead, just unconscious," said Kaid,
slathering antiseptic over Kusac's wounds and making him
yelp. "Go check them out if you don't believe me. When the
Touibans arrive, they will help you take charge of this world
and rewrite the racial memories of your people so they
have no memory of their warlike past, or K'hedduk. We
need you to be their new Governor."

"Fastheal," said Kusac succinctly, reaching for Kaid's
first aid belt pouch and taking out the ampule of the drug.

"No, you need to heal naturally," objected Kaid, trying
and failing to snatch it back. "You expended far too much
energy in that fight!"

"I have my son to rescue," said Kusac, hitting himself
with the hypo on his injured thigh. "I need to be able to
fight again if need be."

"You won't stop him," said Banner wryly. "I know, I've
tried."

Prime world, same time

"Shaidan's missing!" said Kitra, dashing into the office
where Dzaka was closeted with General Kezule.

"What?" demanded Dzaka, looking up. "Has he gone off
on his walkabouts again? I'll tan his hide for him!"

"No, he's really missing. He's nowhere on K'oish'ik!"

"That's impossible," said Kezule. "How could he leave
this world?"

"I don't know!" wailed Kitra, eyes overflowing with
tears. "I promised my brother I'd take care of them all for
him."

"I'll tell you who probably knows where he is," said
Dzaka, getting up, "Gaylla."

"Yes, she has to know!" said Kitra, dashing the tears
away with the back of her hand. "They're never far apart."

They found Gaylla in the bedroom, holding her pet

...get tightly, surrounded by her brothers and sister, sob-
...ng her heart out.

"They's taken Shaidan!" she wept. "They's taken him
away from me!"

Kitra sat down on her bed beside her. "Shishu," she said,
looking up at the nursemaid, "Take them all round to the
Brothers' and Sister's rooms, please. I need to talk to Gaylla
alone."

Shishu nodded, and rounding up the other four cubs, led
them off to M'Nar and Jerenn's common room.

"Gaylla, who's taken Shaidan? Where did he go?" she
asked quietly, taking the distraught cub into her arms.

"He went to help his mama and papa," she wailed, "but
while he was there, they tooked him away."

"He can't possibly have gone to help his parents," said
Kitra. "It would take him weeks on a spaceship to get there!"

"He got taken there, I felt him go," she wept. "Then
they's tooked him from there to somewhere else!"

"Gaylla, it's all right. He's probably hiding down in the
grand courtyard," said Dzaka, trying to help.

The cub began to shriek and wriggle in Kitra's arms, demanding to be put down. The poor jegget was even squeak-
ing in distress. Kitra released her, and Gaylla slid off her lap
and down onto the floor.

Standing there, Gaylla stamped her foot hard. "He's
gone to M'zull to be with his mama and papa, to help them
against the bad man who made us," she said, rubbing her
wet face on her sleeve. "He told me so!"

"How is that even possible?" asked Kezule, looking at
them.

"I could tell you if anyone bothered to ask me," said
ZSADHI. "But I'm just an ignorant AI, aren't I? I know
nothing."

"What the hell?" asked Dzaka, looking around the room
for some manifestation of the voice.

"ZSADHI, what do you know?" asked Kezule.

"Another AI took him, one more powerful than me."

"What?" demanded Dzaka. "Another AI?" He looked at
Kezule. "I thought you only had one AI here, ZSADHI."

"We do," said Kezule grimly. "ZSADHI, explain yourse[lf] before I have your personality overwritten!"

"Very well! If you feel like that about it. I am only trying to help, after all."

"Get on with it!" roared Kezule.

"Another AI has been communicating with Shaidan for some time. It has a presence here due to a transponder he wears braided into his hair. It has the ability to move people and objects almost instantly over vast distances."

"Why have I never been made aware of this before now?" demanded Kezule.

"I wasn't aware of it till now. It wasn't until Shaidan actually disappeared this time that I knew."

"This time?" asked Dzaka ominously. "Has it happened before?"

"Looking back on my records of past events, I see he has gone missing some four times before," said ZSADHI.

"Who does the computer belong to?" asked Dzaka.

"That I cannot tell you," said ZSADHI.

"Likely it belongs to one of the two races you have been working with here, General Kezule," said Noni, entering the nursery. "The TeLaxaudin and the Cabbarans, isn't it?"

"How do you know of this? What makes you so sure it's one of them?"

"Well now, it could be because we don't know anyone else it is likely to be," she said sharply as she pushed her way through to the cub's side.

"Well, precious, I see you have a pet jegget!" she said. "What's it called?"

"Snow," said Gaylla with a hiccup. "A Brother gave her to me."

"Ah, Brother Vartra would that be?" she asked, sitting on the edge of the bed and reaching out to pet the jegget.

A smile wreathed Gaylla's face. "You knows him? He gave me Snow as a pet."

"I knows him," agreed Noni solemnly. She looked up at the other adults gathered round Gaylla. "I think our young lady has told us all she can. Perhaps now is the time for you to go and leave her to me. There's nothing we can do here haidan is indeed either on M'zull or has been taken as a captive. That's down to his parents now."

"There must be something we can do!" raged Kezule. "They left me to look after their son, and I haven't!"

"It would take three weeks to get there on the fastest ship," said Noni. "Not just that, you could find yourself surrounded by enemies and be taken captive. Far better to leave it to Kusac. Trust me, he will know his son is in danger. Now go, and leave Gaylla to me." She reinforced her order mentally, telling Kitra that all the adults worrying like this was only making Gaylla hysterical. *Vartra brought her the jegget to ease her pain and the separation,* she sent to her. *We can do nothing from here; make the males understand this.*

"I think we should go," said Kitra, getting up. "We can talk about this in the lounge."

"Am I expected to believe that an AI from another species has been talking to Shaidan all along, and whisked him off to help his parents on M'zull?" demanded Kezule as they settled down in the lounge. "ZSADHI, ask Doctor Zayshul to join us. She knows exactly who's working in the labs right now."

"It seems we have more at work than just an alien AI," said Dzaka. "We have Vartra, too."

"Vartra?" asked Kezule.

"One of our Entities," said Dzaka. "God of Warriors, seen as a warrior laying down or picking up His tools of war. He's surprisingly active for an Entity!"

"He gave the jegget to Gaylla," said Kitra. "There is no way that the creature could be here unless He gave it to her. They only exist on Shola, and are the only other telepathic species on our world."

"They're considered vermin and are very adept at avoiding capture, believe me!" said Dzaka. "It would take an Entity to capture one."

Kezule looked confused. "Why would an Entity like him give a creature that's seen as vermin on your world to Gaylla as a pet?"

"To divert her and comfort her when Shaidan went miss-

ing," said Noni, coming in. "There's method in the madne
of this Entity, mark my words. I feel He may not like th
role that has been created for Him!"

Doctor Zayshul came in then and they quickly updated
her as to what had happened with Shaidan.

"There was a TeLaxaudin working in the labs until earlier this week, but no one has seen him this last day. We
don't keep a strict watch on them. ZSADHI does that and
only alerts us if they go into proscribed areas."

"Seems to me that the TeLaxaudin are good suspects for
having their own AI here," said Noni. "Do they have a ship
on K'oish'ik?"

"ZSADHI?" asked Kezule.

"No, they get dropped off by a ship which then leaves.
They don't maintain one here."

"Is Kouansishus on our world?" asked Doctor Zayshul.

"No, Doctor Zayshul, the TeLaxaudin doctor is not on
this world, and no vehicles have lifted off our world in the
last five days."

"So someone else is missing without having left K'oish'ik
in the normal way," said Kezule, "just like they did during
K'hedduk's brief reign."

"All we can do is to keep a good eye on Gaylla and ask
her to tell us if Shaidan shows up back on K'oish'ik," said
Dzaka with a sigh.

"I already asked her to do that," said Noni. "It's all we
can do, unless you fancy praying to Vartra and asking what
is going on?"

Looks of astonishment greeted her comment.

"What? I thought that would be the only obvious thing
to do," said Noni tartly.

CHAPTER 11

KARMA

Ghioass, Isolationist HQ

THE world around him disappeared suddenly, and Shaidan found himself adrift in the darkness of nowhere. Just as suddenly, he materialized again and fell to the floor with a crash that knocked the breath out of him.

A black-furred hand reached for him, but instinctively, still on his hands and knees, he crabbed away backward. The mind did not feel Sholan; it felt different, alien. He sensed the presence of other alien minds, two of them, both facing him.

Looking up, he saw a being similar to his people, but the legs were straight, and the hair was like a mane, full and long.

He pulled his knife, slowly coming up into a crouched fighting stance. "Who are you? You aren't of my people." He heard the wobble of fear in his voice and tried to banish it. "You're U'Churians. What do you want with me?"

Prime world, morning of same day

The cubs were full of it, almost bouncing off the walls with a mixture of horror and excitement that Shaidan was missing.

M'Nar excused himself and came back with N'Akoe to help. At least that's what Jerenn thought until his sword-brother again excused himself.

"I've got something I have to do," he said apologetically.

"Right now?" asked Jerenn, trying to comfort Zsayal. "Can't it wait till Brother Dzaka and Sister Kitra come for them?"

"Right now," insisted M'Nar. "You'll understand shortly." With that, he left their common room and headed for the library.

It was empty at this time of the morning, and he slipped in, quietly closing the door behind him.

Now he was here, he wasn't sure where the panel with the secret catch on it was. He remembered Shaidan saying something about it being like a raptor, or a dragon—dragon, it was like a dragon on a nest!

The only place there were carvings of draconic creatures was round the fireplace that wasn't used now. M'Nar pressed every part of the carving on the right-hand side of the fireplace, but nothing worked. Then he tried the left-hand side. Almost at once, he heard the slight click and saw a panel in the wall spring open slightly.

Heart in his mouth, M'Nar pushed the panel open and looked in. It was as dark as the inside of a Highlander's pouch, as the saying went. He reached in his pocket for the flashlight and, taking it out, shone it down the passageway. It was dusty and cobweb covered, but he couldn't see anywhere that a journal could be placed. There was no help for it. He would just have to explore this fascinating secret passage!

He pulled the panel closed behind him, then started walking, keeping his eyes on both sides of the walls as he did. It was just a tad wider than his shoulders, and he was well muscled for a Sholan. For a Valtegan—well, the Primes would be able to go down like he was, but the commandos, Kezule's offspring, would have to go down it sideways.

Then he saw it: a hard-bound blue book sitting on a small shelf made by a missing brick on the inside of the passage. He grabbed it, putting it inside his tunic where it would be hidden from prying eyes. He wanted to read this by himself before he involved Jerenn—he had to know what he was getting himself involved in before telling his sword-brother.

Retracing his steps, he stopped at the panel, listening for any sounds of occupancy in the room before releasing the catch. Slipping through the gap, he entered the library again and closed the secret entrance. He could follow the tunnel to its end another day when something more important didn't demand his attention.

Heading back to their common room, he found the cubs gone and Jerenn and N'Akoe chatting about where Shaidan could be.

Jerenn looked up as he walked in. "Have you finished this important task?" he asked.

"Yeah, all done," said M'Nar. "Just need to work on that plan for the MUTAC for a few. I'll be down there if you need me." He waved his hand and, oblivious to Jerenn's objections, left for the barracks where the MUTAC was stored.

Once there, he climbed up into the cabin and sealed the doorway. Sitting in the control harness, he pulled out the book and began reading.

What he read made the hair on the back of his neck bush out and his blood run cold. Shaidan was young enough not to notice all the implications, but this journal hinted at an alliance of other alien species to rival the Sholan one with, as its member races, two of the most adaptable and tech-minded species he could think of. They were also the most devious as they were intertwined deeply in the Primes' lives. The Cabbarans, the mysterious TeLaxaudin, and the U'Churians were woven into the fabric of each other and the Valtegans in a way he found discomforting.

Then there was this AI called Unity, a computing device of infinite size and knowledge, not only of all their species in the Alliance, but of its own three-member species. The journal also gave him a way he might be able to contact this Unity. Now that he was unsure of. There was no telling what can of worms that contact between him and Unity would open. It gave him food for thought, though, and the knowledge that he couldn't tell Jerenn what was in the book yet, even though he still needed to find a way to discuss it with him at some point.

Hiding the journal inside his tunic again, he headed back to the Palace.

Ghioass, Isolationist HQ, same day

"Put that knife down, child," said Naisha, not unkindly. "You might get hurt if you try to use it."

"I know how to use a knife," said Shaidan. "Stay back, or I will!"

"Don't make threats you can't keep," laughed Tyakar, standing just behind Naisha. "You lose all credibility that way,"

"Why am I here? What do you want with me?"

"We were told to capture you, and that's what we did," said Tyakar, elbowing his colleague out of the way and coming toward Shaidan. "Now give me that knife before you regret it!" He held out his hand for the knife, expecting Shaidan to comply and hand it over.

Instead, Shaidan lashed out with his blade, cutting the male across the palm of his hand before darting back again.

"You little . . ." began the U'Churian, pressing his good hand over his bleeding one. "Get him, Naisha!"

"That's not the way to behave," said Naisha, shaking his head. "You'll only make Tyakar angry, and that's not something even a grownup wants to do."

"*I'm* angry!" shouted Shaidan, his face creasing in rage. "You stole me from my papa! I was just about to see him, and you stole me!"

"Master Zaimiss wants to see you," said Tyakar, taking a rag out of his tunic pocket and wrapping it round his hand.

"And what he wants, he gets. You made a big mistake when you cut me with that knife! Naisha, grab him!" he said and they both suddenly rushed at Shaidan.

He managed to get in another slicing wound, this time to Naisha, before they held him down and prized the knife from his grasp. He was then let go, but as he got to his feet, Tyakar lashed out at him, delivering a blow to the side of his head that sent him spinning across the room to hit his head hard against the wall.

Stunned, he fell to the ground, lying there while Tyakar came up to him and gave him a kick in the ribs.

"Let that teach you not to play with pointy things," he growled before leaning down to haul him to his feet. "Now get moving! Master Zaimiss wants to talk to you!"

Zaimiss sat in a pile of cushions with Elder Tinzaa beside him on her sloping chair. "So you are the young one who has been cutting my helpers. I know they aren't happy about it, but I am less than pleased. You show regrettable manners for a child."

Shaidan peered at the TeLaxaudin, unable to focus on anything except for the dark red draperies. Everything else was blurred. He felt dizzy and nauseous, and wanted dreadfully to sit down so the room would stop spinning.

"You are a nexus. Around you the potentialities swirl. Why is that? What do you know that makes you so important to the future?"

Naisha nudged him in the side and Shaidan mumbled something incoherent.

"What did you say?" snapped Zaimiss. "Repeat yourself! What's wrong with him?"

"Master Zaimiss, he's gone pale and his hand feels clammy," said Naisha after examining him. "He hit the wall during our capture of him. I think maybe he has a concussion."

Shaidan fell to his knees and started vomiting.

"Get him out of here," hummed Zaimiss in disgust. "Put him in the room you prepared for him and get the doctor to see to him! I don't want him dead."

"Yes, Master Zaimiss," said Naisha as he waited for

Shaidan to stop vomiting before picking him up and limping out of the room with him and Tyakar.

"Damned child had no business having a blade on him," said Tyakar. "You got sliced up by him, too. What was it, your leg?"

"Yes, but it's shallow, thank goodness. It's already stopped bleeding. We need to get information from him, Tyakar, and we can't do that if he's unconscious or dead! Think ahead before acting."

Tyakar grunted at him and sped up, walking quickly to the room they'd turned into a cell, opening the door for Naisha.

"Hurry up! I want to get my hand seen to."

"We need a medic to see to him as well. Let me put him in the recovery position so he doesn't choke if he vomits again."

That done, and the door locked, both of them made their way to the common room where the Cabbaran medic was. There they got their cuts attended to before they escorted him to Shaidan's room and stayed with him while he examined the cub.

"It's a concussion," Sivaar said after using his portable scanner on the unconscious cub. "Nothing serious, but you should keep him quiet for the rest of the day. Likely he will be disoriented and problems understanding what you say at first may have, due to concussion. A lot better tomorrow he should be. His ribs will take longer before the bruising goes down, about a month. Really necessary to throw him at a wall, then kick him?" he asked Tyakar. "Your violence counterproductive. Punching it insensible not solve everything!"

"You stick to your job, Sivaar, I'll stick to mine," said Tyakar.

Ghioass, Camarilla chamber, same day

Needaar was trying in vain to keep order in the Council chamber as they discussed the latest potentialities. The new nexus and the one they knew to be the Hunter had clashed spectacularly. In fact, they had been able to see it as it happened. Then a third nexus had appeared, been identified as the child of the Hunter, only to disappear completely from their projections.

Annuur was speaking to the assembly, and he wasn't mincing his words.

"Instantly removed from M'zull cub was. Only two ways—use of translocators, which he didn't have, or through Unity. Unity cannot initiate contacts or transports, so must have come from us. Which party would find cub of use? Isolationists, I say!"

Khassis was picked to speak as Needaar reminded the assembly that those who made too much noise would be removed from the hall.

"How would Isolationists use the Hunter cub?" asked the TeLaxaudin Elder. "We Moderates wish to know."

"Cub can disappear. Not visible in potentialities at some times, there at others. This I have seen. Knowing how to conceal themselves from Unity be useful for Isolationists. Already they manage to make and use device to look like Phratry leader Kuvaa." There was an outcry at this, with Leader Needaar calling for silence.

"Unity, confirm what I said about Isolationists masquerading as Kuvaa," said Annuur.

This I can confirm. Protocols were initiated by Phratry Leader Kuvaa to stop this happening again. The person affected by this subterfuge was Giyarishis, who is now missing from sand-dweller world, and this one.

"I say Giyarishis been abducted by Isolationists same as Hunter cub because monitoring the cub he was, had information on him for Camarilla. Now he prevented from giving us information—information that could allow others to hide from Unity! Who would want this information?"

Again the clamor of voices, all in their own tongues, and all translated simultaneously by Unity.

When the noise died down again, Khassis was able to continue. "I see pattern here, desire for ways to work under cloak of secrecy. This is not Camarilla way."

Annuur pointed to Dhaimass, a TeLaxaudin Elder, indicating she was next to speak.

"As Elder in Isolationist party, object do I to this assumption our members are at fault. What proof is there of deceiving Giyarishis of Kuvaa's identity? Only your word!"

"Unity, show images of Kuvaa on day "she" spoke to Giyarishis, but it was not her," said Annuur. "Show image of real Kuvaa same day side by side."

On the large screen was the image of Kuvaa with her new tattoos while on the other side was "her" talking to Giyarishis without the tattoos.

"As clear to see, Kuvaa had new tattoos, but Kuvaa who spoke to Giyarishis did not," said Annuur. "Date on each image also clear."

"Not aware of this was I," said Dhaimass, eyes whirling as she focused on Annuur after looking at the screen. "Who responsible?"

"Not one person," said Annuur. "Giyarishis felt different handlers, different times. Not easy being agent, not needing this happening!"

Needaar came running over to the lectern. "Stop, Shumass! Or arrested you will be!"

Annuur looked to the exit where the TeLaxaudin was beating a hasty retreat toward the doorway.

"Halt, on order of Camarilla," said Annuur, but the TeLaxaudin kept going.

A signal from Needaar and the two U'Churians nearest the exit immediately placed themselves where they could apprehend him.

Shumass stopped then, looking around for another way out of the chamber.

"Prevent translocator from working," snapped Annuur, guessing correctly what the panicking member would do next.

The two U'Churians moved swiftly forward to apprehend him, grabbing his arms and holding firmly onto him.

"You will surrender your weapons to the duly appointed lawkeepers, and accompany them to the detention center," ordered Needaar. "We will know why you tried to flee the council hall when duplicity from your party over Kuvaa was disclosed!"

In the uproar, Elder Khassis came up to the lectern to talk to Needaar, then took over from Annuur.

"In view of these events—disappearance of Hunter cub, and person masquerading as Kuvaa, I say we imprison all Isolationist leaders until truth of matter is known. Those for my motion?"

A forest of hands went up at this.

"Those against?" A few hands, mainly those of the Isolationists, went up as once again the babble of voices threatened to drown out any speakers.

"Silence!" Khassis called out. "Unity, what is the result of the vote?"

Thirty against the motion and one hundred and sixty-five for it. The motion is passed. Records will show that the leading members of the Isolationist party will submit to the lawmakers until the truth is known about the disappearance of the Hunter cub and who was involved in pretending to be Phratry leader Kuvaa.

"Lawkeepers, you know your duty," said Khassis, standing back from the lectern as the U'Churians around the hall stepped down to take the leading members of the Isolationist party into custody.

Azwokkus and Shvosi were going frantic, using Unity trying to search out all the areas they could think of where the Hunter cub could be concealed. At last Kuvaa came to join them at the Reformist HQ office.

"Kuvaa, ask Unity if anything more about the Hunter cub can it disclose," said Azwokkus. "Have searched all known locations for him and nothing."

"I have more to tell you of cub," she said, grabbing a handy lounging seat and stretching out on it. "Have not this mentioned before. Hunter cub found Unity on sand-dweller home world at node left in pool area. Isolationists put there to track Hunters and sand-dwellers both. Unity initiated contact with cub."

"What?" asked Azwokkus, his large eyes swirling as they focused on her and not on the screen before him.

"You must be wrong," said Shvosi. "Unity cannot initiate anything without our instructions!"

"Unity, did you communicate with Hunter cub?" asked Kuvaa.

I did communicate with the cub known as Shaidan, said Unity.

"Who initiated this contact?"

I did, Phratry leader Kuvaa.

"Why did you do this?"

I wanted to learn more from him.

"What did you discuss?" asked Azwokkus.

I taught him the history of the U'Churians and about how the sand-dweller home world had been—the plants, trees, and animals.

"Did you bring him to your core, Unity?" asked Kuvaa quietly.

I did. I wished him to know my nature.

"Unbelievable as it may seem, I think Unity was making friends," said Shvosi.

Kuvaa nodded her head. "I think this, too. Teaching he was. More advanced than we thought has Unity become."

"Can you tell us who brought Shaidan here, Unity?" asked Azwokkus once again.

I am not at liberty to tell you who brought him, or where the Hunter cub known as Shaidan is. I can only tell you that the order to transport him here did come from an Elder.

"Which Elder?" asked Kuvaa. "Your records should show this."

Elder Tinzaa requested Shaidan's transfer.

"At last!" muttered Azwokkus. "Where was he transported to?"

I cannot say because the location is not known to me. I sent the cub there, and the location was gone from my memory. If possible, Unity sounded perturbed at this.

"Have you asked for lists of known Isolationist-owned buildings?" asked Kuvaa.

"Yes," hummed Azwokkus. "And asked Unity to list who was in them."

"Did you hear that all Isolationist leaders have been arrested?"

Azwokkus nodded his head, mandibles clicking. "About time. Also I asked for list of all people in those buildings. Seems not only Hunter's cub missing, also several of the top Isolation personnel as well. I now believe them to be in the same location."

"We need to find where that is," said Shvosi, her long, mobile snout wrinkling in distress. "If Hunter arrives here distressed at missing cub, then prey for him we will surely be!"

"We will have many of perpetrators of kidnapping for him at least," said Azwokkus.

"Would that be enough for one of us if offspring involved? Not known for subtlety, cub may be injured by them as well. Have to find him!" said Shvosi.

"Unity, watch movements of all major people in Isolationist party. Watch where supplies are moved to, anything unusual happens connected to Isolationists, inform each one of us here," said Kuvaa. "That should give us some information."

I shall be pleased to do as you ask, Phratry leader Kuvaa. I am anxious to find Shaidan, too.

The Council Hall was quieter now that, one way or another, the Isolationists had left. The rest of the members had either gone outside to gossip about what had happened or were sitting relatively quietly to see what the potentialities showed.

Khassis and Needaar looked at the large screen. There were two nexuses now, one they knew was the Hunter, and the other was the Hunter's cub. There had been a third one briefly, but it had flared then died as the Human Carrie had been defeated by her son.

"As can be clearly seen, the second, smaller nexus is located on this world, and the larger one is still on the sanddweller world," said Khassis, her eyes swirling as she changed her focus from the screen to the people in the hall.

"Obvious it is that the Hunter will come to Ghioass. Not

long will it take him to realize son here," said Needaar. "Yes Htomshu." She indicated the Moderate Party Elder.

"How will the Hunter know to come here?"

"Cannot say. Will have to do with something Hunter cub, his son, has already done, probably on sand-dweller home world. There he finds clue to us."

Needaar indicated Shoawomiss.

"Should we not try to destroy such a clue? Prevent him from coming? On Prime world I work."

"No," said Khassis and Needaar together. Khassis bowed her head to the Cabbaran.

"Worst we could do is that. Cooperate we must, or all we work for is naught. Destruction of Camarilla not best for everyone," said Needaar.

Zoasiss of the Moderates was next. "M'zull world—were the sand-dwellers there not to be poisoned on vote won by Isolationists? Seems they are not dead."

Needaar looked to Annuur for clarification. "Ah, well," he said, dipping his long mobile nose down and wrinkling it. "Seems nanites we gave to Hunter were not poisoned. Memory wipe they will do instead so sand-dwellers can be reprogrammed. One caste not three they become in time, but to forget their dreams of conquest now."

"How we know this works?" demanded Htomshu once she was recognized to speak. "Distasteful was idea of poison, but at least an ending of their empirical ways."

"Touibans will monitor and help reprogram them," said Annuur. "They make it work."

"Hmm. Will see from potentialities after current crisis is over," she said, sitting back down on her nest of cushions.

M'zull, outer grand courtyard, midafternoon

His wounds dressed Kusac headed over to check on Carrie, who was beginning to come round.

"Ohh, my head," she moaned, putting a hand up to her forehead. "I have a hell of a headache. What happened?" Then she realized where she was. "Oh, Gods! We're in the city, and I'm Human—and you're all Sholans!"

"It's all right," said Kusac, crouching down beside where she was sitting and reaching out to touch her cheek comfortingly. "The nanites have activated. Annuur's plan worked."

"Kusac," she said tentatively. "Why am I in all this metal armor?"

"Someone gave you the crown of Tashraka and it morphed you into her," said Kaid, handing her something for the headache.

"Who gave me the crown? And I turned into her?" Carrie looked at Kusac's wounds. "The legend. Tashraka. She . . . I . . ." Her look was one of growing shock. "Did I hurt you?"

"A little, but not badly," said Kusac. "It was Shaidan that stopped you. He jumped onto your back and dragged off the crown. It looked like the legend had to play itself out once more. Let's just be thankful the result wasn't the same as the first time." He pointed to the forgotten pain medication in Carrie's hand. "Take it. You'll feel better."

She took the pill and let it dissolve on her tongue, pulling a face at the taste of it. "Have I anything else to wear here, or is it all back at the den?" she asked.

Kaid gave a small laugh. "Trust a female to worry about that."

"You're not the one dressed in uncomfortable chain mail," she retorted. "So that's it?" she asked. "It's all over now? Where's Shaidan? I thought you said he was here."

"No, it's not over," said Kusac, his voice heavy. "Shaidan's been taken. The matter transformer was damaged by K'hedduk attempting to blow it up, and somehow Shaidan was the one who came to bypass it. He helped to break the spell on you, and then he just vanished. Now the matter transformer's vanished, too!"

"How did Shaidan get here in the first place?"

"I wish we knew," he said. "He should have been safe at

home—unless someone like Vartra brought him here!" They could all hear his anger building again.

Kaid shook his head. "Not Vartra's style. He'd take one of us in a heartbeat, but not a cub. It is Shaidan's style, though, volunteering to do this."

"But how would he know we needed that help? Who could have told him? No one but us knew that the transformer was broken," said Kusac. "And where is it now?"

"The answer to both is likely to be on the Prime world," said Kaid.

"It didn't take Shaidan three weeks to get here," said Kusac harshly. "It damned well better not take me three weeks to get to K'oish'ik!"

"Looks like the Touibans are arriving," said Rezac, pointing to the sky as a fleet of ships began to descend.

Within half an hour, what remained of the courtyard was full of units of the Touibans, marching off to set up processing centers where the soon to be awakened M'zullians would receive their new memories. Other units were heading for areas like the underground Palace to get those people still there to the surface, then to set charges to destroy it once and for all. Through it all, Kusac paced like a caged beast at the necessary delay before he could start looking for his son.

"Stop pacing, Kusac," said Kaid, reaching out to grab him by the arm and hold him still. "You'll wear yourself as thin as you're wearing this concrete. You'll be in no fit state to deal with any emergency that comes up. Look at Carrie. She's as worried as you, but at least she's sitting down with T'Chebbi and Jo and talking about it!"

"She went back to the den with the others to get changed and collect her things," he said, nodding to where his wife sat. "I've had to wait here!"

"I think I recognize that swarm," said T'Chebbi getting their attention. "Toueesut, if I'm not mistaken."

Kusac looked round. "Shazzuk, I need you to meet a friend of ours. He's an Ambassador for the Touibans to Shola, my world."

"This is the Touiban you spoke of?" asked Shazzuk.

"What do I have to do and say?" There was a note of panic in his voice. "I've never had any dealings with alien races!"

"Yes, you have, with us," said Rezac. "Just be yourself with them. They can't expect anything else."

"Friend Kusac!" said Toueesut, dancing up to him. "Glad I am to be seeing you so well even if covered in bandages and wearing a most peculiar garment. Is this being the fine male you said would be our contact on this world?"

Kusac looked down at himself, realizing he was still wearing a loincloth from when he'd been fighting Kezule. He shrugged and put his hand on Shazzuk's shoulder.

"Shazzuk is the leader of the villagers you see here. They're all awake because they're already all three castes merged into one, unlike the rest of the population. Shazzuk is also the direct descendant of the last Governor of M'zull, so it's fitting he take over governorship under your people until the population is ready to go it alone."

"Pleased to be meeting with you, Shazzuk," said Toueesut, his mustaches bristling with pleasure. "Be coming with me to meet the Admiral in charge of this operation as he be wanting to meet with you."

"Just look at them out of the sides of your eyes till you get used to them," Kaid whispered clapping the stunned M'zullian on the back. "You'll get used to their constant movement, I promise. And, congratulations, Governor Shazzuk!"

Toueesut bowed deeply, taking the new Governor by the arm. With Shazzuk in tow, he danced off with his swarm, his bright turquoise coat with the maroon-and-gold embroidery on it eclipsing the large number of gold chains that he wore.

"Annuur," said Kusac, calling their Cabbaran friend on the translocator.

A hologram of him appeared in front of them. "Friend Kusac, what can I be doing for you?"

"We need to get to the Prime world instantly. Shaidan has gone missing. I might be able to find a clue to where he is there."

"Can send you and others there by translocator," agreed

Annuur. "In barracks courtyard you will materialize. Will this be acceptable?"

"Just send us now," said Kusac, his voice harsh with worry and anger at whoever had taken his son. "Do you know anything about him? He appeared suddenly to bypass that matter transformer."

The world around him began to fade, plunging him into nothingness where all that kept him focused was his link to Carrie. Just as suddenly, he materialized in the barracks courtyard, as Annuur had said he would.

Prime world, midmorning.

M'Nar's first stop was the library where he found a high shelf at the back of the room filled with what he considered boring books. He hid Shaidan's journal there. Then he went to the pool room and, stripping off, headed for the showers. It was a token shower, and then he was running down the slope into the pool and swimming strongly toward the island where the small jet pool was. Luckily, there was no one else there at that time of day.

Once there, he hauled himself over the ledge into it, waded across it, and climbed out on the other side among the ambient greenery. He tried to look nonchalant, just in case anyone was looking, as he felt along the wall behind the plants, searching for anything that just didn't feel right.

He found it, a tingling sensation under his fingertips. *Unity,* he sent, hoping that the fact he wasn't a telepath wouldn't stop him contacting the AI. *Unity, are you there?*

An adult Sholan? The voice in his head was clear and totally unexpected. *On the sand-dweller world. Not a telepath. M'Nar is your name. I have heard Shaidan speak of you.*

I'm in the Brotherhood, and a friend of Shaidan's, he thought back, unnerved by the way it knew his name.

A sensitive, though. You will want to know about Shaidan, won't you?

Yes! Where is he?

He is here, on Ghioass, but where on this world I do not know. His location is hidden from me.

Who took him? demanded M'Nar.

I did. The matter transformer had been damaged by the sand-dweller Emperor. A bypass was needed. He also sensed that his parents needed help. Shaidan offered to do the bypass if I took him to his parents.

Sand-dwellers? asked M'Nar, confused.

You call them M'zullians.

Wait, you took him from here to M'zull? M'Nar was incredulous. *What gave you the right to take a cub away from his family and minders like that?*

Would you rather I had let his parents die? They would have had he not intervened. Shaidan didn't wish that, and I had to take his wishes into account.

Look, I just want to know where Shaidan is! sent M'Nar. *Can you tell me?*

No, I am unable to tell you. His location is hidden from me.

M'Nar could swear he heard regret in the mental tone. *Can you only be reached from here?*

Shaidan has a transponder braided into his hair so he can reach me from anywhere. His captors are blocking him, preventing him from reaching out mentally to me or anyone.

Can you give me a transponder? M'Nar sent eagerly. This was the first piece of good news he'd heard.

You cannot keep it on you as you are not a telepath, but you can place it in a safe spot for me to create a web so that we can contact each other.

I can live with that. Give it to me.

You will have to return here in an hour. I cannot manufacture it instantly; it takes time, replied Unity.

I'll return in an hour, M'Nar sent.

He let his hand fall off the wall and took a deep breath. This was almost beyond comprehension. He'd just been talking to an AI on a planet Vartra knew how far away! And one who had at least a starting point for their search for Shaidan. Now it was time for him to go and tell Jerenn.

"You left me and N'Akoe to deal with the cubs on our own for over an hour, M'Nar," said Jerenn, polishing his sword with the feline-headed pommel.

"Are you even listening to me?" asked M'Nar. "I told you I have a lead to where Shaidan is!"

"We have a crisis on our hands with Shaidan missing and you go tearing off on your own, chasing after blue jeggets! It's not appropriate, M'Nar! You're the one with the parenting experience, yet you leave it to me and N'Akoe. Shaylor and Vazih were crying they were so upset that you weren't there."

"Jer, stop polishing your damned sword! I get your point, you're mad at me!" M'Nar pulled the oily rag from Jerenn's hand and flung it across the room. "Will you at least come with me and make up your own mind? We've nothing to do right now for the next hour or two."

"If it means you'll shut up about it, yes! Secret passages and alien voices in your head—I don't know what you've been drinking, but it's far too early for it!"

"Do you want to see Shaidan's journal first?"

"No, because it will only turn out to be a story he's writing for himself. Trouble with you is sometimes you can't tell fact from fiction!"

"I'm going to make you eat your words," said M'Nar as Jerenn followed him out of the door of their common room. "I don't understand why you are so skeptical of what I'm telling you! This is not like you."

"You don't usually go off and leave me to do the work alone. You did this time and then came back with this unbelievable tale. It'll turn out to be nothing, mark my words," he said as they entered the pool room.

This is Jerenn? You share a close bond, sent Unity.

"What the hell . . ." began Jerenn, almost falling into the jet pool as he backed away from the wall. "You're . . . it's real!"

No need to talk. Just say what you want in your mind instead. I can hear it.

M'Nar says you took Shaidan from here to M'zull to help his parents, sent Jerenn.

I did, but I am not responsible for him vanishing from M'zull. He is now somewhere on my world, but I don't know where. I have been asked to search for all the Isolationist houses and track their orders over the last few days to see if one of them is expecting a prisoner and planning for the inhabitants to lie low for several months.

Last few days isn't long enough, said Jerenn. *Look for longer, at least over the last month.*

If you took Shaidan to M'zull, can you take us to Ghioass? asked M'Nar.

I can take a small group of you, yes.

How many? asked Jerenn.

No more than twenty.

Any restrictions on weapons or armor?

No, but I must warn you that I will defend the Camarilla, myself, and my people.

What about Shaidan? asked M'Nar. *Will you defend him?*

He is my . . . friend. I will defend him, yes.

Good enough, said M'Nar, satisfied. *Who lives on Ghioass?*

The world belongs to the TeLaxaudin, but on it live Cabbarans and U'Churians. The Camarilla is comprised of only the TeLaxaudin and the Cabbarans.

"We need to go see Brother Dzaka," said Jerenn. "Let him know we have a lead on where Shaidan is."

"That's going to be a fun conversation, given how difficult it was to persuade you I was telling you the truth," said M'Nar dryly.

"There was a reason for that," Jerenn reminded him.

"Agreed," M'Nar admitted with a sideways glance at his sword-brother. *Will you talk to Brother Dzaka, our superior?*

No. Enough people know about me for now. Here is your transceiver, with a device to enable me to speak if need be.

A slim palm-sized device fell to the soft earth just below the node.

Place it down before you try to contact me, Unity said.

M'Nar picked it up. *We have to go now and alert our superiors, tell them we know roughly where Shaidan is.*

When I have news, I will tell you the next time you contact me.

Till then, thank you, Unity.

"Let's get moving," said M'Nar, turning to jump into the jet pool. He hesitated. "Do you think this device can get wet?"

"I doubt it," said Jerenn. "Carry it in your mouth, why don't you? You put your foot in it often enough."

"Very funny," said M'Nar, gripping it carefully with his teeth before entering the water.

They tracked Dzaka down to General Kezule's office.

"Should we wait until he's done with the General?" asked Jerenn. "Might be easier to talk to him alone."

"No. Every minute we waste is another one that Shaidan is in the hands of an enemy we can't reach," said M'Nar. He took a deep breath, then with the smallest of hesitations, he pushed open the door to the General's office.

"General Kezule, Brother Dzaka," began M'Nar as he walked right into the room. "We know where Shaidan is."

"We're listening," said Kezule grimly as Dzaka turned round to stare at them.

"Shaidan told me about a journal he was keeping," began M'Nar.

"Too long-winded," interrupted Jerenn. "We found out he's on the TeLaxaudin world of Ghioass. His journal told us how the TeLaxaudin have been watching us all here."

"And they left a node in the King's swimming pool room, so we went to it and talked to their AI called Unity," said M'Nar.

"It told us he was kidnapped from M'zull by a group called Isolationists." said Jerenn

"Unity couldn't tell us exactly where on the world he was, but it was busy looking for him when we left it to come and tell you. It will tell us when it does find him," said M'Nar, grinding to a halt as he saw the incredulous looks on the faces of the General and Dzaka.

"Let me see this journal," said Kezule, his tone clipped and businesslike.

"Shaidan trusted me with it," said M'Nar, then he saw the look that Dzaka was sending his way.

"Give it to them," hissed Jerenn, digging him in the ribs.

M'Nar reached inside his tunic and pulled out the blue-bound book. As both Dzaka and the General reached for it, he put it on the edge of the table and slid it into the center.

Kezule got it just before Dzaka and began reading it.

"A summary, if you please," demanded Dzaka.

"Seems your two here were teaching Shaidan how to fight," said Kezule, looking up from the journal.

"You were doing what?" asked Dzaka.

"Shaidan was afraid of being in a situation where he would need to defend himself and be unable to do it. He got really worked up about it, so we gave him extra lessons; that's all," said M'Nar.

"Extra lessons with firearms and throwing knives," said Kezule, putting the journal down.

Dzaka snatched it up and began reading.

"You taught a ten-year-old child how to strip down and fire energy weapons?" demanded Kezule. "You were supposed to be looking after children, not young warriors!"

"With respect, sir, it shows that our training may have been of use to Shaidan. He was right," said Jerenn. "He was abducted by alien people and was taken to an alien world. Right now, all that may have kept him alive is his knowledge of hand-to-hand and weapons fighting! What would you have done had we told you? Put a twenty-six-hour security detail on him and made him a virtual prisoner?"

"Somehow Shaidan had a premonition that something would happen," said M'Nar. "We just helped him face his fears by teaching him what we thought was appropriate for his age."

"You should have told us," said Dzaka angrily. "The

decision wasn't yours to make. You are not his guardians—Kitra and I are!"

"If he'd come to either of you, what would you have said?" demanded Jerenn, looking at both of them. "Disbelieved him and told him it was his imagination, when events have now proved it wasn't! You'd have had him living for weeks terrified of the future whereas we helped him put his fears to rest. Besides, you were brought up in the Brotherhood from a very young age, weren't you, Brother Dzaka? I bet you were learning unarmed combat and other skills by the time you were ten, along with the other sons and daughters of the Brothers and Sisters."

Dzaka looked away and went back to reading the journal while Kezule looked ready to snatch it away from him.

"You say you've talked to this Unity," demanded Kezule.

"Yes, we both have, but it says it won't speak to anyone else," said M'Nar. "It took him from here to M'zull to run a bypass on the matter transformer that was needed to switch on the nanites. The Captain saw him then and when he helped save his mama from . . ."

". . . possession by an ancient Valtegan Entity," said Jerenn smoothly. "It was after this that Shaidan was kidnapped."

"So not only do we have Shaidan missing, but we have his father on M'zull aware he is missing, and unable to do anything about it!" said Kezule.

"Captain Kusac Aldatan and his team have returned from M'zull," said ZSADHI. "They are on their way up here."

"Wonderful," hissed Kezule. "I promised him his son will be safe here while he's away on a mission, and here we are with his son kidnapped!"

"But we do know which planet he's on, and we have a way to get there," said Jerenn.

"Explain yourself," snapped Dzaka, passing the journal to Kezule.

"Unity said it can take a small group of up to twenty people and weapons to Ghioass."

"And it is looking for him on the planet," said M'Nar. "I know it will find him and tell us where he is."

"Why should this AI help us? It's bound to its owners, unable to act independently, unable to do anything it isn't programmed to do," insisted Kezule.

"Unity isn't like that," said Jerenn. "It has been talking to Shaidan as you can see from his journal, making friends with him. It offered all this information on him to us; we didn't ask for it. I think you'll find it has gone beyond its programming in many ways."

"I think we better get ready for Captain Kusac," said Kezule, putting the journal down.

Still gripping the Zsadhi sword in one hand, Kusac took the stairs two at a time, Carrie not far behind him.

"Where's the General, ZSADHI?" he demanded. "And Dzaka?"

"They are in the General's office on the third floor."

"Is Shaidan here?"

"Shaidan hasn't been here since he went missing just over two hours ago, Captain."

"Are the other cubs safe, and my sister and Dzaka?"

"All are safe, Captain. Brother Dzaka is, as I said, currently in the General's office."

"Kusac, slow down," said Carrie as he took the staircase to the third floor at a run. "You're leaving us all behind. Shaidan isn't here."

They might know something we don't, sent her life mate. *Perhaps they know how he managed to travel instantly to M'zull. I need to know what they know, Carrie.*

Security tried to stop them, but they backed off after one look at Kusac. It helped that Cheelar was there with them and they recognized him as well.

They came to a stop at Kezule's office. "Carrie, Kaid,

come with me. The rest of you wait here," he said an. opened the door.

"Welcome back," said Dzaka, getting to his feet. "We know Shaidan's missing, but we have some leads on where he might be, thanks to Brothers M'Nar and Jerenn."

Kusac nodded to them and Kezule. "Everything is well on M'zull," he said, "except that my son suddenly appeared to do a bypass we needed on the matter transformer. He then helped his mother," he indicated Carrie, "and disappeared. You have some leads?"

"Yes, your son wrote a journal which he entrusted to Brother M'Nar," said Dzaka. "It told of an unlikely friendship he struck up with an AI on a world called Ghioass, the home world of the TeLaxaudin, and host to the Cabbarans and some U'Churians."

Kusac sat on the edge of the desk. "Go on," he said, staring at them intently.

"They have been watching us by setting nodes at various locations," said Jerenn. "Shaidan found one in the King's swimming pool which is how he was able to talk to Unity."

"Why were they studying us?" demanded Carrie, resting against Kusac's uninjured leg,

"That we don't know, but we know that the two main races, the TeLaxaudin and the Cabbarans, formed a group called the Camarilla. They're bound into the fabric and life of the Primes," said M'Nar, "and with the U'Churians as well, they form an Alliance that is arguably more powerful than ours."

"They knew we needed help with the matter transmitter through Annuur," said Kusac, his tone taking on a deep growl of anger. "His people gave us translocators to move from place to place on M'zull instantly, and when asked, they brought us here! He has to have been in contact with Shaidan!"

"Surely, if he had been, he would have told us," said Carrie, reaching out to touch his arm. "How does this AI fit into all this? Can we talk to it?"

"It was Unity that sent Shaidan to you, not Annuur,"

...aid M'Nar. "Unity admitted that Shaidan contacted it, saying that you, Sister Carrie, were in danger and he wanted to help you. It told us that in return for sending him to you, Shaidan would apply the bypass to the matter transformer."

"So who took Shaidan off M'zull?" demanded Kusac angrily.

"Unity said it didn't know who, but that he was taken to Ghioass," said M'Nar. "It's been searching all the known Isolationist houses for one buying large amounts of provisions and supplies that could hint at the inhabitants wanting to lay low for some time, perhaps even expecting a prisoner."

"Isolationists?" asked Kusac, eyeridges meeting in a frown.

"A party within the Camarilla. I got the impression that they don't all agree on matters all the time," said Jerenn.

"Right," Kusac got to his feet. Putting an arm around Carrie's shoulders, he said, "Kaid, take Banner and Rezac and get us the weapons and explosives we'll need—a mix of longer-range and close, projectiles and energy weapons, maybe even a smart machine gun."

M'Nar stepped up to Kusac. "That's my kind of weapon," he said. "We were training the cubs and are very attached to Shaidan. Permission to accompany you, sir. We have a means of communicating with Unity and asking it for immediate transportation to Ghioass."

Kusac glanced over at Dzaka.

"They were teaching Shaidan how to fight with knives and guns," Dzaka said.

Kusac turned back to M'Nar, his myriad braids swinging as he brought his amber eyes to bear on him. "You were doing *what* with my son?" he asked very quietly.

"What Brother Dzaka didn't tell you is that Shaidan begged us for extra lessons as he was convinced he would face a life-or-death situation," said M'Nar, standing taller. "Seems he was right. Yes, we taught him how to use anything that came to hand as a weapon, but we also taught him when not to fight as well."

Kusac stared at him and M'Nar felt the faint prickling sensation as his mind was read. "Kaid, take M'Nar and get him his gun," Kusac said. "Tell Noolgoi to go with you. He can handle one of those." He looked at Jerenn. "You can come, too. We might need a sniper. Meet me in the audience hall opposite in fifteen minutes."

"Aye" said Kaid, leaving with M'Nar in tow.

"Kusac," began Dzaka.

"Stay here with Kezule and keep my sister and the rest of the cubs safe," interrupted Kusac, putting a hand on the other's shoulder briefly. "You aren't going to stop me taking the weapons I need, are you?"

"No, take what you need. There is a very real threat to all of us here if they are spying on us as this Unity says they are."

"Kezule, no blame is attached to you. Seems my son has his own ideas when family is at stake," Kusac said to the General.

"Very like his father."

Kusac gave a brief smile. "I want to take my commandos with me. I'll be taking all my people with me as well. Sixteen of us in all."

Kezule nodded. "Understood. I'm sure they'll wish to accompany you."

Drawing Carrie with him, Kusac left the office and headed for the audience hall. His people were already beginning to gather there, checking over their gear, getting new energy packs and ammo for their projectile weapons, and fastening on body armor.

"You should get out of the Zsadhi outfit, Kusac," said Carrie, accepting body armor from Jo and turning round so the other woman could fasten it on her.

"I haven't time to go to our rooms . . ." he began, then stopped as he saw Lieutenant M'kou coming toward him carrying a gray tunic and belt.

"I saw you arrive, Captain, and thought you would need these," he said, handing them to him.

"Thank you," said Kusac, unfastening the loincloth and throwing it aside. He passed the sword to M'kou and, grabbing the tunic, put it on and fastened the belt with its pouches around his waist. Accepting the body armor from Cheelar, he let him fasten it. Kaid handed him his preferred

...ns, which he fitted into their holsters. Finally, he accepted ...ne sword from M'kou and slipped it through his belt.

"You know we might not come back from this one," he said quietly to Carrie, pulling her close. He rested his forehead against hers.

"We nearly didn't come back from M'zull," she said equally quietly. "He's our son. I want to bring him home as much as you do." Her voice hardened. "And to rain down death and destruction on those who took him!"

Everyone was ready at last, Garras being one of them. "I'm coming and you can't stop me," he said, snagging body armor from Cheelar.

"Some of us might not be coming back," Kusac warned.

"What better reason to fight than for our young and our future," said the older male.

"Very well," said Kusac, stepping away from his troops. "Garras, you take command of comms," he said, accepting a throat mic from Kaid and fitting it round his neck. "Rezac and Cheelar, you're on point. M'Nar, bring that contact device over here, I want to talk to *Unity*."

"Yes, Captain," said M'Nar, following him, one hand on the gimbal-mounted weapon, the other reaching into his pocket. He handed the palm-sized object to him. "Unity said I couldn't carry it and use it as I wasn't a telepath. It should work for you, though, without the web he said I'd need."

Kusac took the object and closed his hand around it. "Form up beside and behind me," he said to his people. "I'm going to talk to this Unity now and ask it to transport us to where Shaidan is." *Unity,* he sent. *I'm Shaidan's father. Answer me! I'm looking for my son.*

Captain Aldatan, came the voice in his mind. *They said you would come.*

Where is my son?

I know he is on Ghioass. I'm looking for him now.

What are you? demanded Kusac.

I am an AI, and I plot the potentialities of the future so that the Camarilla may decide which course to steer. Every decision taken involves life and death, or no decision would be needed.

Kusac let that revelation pass. Right now, he wanted information that would help him find Shaidan. *The Camarilla, what's that?*

It's the council of elder species that guides the future for both the younger species like yourself, and for themselves.

What species make up the Camarilla?

The TeLaxaudin and the Cabbarans form the Camarilla, but their helpers on Ghioass are U'Churians who live there.

What does it do?

It exists to make the future as harmonious as possible. The rise of the sand-dwellers on M'zull was not harmonious, and so a solution was sought for them.

So the nanites Annuur put in my wrist were part of the solution?

They were the solution, though not the one the Camarilla voted for. The Isolationists wanted the sand-dwellers wiped out, poisoned by the nanites. Annuur and the group he belongs to decided to wipe their memories instead.

The Isolationists?

One of three parties in the Camarilla. There are the Reformists, the Moderates, and the Isolationists. The Isolationists wish to isolate themselves from every other species, but still monitor the potentialities to guide the future.

And the Reformists? asked Kusac, his anger building.

They wish to stop interfering so much in the potentialities and to include other species in the Camarilla.

So all this trouble with the M'zullians and their representative Lassimiss, who made nanites for them in the matter transmitter, could have been avoided if not for the meddling of which party?

Isolationists.

Why was my son taken? he demanded.

I believe because he could be invisible to the tracking program used by the Isolationists. Part of that is my fault because when we talked, I shielded him from any listening ears. But there were times when he did vanish.

Then it is likely the Isolationists that have taken him, sent Kusac.

It is. I have searched the records of supplies ordered by all properties they own, looking for ones to either suggest a pris-oner was expected, or that they would be remaining there for some time, but have found nothing of note.

Check for several months, sent Kusac. *This may be part of a long-term plan.*

"The Camarilla is a council of TeLaxaudin and Cabba-rans," said Kusac loudly to his gathered forces. "Of the two, the TeLaxaudin are more dangerous. If you injure one, ei-ther make sure it's dead, or strip it of all jewelry and belts as they all have a miniaturized arsenal of deadly weapons. Do not shoot until I give the command."

Unity, I want you to transport me and my people to Ghioass. To the Camarilla meeting place.

Know that I will defend myself and my people from you if you should try to harm them.

"I want those who stole my son and put his life at risk," snarled Kusac aloud. "Stay out of my way, Unity, and no harm will come to you! Now transport us to Ghioass!"

Ghioass, Isolationist mountain retreat

"Bring the child," said Zaimiss to Naisha. "Our officers in Camarilla been arrested. Need to know now how he hides himself."

"Has only been an hour since you last spoke to him," said the U'Churian. "He's still suffering from that concus-sion. You might not get any sense out of him."

"And we might. Have to try. Didn't expect them to move against us so quickly. Fetch him."

"As you wish," said Naisha, inclining his head.

Shaidan opened his eyes slowly, aware he was being shaken. He stared up at the face looming over him. Instinct took over as he tried to back away, but there was nowhere to go on his cot.

"It's all right," said the U'Churian. "I don't mean you any harm. They want to see you again." A hand was held out to him.

"You're a U'Churian," he said.

The male bobbed his head in an affirmative gesture. "Yes. Come along. If you take too long, they'll send Tyakar, and neither of us want that."

Taking hold of the hand, he allowed himself to be gently drawn to his feet. "Can I have some water?" he asked. "My mouth feels terrible."

Still holding his hand, Naisha led him to the washbasin and filled the drinking bowl that was there.

"Here you are," he said, handing it to him. "My name is Naisha."

Shaidan drank deeply then handed the bowl back. "Why am I here?"

Naisha led him to the doorway and out into the corridor. "I couldn't say as they don't tell me these things. Just answer their questions as best you can," he said, catching him as he stumbled.

"I feel dizzy," said Shaidan. "I want to lie down."

"Once you've talked to them," said Naisha, picking him up and carrying him.

"Who are they?"

"They are Leader Zaimiss and the people from the Isolationist party of the Camarilla. Now enough questions," he said not unkindly.

The rest of the journey to the room full of cushions was conducted in silence. Just outside the door, Naisha put him down onto the ground. "Try not to throw up this time," he said quietly, before opening the door.

"I tell you I don't know how I became invisible to your sensors!" cried Shaidan, holding his throbbing cheek where Tyakar had just hit him.

"Try other questions," said Tinzaa. "How came you to know about us?"

"Unity told me. I could feel him at the node in the swimming pool room."

"You sensed the node?" demanded Zaimiss. "How? Well hidden it was."

"It wasn't. I felt it the first time I went to that part of the pool," said Shaidan.

You strong telepath? sent the TeLaxaudin, boosting his mental talk with the web of energy laid throughout the house.

The look of surprise he gave his captor gave away his ability, so there was no use denying it. *Yes,* he sent back, strengthening his mental shields so he couldn't be reached again.

"So you won't talk mentally," said Zaimiss. "No matter. We know how you were contacted by Unity. What did you learn from it about us?"

"Nothing. I don't know who you are, or what you want from me," he said, sitting down on the floor. He began to cry, covering his face with his hands. "I want my mama and papa!"

"Nothing more you will get from him," said Tinzaa. "Truly, I believe he doesn't know anything about how he appears invisible to us, or that he knows anything about us."

"Take him back to his room," said Zaimiss, mandibles clicking in annoyance. "Done with him for now are we."

As he was pulled to his feet by Naisha, he risked a quick look at them through his fingers. It did look like they had given up on getting any information from him.

Ghioass Camarilla chamber

Needaar and the leaders of the Reformist and Moderate parties, Azwokkus and Htomshu, along with Annuur, stood clustered round the screen. There the potentialities, a roiling red and yellow of anger, were firmly seated over Ghioass.

"They will arrive any time," said Htomshu. "Are all the Isolationists taken into custody?"

"Yes," affirmed Annuur. "All are in the holding cells grown by yourselves adjacent to this chamber."

"We must be here to greet them, explain ourselves . . ." began Azwokkus.

"They are here," interrupted Annuur. "Move back and give them room."

The darkness that surrounded them gave way suddenly to a room full of plants and trees, among which were islands of cushions and the sloping chairs of the Cabbarans. The hall was perhaps half full. Right in front of them waited a small group of four people. A glance beyond them showed the hall ringed by U'Churian warriors, all armed and standing with their backs to the wall. A group of six U'Churians detached themselves from there and moved forward to flank them. Instantly recognizable was Tirak.

"Captain Aldatan," he said, "we're here to support you."

"Deploy," said Kusac as, sword suddenly in his hand, he stepped forward. Around him, his troop fanned out to face the assembly.

"So this is where all that help on M'zull came from, eh, Annuur? Guilty consciences much? There was the Isolationist Lassimiss giving all that aid to the M'zullians against the will of your Camarilla. You had to take him out to minimize the damage he was doing, didn't you?"

"We gave you aid to counteract what had been done against you by Isolationist policy," said Annuur. "You know this. You helped arrest Lassimiss."

"When were you going to tell me about my son being brought here?" he asked, his voice deadly calm. In the silence that followed, no one even breathed. "WHEN?" he roared, pointing the sword at the Cabbaran. "You hid your knowledge from me! Tell me why I shouldn't hold you responsible for his disappearance!" Energy seemed to surround him, crackling down the sword toward Annuur.

"We are looking for him now," said Annuur, keeping

very still as he sat there on his haunches. "You think I would put cub at risk when recently I have young, too? No, friend Kusac, we try find Shaidan."

"Too many say 'friend Kusac' and mean the opposite. You lied to me, Annuur! Where is he? Where are those Isolationists?"

"Most Isolationists in cells waiting interrogation," said Annuur. "We police our own, Kusac. Welcome are you to interrogate them. Are not my own family supporting you?"

Kusac made a negative gesture with the sword, passing it just in front of Annuur's face. "I haven't the time for that now! Unity! Have you found him yet?"

I have found an Isolationist property that has been ordering excess supplies for the last two months. It is on Leader Zaimiss' land, a mountain retreat.

"Unity speaks to you?" exclaimed Htomshu.

"Yes." A sudden movement to his right drew his attention As a flare of energy blasted toward him, he retaliated with one of his own. Like lightning, it crackled down the length of his sword, catching the TeLaxaudin full in the chest and sending him flying.

"Shoot at will if we are threatened," ordered Kusac, turning his attention back to Annuur. "Foolish of that one to try and attack. I suggest you all remain calm. Who's in charge here?"

"No one," began Annuur.

A TeLaxaudin near the front stood up. "The Elders are," she said. "We form a small multi-party group within the Camarilla."

"Then make sure you do nothing to cause my people to harm you while I go after my son," he said. "M'yikku, Noi'kkah, J'korrash, and Kushool, remain here and see they don't interfere. Shoot if you have to. Annuur, you're coming with me as insurance of good behavior." He reached out and grabbed the Cabbaran by his harness, dragging him closer.

Annuur allowed himself to be pulled. "Kusac, we friends. Tirak and crew come with us, as well as my sept."

Kusac turned to face Tirak, reaching out with his mind to

scan him and his group. "Tirak, Manesh and Mrowbay, come with us. The rest support M'yikku," he said. They could do with another medic, and Mrowbay was a good one. "As for your group," he said to Annuur, then stopped.

"Always have I helped you and yours," said Annuur quietly. "Now no less."

"You withheld knowledge of what had happened to my son," snarled Kusac.

"We tried to find him before you came," said Annuur.

"You lied to me!"

"No, I didn't answer you. Different."

Kusac flung him aside, making him stumble into M'Nar, who took a couple of steps back to compensate.

"Who pushed for your mental treatment by Kizzysus?" said Annuur, trotting back to him and sitting down before him again. "Who helped you with it? Who at your side during retaking of Prime world? Tirak and me. You trust me same as him. I give you my word."

Again, Kusac reached out with his mind, scanning the alien. Reluctantly, he nodded. "Come then, but one false move . . ." He left the rest unsaid as the other three members of Annuur's sept trotted up to join him. They edged around M'Nar to stand in the middle of the group, creating a V formation with the addition of the three U'Churians.

"Captain," said Annuur. "Safe house is this. Protected by nanites that can remake walls as they wish. Will also have AI. Plan you must have before leaving."

Kusac swung round to look at the small Cabbaran. "What do you suggest?" he asked after a moment.

"Not designed for all-out attack like this. Divide troops, make three attacks to force way in, makes AI spread thin, easier to gain access to house. Keeps attention on defenses not attacking us."

He glanced at Kaid.

Do you trust him or not? sent his sword-brother.

"Unity, show me plans for the house," he said. As they came up on the large screen, he and Kaid studied them.

"Jerenn, take Noolgoi, Manesh, and Cheelar with you. You'll be Team Two. Tirak, you'll be Team Three with

Mrowbay, Banner and Jurrel, Kaid and T'Chebbi with you. With me in Team One will be Carrie, M'Nar, Rezac, Jo, Garras, and Annuur and his sept. Unity, land us outside the house. Team One's target will be the front door. Team Two, your target is the patio door on the west wall. Team Three, your targets are the large windows in the east wall. You," he snarled, drawing an arc with his sword that took in everyone in the council hall, "remember this isn't over yet. Unity, take us to where Shaidan is."

CHAPTER 12

Ghioass, mountain safe house

"HUNTER cub!" The translator rendered the voice from a series of melodic hums and clicks into Sholan. "Hunter cub! Come close."

The sound was coming from the wall opposite him, by the door. Shaidan got up and went over to it. "Who is it?" he asked quietly.

"Giyarishis I am. Watching you I was till the Isolationists kidnapped me."

"Kuvaa told me about you. Why were you spying on me?" he asked.

"You would disappear from Prime's world where I was watching you. Was tasked to find out why."

"I have no idea how that happened!" he snarled back. "Leave me alone!"

"No! Escape we have to. Together. House here has security system watching us, disable it I can if free."

"So it makes sense to talk about it while the house can watch and hear us," said Shaidan sarcastically. "I think I'll pass for now." He headed back to his bed and lay down again, resting his throbbing head on the pillow.

What the TeLaxaudin had said, though, got him thinking. If he was being watched by a security system, it must be like Unity in that it allowed interaction with it from nodes placed throughout the house. If, as everyone seemed to think, he could disappear from sight every now and then, then if he could work out what it was he was doing, he could do it here and get the AI thinking he'd escaped. While they all went mad looking for him, he could maybe evade them and really escape.

One way he could have been "missing" from the Prime world was when he was actually with Unity on the AI's world, which was this world. But he couldn't reach out with his mind to Unity here as there seemed to be some kind of barrier up that he couldn't penetrate. Was there any other way he could seem to disappear?

Visit me, little one, said a voice in his mind. *You know the way. Your father and Kaid have used my doorway before now. Look inside to find it.*

Vartra! He called out mentally, but Vartra was gone. Now he had to go and look through his papa's memories and find out what to do.

He closed his eyes and trying to ignore the pounding of his head, turning his thoughts inward. Eventually, he found a memory of a wooden door with two trees carved on it, one on either side of the triple spiral of the Brotherhood. In the center of the spiral was a blue-white crystal.

Making his breathing slower and gentler, he imagined the door in front of him. When it became so real he could see the grain of the wood, he reached out to touch the crystal. There was a flare of light from it, and the door opened.

Ahead of him was a peaceful woodland scene. He was on a grassy pathway that led to a clearing not far away. As he began to take hesitant steps down the path, he saw a cottage with a thatched roof. To one side was a lean-to where a forge had been built. A curl of smoke came from its chimney, letting him know that someone was at home.

Shaidan walked into the clearing and, seeing no one in the forge, went to the cottage door. He hesitated for a moment, then raised his hand to knock. As he did so, the door opened and there stood Vartra.

"Well done, Shaidan! I don't know of any other cub who

could have come here so easily. Welcome to my home." Vartra held the door ajar and stood aside for him to enter.

Shaidan stepped into the small living room. It was simply decorated, with a wooden table in the middle and chairs set round it.

Vartra pulled out a chair for him and waited while he sat down, then took the one next to him.

"I know it's pretty frightening being captured by these aliens, especially when they are hitting you, but you have to keep on being brave for a while longer, Shaidan," said Vartra gently. "What you need to do now is let them believe you've died. If they think you're dead, they may stop monitoring you, which will leave you free to escape from that room."

"How do I play dead so as they'll believe it?" asked Shaidan.

"You can do this by triggering your Valtegan side and the healing trance that was explained to you by General Kezule. Once you're in that trance, because it slows down everything in your system so that you hardly even seem to be breathing, they'll think you're dead."

Shaidan frowned. "I don't remember how to access that part of me."

"Everything you need to know is inside your mind, youngling, either from your papa or from Brother Jerenn. Just reach and you'll find it. Now it's time for you to go back to your realm." Vartra got up, placing a hand on Shaidan's shoulder.

"But aren't you going to help me?" the cub asked plaintively, looking up at him.

"I have helped you, and I'll wake you from your Valtegan healing trance when they wrongly decide you are no longer alive. You can do the rest on your own, you know. Just look inside yourself . . ." The voice seemed to echo inside his head as he opened his eyes and found himself back in the room that was his prison.

This time, when he reached inside, he was looking for his Valtegan heritage. Finding it, he began to allow himself to sink into the deep healing trance that was near death.

Kusac and his troops materialized a few hundred yards
from the safe house. It was a square building, with defensive
walls fronting the roof area. A driveway led to the front
door and parked in it was an aircar.

"Head out," Kusac said quietly into his throat mic to the
other two team leaders as he and his team took up offensive
positions behind the aircar but facing the front door.
"M'Nar, get that door down."

"Aye, sir," M'Nar said, bracing himself before opening
fire. Moments later, the door was gone—only to reform
again almost immediately.

"Nanites," said Annuur succinctly. "House made with
them, can reconfigure walls, everything. Likely controlled by
house AI which is limited in capability. Stretch its resources,
we need to do, which is why we attack at three points."

From the roof, enemy fire rained down at them, making
them keep their heads down.

"Keep targeting the door," said Kusac. "Controlled short
bursts. Inform the others, Garras, to keep pounding their
entry point when it tries to reform. Rezac, I want grenades
up on the roof. Take those shooters out. If you can get a
shot, Jerenn, take it."

"Aye, Captain," said Jerenn, sighting on the rooftop.

"Copy that," Rezac said, moving to the rear of the vehicle to get a better line of sight on the roof. The grenade
launcher arced a grenade into the air. It came down right on
target with a satisfying crump and cloud of debris. A second
one followed, and the shooting from the roof stopped
abruptly.

Meanwhile, the door again disintegrated in a shower of
sparks and flakes of what looked like metal, only to reform
within moments. Kusac found it surreal watching the parti-
cles form streams of liquid metal which ran together before
flowing back to become the doorway.

When the door reformed the third time it was blown

apart, there was noticeably less of it. Instead of reaching the top lintel, it stopped a good foot below.

"Ah," said Annuur. "Now we seeing that other sites doing equal damage. Soon the door will not reform."

"Hold your fire, M'Nar. Rezac, lob a grenade there," Kusac said.

Crouched down, Rezac moved up to the front of the aircar to throw one. This time, the hole left was larger, taking out some of the brick-and-mortar construction around the doorway.

"And another," Kusac ordered.

When the smoke and dust cleared, they could see that only the first two feet were able to reform—it was easily low enough for them to step over.

"Jerenn, keep guard out here, just in case anyone tries to escape us. M'Nar, take point," Kusac said, getting cautiously to his feet. The rest of his team fell in behind him as he made his way to what remained of the front door.

"Teams Two and Three are inside," said Garras quietly as they stepped over the remains of the door.

"Take it nice and slow," said Kusac, looking past M'Nar to see the open doorway at the end of the pillared entry hall. "Rezac, Jo, check the room to our left."

Without a sound they peeled off from the team and went to the doorway. The door was closed, but Jo and Rezac, as well as Kusac, knew the room was empty. Still, Jo stood to one side as Rezac kicked the door open. "Empty," said Jo giving the room a quick once over before they rejoined the team.

By the time they reached the main hall, the other two teams had rejoined them. There they kept close to the west wall, seeking protection from the balcony above. No sooner had they stepped into the hall than they were hit from above by laser fire. Backing off, Kusac signaled to Rezac and Noolgoi to fire grenades up into both balconies.

Under cover of this attack, Kusac led them at a run under the east balcony. A small staircase there gave access to the floor above. Laser fire blasted down the stairs at them but was promptly stopped by M'Nar and Noolgoi with their machine guns. With those two taking point, they took the

airs two at a time, gaining the landing, then turning right
into the passageway there.

Zaimiss was angry. "How they find us?" he demanded. "We
left no traces!"

"House is telling us the Hunter cub is dead," interrupted
Sivaar. "I need escort to go check on him."

"Go!" hummed Zaimiss angrily, mandibles clicking and
eyes swirling as he regarded his Cabbaran colleague. "If
dead, turn off security node for it and other captive. Maybe
our defenses come back online! One can hope!"

Sivaar trotted off between two U'Churians, heading
along the passageway to the western bedrooms where
Shaidan and Giyarishis were being kept. The two U'Churians went in front of him. Rapid gunfire could be heard coming from the southern corridor.

"Hurry," said Sivaar, butting the legs of the U'Churian in
front of him with his head. "We must not get caught by
these intruders!"

The door unlocked, Sivaar entered while the two U'Churians kept guard outside. He scampered over to the bed
where Shaidan lay sprawled. A cursory exam yielded no
discernible pulse and breathing, To all intents and purposes,
his patient was dead.

With a sigh, Sivaar covered the body with the blanket
and turned to his escort. "We be leaving now," he said. "Cub
is dead from the head injury."

Once out of the room, he used the node to contact the
house AI. "Turn off surveillance of this room and the next.
Hunter cub patient is dead," he said before leaving the area
as fast as he could.

"Shaidan." The voice was insistent and familiar. "Wake Shaidan. They've turned off the node outside your roo and left the door unlocked."

Shaidan stirred, not wanting to come out of the warm and comforting place he was in. He needed to be there while his concussion healed.

"Wake, youngling. Your papa is not far away." The voice was very insistent.

He nırred in his sleep, stretching, and finally cracked his eyes open. Over him stood Vartra.

"I said I would wake you," the Entity said. "They think you're dead and have turned off the monitoring node outside your room. This means you can release the TeLaxaudin next door if you wish. Be careful whatever you do. There are many armed people about, some defending this house, ready to shoot at even you."

Sitting up, Shaidan yawned and nodded, hearing the gunfire. "Be careful, lots of shooting." Suddenly he realized what Vartra had said. "Papa's here?" he said, looking up, but the Entity had gone.

Getting to his feet, he staggered toward the door. His head still hurt dreadfully, but at least even the short time spent in the deep healing trance had stopped him from feeling nauseous.

The gunfire sounded nearby but not too close. Softly, he padded to the room next to him and stopped at the door there. It was locked but with a conventional lock. Reaching up into his hair, he managed to pull free the sliver of metal that Unity had given him. Praying that it wouldn't break, he inserted it into the lock and began to carefully jiggle it. After a minute or two, the lock snicked open. Putting the transceiver back into one of his braids, he opened the door. M'Nar would be pleased to know his teachings had proved useful.

Giyarishis stood there waiting for him.

"They treated you pretty bad, too," said Shaidan, taking in the bruises and cuts on the TeLaxaudin's face and arms.

"It will heal. I hear weapons' fire. Is rescue imminent?"

"I don't know. I do know there are lots of U'Churians here fighting my papa."

Then let us aid them," said Giyarishis. "We need to be ⸱e to access the house AI and subvert it."

"They turned off the node outside our rooms," he said, pointing to a small box-shaped object mounted low on the wall between the two rooms.

"Ah, a physical node! I can do something with that!" Giyarishis scuttled over to the node and began examining it. On him, it was at a comfortable waist height. "If I can get into it," he muttered.

Sighing, Shaidan reached up into his braid, and pulled out the transceiver. "Try this," he said. "It isn't strong, so don't break it. We may need it."

Giyarishis' eyes spun as he focused in on the sliver of metal. "A transceiver," he said, looking up at him, eyes swirling again. "Now who would that connect you with? Not that it would work in here at the moment."

"It doesn't matter, I just want it back," he mumbled as Giyarishis began attacking the small nodule.

The lid came off easily. After all, thought Shaidan, it wasn't designed to be tamper proof because who in this house would tamper with it?

"Should be diagnostic screen installed," said Giyarishis to himself. "If so, can reprogram this node to do something more useful to us."

Shaidan looked over his shoulder as the other poked and prodded at various parts of the electronics in the box, then jumped back in shock as a holographic screen suddenly appeared.

"Aha! Now can I be helping us!"

The doorway opposite them suddenly dissolved, becoming a solid wall as the house began to respond to their presence.

"Shoot it out," ordered Kusac gesturing the others to back down the stairs a short way.

A short pulse of bullets, followed by a second one, and

the hole in the wall was low enough to step over. "Noolgoi, you're last through in case it reforms," ordered Kusac as his team began stepping through the gap, straight into the path of fire from two U'Churians.

Pushing Carrie back, Kusac flung himself against the wall and peered through the gap, leaving room for his people to retreat. The gun battle was furious for as long as it took M'Nar to spray the end of the corridor with his projectiles. The silence that fell was filled with a moan as Rezac, limping from a wounded leg, pushed his way back through the wall, carrying Jo. She was bleeding heavily from a wound in her side.

"She's bad," he said, looking at Kusac. "It pierced her armor. We'll stay here, you go on."

Kusac looked at the other's face, pinched and pale round the nose with pain, and nodded briefly, reaching out to grasp his shoulder. Mind linked as Leskas, he knew that Rezac and Jo were both experiencing each other's pain as well as their own. Unspoken by him and Rezac was the knowledge that if Jo died, so would Rezac.

"Mrowbay," he began.

"On it, Captain," said the other, leading Rezac to one side and helping him lay Jo down before reaching into his first aid satchel.

"Manesh, Cheelar, protect them," he ordered before pushing through the wall and following M'Nar cautiously down the hallway.

Ahead of them, a tide of silver flowed across the floor, gaining height as it traveled, trying to form a wall in front of them. A quick burst of fire from M'Nar scattered it, but not before they could see that the nanites were having problems.

"Looks like we're wearing them down," whispered M'Nar as he carefully approached the end of the corridor.

A blast of energy met them as the U'Churian on the other side opened fire.

"Stop firing and think about this," Annuur called out as he trotted forward to where Kusac was. "This not your battle. Ours it is, with the TeLaxaudin and Cabbarans of the

Isolationists. Lay down your weapons. Do not die for them like your colleagues."

A fusillade of shots followed his speech. Annuur looked up at Kusac and wrinkled his long, mobile nose. "I tried," he said. "Kill them we must."

Kusac nodded at M'Nar. "Try to leave one alive long enough for us to question about Shaidan," he said quietly.

"Yes, boss," said M'Nar before peering round the corner and taking aim.

A yowl of pain followed his short burst of fire, and with that, Kusac ran round the corner, flinging himself into the space between two pillars. He was closely followed by Garras.

"I'll grab him," said the older Sholan, going down on his belly and cautiously edging forward toward the fallen U'Churian. "Cover me!"

Kneeling by the pillar, Kusac pointed his blaster down the corridor, watching for the slightest aggressive move from either their downed enemy or anyone else.

Grabbing the U'Churian's weapon, Garras threw it back to Kusac, then began to wriggle backward, towing the barely conscious male with him, using his body as a shield between himself and the end of the corridor. It was only a few feet; as soon as he was close, Kusac reached forward and helped haul him into their small alcove.

The U'Churian was fatally wounded, and he knew it. He lay there glaring helplessly up at Kusac and Garras.

"Where's the Sholan cub?" snarled Kusac, grabbing him by the neck. "Tell me where my son is!"

The other grimaced at him. "Think I'm going to tell you? You'll never find him!" He stiffened, then as his eyes rolled back, went limp in Kusac's grasp.

Kusac shook him. "Where is my son?" he demanded again.

"He's dead, Kusac," said Garras. "He can't tell us. But it's likely they have him well guarded. Find them and we find Shaidan. I'd say it's not down this corridor, I didn't see any other guards."

Letting the dead U'Churian go and nodding slowly,

Kusac said, "You're right. They'd have more guards round him. Let's head down the other corridor."

They moved down the southern corridor, making their way toward where it turned right to the west.

Still on point, M'Nar took a quick look round the corner, seeing telltale signs of two U'Churians, one at either end of the corridor. He held up two fingers to Kusac, letting him know before darting past the opening. Nothing happened, but now M'Nar had a good line of sight to both enemies. Noolgoi followed him as soon as he received the other's hand signal.

Taking aim, he sprayed the entrance to the west corridor. It was a quick burst and he waited to see if there was return fire. All was quiet until he edged his way round the corner, then all hell broke out.

Guess we've found where Shaidan is, sent Carrie as she hunkered down behind Kusac.

Yeah, he replied briefly, watching M'Nar back rapidly away from the entrance followed closely by Noolgoi. *Still can't reach him mentally. They must have some damper field on around him.*

The shooting stopped and, in the silence, Kusac heard a small voice calling to him and Carrie.

"Papa! Mama! I'm here!"

Kusac immediately looked round the corner, pulling his head back just as another barrage of shooting broke out. "He's in an opening about halfway up that corridor," he said. "But there's two shooters between us and him."

Suddenly, his son's mind flooded his with its fear, making him rock back on his haunches and almost fall over. Carrie was there to support him as she also picked up Shaidan.

Papa, there's two guards here, the cub sent.

I know. Stay back and be safe. We'll get you, don't worry! he sent in reply before turning to Garras who was behind Carrie.

"Can you get past the opening to join M'Nar?" he asked in a low voice. "I need a couple of grenades in that first alcove. Jurrel, you go, too. That rifle of yours might make all the difference."

Garras and Jurrel both nodded. Using the Brotherhood hand signals, Kusac let M'Nar know what was happening and asked for covering fire. Getting an affirmative in reply, Kusac moved back to allow Garras and Jurrel to take his place.

M'Nar poked his nose and his gun round the corner and began spraying the wall opposite, working his way toward the opening. Noolgoi gave him covering fire as he darted forward. Seeing his opportunity, Garras, followed swiftly by Jurrel, did a mad dash over, landing in a pile against the end wall.

Kusac watched as they picked themselves up. Crouching low to the ground, Garras came up under M'Nar and his gun and lobbed a couple of grenades into the opening opposite before they both pulled back. A high-pitched scream followed as the grenades exploded with a satisfying crump.

A fusillade of energy bolts came down the corridor at them, forcing them to keep their heads down and back in cover. Jurrel tapped Garras on the shoulder and signed that he wanted to take his place. With a gesture of acceptance, Garras moved backward, letting the other pass him.

"Papa, he has me!" screamed Shaidan, terrified.

The sword in one hand, blaster in the other, Kusac rose to his feet and stepped into full view, snarling his fury. In the center of the corridor, a U'Churian stood with his arm locked round Shaidan's throat.

"What do you want?" Kusac demanded.

"Safe passage out of here, then you can have your brat," said Tyakar.

"What guarantee do I have you'll keep your word?" he demanded, slowly pacing forward.

"That's close enough!" hissed the U'Churian, backing away from Kusac.

Suddenly, the cub reached up and grabbed the restraining arm with both hands, digging his claws in deep and twisting his body till he dropped out of the grip.

Not stopping to think, Kusac rushed the U'Churian as a crack sounded from Jurrel's rifle. Stepping over his son's curled-up form, Kusac swung the sword in an arc that ended at the other's neck. Blood sprayed into the air as the head went flying in one direction. Slowly, the body toppled over, blood still gouting out from the severed neck.

Kusac stooped down just far enough to sweep Shaidan into one arm, then pass him back to where Carrie now stood behind him. He pushed them into the alcove between the two pillars.

"I remembered, M'Nar, I remembered how to get away from him!" said Shaidan, his arms clutching tightly round his mother's neck. "Papa, Giyarishis is there, he's a friend."

Kusac spared a questioning glance at M'Nar before turning his attention to the TeLaxaudin standing in the opening of the corridor leading off theirs.

"Prisoner I was, like Shaidan. Managed to damage house AI we did. Hope it was of help." He scuttled quickly to join them and reached out a hand to Shaidan, holding up the slightly bent transceiver. "Thanking you for its loan. Maybe now you can reach Unity on it."

"Annuur, have one of your people take Giyarishis to the rear," Kusac said then turned to look at his son. "You can contact Unity?"

"I think so," Shaidan replied. "Do you want me to try?"

"Not just yet," he said. "We need to find the control room and put an end to this nest of snakes. Stay to the rear with Shaidan, Carrie. I don't want either of you too far back, just in case. Tirak, you and Manesh guard them."

M'Nar, followed by Noolgoi, Kusac, Garras, and the other teams, made their way carefully up the corridor, darting quickly between the remaining pillars. Once at the top, M'Nar and Noolgoi quickly moved into the room opposite, checking it out.

"Empty," said M'Nar through their mic system. "The first alcove is also empty."

I sense one more guard ahead, sent Carrie. *Thank goodness the damper field is down! Ahead of him is a room with three people in it, two TeLaxaudin and a Cabbaran. That has to be the control room.*

Agreed, sent Kusac, relaying the news verbally to the

others. "More alcoves we can duck into round the corner. Noolgoi, take point here," he ordered quietly.

"Aye, Captain." Noolgoi peered cautiously round the edge of the doorway, then ran into the first gap. From there, he gestured the others to follow him.

Bolts of energy started up immediately, only to be countered by Noolgoi's suppressing fire. Under cover of that, they were able to get Kusac, M'Nar, Garras, and half of Team Two into the alcove.

"M'Nar and Noolgoi, advance to next gap," he ordered. "Suppressing fire, keep with the short bursts."

As the two gunners moved out, each one shooting only when the other stopped, they were able to advance to the next alcove, leaving the first one free for the Cabbarans and Team Two.

"Garras, roll a grenade along the floor. We need to take out that gunner. M'Nar, Noolgoi, you know what to do. Jurrel, follow them."

"Aye," said Garras, taking a grenade from the pouch at his side. Pulling the pin, he sent it rolling along the floor.

Every ear was swiveled forward, listening to the sound of the grenade traveling along the floor. They all heard the exclamations of shock and then the rapid crack of Jurrel's gun as he fired at the single shooter. A scream, followed by the explosion, and their way to the command room was clear.

"Giyarishis says the three in there are likely to be Zaimiss, the TeLaxaudin leader of the Isolationist Party, Sivaar his medic, and Tinzaa, a Cabbaran Elder," said Kaid as thick dust and pieces of plaster and wood continued to fall around them. "He's been visited by each of them. Beware of the arsenals of the two TeLaxaudin, he says."

"Copy that. Everyone, they have miniaturized weapons systems concealed in rings and bracelets. They are nasty—flechettes, poisons, and energy weapons. Shoot to kill, we don't need prisoners."

"What if they surrender?" asked Carrie.

Kusac made a sound of annoyance. "Get them to throw down all their jewelry first, then we'll see. M'Nar, Noolgoi, advance. Take no risks!"

"Aye, Captain," they both said, entering the remains of the corridor side by side. Behind them, Kusac was accompanied by Garras, Kaid, and T'Chebbi, followed by Carrie, Shaidan, and the Cabbarans with Tirak and Manesh. Banner and Jurrel provided rearguard protection.

The entrance to the control room had been blown open. There was no sign of the nanites trying to block the doorway, but they stayed back from the opening to be safe. Those inside were coughing and spluttering.

"Surrender now or die," snarled Kusac. "I don't care which."

"Surrender!" came the high voice of the Cabbaran, laying down his weapon and scuttling out to flatten himself to the floor in front of them.

The hums and clicks from one of the TeLaxaudin were translated into Sholan moments later.

"How dare you attack peaceful house! This calumny will be reported to Camarilla!"

"Throw down those weapons, or you won't get the chance to complain!"

"Coming out to do that, Sivaar I am."

"Throw the weapons down first," said Kusac, aiming directly at the spindly TeLaxaudin as he began to strip off rings and other jewelry and throw them toward Kusac.

"Belt, too," said M'Nar.

"Only belt it is! Naked you leave me," Sivaar complained, following the order.

"On the ground," said Kusac, gesturing with his gun.

The small alien squatted down, then lay prone on the dusty floor.

"Zaimiss, you now," said Kusac, gun aimed on the doorway, waiting for the last TeLaxaudin to emerge.

"You are dust beneath the feet of the TeLaxaudin people! Never should you be elevated to the Camarilla! Barbarians you are! I will not surrender!" As he spoke, Zaimiss raised his arm and let off one shot before he rushed toward the window and leaped out.

"No! Papa!" screamed Shaidan, rushing up to his father and pushing him aside. The shot, meant for Kusac, hit the cub instead.

As it did, both M'Nar and Noolgoi rushed to the window.

"Shaidan!" Kusac fell to the ground, watching as his son was sent flying into the air to hit the stone pillar behind them.

"No!" shrieked Carrie, rushing forward to her fallen cub. "I only let go of his hand for an instant!"

Kaid and T'Chebbi raced up to stand between them and the prisoners when another whine of energy rang out.

Caught like an insect in a candle flame, T'Chebbi let out a grunt of pain and fell to the ground, bleeding from a hit to her arm and her side.

Before his two gunners could react, Kusac fired on both of the prone captives, killing them instantly then scrambling to his feet. "Check for any others," he ordered. "Jerenn, get that son of a jegget! He shot Shaidan!"

"Got him in my scope, Captain," came Jerenn's harsh reply.

"Banner, take command. Kaid, see to T'Chebbi!" continued Kusac.

"Aye, Captain," said Banner, quickly issuing orders to search the whole area thoroughly and calling for Mrowbay and his medikit.

Jerenn had pulled back from the aircar when the others had entered the house. Now he was crouched down behind a group of ornamental rocks, his rifle resting on the highest one.

He spotted the TeLaxaudin leaping through the window and heading for the vehicle just as Kusac's message came through his comm unit. Before he could take a shot, the aircar had powered up and had taken off.

"Damn!" he muttered as he changed position and flipped out the rifle's stabilizer. Eye to the scope, he pointed the rifle at the aircar and let it auto lock onto his target. "Yeah," he breathed as he lined up his shot. There were still good odds that he'd get the bastard.

He stopped breathing, making sure that not even the slightest movement could spoil this shot. He had a personal interest in getting this piece of animal dung—shoot Liege's son, would he? Not and live to tell about it!

Slowly, he squeezed the trigger. Muzzle flash followed swiftly by the sound of the shot, then silence. He started counting.

One-thousand one, one-thousand two . . .

A flash of light beneath the rear thruster on the aircar showed he had hit his mark, but was it enough?

"You got it!" M'Nar's voice came loudly over his mic, making him jump and bang his face on the scope.

He looked away, rubbing his eye, missing what M'Nar, leaning out of the window, was seeing. He telegraphed that he was switching to their private comm channel.

"I *know* you got it," M'Nar shouted. "Look!"

It looked like the aircar was losing altitude. "If it lands, we'll have to go get the bastard," snarled Jerenn, looking across to the window that M'Nar was hanging out of. "He's not getting away from me!"

"Told you that you got him," said M'Nar, waving his arm toward the trail of smoke that was now coming from the vehicle. "No need to go after him on foot."

A resounding boom had Jerenn turning back to the scene. A cloud of black smoke laced with red now occupied the space where the aircar had been. Pieces of it were being flung in every direction.

"Great shot!" M'Nar exclaimed.

Jerenn allowed himself a small smile. "I wasn't all that happy as a terminator operative," he said, watching the falling debris. "But that's one 'termination' I really enjoyed." He flicked his comm back to the main channel again. "Captain, escapee terminated," he said more soberly.

Mrowbay rushed forward, checking briefly on T'Chebbi as the nearest victim, throwing pressure bandages to Kaid before moving on to where Shaidan lay in a slowly widening pool of blood.

"Shaidan, baby," said Carrie, her voice trembling as she reached out to touch his face.

Kusac landed on his knees beside them. "Cub," he said, his voice breaking as he tried to assess his son's injuries.

"Let me see him," said Mrowbay, elbowing his way between the two adults to examine Shaidan properly.

"Bleeding from the ears and nose, possible skull fracture," the U'Churian medic muttered, before lifting the cub's small arm aside from the stomach wound. "Captain," he began, then hesitated.

"Do what you can," said Kusac harshly, reaching out to stroke his son's cheek.

"Can't you heal him, like you healed Zsurtul?" Carrie asked, grasping her husband's other hand. "There must be something you can do!"

Kusac shook his head. "He's too badly injured," he whispered, tears filling his eyes. "Zsurtul only had one life-threatening wound, Shaidan has two, and the fight with K'hedduk weakened me."

Mrowbay busied himself trying to stem the blood loss from the stomach wound, cutting Shaidan's tunic away and putting a pressure bandage on him, preparing an analgesic injection.

"Captain, he's unconscious and unlikely to be feeling any pain. I can give him a regular shot just in case, or I can give him a heavier dose to . . ."

"No!" said Kusac, bearing his teeth in a snarl and turning on him. "He has to have every chance to live!"

Meanwhile, Annuur and his sept had been busily checking on Jo as well as T'Chebbi. As Annuur approached Kusac, Rezac limped over to join them, Jo cradled in his arms. One look at them, and they knew she was dead.

"Oh, Gods, not Shaidan, too," Rezac groaned, crouching to set Jo's body down on the ground. "I'm sorry, Kusac. I came to say farewell, to you and my son," he said, passing a shaking hand over his forehead.

"You can't go," said Kaid, looking up from where he was still wrapping the pressure bandage on T'Chebbi's arm. "I won't lose you today!"

"I've lived two lives, Kaid. Fifteen hundred years ago I should have died. The last few years have been a bonus for me. I'm ready to let the link take me since it's all taken Jo."

Annuur nosed his way between then. "Friend Kusac help you we can, but you will have to decide. Naacha says we can heal either Shaidan or Jo, but not both. T'Chebbi we can help afterward."

"Help Shaidan," said Rezac, slumping back against the wall. "Jo and I came on this mission to save Shaidan. We knew the risks, we took our chances. Save the cub, Annuur. His life is still ahead of him."

"It's decided, then," said Annuur, sitting up on his haunches and gesturing the other three of his sept forward. "Step back, Carrie and Kusac. We must be only ones touching him, if you please."

Tirak grasped Kusac by the shoulder, making him look up at him. "He can save him if anyone can," said the U'Churian quietly. "I saw Annuur dead when our *Watcher* ship was attacked and damaged, and yet they brought him back to life."

Kusac nodded, dashing the tears away from his eyes on his forearm as he helped Carrie to her feet. "Let them work," he said, pulling her into his arms as they stepped back from their son's small broken body.

Mrowbay knelt down beside Kaid and began taking over from him. "I have a shot for the pain," he said, putting the hypo against T'Chebbi's thigh and pressing it.

T'Chebbi hissed in pain. "Hope Annuur can help Shaidan," she said between gritted teeth. "No cub deserves to have life cut this short, especially Shaidan."

"You're going to be some time recovering from your own wounds," said Mrowbay, putting the syringe aside and checking the bandages on her arm and side. He looked over his shoulder at Kaid who was hovering between her and his father. "Go see to Rezac," he said compassionately. "T'Chebbi is in no danger now."

"See to your father," echoed T'Chebbi, the relief that the drug gave her from the pain visible on her face. "I'm fine." Her voice had degenerated to a slow drawl by now. Closing her eyes, she drifted into unconsciousness.

rowbay looked up at the others clustered round them.
t me something to put under her head," he said.

Kaid knelt down in front of his father. Rezac was fading
fast now as he was pulled closer to death by the strength of
the Leska link he'd had with Jo.

"Father," said Kaid, his voice low as he reached out to
hold him close. "Are you sure this is what you want?"

"I've only known war, Kaid," Rezac said quietly, lifting
an arm to put round his son. "Now it's time for me to have
peace. I loved Jo, you've no idea how much." He gave a little
laugh. "I reckon you do know how much at that. I can't let
her travel to the other side alone. I've had a great gift in
knowing you against all odds." His hand cupped Kaid's
cheek before it fell away back to his lap. "Look after your
T'Chebbi. I love you," he whispered.

Still holding Carrie close, Kusac turned to Kaid. "I am so
sorry," he said quietly. "I had no idea the cost would be so
great to us."

"It had to be done," said Kaid, rubbing his hands across
his face, wiping away the tears. "It was never just about
Shaidan, it was also about a body of people determined to
run our lives. We had to stop them. We still have to. Once
our wounded have been treated, and our dead sent home,
we have to go back to that meeting room and give them
hell!"

*Captain, I am Unity. I can take care of your injured and
dead until you are ready to take them home,* said a voice
they had never heard before.

Unity! Kusac swung round, looking for an outlet for the
voice.

Giyarishis stood up from where he was taking possession
of some of the armaments dropped by his enemies. "I
opened a node for Unity, Captain. Have need of its help if
you want to leave here and travel back to the Camarilla
Council chamber."

An insistent tugging on his arm finally got Kusac's attention, and he looked down at Carrie's tearstained face.

"What is it?" he asked fearfully, looking across at the ⟨ dle of Cabbarans.

"It's Shaidan," she said, her voice a disbelieving whisper "Look!"

He looked, but Shaidan was still almost completely hidden by the four Cabbarans who ringed his still form. He heard the cub gasp for air once, then a second time, then begin to cough and moan.

Kusac made to move forward, but Tirak forcibly held him back.

"No, wait till Annuur says it's safe," the U'Churian Captain said.

"How is this possible?" asked Kusac disbelievingly.

"They manipulate matter, Kusac. All matter, including living tissue. It's like what you did when you healed King Zsurtul, only on a greater level."

Gradually, the four Cabbarans pulled back and on the floor between them, Kusac and Carrie could see their son's body beginning to move.

"Still hurt is he," said Annuur in a voice that was a thread of his usual one. "But now he will live."

Kusac and Carrie fell to their knees beside their son.

Shaidan's eyes flickered open. "Papa, Mama" he whispered, reaching out toward them. His small hand closed on Kusac's. "Annuur made me better."

"We can't thank you enough," said Carrie, reaching out to touch Annuur on the head. "Shaidan is very special to us."

"As all our children are," said Annuur tiredly. "Now we will see to T'Chebbi. Less we can do for her because drained we are working on Shaidan."

"Anything you can do for her is appreciated," said Kusac before Kaid could. "I owe you for this, Annuur. I'm sorry I ever doubted you."

"Not always have our goals been the same, but compatible always they have been," said the Cabbaran, leading his sept over to the unconscious T'Chebbi.

Kusac carefully lifted Shaidan up into his arms. The cub was still covered in blood and all the visible skin on his

—around his eyes and nose, and inside his ears—was
er than usual, but he was alive and conscious.

"You shouldn't have run between me and that shot," said
Kusac, holding him close.

"I had to," whispered Shaidan. "We need you alive to
deal with the Camarilla," he said with the logic of a child.

Jurrel came up to them and handed Carrie a blanket for
Shaidan. Kusac took it from her and while Carrie helped to
remove the pieces of his torn and bloodstained tunic, he
carefully wrapped their son up in it.

"We nearly lost you today," said Kusac. "You will not do
that again," he said sternly.

"I'll try not to, Papa, so long as you aren't in danger
again," said the cub, cuddling up to his father.

"No conditions," said Kusac, putting a finger under his
chin and making Shaidan look him in the eyes.

"Yes, Papa."

"Good. Kaid." He turned to his sword-brother. "We
need to go to the Camarilla Council chamber," he said gently.

"I won't leave them here," said Kaid, looking up from
where he crouched beside T'Chebbi. "Not Rezac and Jo, or
T'Chebbi."

"I'm not asking you to," Kusac began.

*Captain, I can take your dead to my core where they will
be safe and untouched by anyone till you request them,* interrupted Unity. *Lieutenant T'Chebbi will be able to walk
when Agent Annuur and his sept are finished.*

"She can visit with my sept," said Annuur. "She be safe
there, can see our younglings."

"Can make up own mind," said T'Chebbi, conscious
again, her tone acerbic despite the tiredness apparent in her
voice. "I go with you."

"Would that be acceptable for Rezac and Jo?" asked Kusac.

Kaid nodded silently, watching as his father and Jo faded
slowly from their view.

All honor will be shown them, said Unity.

"Your sword," said Carrie, handing it to Kusac.

One-handed, he slipped his blaster into his holste[r] got to his feet, taking the sword from her. "Form up on [r] he ordered. When they had formed a V shape behind h[im] he spoke to Unity. "Take us to the Camarilla."

They materialized where they had before, on the raised area by the podium, the large screen showing the potentialities at that moment, their backdrop of angry roiling reds, oranges, and blacks.

Waiting for him were M'yikku, Noi'kkah, J'korrash, and Kushool, supported by the two U'Churian females, Sheeowl and Thyasha.

"I said I'd return," he said loudly. "I said I'd rescue my son, and I have. Tell me who else is responsible for his kidnapping and torture!"

Khassis got slowly to her feet. "The Isolationist party were the only responsible ones," she said, her humming and clicks translated into Sholan. "Arrested them we have. In cells are they, along with the one who was traitorously aiding the false sand-dweller Emperor."

"I demand they be turned over to face trial for their actions," snarled Kusac. "A war crimes jury will be assembed by the Alliance species and they will appear in front of it!"

"Agreed, but we must also be represented," said Khassis.

"And us," said Nkuno, a Cabbaran Elder, getting to her feet.

"Diplomatic relationships are already underway with both your peoples," said Kusac. "Our Ambassadors will decide these matters, not us. As far as I'm concerned, you are all guilty of meddling in our lives!"

He stopped to hand Shaidan to Kaid, who was waiting at his elbow to take the cub. "Who pushed the M'zullians into reforming their empire?" he demanded, stepping forward and extending his sword to sweep it in an arc around the oly. "You had one of your people—Lassimiss— aled in K'hedduk's court! They had a matter transformer m you to make the nanites that utterly wiped out all the eople on the planet of J'kirtikk! You spied on us on the *Kz'adul*, on the Prime world, and the Gods know where else! Somehow, far in both our pasts, you mixed our DNA with the U'Churians! And that is only what I know about, I'm sure there is more!"

Nkuno the Cabbaran, sat up on her haunches, rubbing her face in embarrassment. "Was us who adapted the U'Churians, our Children, in order to prevent them from dying out as a species," she said. "This was before we joined the Camarilla. Solar flare did genetic damage, we repaired it best we could."

From the corner of his eye, Kusac saw Tirak's shocked reaction to this news.

"The TeLaxaudin took some of our people and transplanted them here," said Tirak. "There are generations of U'Churians who don't even know about Home, or the trading ships we live in, don't know about our links to the Cabbarans!"

There was a shuffling sound as dozens of the U'Churians stationed round the room as guards, moved their positions, turning briefly to look at each other.

"Not all these decisions were taken by the Isolationists!" snarled Kusac as once again the energy coursing through him could be seen crackling in his sword. "Few of these decisions benefitted those affected by it! Give me any good reason why you should be allowed to continue in this selfish way?"

"Not all our decisions were selfish," said Khassis.

"Saving the U'Churians was altruistic," said Nkuno. "It benefitted us not at all at the time. Only thousands of years later were we able to help them into space and form trading families with them. Their use by the Camarilla was not our doing."

"That was ours," admitted Khassis. "We needed strong backs and sensitive dispositions to help do that which as fragile beings we could not do."

"So you made servants of them!" said Kusac.

"Not so! They are trusted members of our households. Many own and run their own businesses as they are a trading people by nature."

"Show me any independent U'Churians here who own their own ships, or who can go off planet if they wish to!" interrupted Tirak, stepping forward. "There are none!"

Kusac turned to look at the large screen behind him, pointing his sword at it. "I see two large centers of movement there, and guess they are right in this Council chamber."

"You are correct. They are the nexuses representing you and your son," said Khassis.

"You plot disasters before they happen, with no real knowledge of if they will! Just looking at this representation makes me think that to stop this disaster you foresee, all you need to do is kill me! Only I have no intention of lowering myself to the level of your Isolationist Party and assuming you will try to do that. You spy on people you suspect of being a nexus, never taking into account properly that perhaps, just perhaps, your interference will make what you fear happen! Events need to play out in most cases. Not every event that initially looks bad will be a disaster."

"We try to let events play out. Most of what we do is gathering information on situations that potentially could . . ." began Khassis.

". . . affect you and the Cabbarans," said Kusac. "That has to stop now! I grant you may have fallen into complacency over the centuries." He lowered his sword till its tip rested on the ground. "I will tell you how it is going to be for the Camarilla from today! All our species matter as much as any one. It's time that you admitted all the other races whose lives you have been playing with. The U'Churians for one, and ourselves and the Primes. For too long you've had a say in how our lives will be run, time the favor was returned."

Azwokkus rose to his feet from the midst of the Reformist Party. "Agreed," he said. "For this have we been working."

"Too soon is it for the inclusion of junior species," began Htomshu, leader of the Moderates.

"This is not open for discussion," said Kusac, glaring at the TeLaxaudin female. "It is what *will* happen!"

As he spoke, Kusac was aware of two things. He felt a cool breeze that smelled of summer flowers, and those who were facing him, who'd been standing, suddenly either sat down, or began to back away.

Kusac swung round, raising his sword again, only to face a group of three Sholans, one of whom he knew.

"Vartra!" he said in shock as the Entity moved toward him, holding out his hand for the sword.

"Indeed, it is me," said the black-clad Sholan, taking the sword from Kusac's now limp grasp. "So you decided to be their savior, not their destroyer. I'm glad my confidence in you wasn't misplaced." Vartra turned, and with a bow to his two companions, he handed them the sword.

L'Shoh, the dark Entity of the afterlife, took it, planting it point first onto the ground, and resting his hands on the quillons.

There was an aura of power about the Entity, and Kusac was aware of his visage changing, altering subtly, to become first U'Churian, then Cabbaran, and finally TeLaxaudin before returning to that of his Sholan self. He was sure that each species saw the Entities in their own form.

"Your Camarilla has overreached itself when it went as far as to imprison our brother, Vartra. It's time that your monopoly be ended and that the younger species have as much of a say in the running of your group. Diverting disasters is one thing, meddling in the natural progression of a species is not acceptable. The Sholans have earned their place among you, as have the U'Churians for their loyalty."

Ghyakulla took a step forward, setting her hand on Vartra's bowed head. "Your geas is ended, faithful one," she said slowly in a voice obviously unused to speaking. "The Valtegan problem is solved once and for all. Choose your future as mortal or immortal."

"You can live out a normal span of years, or choose to become an immortal," said L'Shoh. "If you choose to join us, you will have to decide whether or not to remain as consort of Ghyakulla."

Vartra knelt before Ghyakulla and reached out for her hand, which she gave to him. "I choose to remain as your consort, if you'll still let me," he said. "Like you, I'm tired of the constant conflict between myself and Kuushoi. It's time I chose, and I choose you."

Ghyakulla smiled, raising him to his feet and setting him beside her. "Keep an eye on this Council you will, guide them if they overstep again," she said.

"And you, Kusac," said L'Shoh. "Now your time as the Avatar of Justice is over, what would you do?"

"Go home to my Clan and be a father to my people," he said instantly, reaching for Carrie, Kaid, and Shaidan. "Take the extra abilities away, I don't want them, I only want to be me!"

"Hey, I like being able to shape change into a Sholan," said Carrie, tugging on his arm.

Ghyakulla smiled and reached out to touch her cheek. "Then once a year at midsummer, little Human, you can become Sholan for a day, if you wish. Time now to return to the Prime world with honored dead and injured. Much to see to there before you can go home." She gestured, and a gateway appeared just beyond where Kusac stood.

"Vartra, now as Avatar of Justice, will see to it that those responsible will be dealt with through your judicial system," said L'Shoh.

Kuushoi's realm

Kuushoi passed her hand across her viewing pool and stepped back among her Dzinaes. "Well, that was mildly amusing," she said to Gihaf. "Pity they didn't fight for longer, I wanted to know who would win. But their son stopped it."

"You've watched the fight several times now, Lady," said

_af, fingers idly twining around one of the many fine
_aids he now wore framing his face. "Did you find what
_ou were looking for?"

She frowned, reaching out to smack his hand away from
the braids. "So you're copying our Avatar's hair, are you?"

"Only a few braids," he said, putting the back of his hand
to his lips and licking it where she had hit him. His deep
blue eyes gazed at her all the while. "I like the look of them.
Nefae did them for me." He turned his head so she could
see the back of his long hair. "See, the rest is as you like it,
long and loose."

"Hmm," she said, pulling one fine braid. "It'll do for
now," she said. "Yes, I found what I wanted. The look on his
face when the little Human appears, and when she attacks
him, is priceless!"

"Lady!" Rojae's voice was high-pitched in concern as
she came running into the viewing room, closely followed
by Nefae. "He comes, Vartra comes for you!"

"That's Lord Vartra now," said Vartra as he swept into
the room, his long gray robes just reaching floor level. "You
are to present yourself before your husband, Lord L'Shoh,
for judgment. Your untimely meddling in the affairs of the
Avatar was not appreciated."

She pouted. "You make such a fuss over it. I was only
amusing myself because I was bored. It's summer and you
aren't with me."

"I won't be with you again," he said, reaching for her arm
and taking hold of her. As he did, she saw the sword that
hung on his hip, the Avatar's sword. "I am released from my
geas and have chosen to be Ghyakulla's consort. Another
will play the part of Winter's Father and Child. Now come,
L'Shoh is not pleased you interfered with the human called
Carrie."

"I won't go," she said, stamping her foot and glaring at him
as she tried to pull her arm free. "And you can't make me!"

"Oh, but I can," said Vartra grimly, bending down to lift
her up into his arms. "I'm no longer a lesser Entity, Kuushoi,
I now rank with you. You'll have to find another plaything
to amuse you in the winter!"

He turned and, carrying his squirming and protes.
burden, walked briskly to L'Shoh's portal and stepp.
through.

The Prime world

Kusac and Carrie and their teams materialized in the temple on the Prime world, with Noni and Conner waiting for them. The bodies of Jo and Rezac had already arrived and lay on twin trestle tables, dressed in the Brotherhood grays, with garlands of sweet-smelling summer flowers around their necks.

"Welcome home," said Conner, stepping forward to greet them. "Rezac and Jo were returned to us like this. Noni sees the hands of the Entities in it."

"She's right," said Kusac somberly, stepping up to the bodies to lay a hand briefly on each one's head before turning his attention to them.

Kaid, supporting the limping T'Chebbi, touched each one on the chest, letting his hand linger on the flowers for a moment.

"We're sorry for your loss, especially for you, Kaid," said Noni. "Our family has just gotten smaller again. They will be sorely missed."

From the front of the temple, King Zsurtul and Queen Zhalmo, accompanied by Dzaka, Kitra, and General Kezule, entered at an undignified run.

Kitra stopped suddenly when she saw Kusac was carrying Shaidan. "Is he all right?" she whispered, hand to her mouth in shock at his pallor and the fact he was still wrapped in a heavily bloodstained blanket.

"He was badly hurt, but he'll recover," said Carrie, putting a proprietary hand on Shaidan.

"Gaylla," said Shaidan. "Where's Gaylla?"

"We left her with Shishu," began Kitra, only to be cut

t by a screech from that young lady as she ran pell-mell wn the temple nave to her brother. "Shaidan!" she obbed, tears coursing down her little face, turning her light gray fur dark. "You got hurted! I felt it!" She flung herself at Carrie, reaching up to try and touch Shaidan.

Carrie bent down and picked her up, allowing her to see that Shaidan was safe. "It's all right, Gaylla," she said, rocking her. "Shaidan is fine. He'll need a few days in bed, though, to get properly better."

Following a distance behind her was Shishu, obviously out of breath. "I'm sorry, Captain Kusac, but she runs so fast!" she panted.

"Who's looking after the other cubs?" demanded Kusac, his voice harsh. "I hope you didn't leave them alone!"

"Lieutenant M'kou is with them," she faltered. "I thought he'd be fine with them, and I couldn't let her run off on her own."

"You did fine," reassured Carrie, continuing to rock the cub. "They'll certainly be safe with Lieutenant M'kou."

"We're so sorry for your loss," said Zsurtul. "And for the injuries the rest of you have suffered."

"My wife is waiting in the hospital for the injured," said Kezule. "How many are there?"

"Two," said Kaid tiredly as a group of EMTs came running up with floaters and field medical packs. "T'Chebbi and Shaidan. Both are stable but still injured and need hospitalization."

"We'll see to them," said Kezule. "As for your lost ones, would you allow the Palace embalmers to look after them until you are ready to hold a funeral?"

"It would be best," Kusac said quietly to Kaid.

His sword-brother nodded, helping T'Chebbi over to one of the floaters. "It would be best," he agreed, tired beyond even talking.

Kusac shook his head as the medics came over to him. "I'll carry Shaidan up to the hospital myself," he said, adjusting his grip on his son as Shaidan exchanged a hand clasp with Gaylla and then snuggled back up to his father.

He looked over to his troops. "Dismissed. Well done,

everyone. Get the weapons cleaned and stowed, get washed and fed, and sleep. We'll debrief tomorrow morning." He began walking to the back of the temple with Kezule. "The plans went as we hoped they would. The Touibans are now in control of a planet full of M'zullians who have no memory of wars or empires or conquest."

"And K'hedduk?" asked Kezule.

Kusac stopped and faced the general. "Dead," he said with a feral grin. "Burned from the inside out. He was a smear on the ground when I left. We are finally both avenged, Kezule."

EPILOGUE

Prime world, the hospital, Zhal-Oeshi 17th (August)

THE day after they arrived back on the Prime world, M'Nar and Jerenn made their way along to the security post outside the hospital area on the fourth floor of the Palace of Light.

"We'd like to see Shaidan," said M'Nar, going up to the officer on duty. "Brothers M'Nar and Jerenn. He'll be expecting us," he added as an afterthought.

The guard consulted a list on his desk. "Brothers M'Nar and Jerenn. Ah, I see your names." He looked up at them, mouth widening in a smile. "You're expected," he said. "He's only allowed short visits for the moment, but Brother Kaid will tell you when it's time you need to leave."

"Thank you," said M'Nar, nodding briefly to him as he entered.

Jerenn caught at his arm, pulling him to a stop. "Did you hear what he said?" he hissed. "Kaid's here!"

"So? You heard the guard, we're expected." He started walking again.

"But Kaid!" said Jerenn, still pulling him back.

"You worry too much," said M'Nar, trying to disentangle himself from his sword-brother. "What's he going to do?"

The sound of a curtain being pulled back drew both their attention as a nurse emerged from the most distant room. Seeing them, she smiled brightly and came toward them. "Good day, Brothers. How can I help you?" she asked.

"We've come to see Shaidan."

"He'll be pleased. You must be the Brother Jerenn and Brother M'Nar he keeps talking about."

"Ah, yes," said M'Nar, beginning to feel some of Jerenn's uncertainty for himself.

"Follow me, then," she said, leading them to the room nearest the nurse's station at the far end of the ward.

Shaidan was sitting propped up in bed playing a game of squares with Gaylla. On seeing the two Brothers, she let out a high-pitched squeal and launched herself at the nearest one. Jerenn stumbled back into M'Nar as he grabbed hold of her.

"You's came to see Shaidan an' me!" she squealed. "Good! We's so *bored* here!"

"It is a hospital," said Jerenn, giving her a hug before setting her down on the bed. "Shaidan's supposed to be getting better."

"He's lots better today, aren't you?"

"Actually, I'm a lot better," said Shaidan, looking up at them both.

M'Nar sat down on the edge of his bed beside him and peered carefully at the cub's face. "Hmm, you do look better than when we last saw you," he admitted. "You looked pretty beat up."

"I was. They were not nice people." Shaidan's ears sank level to his head before perking up again. "But I remembered what you taught me," he said. "I didn't tell them anything they actually wanted to know, and when one of them had me in a head lock, I knew how to get out of it."

"We saw, youngling," said M'Nar. "Well done. It gave us the opening we needed to take him down."

The cub nodded briefly, then groaned and put a hand to his head. "It still hurts a lot," he said. "Doctor Zayshul says it will take a week or two before I'm fully healed. She said the wound in my stomach was much worse, but luckily Annuur was able to heal that completely."

M'Nar glanced at Jerenn, sitting on the chair by the bedside.

"You were pretty badly hurt," said Jerenn, leaning

ward to pat the hand that lay nearest to him on the blanket.

"Papa said I was very lucky that Annuur was there to help."

"You were, but that's all behind you now," said M'Nar briskly. "Your father has told us we're going back to Shola with you all and continuing on as your trainers."

"For all of you," added Jerenn as Shaidan's mouth widened in an excited grin.

Gaylla bounced on the bed in joy. "Oh, good! I gets to keep playing wif you!"

M'Nar saw Shaidan wince and grabbed for the young female, pulling her into a cuddle and sitting her on his lap. "No jumping, young lady!" he said.

"That's great news," said Shaidan. "I was afraid that I'd got you into trouble with my papa for what you'd taught me."

M'Nar grinned and reached out to gently ruffle Shaidan's hair, which was lying loose about his shoulders. "That was for us to worry about, not you, youngling," he said as Gaylla squirmed off his lap onto the bed again. "Your father was just glad our training had been useful to you."

"Very glad as it happens," said Kusac.

M'Nar and Jerenn shot to their feet and turned to face him, saluting.

"Captain Aldatan. They said we were expected," said Jerenn.

"Relax," said Kusac, stepping into the room. "I gave those instructions because I knew your minds wouldn't be at ease until you'd seen Shaidan for yourselves. Thank you for helping to look after him, and the other cubs, while we were away."

"Our pleasure, Captain," said M'Nar. "When he came to us with a premonition of danger to himself, we could do no less than help him be ready for it."

"I'm intrigued as to why you didn't let Brother Dzaka know," said Kusac moving past them to sit on his son's bed.

M'Nar and Jerenn exchanged a glance.

"Security can only do so much," said Jerenn. "There will always be that moment of opportunity for someone deter-

mined enough to get through to their target. We deci~~ded~~
that since Shaidan's premonition was so vague, it was bett~~er~~
to prepare him to meet trouble than to try and prevent i~~t~~
from happening."

"Plus we knew how good that security was," added M'Nar.

"Not that good when this young male was able to escape
through secret passages out into the main courtyard at
night!" said Kusac, turning a stern look on his son, who
hung his head.

"Not to tell Shaidan off," said Gaylla, crawling over to sit
on Kusac's knee. "He's been hurted bad, but he's getting
better now."

Kusac put an arm round her and held her close for a
moment. "I'm not angry with him now, Gaylla," he said.
"Just reminding him that he'd better not do any more disappearing now that his mama and I are home!"

"No, Papa," said Shaidan, scooting closer to him. "No
more disappearing." There was a slight hesitation in his
voice that they all caught.

"But what?" asked Kusac, putting his other arm around
him.

"Can I still talk to Unity if it promises not to disappear
me unless it's arranged with you first?"

"Will you be able to reach Unity from Shola?"

*I can talk to Shaidan no matter where he is, if he uses the
transceiver I gave him,* came the voice of Ghioass' AI.

"Are you listening in to our conversations?" demanded
Kusac, holding onto the cubs more tightly.

I was only concerned for the safety of Shaidan, it said, the
artificial voice almost managing to sound apologetic. *Now I
know he is well, I will leave you in privacy until you or
Shaidan contact me.*

The three adults all looked at each other, various degrees of worry on their faces until Gaylla broke their somber mood.

"Owie, Uncle Kusac! Your hug is too tight, you're hurt-
ing me!"

"Sorry, little one," said Kusac, relaxing his grip on them
both. "I think we'll not contact Unity for the next few

ks, Shaidan. Let's get ourselves home first. You've got
o sisters and a brother to meet, not to mention any num-
er of other relatives! Then we can sit down and discuss you
and Unity. Deal?"

"It's a deal, Papa," said Shaidan.

Prime world, Zhal-Oeshi 19th (August)

The funeral for Rezac and Jo was a state affair, with the
funeral pyre built in the main courtyard. Conner and Noni
conducted the service, a simple one that celebrated their
life together.

When the flames died down, their ashes were collected
and put into a beautifully carved wooden box and presented to Kaid to take home to Shola.

"We have a wall on the estate where such containers are
placed," said Kusac. "The outer plaque is then inscribed
with their names. Your father and Jo have certainly earned
a place there, and not just as members of our Clan."

"Thank you," said Kaid, holding the box. "I know they'd
be proud to rest there."

The following days passed both quickly and too slowly for
Kusac and Carrie. Slowly in that there were numerous de-
briefings on what they had been doing on M'zull. It seemed
everyone wanted to know about their time there and how
it had gone down. Kusac made one debriefing document
that he gave to everyone who needed or wanted it.

"I don't want some bits of paper!" said Noni, throwing
them back at him. "I asked how it went! I expect you to
tell me!"

"It went fairly well," he said grabbing for the sheets of paper before they fell to the floor. "No plan remains intact, especially when you can't get enough intelligence on the enemy ahead of time."

"Then I take it you did a few things you wouldn't normally do."

"I did a lot of that! But everything I did was necessary at the time. It kept either me or those with me alive."

"Is there anything you regret doing?" asked Noni, bustling about making a pot of c'shar. The rooms she and Conner occupied in the temple were small but comfortable, and Noni had made sure they had as many of the comforts of home as possible.

Kusac sat down at the table, shuffling the pieces of paper into a neat stack before putting them back into his folder. "Not really," he said, "unless it was setting fire to the old Lord Nayash's remains. Seemed the old male was a fairly decent person as M'zullians go. I hope I didn't deprive him of his afterlife. All the Valtegans believe that if their bodies are burned, they don't go to their next world."

"I know that," said Noni, pouring boiling water into the brewer. "I doubt that your actions made much difference to him. He'd already have faced his judgment day."

"I suppose," said Kusac. "Good to think I didn't affect him then."

Noni brought the brewing pot over to the table and set it down on a heat-resistant mat, then took her accustomed chair at the table. She reached out and clasped Kusac's hand where it lay on the table.

"You're thinking of Rezac and Jo," she said. "Fret not about them, lad. Any debts that Rezac owed were more than paid when he died. Same for young Jo. Tragic their deaths were, but I know L'Shoh will have judged them well, and I told Kaid that."

"It's the cost of getting Shaidan back that bothers me," he admitted. "It seems others have paid dearly for that. Rezac and Jo dead, and T'Chebbi invalided because of her damaged arm. Kaid's lost his father, and his mate will never be on active duty again."

"Do any of you plan to be on active duty again?" asked Noni, raising her eyeridges at him.

"No, but . . ."

"Then it shouldn't matter so much. It'll be a good excuse to keep Kaid home. And you have four children in your triad—six now that Zsayal and Vazih have lost their father."

"We're keeping all the cubs together in our nursery on the estate," said Kusac. "All they really know is each other. Their parents aren't even adult couples, except for us."

"I hope you intend to keep that little lass, Gaylla," said Noni, lifting up the brewer to pour out the c'shar into two honest-to-goodness mugs. "Kate and Taynar are barely adult themselves; the child needs older parents who understand how special she is."

Kusac nodded. "It would be cruel to separate Shaidan and Gaylla. We intend to make sure she stays with us as a member of our immediate family. The others will belong to their parents, but we plan to keep them together at our nursery on the estate. Their parentage is so mixed as to prove it almost impossible to give them to a family unit. Kaid has already claimed Dhyshac as his son, so he's settled. That leaves Vazih and Zsayal who were Rezac's daughter and son. As Zsayal has Carrie as the mother donor, we'll share him with Kaid. He's actually their older brother! He can share Vazih with Kate, if she's up for the task of being a mother to her. Kate and her Leska Taynar also have Shaylor who's their son, but I doubt they want to be full-time parents when they are still young themselves. Being a Human and Sholan Leska pair is hard enough work as adults, never mind for teenagers."

"Complicated," nodded Noni, pushing Kusac's mug of c'shar toward him. "Better that they all live together and are visited by their parents. Even a day or two a week staying with their donor parents won't go amiss, though, and each cub will feel cared for by them."

"Agreed. Only they know what it's like to be so advanced at their age, so it makes sense to keep them together. I also plan on continuing the Brotherhood education they've been getting, including their training in martial arts. M'Nar and Jerenn did a good job with them, and with

Shaidan, so I plan to keep them on as instructors. They'r clan members anyway." He picked up his mug and took a long drink. "Ah," he said, grinning. "I've missed c'shar, and drinking from regular mugs!"

"I expect just being Sholan all the time is a blessing," Noni said, sipping her drink.

"You have no idea," he said, putting the mug down. "Thankfully I kept my mental powers, but to lose the use of the senses that I've relied on all my life for those of the Valtegans . . ."

"I'm sure they'd feel the same if they were given the chance to morph into one of us," said Noni placidly. "How's Kaid doing?"

"I thought you'd be one of the first people wanting to see him," said Kusac more somberly. "He's grieving over the loss of his father, as is Carrie over Jo, but it's a normal grief, completely understandable."

"I was one of the first to see you all," said Noni. "I went up to the hospital after everyone was settled in, and examined them myself. But that was two days ago now. I wanted to know how he's been in the meantime."

Kusac picked up his mug again. "As I said, grieving in his own way, and spending time with T'Chebbi since they won't let her out of her bed because of her surgery."

"She'll be all right," reassured Noni, catching his underlying concern for T'Chebbi. "Her arm will be fine for normal life, she just won't have the strength she needs to be a fighter again."

"She'll find that very hard," said Kusac.

"At first, but when she sets up as a trainer and has those berrans of her own with Kaid, she'll find life sweet again," said Noni with confidence.

"Kaid a father with a young cub," said Kusac with a slow grin. "This I have to see. Actually, I will. There's his daughter Layeesha that I haven't met, and Dhyshac, my son with Carrie. They'll be what now? Just short of two years old?"

Noni nodded. "And Kashini is creeping up on three soon," she said. "Proper little miss she is! You'll have your hands full with them as well as the other older cubs."

Kusac leaned forward, all traces of humor gone from him. "How will the authorities on Shola see the cubs? Will they want to take them into their care and away from us? Do you have any idea what they plan?"

"I'm glad you asked," she said, eyes twinkling at him over the top of her mug. "I think you need to make a public arrival on Shola. Very public, and very ostentatious. I heard how your entry with Shaidan at the royal banquet went. You need to do something like that. Get some of your alien friends to arrive with you." She put her mug back on the table. "Land at Shanagi Spaceport. Some friendly press agent getting an exclusive would also help to get the news out to all of Shola."

Kusac began laughing. "No one could call you naive, Noni," he chuckled. "If we arrive like that with the cubs, all done out in the open, there is no way they could touch them without a public outcry. Do we tell the truth about their genesis?"

"Yes. Then the authorities can hold nothing about them over your heads. See if you can get that newscaster you had for you and Carrie back in the day to interview you when you arrive. You've time enough for her to start a campaign of your organizing in return for her exclusive news of the cubs, and the new alien treaties."

"You mean that Vorkoh female, Rhaema Vorkoh of Infonet," he said, dredging up her name from memory. "Yes, I could call her from here and set this up. She'd need a special pass to get access to us, though, and I don't see the Governor's office granting her that."

"Oh, you don't tell the Governor what you're doing, lad," said Noni. "Only person who knows is this Rhaema lass. She's waiting for you on Chagda space station where you pick her up, then you alert the Governor's office you plan to land with delegates from the various alien species."

Kusac stared at her, still laughing, then shook his head. "Talk about making an entrance," he said. "I'll need to get Kezule involved and get him choosing a delegation to discuss treaties with Shola. You don't plan small, Noni."

"I took a leaf out of your book, Kusac," she said. "And I

can't take all the credit for it. Conner had more to do w
this idea than me. He's used to that kind of thing, after all.

"If we make it all public before we even land, and they
see who we have as friends and allies, they won't dare try to
hide the cubs from the public, or to take them away from us.
They'll be safe."

Noni nodded. "Safe to be the cubs they are and grow up
knowing the security of Clan and family. How you planning
to get home?"

"My ship the *Venture*'s been here for months. Right now,
a Prime work crew is changing the Captain's lounge and
office into a dorm and play area for the cubs. They'll be
sleeping right beside Carrie and me. Most of my people will
travel back with me—she's big enough to carry nine folk,
three as passengers, the other six will be needed as crew. I'm
getting Banner and Jurrel to travel with the Prime scouter
as they know the finer points of navigating to the space
station, while two of them, probably Cheelar and Noolgoi,
travel with us. Toueesut is returning with us, so Kitra and
Dzaka are traveling with him."

"Sounds like you're able to change out your crew to give
everyone some down time. And with a fine escort of your
alien friends' ships, you should easily get home safely."

Kusac got to his feet and leaned over to plant a kiss on
Noni's forehead. "Bless you, Noni, we'll be fine. I'll get right
on with contacting Infonet and Toueesut now. When do you
plan to go home?"

"In a month or two, when our work here is done."

The *Venture*, Zhal-Nylam 6th (September)

The *Venture* sat on its launch pad at the Prime spaceport just
outside the City of Light. The *Couana*, their crew having
already said their good-byes, waited for them at the orbital
space station along with a ship belonging to the TeLaxaudin.

...it, as Ambassadors, were Azwokkus and Khassis, as well the Cabbarans Shvosi and Kuvaa. Ready to join them were the *Watcher* ship crewed by Tirak and Annuur and their crews, and the *Vanguard*, a Prime scouter, crewed by Cheelar and his brother M'yikku.

Public leave-taking had been done back at the Palace, but Kezule and his wife, Doctor Zayshul, had been joined by King Zsurtul and Queen Zhalmo to actually see them off.

Banner nudged Jurrel. "Let's get settled on the *Vanguard*," he said. "Leave the brass to say good-bye."

"Aye," said Jurrel. "Be good to get home and drink c'shar from real mugs again!"

"I grabbed a couple mugs and some brew from the *Venture* for us," said Banner. "It's in my backpack. I figured since they'd have to have a couple of those bowls and some maush for M'yikku and Cheelar, we could have our share of the drinking rations!"

"Sweet," said Jurrel. "Maush is all right, but I'm used to c'shar."

"I didn't get a lot of it, so we'll likely have to drink maush as well, but at least it will be from mugs."

Banner caught Kusac's eye and signaled to him they were going to their berths on the *Vanguard*. Kusac nodded his assent and turned back to his conversation with Zsurtul.

"I enjoyed my time on Shola," the young King was saying reminiscently. "I would like to visit again some day." He smiled as Zhalmo reached out to touch Gaylla on the cheek. "We will both miss the cubs a lot."

"You can come to visit us any time you wish," said Carrie, adjusting her hold on Gaylla as the young female leaned over to return the gesture with a pat of her own to Zhalmo's cheek.

"Come visit us when you has your baby an' we's can play wif him," said Gaylla with a smile. "Be more fun then."

Shocked exclamations from Carrie and Zsurtul were met with embarrassment from Zhalmo, and a knowing look from Kusac, over the top of Shaidan's head, to Carrie.

"I was going to tell you later today," the young female murmured to her husband. "I didn't want to overshadow the leave-taking with my news."

"It's wonderful news," said Zsurtul, putting his arm around his wife and pulling her closer to his side.

"You shouldn't tell people that kind of news," Shaidan said quietly to his sister. "That's too personal."

"I'll explain it to her later," Kusac said quietly, settling Shaidan on his hip again. "You're getting heavy," he said. "Must be all that good food you've been eating! Time we got you back to doing some exercises with M'Nar and Jerenn."

"Can we do that in the *Venture*?" asked Shaidan hopefully. "It's so boring being ill."

"There's enough room in the cargo hold for some practice," said Kusac. "It would be cold down there, but I'm sure there's a way to get it heated. We'll talk about that later." Kusac held his hand out to Kezule. "Thank you for your help in getting Shaidan back," he said. "It took us a while, but eventually we grew to appreciate each other."

Kezule took the offered hand and shook it. "It was a rather trying relationship for a long time, mainly because of me," he admitted. "You taught me a lot about myself that I won't forget."

"Thank you for looking after our cubs," Carrie said to the Doctor. "Without your and your husband's care, neither Shaidan or Gaylla would be with us today."

"They were just children. What K'hedduk planned to do with them was just dreadful," she said. "We had to help them, that's why Kezule went to rescue them."

"Not everyone would have done that for the children of their enemies, as we were seen at that time."

Zayshul made a gesture of negation. "Kezule never saw the cubs like that," she said. "Only as children in need of rescue."

"Time to go," said Kusac. "Garras is telling me Tirak and M'yikku are ready for liftoff, as is he."

"Good-bye and we will come and visit you soon," said King Zsurtul, clasping Kusac by the hand.

'Good-bye, Zsurtul and Zhalmo. Be well," said Kusac as arrie gave the queen a hug.

Sholan Space, Zhal-Nylam 27th (September)

"Approaching Shanagi Spaceport," said M'Nar's voice over the ship's com. "Coordinating landing with the *Couana*, *Vanguard*, *Watcher,* and the Telaxaudin's *Ambassador*. Telling Shanagi we want five adjacent landing pads. Waiting their reply now."

"Acknowledged," said Kusac, raising his voice slightly before turning his attention back to Rhaema Vorkoh who had been talking to the cubs.

"Okay, younglings," said Carrie, getting to her feet. "We're landing shortly, so it's time you got yourselves ready. Hair brushed, clothes clean and tidy. Yes, that includes your dolly, Gaylla," Carrie said in response to a look from the young female. "Then when the command comes, get yourselves onto your designated bed or seat and pull the crash net over you. I'll come round to check you've all got it right."

As they sat there looking at her, she clapped her hands together. "Scoot! I want you to do this now!"

A chorus of "Yes, Aunty Carrie," with a "Yes, Mommy," in there, greeted her as they began to get up and scatter to their room.

"I can't believe it," Rhaema said, scribbling on her tablet. "And they really are only about a year old?"

"As near as we can work it out," said Kusac. "Don't be misled though, they have the functioning minds of ten-year-olds."

"Oh, I can see that!" she said. "Apart from the one called Gaylla, that is."

"Yes," said Carrie, getting to her feet. "We think there was a fault that caused a delay in her being birthed from the tank and she suffered some oxygen deprivation. Whatever the reason, we are keeping her with us as a member of family. Kusac, I'm going to see to Shaidan. He's wanting to see to his hair. One of his braids has come undone." S. laughed gently. "He does so like to have his hair done the same way as his father."

"Shaidan does seem very different from the others— more mature."

Kusac nodded. "He's been their leader, watching out for them all, but especially Gaylla. But every now and then, like the others, he has a childish meltdown as if he was a four-year-old. They're becoming more normal every day."

Rhaema looked up at Kusac. "I'm sure they are. And sure that having fine braids at the front of your hair will become a new fashion," she said. "Where did that idea come from?"

"The Primes," said Kusac. "Not having hair, they often have circlets with fabric braids that they'll wear. While they were helping to look after Shaidan, they braided all his hair to make it easier for them to cope with."

She nodded, and finally put her tablet away. "So does Governor Nesul know you are arriving today with Ambassadors from four alien cultures?"

"If you contacted his office, then he'll be sure of what's happening," said Kusac. "I called my father, Konis Aldatan, a day ago, to let the Governor know what we were planning. So far, Governor Nesul hasn't contacted me."

"Am I right in saying your hope is that by arriving so publically, with the story of the cubs and their genesis not only on the front pages of Infonet, but also going out live as we speak, that your children will be allowed the peace and privacy to grow up on your estate with their parents?"

"Yes, we want to ensure they don't become test subjects for the medical profession to examine and poke and prod. These are our cubs, our sons and daughters, they deserve a life of quality and family after such an uncaring beginning. And we plan to make sure they get it."

"Thank you, Kusac Aldatan, of the En'Shalla Clan, for sharing not only your hopes but letting me meet your cubs for myself."

...e recording light on the small drone camera she had
...ght with her winked out. "I appreciate your contacting
... with this story, Captain Aldatan. It's going to make the
...ther networks absolutely mad with jealousy! You are going to be the main topic of news for several days now."

"Well, we don't want to deal with any other stations,
Rhaema, so if you need more information from us, please
contact me at the number I gave you. If you can keep the
others off our backs, you can have the exclusives."

Kusac got to his feet. "I have to go to the bridge now.
Lieutenant T'Chebbi will look after you as we make our
approach to the spaceport and land there."

Kusac walked smartly down the corridor to the bridge,
keying in the security code and letting himself in. He slipped
into his seat at the main console, ready for the chatter with
the flight tower.

"Tower to *Venture*, you and your party are clear to land
at bays twelve through sixteen. Bay twelve has been allocated for you."

"Thank you, tower," said M'Nar. "Proceeding to bay
twelve. Incoming call from Governor Nesul," he added.

"Put it through to my board," said Kusac. "Governor,
how can I help you?" he asked.

"I'm disappointed in you, Kusac. I thought you would
have landed quietly in your own estate, not go for something this public."

"It was the only way to be sure our cubs are treated like
the children they are and not have them end up in some
laboratory."

"They are unique, Kusac. I am already inundated with
requests by various departments, all wanting to study
them."

"Then this makes it easy for you. They are our cubs, but
will also be part of the trade and peace treaties with all the
species accompanying me today. You will be given full tran-
scripts of the cubs' genesis, and all the particulars of their
early days, but that is all. They will not be subject to any
tests or interviews by anyone. They will be left alone to

grow up as normally as possible, given they are physically ten years old with minds that have only been awake for about a year."

"What about the technology to grow them to that age? I know our medical experts badly want that. It could be invaluable for organ transplant alone."

"Nothing to do with me or the cubs. That technology belongs to the TeLaxaudin. I don't know if they plan to make it available to you. That is something you will have to discuss with them."

Kusac caught a hand signal from M'Nar and abruptly ended the conversation . "Sorry, Governor, but I am needed on the bridge. This will have to wait till later." He cut the connection and began to ready his board to take over the landing sequence from Garras.

"Keep her engine ready to take off, Garras. This is only a short stop till we head back to the estate with Toueesut and my sister and Dzaka."

"Aye," said Garras, powering down the engines to an idle.

"Home," said Jerenn. "Hardly seems possible. Must be worse for you, you've been away so much longer."

"Nearly two years for me," said Kusac, unfastening his restraints and getting to his feet. "How long for you, Garras?"

"Coming on eight months, I think," he said, getting up from his post and stretching from head to tail tip. "Vanna's got them into a frenzy of cooking at the main house. We'll be eating till our sides split if they've any say in it. Who you taking out with you?"

"Kaid, M'Nar and Jerenn, and Cheelar. I want you all armed and ready to form a barrier between the cubs and the authorities if need be. Carrie will be in charge of the cubs, I'll be with you as the spokesperson. Garras, be ready to take off at a minute's notice, just in case it all goes wrong out there."

"Will do," said the older male, sitting back down at his post and pulling up the view outside the *Venture* so he could watch everything for himself. "Your father's there," he said a moment later.

Kusac nodded as he headed toward the bridge door. "I know, we've been chatting mentally for a few minutes," he said. "We should be all right as they've not had the time to put any kind of opposition together. This has been as sudden for them as we hoped it would be. Now let's get outside and get this over with," he said, activating the bridge door.

"You said I wouldn't have to do this again," said Shaidan, as he stood with Kusac before the closed air lock door.

"Last time we were alone," said Kusac. "Just you and me. This time it's all of you cubs, and you have both Mama and me with you."

"There's also your friends, M'Nar and Jerenn," added Carrie as she came up behind him carrying Gaylla. "And all the other aliens here to make sure your privacy is protected."

"This is definitely the last public appearance you'll make," promised Kusac, gripping his son's hand just a little bit tighter in reassurance. "After this, we are heading to our forever home."

"We gets to meet our little brothers and sisters, don't we?" asked Gaylla, wrapping one arm round Carrie's neck and holding tightly to her dolly with the other one.

"Father's brought Kashini!" Kusac exclaimed, looking at Carrie. "I thought he was hiding something from us! He and Mother brought Vanna with Kashini!"

"Well, we better get outside, then," said Carrie as she stepped aside to allow Rhaema to go first. "I think it was a wise move on your father's part to bring Kashini here. That way, everyone can see there's no difference between them."

Kusac activated the air lock, opening both doors.

"Give me about twenty seconds and then you can come out," said Rhaema, fitting her microphone round her ear.

Kusac watched her walk down the ramp to the landing pad, starting her commentary on the arrival home of the heroes of M'zull.

"Everyone ready?" Kusac asked as he and Shaidan began to move forward.

A crowd had gathered behind the barriers set by security, probably travelers already in the center when they heard Rhaema's broadcast.

Shaidan welded himself to Kusac's leg. "It's scary, Papa," he whispered.

"I'm here," he said reassuringly, "So's your mama. They aren't going to be talking to you, so don't worry."

As soon as they cleared the ramp, they spread out, a small but defiant group, standing there with the six cubs. Then the occupants of the other craft began to join them, and suddenly they weren't such a small group after all.

They could see their family kept back by security, but suddenly there was a stir and a small blonde figure dodged between the officials and streaked across the empty landing pad to Kusac, yelling "Papa! Mama! You is home!"

She skidded to a stop in front of Kusac and Carrie, looking at Shaidan, then up at Gaylla before flinging her arms around her father's other leg. "You'se home," she said happily, before moving to her mother and likewise attaching herself to her leg. "Missed you both, Mama," she said, hugging her tightly.

"I'se Kashini. You're Shaidan," she said, looking at him from the safety of her mother's side. "Aunty Vanna tole me all about you. You my brother like Dhyshac is, but bigger."

"Hello, Kashini," Shaidan said.

"You my sister, too?" asked Gaylla, leaning down to look at her.

"She's your cousin," said Carrie, gently setting the cub down onto the ground beside Kashini. The two little females looked at each other as Carrie managed to grab each of them by the hand.

Kashini's mouth dropped in a smile. "I like you," she said. "We be friends."

"I has a dolly," said Gaylla, thrusting her Valtegan doll toward Kashini. "An' a pet jegget called Snow. Do you have toys, 'Shini?"

"Looks like little ones soon be fast friends," said Annuur as they watched Governor Nesul, accompanied by Kusac's parents and Vanna start to make their way toward them. As soon as they were close enough, Vanna came running over.

"Please tell me Garras is with you," she said anxiously.

"On the bridge," said Kusac quietly as the official welcoming party stopped in front of them. "Up the ramp and you'll find him."

"Thank you!" She disappeared into the ship.

"Ambassador Nesul," began Annuur before anyone else could speak. "Introducing I am to you the Ambassadors from Ghioass. Elder Khassis, the TeLaxaudin representative you have not been meeting before, neither Elder Shvosi who be representing the Cabbaran people. With her is her aide Kuvaa. For present, Captain Tirak is U'Churian delegate until Home decides on their Ambassador."

Shvosi rose up on her hind legs. "We stay on En'Shalla estate until accommodations suitable you have for us. There we watch our friends and their young ones settle back home. Special are these cubs, with parents and siblings they must be." There was more than a hint of warning in the tone the Cabbaran used, and the Governor was not backward in picking up the implicit threat.

"We're delighted to greet you, Ambassadors. You are our honored guests. However, I'm sure we can find adequate quarters for you at the Palace until we have converted rooms for your use in the Ambassadorial quarter. We already have members of the TeLaxaudin there."

"We stay with the Captain," said Khassis. "We come to consult with our people. When quarters ready, then we move." Her tone, even through the translator, was an indication that the discussion was at an end.

Where are we going to put them? Kusac sent to his father.

Have no fear, sent Khassis, using her artificially enhanced mental senses to speak to him. *We stay in ships till then, on your landing area. Annuur tells us he did this once.*

"In that case, shall we schedule some initial talks two days from now?" asked Nesul.

"That will be appropriate," agreed Khassis.

Nesul turned his attention to Kusac. "We received a report on the events on M'zull from Master Lijou," he s "Is their expansionism really at an end? Is there truly more risk of a war with them?"

"Totally at an end," said Kusac. "You only need to ask Toueesut and his swarm about that. The Touibans are taking charge there for the moment, though they hope to have working groups from every species there within the next few weeks, our Brotherhood being next."

"I'll be in touch shortly with you, Toueesut," Nesul said, nodding toward the group of Touibans swarming slowly round the cubs. "Will you not at least introduce me to this youngling?" he asked, gesturing at Shaidan.

"My bruvver don't want to talk to you," said Gaylla, turning the full power of her gaze on the Governor. "You thinks we's dangerous," she said, squirming her hand free from Carrie's and stepping up to him. She planted her hands on her hips, doll dangling from the right hand. "We's just cubs. We wants to go home now, not live ever again in labs."

Shaidan, ever her protector, let go of his father's leg and joined her. "We want to be with our family, meet our brothers and sisters, and just be cubs," he said, taking Gaylla by the hand and tugging her back to his father and mother. "We don't want to be different anymore."

Kusac scooped Gaylla up into his arms and took Shaidan by the hand again. "They're only children, children who have been kept as captives for much of their short lives," he said. "As their Clan Leader, I plan to make sure they get to grow up in safety among our clan, and their parents."

"I believe my son and his people, including the cubs, have earned this respite," said Konis. "He's achieved more than even you could have dreamed of, Nesul. Conflict with the M'zullians is now a thing of the past, with what survives of their war machine being destroyed even as we speak."

"You'll get all your reports through my father in the next few weeks," said Kusac. "Our new allies will also be able to update you on the M'zullian situation, and the birthing tanks used for the cubs. Until then, we're going home."

sul looked at Kusac, then slowly smiled, holding out hand. "How can I argue with such a determined young nale as your Gaylla? I'll look forward to your reports," e said. "Take what time you need to prepare them as I am sure we have more than enough to keep us busy. I don't suppose you'd like to be an Ambassador?"

Kusac threw him a horrified look even as he shook his hand. "Absolutely not! I will happily work as an aide interfacing with our new allies, but I don't intend to leave Shola for several years! I want to enjoy watching my cubs grow up!"

"As your father says, you have earned that right."

Kusac turned back to his people. "Load up," he said. "We're finally going home!"

Lisanne Norman

The *Sholan Alliance* Series

"This is fun escapist fare, entertaining..."   —*Locus*

"Will hold you spellbound."
—*Romantic Times*

To Order Call: 1-800-788-6262
www.dawbooks.com

DAW 29

Tanya Huff
The *Confederation* Novels

A CONFEDERATION OF VALOR
Omnibus Edition
(Valor's Choice, The Better Part of Valor)
978-0-7564-1041-4

THE HEART OF VALOR
978-0-7564-0481-9

VALOR'S TRIAL
978-0-7564-0557-1

THE TRUTH OF VALOR
978-0-7564-0684-4

To Order Call: 1-800-788-6262
www.dawbooks.com

DAW 73

CJ Cherryh

Complete Classic Novels in Omnibus Editions

THE DREAMING TREE 978-0-88677-782-1
The Dreamstone | The Tree of Swords and Jewels

THE FADED SUN TRILOGY 978-0-88677-869-9
Kesrith | Shon'jir | Kutath

THE MORGAINE SAGA 978-0-88677-877-4
Gate of Ivrel | Well of Shiuan | Fires of Azeroth

THE CHANUR SAGA 978-0-88677-930-6
The Pride of Chanur | Chanur's Venture | The Kif Strike Back

CHANUR'S ENDGAME 978-0-7564-0444-4
Chanur's Homecoming | Chanur's Legacy

ALTERNATE REALITIES 978-0-88677-946-7
Port Eternity | Voyager in Night | Wave Without a Shore

THE DEEP BEYOND 978-0-7564-0311-9
Serpent's Reach | Cuckoo's Egg

ALLIANCE SPACE 978-0-7564-0494-9
Merchanter's Luck and 40,000 in Gehenna

To Order Call: 1-800-788-6262
www.dawbooks.com

DAW 9

Gini Koch
The Alien *Novels*

"Told with clever wit and non-stop pacing, this series follows the exploits of the country's top alien exterminators in the American Centaurion Diplomatic Corps. It blends diplomacy, action, and sense of humor into a memorable reading experience."
—*Kirkus*

"Amusing and interesting...a hilarious romp in the vein of *Men in Black* or *Ghostbusters*."
—*VOYA*

To Order Call: 1-800-788-6262
www.dawbooks.com

DAW 160